# Intrepid

Rafe Gray

# DEDICATION

To my wife, family and friends.

# CONTENTS

i

# ACKNOWLEDGMENTS

I would like to thank my family and particularly my grandma and uncle's twin sister for recalling and recounting the story to me so that I could put together the pieces of the jigsaw. I would also like to thank Tony for proof reading and editing the text.

# FOREWORD

The events in this book are based on a true story.

The names of the protagonists have been changed to protect the identity of family members, as well as others.

It recounts the life of my uncle, Horace Gray. The events take place mainly in Staffordshire in and around Burton-on-Trent, my birthplace and where I have lived ever since. I was not yet born when the story begins but I do have vivid memories of many of the people involved whom I got to know as I grew up. I revisited many of the places mentioned as I wrote the book, such as Sinai and Bladon woods.

The story begins with my uncle Horace, aged thirteen and a half, when he was thrown out of school for hitting a teacher who had attempted to sexually abuse him. The Principal didn't believe a word of what my uncle said and expelled him immediately. This was the first of a chain of events that changed my uncle's life forever, including him becoming entangled with a local small-time but ambitious villain called Brian Fisher who had already been detained at Her Majesty's pleasure on two occasions

My great uncle Bill, Horace's uncle (henceforth referred to simply as 'Uncle Bill'), had a big influence on Horace throughout his life. Uncle Bill was born in 1914. His father was absent for the first four years of Bill's life fighting in France in The Great War alongside Horace's dad, George, and George's four brothers. The brothers never returned, all having being killed within three months of each other.

George came back a broken man. He had been gassed in 1916 and a year later shot in the back injuring his left lung. When he returned home he could not be the active father he wanted to be for his two boys, Horace and Ron. Bill, being a strong fit man and, from an early age an outdoors person who enjoyed living off the land, assumed a father-figure roll in Horace's early life.

Uncle Bill had been a sergeant major in the commandos in World War II serving all over the Far East but principally Japan. He returned to Korea in 1949 for a brief period to train the army in the south when it appeared that war would be inevitable. He was very proud of Horace because of his natural ability and willingness to work hard. Uncle Bill taught a ten-year-old Horace to shoot and to strip down, clean and reassemble a gun. Horace was a much better all-rounder than his older brother Ron and his two cousins Bill and George, Uncle Bill's two boys.

Horace's mother, Eva, was the eldest of six children with an age difference that spanned twenty years. She was aged fifty one in 1949 when the story begins.

There were two other very important and influential people in the story of Horace's early life. These were Sir Humphrey Cartwright and Commander Stanley Carpenter (Sir Stanley), both wealthy aristocrats. The vicissitudes of Horace's life led to him befriending a wide variety of people, including working boaters (those who lived and worked on the canals), gypsies and the aristocracy.

Horace was a real fast learner. He was a clever lad at school and was good at maths, English and history. He left Shobnall Junior School after passing his Eleven Plus and was eligible to go to the local grammar school. Horace would rather have gone to the technical school instead, a desire supported by his dad and Uncle Bill, but his mum insisted he went to the grammar.

He absolutely adored cars and loved anything mechanical. At the age of ten he would walk half a mile up the road to ask Gordon Rush, a local garage owner and mechanic, if he could have a job. Gordon gave Horace a few things to do around the garage at evenings and weekends, mostly just tidying up after him and his assistant mechanic, Martin. But Gordon knew of Horace's passion for mechanics so gave him simple jobs like replacing spark plugs. He even gave Horace an old engine to strip down on the floor because he was too small to reach the bench.

Horace started off in life with sound morals and strong motivation. He was surrounded by good, courageous and hard-working family members and friends....all of the right ingredients to lead a successful and fulfilling life. But things outside of Horace's control would change his destiny forever. The story begins in 1949. King George VI was on the throne and Clement Attlee was the Prime Minister. Winston Churchill was soon to replace Attlee.....on the 26th of October 1951.

# CHAPTER ONE

This is the story of my uncle, Horace Gray. He was just over fourteen years old and attending the local grammar school. He was a clever lad and high achiever in all subjects, especially maths and science.

It was Tuesday, 1ˢᵗ of March 1949. Horace was in a science lesson when the maths teacher, Mr. Osborne, knocked on the door and walked in. He asked Mr. Prichard if he could take out Horace Gray to talk to him, Mr. Prichard consented.

Osborne showed Horace into his office shutting the door behind them. Horace was sure that he felt Osborne's hand touch his backside but didn't react believing it to have been nothing more than an accident. But when they approached the large desk there could be no doubt about Osborne's motives, he reached down and touched Horace's rear-end whilst simultaneously grasping the boy's crotch. Horace was astounded and shocked in equal measure. Instinctively, he turned and punched Osborne full square in the nose and mouth causing Osborne's nose to bleed profusely.

Osborne yelled out in pain, perhaps screamed is a better description. The Principal, Mr. Reynolds, and his secretary heard the commotion and burst into the room.

"What the hell is going on?" the Principal bellowed. The blood from Osborne's nose was dripping off his chin onto his white shirt and patterned tie.

Osborne exclaimed that Horace had just "lashed out" at him for no reason whatsoever.

Horace was beside himself. "He just touched me on my arse and crotch, sir, so my instinct was to lash out. What he did is not what normal people do to young kids".

"Go to my office immediately and wait for me there, Gray, while we take Mr. Osborne to get cleaned up". Horace did what he was told and waited for Mr. Reynolds to return.

"I do not know what you are playing at, Gray, but you do not hit a teacher of mine and get away with it. Why are you lying about this incident? You will go home and come back in the morning with one of your parents when you will be expelled from this school. Now, get out of my sight".

Horace was as mad as he was shocked, he couldn't believe what had just happened to him.

It was lunch time when Horace got home. In the kitchen were his Mum, Eva, his Dad, George, and Uncle Bill....who was like a second father to him. His dad worked at the local brewery and the family lived in one of the brewery cottages on Shobnall Road. The front of the cottage faced the road with a small brook running along its front. The cottages were modest but in good order and the residents kept them clean and tidy.

"What are you doing home this time of day, are you not well?" asked George.

"No, dad I was sent home for punching the maths teacher, Mr. Osborne, on his nose".

"Why on earth did you do that, son?"

"Well dad, the bastard......"

"Watch your language in this house" said his mum.

"Here, our Eva" said Uncle Bill to his older sister, "let him finish before you chastise him. He's a good lad. He wouldn't do that for no reason. Come on Horace, what happened?"

"I was in the science lesson when I was called out by Mr. Osborne. He took me into his office, shut the door behind me and touched my backside. I thought it was an accident but when we got over to his desk he grabbed my arse and crotch".

George was outraged, "That dirty, filthy little bastard doing that to my son. We will go up there after lunch. I will ask Robinson for the afternoon off. Touching kids....that bastard wants the birch and I will do it".

George's face went grey, he grabbed at his chest; Uncle Bill jumped up and laid him gently on the floor. "Bugger off, our Bill, you needn't start trying to mollycoddle me. It's just the shock of a teacher doing that, for God sake!"

"Just take it easy" said Uncle Bill.

"I'm going up to the school to find that excuse for a man and stick my bayonet up his backside".

"Well that wouldn't be wise, George, now would it? Look, both of you. I have a couple of hours to spare this afternoon. Do you want me to go up there with Horace to sort this out?"

Eva had remained silent until now "Yes, our Bill, yes please. You know it will probably kill my George if he goes up to Horace's School. In fact, he wouldn't even get there in his condition; the walk alone would kill him. I would be so grateful if you would go, Bill".

George was in the Somme offensive in France when he was gassed along with hundreds of English and French soldiers. He was sent to a field hospital where he was treated for a few weeks until he was deemed fit to fight again. His lungs were really bad but they sent him back anyway. He fought there for a few more months until he was shot in the back during a retreat.

The bullet penetrated his already damaged left lung. He was in the field hospital for a further two months before being transferred back to England to the Great Hall at the University Hospital of Birmingham. This facility didn't exist until August 1914 and the start of The Great War. It was the main medical building in the Midlands, which was convenient for the family to visit him, otherwise they would have had to go Aldershot or London and Eva wouldn't do that. In fact, she only went to see George once and that only when he was well enough to go out to the garden. She wouldn't set foot in a hospital. The only other time she did was when she had her first child, but that's another story.

Uncle Bill told Horace to get some lunch then they would go straight back to school to sort these damn people out. "Come on, young Horace. Put your jacket on again, you must look smart when we see the principal".

"But the principal said we have to go back in the morning, Uncle Bill, with one of my parents".

They drove to the school through Burton and Horace noticed something wrong with the engine in Uncle Bill's van.

"Uncle Bill, your timing's out on the van. Can't you hear it's 'missing'? It's worse than before".

"Well, it's been like this since it was last serviced at Plenty's garage. I didn't think it sounded right".

"Well you're taking it to the wrong garage. You want to take it to Mr. Rush. He will sort it out for you".

"Well if you know what's wrong with it why don't you do it? You're going to have plenty of time on your hands if you're thrown out of school later. Let's see what Mr. Reynolds has to say, old son".

"I didn't think you would trust me to mess about with your beloved van".

"Well, if you can put it right one good turn deserves another. Come on let's see what he has to say, Horace".

They pulled up outside the school and walked into the building. The Principal's secretary greeted them in the hallway.

"Can I help you? What are you doing here, Gray? You were told to come back in the morning with your father. Didn't you understand what Mr. Reynolds told you? Sorry, Mr. Gray, you've had a wasted journey".

Uncle Bill chimed in, "I'm sorry, good lady, but things like this have to be nipped in the bud, before they get out of hand".

"No! I am sorry you cannot see the Principal until tomorrow morning, Mr. Gray. The Principal is far too busy to see you today. I cannot allow you to disturb him. Now, if you will please leave the building".

"Good lady, this is far too serious to leave until tomorrow". Uncle Bill looked at the name plates on each of the doors. Having identified Mr. Reynolds' office, and not wishing to be impolite, he knocked on the door before walking straight in. Reynolds had his feet on his desk. He was smoking a cigarette and drinking a cup of tea.

"Excuse me! You can't just walk into my office. You need an appointment to see me. I'm far too busy to see you now".

He then saw Horace behind Uncle Bill.

"I told you I would see you in the morning, Gray. Are you not in enough trouble as it is?"

The secretary ran in behind them. "Sorry, Sir, I did say that you were not to be disturbed today but Mr. Gray wouldn't take any notice of me".

Uncle Bill was furious.

"Horace, in trouble after what he told me had happened? You have the audacity to sit there with your feet up while you have a teacher in this school touching boys in inappropriate places, and you're far too busy? Have you been in touch with the Education Board or the police? Having a man like that on your staff".

"Mr. Gray, please. I will see you both tomorrow".

"You really know the boys and their families well do you? I am not his father and you will see us now you pompous arse!" Uncle Bill always had a way with words.

"You sit there with your feet on your desk while you have a crisis in your school. Hearing about what Osborne did to his son this morning has given Horace's dad a heart attack. What are you going to about that pervert of a teacher of yours? I want to see him now. Let him deny it to Horace's face".

"So, if you are not Gray's father, who are you? He can't just bring anyone here to speak for him, now go".

"I am Bill Reece, the lad's uncle and we want to know what you are doing about this situation".

"Mr. Reece, we cannot take seriously what these boys say. The teachers have a hard enough job without being accused of sexual misconduct. However, if you wish to settle this now, Gray, you are expelled from this school with immediate effect. Go and get all of your belongings and leave my building".

"You are telling us that you don't believe him, so why did you want to see him tomorrow?"

"To formally expel him and that is what I have now done. You will be getting a letter in the post, Gray. We simply cannot have pupils hitting the staff here. Now, please leave before I have you escorted from the building".

"So, who do you think is going to escort me from this school of your homosexual friend? I don't think so. You do know that he has done this before to other children".

"I don't know what you mean. This the first time one of my masters has been accused of such a vile crime".

"I'm glad you think it's a crime. I came with Horace today because others have told me what Osborne has done to some of the children in your care. One lad, same age as Horace, came to work for me because of what one of your staff members did to him and you are just as bad passing it off as a lie. Well, let me tell you, Horace has never met any of these lads. They left this school between four and seven years ago. One of them is Ray Wilkinson who works for me. He told me in his interview, then there are Ian Meers, Denis Alcock and Stewart Parker and that's the ones we know about. Believe me Reynolds, there are more. If you're not going to do anything I will go to the Education Board and get this school sorted out. I am not the sort to lie down and take this kind of crap. You will be hearing from us".

When they were driving back, Horace asked why Uncle Bill had never mentioned these other boys before. "Is it true, Uncle Bill?"

"Yes lad, every word, but I couldn't say. I didn't want anyone to fly off the handle any more than they already had".

"Well, that worked well then, Uncle Bill" said Horace teasingly. "You was as calm as a dog with rabies. I'll have to remember to take you again if we have a similar situation. Would you mind taking me up to see Mr. Rush? I want to see if he can give me a few hours work a week, then I'll get a spanner and sort out your timing for you".

Mr. Rush's garage had a small mechanics workshop with a kiosk and two petrol pumps at the front.

"OK lad. I owe you for losing my rag at the school. He just wound me up from the start denying it all".

"No, I owe you. I'm going to put your van right after Billy Boy messed it up for you, or was it Steve?"

"Not sure which one did it but I think Steve is better than Bill".

"How long is Auntie Mavis away for, Uncle Bill?"

"She is back at the weekend. Her mum is really bad at the moment. I wanted to bring her down here but her two sisters want her to stay in Manchester, which is a bind for me and the boys. Mavis is quite happy up there with her sisters. So, Horace, what will you do now, after you've fixed my van I mean?"

"To start with, ask Mr. Rush to see if he'll have me there full time. Martin's just finished and gone to work at Standard Triumph in Station Street. Mr. Rush was saying on Saturday he's got to get someone else. I think I'll go up on my bike this afternoon".

"Come on, Horace, let's go up there now. I can ask him for you it'll be better coming from me".

Bill and Horace went to the garage and explained the day's events to Gordon. He was really shocked to hear what had happened and, even worse, that it had already happened on numerous other occasions.

"Horace, of course you can work for me. That will save me getting someone else. Always said it's better the devil you know, and don't let that Fisher scare you off like he did to Martin, trying to get him to do dodgy stuff. That's the only reason Martin went to Triumph as a foreman. Do you know, Bill, Horace has been stripping car engines down since he was ten years old....and brakes too?"

"Yes, Gordon but can he put 'em back together again? That's the most important thing".

They laughed. "If I have any more of your lip, Uncle Bill, I will make your van sound worse than it is now". Horace readjusted the timing chain then tightened up the housing bolts. He started the engine and gave it a few revs before shutting the engine off. "Right, try that out".

"It's not going to let me down is it Horace?"

"If it does, Uncle Bill, it'll be nothing I've done".

"Start it up again" said Gordon, "and we'll have another listen".

Bill started the van and took 'the mickey' out of Horace telling him it sounded even worse than before.

"With you being such a tight sod, Uncle Bill, you don't get anything done on the van. Look at the tyres for a start. You're not supposed to see who can get the smoothest ones".

INTREPID

"Yes he's right the whole van wants a good look at, Bill. If the timing chain starts to slip again we will have to fit a new one, or it could be the bearings. See how it goes and come and see us in a week or so".

"It was only serviced last week".

Gordon asked if the garage that serviced it had changed the plugs and the points.

"Yes Gordon. They changed the plugs and points".

Gordon took a look at the points.

"This is part of your problem. Apart from the timing chain, which Horace was right about, they're ten 'thou' out and the points are burnt at the side. Can you see this pit mark? Either they didn't change them or they never set them right. Either way they're buggered Bill".

"So they probably never changed the points then, Gordon, if they're ten 'thou' out. Even I know that's a lot".

"It'll only take two minutes. Horace, take the plugs out, see what shape they're in and get some new ones. They'll be in box number 245".

Horace took the plugs out and showed Gordon. The electrodes were warn right down. One plug didn't even have the 'top on'.

"Well, they had you for a monkey here alright Bill. These have been in there for sometime".

Horace fetched some new plugs and fitted them. "There, it should go better now".

Gordon told Bill he didn't want anything for the parts and told Horace that he would see him at eight the next morning.

"Yes, thanks Mr. Rush I can't wait to tell my mum and dad that I'll be working here full time. It's what I've always wanted to do since I was ten years old, repairing motors. I wasn't sure you would take me on".

Uncle Bill took Horace home and they recounted to his mum all that had happened earlier at the school.

Horace's mum was exasperated. "They have expelled you, for what that man did to you? What on earth is this world coming to when that happens and nothing is done? Mark my words this will not go away, Horace. I always knew a boy's school would be trouble. They should have brought in secondary modern schools years ago and got rid of the grammars".

"I think Uncle Bill was as shocked as me, ma. He went mad but no one can do anything about it. Uncle Bill knows of four other kids it's happened to in the last few years and Osborne's laughing at us all. He wants a bullet in the head. People like him taking advantage of the pupils at the school".

"What did Mr. Reynolds say about them? He can't deny it if others have said things in the past about Osborne".

"He said that we are making it all up, that we must have got together to cook the story up, and when Uncle Bill told him that I don't know these other kids he just looked out of the window hoping all this trouble would disappear out of it".

"Do you know any of the other lads, Horace?"

"No ma. I've seen one of them that works for Uncle Bill but never spoke to him. Don't worry about it ma, Uncle Bill won't let it rest. He told me he will go to the Education Board but he isn't sure when. He'll ask Ray Wilkinson about the others. He told me that he's getting all the facts together first".

Horace was having his tea when his dad came home from work, so he had to go over it all once more.

"I don't want to seem thick, son, but your education is being ruined because of a bloody child abuser. That's not right, that's not right at all, our Eva. What are we going to do about it? What places are we sending our kids to when they are taken out of class and a teacher tries to shove his hand up my lad's arse?"

"Well, dad, I would rather go to work than learn Latin or Pythagoras' Theory. What good is that going to be to anyone, and no one speaks Latin in this country anymore except the bishops and some clergy?"

Horace got on his bike and went to see his best friend Kevin Mason to tell him all about what had happened at school.

"Kev, thought I'd come and see you to tell you about the day I've had. It's been a nightmare I can tell you".

"Where did you get to after Osborne called you out? We thought you were ill or something".

Horace told Kevin all about what happened in Osborne's

office. He was so shocked and confused.

"Why would he do that to you, Horace?"

"Uncle Bill said Osborne's a molester and knows of four others that it happened to and told Reynolds their names".

Kevin shouted to his mum and dad.

"What are you 'yarking' at, Kevin?"

He told his parents what Horace had told him.

"You can't go back there with that sort of thing going on. I'm not even sure we want Kevin to go back there after this. You're fourteen now, Horace, so you'll have to go to work instead. When were you fourteen?"

"About a month ago Mr. Mason. Mr. Reynolds said I was lying about Mr. Osborne to try to get him into trouble but Uncle Bill told him about four other boys the same thing had happened to. Ray Wilkinson told Uncle Bill at his Interview for a job on the building site that he and three others had been molested. As well as Ray Wilkinson the other lads were called Denis Alcock, Stewart Parker and Ian Meer. Mr. Reynolds said that me and Uncle Bill had got together to cook the story up but I'd never met the others because they were at school between four and seven years ago".

"Ian Meer lives in South Street doesn't he?" Kevin asked his dad.

"Yes, I work with his dad, Pete. Look son, I can get you a job at the brewery, you're fourteen too".

"Yes, dad but you know I want to go into the building trade and Horace's uncle Bill said I can have a job up the road building the new council houses".

"Kevin, you know we've put our names down for one of them and we don't want one that you've built". Horace laughed. "Don't encourage him" said Kevin's mum.

Kevin and Horace walked up to Ian Meer's house to speak to him. Kevin knocked and Mr. Meer came to the door. He asked Kevin to tell his dad that he needed a lift in the morning because his car would be at the garage tomorrow. He called Ian for them and went back inside.

"Ian, can we have a word with you about Osborne, the maths teacher?"

"That bastard! Why, what's happened?"

Horace told him what had happened that morning, being called out of class, going to Osborne's office and what he'd done after Osborne had touched him.

"Do you know, he did the same thing when I was there but I was more naive then you were. He went further with me and actually took my trousers and pants down. He told me that he had to check all the boys for infection because we were reaching puberty. He was my teacher for God's sake, my teacher".

Kevin asked him what happened next. Ian said that he didn't want to go into too much detail but told them that Osborne had held his penis and asked him whether he was feeling anything. I said "no" so he kept rubbing harder until I started to get an erection. Osborne's face had lit up and he was so nice to me. "He told me that only his 'special boys' do that. I was so frightened of what he was doing that I ran, well stumbled, out of his office pulling my 'kecks' up. I ran past the sectary just outside his office".

"Jesus, Ian, I was lucky then. Did you tell your mum and dad about it?"

"Yes, I ran straight home, didn't even go back to class. Mum called dad to come home from work to sort it all out. When he got home I told him all about it. You see, I never told mum the full story just the outline to it, but I told dad the whole lot. He picked up a dining chair and threw it against the wall saying he would kill the evil bastard and went straight to the school. I'd told dad where to find the maths room. He went straight in, picked Osborne up by the throat and kept smacking him in the mouth....until the other teachers grabbed him. The police come and arrested dad. He was fined thirty pounds for assault and nearly went to jail, but the judge said that the only ones that know the truth to what really happened were him and me".

"Uncle Bill went mad too, Ian. I thought he was going to hit Reynolds when he said we'd got together to cook up the story but when Uncle Bill told him that I'd never met the others, he just told us to get off the school property. Uncle Bill said that the way Reynolds reacted shows that he knew the truth about what Osborne has been doing".

"Come in and tell my mum and dad". They went into the living room. "Mum, dad listen to this. Go on, Horace, tell my mum and dad what you've just told me".

Horace went through the story from the start.

Mr. and Mrs. Meer were livid that Osborne was still teaching in a school, any school but especially that school. "So, what will you do Horace?"

"Well, I've just been to see Mr. Rush at the garage. I've been working at weekends but now and I'm starting full time".

"Yes, but that's another child's education ruined. How many are there whose lives are being marred by these people?"

"Mr. and Mrs. Meer, I can assure you that one day I will get justice for all of us and hopefully Uncle Bill will help to get it all sorted. He won't take any nonsense off the Education Board. I want to be like him when I get older".

Horace bade them farewell then left Kevin at the end of North Street from where he started to bike home over the Ox Hay. He hadn't got far when he saw a man attacking an older woman. He rode over at full speed, jumped off his bike and pushed the chap to the ground where they both wrestled and punched each other. The assailant managed to get up but Horace grabbed one of his feet and pulled him over again. But the man managed to wriggle free, get up once more and started kicking Horace in the face before trying to run away. Horace picked up the sturdy branch of an oak tree and gave chase. Being younger and fitter, he caught up with the man and struck him on the head with the branch causing the man to fall to the ground where he stayed, stunned.

*Authors Note: The Ox Hay is an area of wash land by the River Trent to the South East of the town.*

By now, a man and a woman had arrived on the scene and were comforting the attacker's victim. Horace turned round and asked if she was alright, to which the man replied "I think so, son, she is just shocked. I can't see any outward problems. It was lucky you were passing on your bike, we couldn't have run over in time to stop him attacking her".

A man wearing a train driver's hat was passing on his way to work at the railway station and, witnessing the commotion, rushed off to fetch a policeman. When PC Richmond arrived he went straight over and handcuffed the assailant. He looked at the man and said "Not this devil again. We've been after him for weeks but he keeps giving us the slip. He's Fryderyk Nowak a Polish ex-prisoner of war".

He thanked the man and woman for apprehending him. "Sorry officer, it wasn't us it was this young lad".

"You son, you're only a child. How the hell did you get him when the whole Burton police force couldn't? He's a nasty character is our Nowak".

PC Richmond asked the lady if she was alright, but she didn't seem to be fully aware of what had just happened. "Son, could you bike round to the ambulance station? It will only take you a minute".

"Yes, sir, I will go straight there".

"Are you sure you are up to it, son? Your face looks a right old mess, your left eye is nearly shut".

"Yes, I'm fine, sir".

Horace rode around the corner as quickly as he could to the ambulance station, told them about the incident and returned to the Ox Hay. When he got back the woman had become unconscious and was not responding to anyone.

"Good lad, you've done well tonight but you must go to the infirmary to get that gash on your eyebrow seen to".

"Its fine, officer, it's not bleeding too much".

"That's what's worrying me". PC Richmond went to ask one of the ambulance men to take a look at it.

"This looks nasty. I saw it when you came to the ambulance station. How did that happen?"

"He kicked me in the face when he was trying to get away".

"I suggest you go round to New Street Infirmary and get it seen to. That cut will need at least six stitches".

"We think the lady has had a stroke. She regained consciousness for a few seconds but her right side is weak and I can't make out what she is saying".

Horace went to the infirmary on his way home arriving before the ambulance. A nurse asked him what had happened so he told her the full story. She called the doctor to see Horace immediately.

"It looks like you have an orbital fracture, Horace. We will need an x-ray to be absolutely sure but your eye socket is definitely damaged".

After the x-ray and stitches, Horace was told that his eye socket may be damaged permanently, but he was young enough for it to stand a chance of healing fully. "But it will be sore for a few days. Come back tomorrow when we have seen the x-ray, we can tell you more then but there really isn't much we can do with a damaged eye socket".

Horace enquired about the old lady and was told that she was very poorly.

PC Richmond came in with a gentleman and went into the cubical in which the old lady was lying. When PC Richmond came out again he asked Horace if he could stay a bit longer.

"Well, I have to go and tell my mum and dad where I am or they will be worried. It's gone nine but I promise I will be back, I will be back, sir."

"Where do you live, Horace?"

"At Marston's cottages, my dad works at the brewery".

"Alright son. We'll be here for a while so there's no rush. You can bring your dad back with you if you wish".

"I am fine, thank you. I'll just go and tell them what's happened and will be back in about thirty minutes".

Horace biked it home and as soon has is mum saw the state of his face she screamed "What the hell have you done, have you been in a fight? What a mess you've made of your eye, our Horace".

"Our George, come and look at Horace's face".

George got up reluctantly out of his chair. His beer was on the floor beside his chair and whatever had happened couldn't be more important than that but he picked himself up and went into the scullery to see what the fuss was about. When he saw Horace's eye he said "It'll be worse than that next time I have to get up out of my chair. How'd it happen, son?"

Downplaying his role as a hero and not mentioning that he'd helped a lady who was being attacked, Horace told them that this Polish bloke had knocked him off his bike and that he'd have to go back to hospital now for a doctor to check it and then again tomorrow to get the result of the x-ray.

His dad said he would get his coat and go with him as it's getting late. "What else is going to happen to you today, Horace? After this morning you would think that would have been it for today".

"No, honestly dad I'll be fine. I should be home within the hour; they said it won't take long. I only came back because I knew you would be worried about me....and because you'd have to fetch your own ale".

"Yes, Bella did mention that I have to do everything myself in this house".

Eva was in the scullery making bread for the following day.

"You are a cheeky bleeder, our George. She would have been talking about me. What do you do around this house? The kids fetch and carry for you and I do all your cooking and cleaning, not to mention washing your smoke-ridden clothes....you dirty, messy old man. It's about time you lifted a finger in this house. You moan when you have to move your backside out of a chair to look at your poor son's face".

"Now see what you've done, Horace. You come home and upset your mother like this and I get the blame for it. Next time stay out 'til you've stopped bleeding all over the place. There you go, our Eva. That told him for you, my love. Haven't you done that bread yet, what you mucking about at?"

"Any more of that, our George, and you can come and make your own bread. You eat the most of it anyway".

"Here our old gel, I keep chickens but I don't lay the bloody eggs, you silly old mare".

Horace biked back to the hospital to see PC Richmond. "What did your parents say about you being the have-a-go hero? They must be very proud of you. I know I would have been".

"Is the lady any better, PC Richmond?"

"She looks a bit better than when she came in. We don't know what the damage is yet, but she is starting to talk. There is someone who wants to talk to you first".

The gentleman who went into the cubicle to see her with PC Richmond came out from behind the curtain. "So, you are the young man that saved my wife's life. I simply cannot thank you enough and when she is feeling better she will want to thank you as well. Could you tell me how old you are, Horace isn't it?"

"Yes, sir, I am fourteen. Do you think she will be alright, sir? She didn't look very well when she came in."

"My name is Stan Carpenter and my wife and I live in Oak House, backing onto the Ox Hay. My wife was just taking a stroll by the river when this happened. We will want to thank you properly when she feels better".

Horace went home after making a statement to PC Richmond and said he would go to the police station the following day at two o'clock for the identity line-up. Horace got home just after ten o'clock. His parents were still up to see how he was. His mum and dad looked at his injured eye. "That eye looks strange, it looks almost square. You can't go to work tomorrow looking like that, it must really hurt as well".

"It does, dad, but it's no good just staying at home. No, I will be going to work as planned but I will need an hour or so to go to the hospital and they think they found the bloke that did it so afterwards I will go to do the identity parade. Goodnight mum, dad. I'll be up at five or before. Probably won't sleep much tonight".

# CHAPTER TWO

Horace was up early the next morning. He had always been an early riser from a very young age but with the pain in his eye was up even earlier. He went for a walk outside to have a smoke and collect some eggs. With forty laying hens there were always plenty of eggs. He went back indoors and lit the fire to warm up the stove so that Eva could bake the bread when she got up. It was always the job of the person who was up first in the morning to light the fire. He put the kettle and pan on the stove and placed the sausage meat and bacon in the pan. Dad was up next. He always was when he smelt breakfast cooking.

"What are we having for breakfast, son?"

"Oh dad, shall we have some bacon, sausage meat and eggs? Do you want me to get some bracket mushrooms?"

Bracket mushrooms are fungi that grow in the shape of what look like flat, semi-circular plates that overlap each other. They are found predominantly on or near tree bark.

"Yes, son, but remember to get the right sort. Bring it all. If there's a lot I will dry some and put it in my tea. I'll finish cooking the bacon and sausage while you're out. Your eye's a bloody mess, my son. It's nearly closed up altogether".

"Yes dad. I can't see much out of it".

When Horace returned with the mushrooms and breakfast was

ready, George put it on the table then made the tea. "I thought Ron would be up by now, he starts at seven. I'll give him a call to come and get his breakfast. Do you know, our Horace, it doesn't take me long to cook the breakfast does it now?"

"No dad, you're like a bloody whippet in the mornings, you're that fast we can hardly see you move".

"Are you sure you will be OK for work with your eye being so bad this morning?"

"Yes dad. I will do what I can. It does hurt but Mr. Rush will understand if I have trouble with it. I've got to go to the hospital and police station later anyway, so will have to leave work early".

When Horace got to the garage he heard someone arguing with Gordon in the workshop. Not wanting to intrude he stayed outside and lit a cigarette.

Christine Rush, Gordon's wife, came outside and bade him good morning. "What on earth's happened to your face it looks like you've been kicked by a horse? What happened to you?"

"I was biking over the Ox Hay when this Polish chap knocked me off my bike and kicked me in the face. I went to the hospital yesterday but have to go again this afternoon, and then to the police station at two o'clock to see the police officer that arrested him. I don't want to go into the workshop yet, Mr. Rush is talking to someone in there and it sounds like someone's very cross about something".

"Don't worry, Horace, it's only my dad. Christopher and I are going for a walk now. Will you tell Gordon when they've finished talking, or should I say arguing, please Horace? I didn't know you smoked, your only fourteen. What do your parents think of it?"

"Yes, but only the odd one from time to time. My dad keeps nicking mine, tells me he's saving my life".

"Well don't make a habit of it and he's right, smoking is very bad for your health. That's what they are saying now anyway".

"So is getting kicked in the head Mrs. Rush".

Christine laughed. "You are funny, Horace. I love your sense of humour. I wish more people were like you, my dad included. He is always in a bad mood and has been for as long as I can remember. Your eye looks very sore and the socket is almost square".

"They told me that the bone in the orbit of my eye is fractured. It's supposed to be round, which is why they call it the orbit, I suppose. The doctor said they don't know if the damage will be permanent or not".

He walked up to the pram to say hello to Christopher. "You're growing into a big boy now. The toddler smiled then pointed at Horace's eye.

Even Christopher had noticed it. It must look bad, he thought, for even a three year-old to notice it. They said goodbye. Horace went inside and said good morning to Gordon. Mr. Fisher was standing there with him.

"Morning, Mr. Rush. I was here at eight but heard you arguing with someone, or should I say, someone arguing with you. When Mrs. Fisher told me it was her dad I thought it was private, well as private as it could be. You could've heard him down the coal mines in Swad".

He got a terse reply and scowl from Brian Fisher. Brian asked Gordon why the boy was here and not at school. "The little bastard should be at school not here. Get rid of him, I don't know why you encourage him".

"It's because I have a happy persona" said Horace. "Oh, sorry, that means a happy person to a thick twat like you".

"Fuck off you little bastard. What are you doing in here anyway? Piss off outside, the big boys are talking about grown-up things".

"Horace, you stay right here. What's happened to your eye?"

Horace went through the story about what had happened the night before and explained that he needed to go to the hospital and police station in the afternoon.

Fisher sniped, "The chap clearly never kicked you hard enough because you're still here. Why are you here anyway?"

"Well, if it's anything to do with you, which it isn't, I have left school and started here full time thanks to Mr. Rush. It means I can get evidence for the police about your dodgy dealings".

"You're not old enough to leave school yet, and get your facts right about my business".

"Well, if you really want to know, I was expelled for thumping a teacher".

"What, a little squirt like you? He should have taken you round the back of the school and did what that bloke did to you last night but kicked you into next week. I'm telling you Gordon, get shot of him, or I will. The little bastard has been coming here bothering you since he was knee high to a snake".

"So you know about snakes and how low they can go, you old bastard".

"Brian, you don't know the whole story. He was molested by a teacher, that's the whole truth and that's why he is working here full time now".

"You should have asked me first before hiring more shit. You've only just got rid of that other useless twat, Martin, but I have a marker out on him. One word from him and I have enough to put him away for ten years".

"Yes, and that's why Martin left, because of you and your scheming. It was the stuff you asked him to move for you, he was as frightened as a baby rabbit in the headlights. If you hurt him it's you I'll have to put away".

"Sorry Mr. Rush. I don't want to be rude but you employ me, what's it got to do with him anyway?"

"Because you little Bastard" interrupted Brian, "this all belongs to me. The garage, the house and seven more houses down this road. So, if I don't like anything or anyone it is up to me to decide what to do, and I don't like you, never have. There is something about you that bothers me so if you don't want to get another clout you will do what I say".

"Another clout, what, off someone like you? You'd never catch me you fat bastard".

"Gordon, you wanted him here, you keep him in line or I will". Brian produced a revolver briefly then left.

"Be careful, Horace. Don't wind him up too much. We're the ones who'll get the backlash if he gets angry".

"Sorry, Mr. Rush, but he's such a horrible person with his big 'I am' nonsense".

"Start on the Alvis, the rear brakes need changing. I'll crack on with the Vanguard while you take the back wheels off".

The next time he looked over at the Alvis, Horace was using a wire brush to clean the drums and back plates. By the time Gordon had finished fitting a rocker cover gasket to the Vanguard, Horace had fitted the brake linings to the rear wheel on one side. "Are they alright lad? You've done a good job cleaning the drums and back plates, how are they?"

"The drums are a bit scored but not too bad". Gordon checked them. "Yes lad, you're right, they'll do. I will help to put the new linings on the other side in a minute".

"It's OK. I'll put them on and leave the drums off for you to check them".

"Good lad".

He worked till one o'clock then left to go to the infirmary and police station, but went home first for a wash and change. Uncle Bill was there for his lunch and laughed when he saw Horace's face.

"You look like your Auntie Mavis now with all that damage".

"Our Bill" said Eva, "it's horrible to say that about Mavis. You would run a mile if I told her when she comes back".

"A mile? Old Mavis couldn't run to the end of this row".

Horace had changed into his best trousers and had his jacket on, his hair was brushed.

"My God!" said Uncle Bill, "is it Sunday already? How the time flies".

"I've got to go to the infirmary and station about last night. This Polish bloke can't get away with doing this".

"Good lad" said George. "You go and make sure they throw the key away with this fellow. They shouldn't have stayed here when the war ended. We have Polish, Germans, Italians and French, all the ones that hated us in the last two wars".

"Well, George, I can't argue with you on that one, but the politicians say it's a good thing to integrate but I don't see how".

Horace said cheerio and left.

He went to the infirmary first to see about the x-ray. The eye socket was definitely broken so the doctor advised him to protect the eye as much as he could. But, like they said the night before, they couldn't really do anything for it. He would have to go back in a month's time for them to check whether it was healing and getting back to its original shape.

At the police station he was shown into an interview room where he was joined by PC Richmond and Inspector Smart.

"Good afternoon, Horace. How are you today? You managed to get out of school then".

"Well, so to speak, sir. I was expelled yesterday morning".

"Expelled? What on Earth for? I like to think that I'm a good judge of a person's character and yours seems to be exemplary" said Inspector Smart. "Could you tell us why you got expelled?"

"Yes, but first can you please tell me how Mrs. Carpenter is?"

"Not very well, I'm afraid. She has a bleed on the brain so it's touch and go for her".

"Do you think I could go and see her later?"

"I will find out, Horace. So, what was the reason for your expulsion?"

"I was called out by the maths teacher to go to his room. I went in first. He shut the door behind me and touched my backside. I thought it was just an accident but when we got to his desk he touched my crotch as well. I reacted instinctively and punched him on the nose".

"I see".

"The Principal said I was lying about the incident but my uncle Bill knows of others that it's happened to, one of them is a lad called Ray Wilkinson".

"That name is familiar" said Inspector Smart. "Yes, I remember now. It was about five years ago that he came to the station with his dad. I was sergeant at the time. I went to the school and spoke to a Mr. Reynolds and he said then that the lad was a prolific liar. I'm afraid we must have let the boy down badly. I will re-open the case. As PC Richmond says, you sound like a remarkable lad reacting the way you did to that attack on the Ox Hay last night. Most lads your age would have just frozen. Tell us about last night, Horace. Where were you coming from and going to?"

"Well, sir, I went to see my school friend well, he's been my best mate since we were at infant school. They lived in Blackpool Street then and moved to Winshill when we started at grammar school. His name is Kevin Mason. He was shocked when I told him that I'd been expelled and the reason why, and so were his mum and dad. When I told them that my uncle Bill mentioned some other lads' names to Mr. Reynolds, and that one of them was Ian Meer who lived around the corner from them, Kev said we should go and see him. So, that's what we did".

"When we got there we told him what had happened to me. Then it all came out. Ian told us how the same had happened to him and ruined his life. He's four years older than us and works at BTR. He had wanted to work in a bank when he left school like his uncle. We then left Ian's and got to the end of the road. I told Kev that I'd see him later that night then biked it back down Bearwood Hill Road then across the Ox Hay where I saw this man hitting an older lady".

"He was hitting her across the face and head, mainly the head, so I biked as fast as I could to try and stop him. That's when I jumped off my bike, grabbed him and pushed him over. We fought on the ground for a few moments then he got up, kicked me in the head three times and ran off. There was this branch nearby so I picked it up, chased after him and hit him over the head with it, flooring him....'til PC Richmond got there".

Inspector Smart told him that it was the best and most thorough statement he'd ever been given. "Thank you, Horace. You might have to go to court as a witness but I think he will own up to it".

PC Richmond asked if Horace would do the identity parade. Mr. and Mrs. Norton, the couple who attended to Lady Carpenter at the scene, will be coming as well.

"You have ten minutes or so before the identity parade if you don't mind waiting here" said Inspector Smart.

"Do you mind if I have a smoke?"

"You cheeky devil, you're not allowed to smoke 'til you're sixteen". PC Richmond threw him a pack of Richmond.

Horace laughed.

"What's the matter?"

"A pack of Richmond, did you make them yourself?"

Both Richmond and Smart looked at each other and shook

their heads.

A constable came to tell Horace that they were ready for him. Mr. and Mrs. Norton were already there. They went in one by one and walked down the line of suspects. They all picked out the assailant by tapping him on the shoulder. When Horace reached Nowak and lifted his hand to tap him on the shoulder, Nowak grabbed him by the scruff of the neck but the police were on him like a bunch of flees on a badger.

After the identity parade, Horace walked out to the front desk, the desk sergeant nodded to him. There was a group of people standing near the entrance to the police station. "They are reporters from the press" said the sergeant, "they want to ask you a few questions".

"Are you the lad who saved Lady Carpenter's life?" one reporter shouted through the doorway.

"I helped a lady" replied Horace, "but I didn't save her life. The doctors and nurses in the infirmary did that. I was just biking home when I saw a man attacking a lady, so I did what anyone would do to help a defenceless person".

"Well, you're right about her being a lady. She is Lady Edith Carpenter, wife of Sir Stanley Carpenter. He's an advisor in the home office and a close friend of the former Prime Minister, Winston Churchill".

"Can you tell us what happened?"

"Sorry, I have nothing to say".

"Well, son, we will fill the paper with whatever we want then. Come on, you were injured, lad, you have to tell your story".

Horace walked over to the desk sergeant and asked him whether the reporters knew his name and address.

"No, son, or they would be camped outside your house. That's why they came here instead".

"How did they know I was here right at this time? It can't be a coincidence can it?"

"No, son, there is someone from this station getting back-handers from the press and what with the lady's husband being a high profile person an' all. If I find out who's doing it, his feet won't touch the ground. I'm Sergeant Simms by the way, if you have any bother with anyone". Now come on he said loudly to the reporters.

"Sergeant Simms, will it be OK if we keep where I live a secret? I don't want any fuss or my family being dragged into it".

"They won't hear anything from us. I will go and tell Inspector Smart to keep your file under lock and key for now".

"Could I please go out the back door? I'll go across the Bass railway tracks they come out near our house".

"Tell you what....just walk across like you are going outside. Jenkins, shout young Gray here and tells him Inspector Smart would like to see him again".

"Excuse me young man" shouted Jenkins as loud as he could, "Inspector Smart wants another word with you".

The sergeant opened the back door to let Horace out and left the press standing at the front of the station. Horace left his bike at the police station and jumped over the wall onto the Bass train tracks. He got home as smartish as he could.

His mum asked him how he got on but he didn't say anything about the press, mainly because he hadn't told his mum about Lady Carpenter. In fact, he never told her about a woman being attacked just that he'd made a statement to the police and gone to an identity parade to pick out the man who'd kicked him.

"I might have to go to court, mum, now that they've charged the bloke".

"Well, he deserves everything he gets for doing that to you, Horace".

"Ma, brother Ron's on his way home from Sharps Joiner's".

Ron worked as an apprentice joiner at Sharps in town.

"There's a letter for you, Ron" said Eva when he came in, "and it looks official. Have you had a good day, son?"

"Yes, thanks ma. The letter should be my national service papers. As you know I applied to join the R.A.F. next year. Did you know that a man beat up a lady last night over the Ox Hay? Apparently he nearly killed her. A passerby intervened and stopped him. People are saying that a foreigner was arrested. That's where you got beat up wasn't it, our kid?"

"Yes, he must have attacked me before her. I never saw an old lady over the Ox Hay".

Strictly speaking it wasn't a lie...Lady Carpenter was only forty six.

Ron remarked that the assailant probably only went after girls and old women. Horace put two fingers up, a bit like Churchill but the opposite way round.

"Thanks, brother. I knew I could rely on you for your kindness and sympathy. Have you learned how to do joints properly yet? Mark said you were crap at mortise and tenon".

"No mate, he's the crap joiner....I'm the best. Nothing wrong with my joints, I have the best marks in the class. Is it me or does your eye look worse?"

"OK, I know. I'm still better looking than you though".

"No mate, I'm being serious. It's gone red around the wound and its seeping yellow pus. What do you think, ma?"

"It looks like it's infected to me, son. If I were you I would go back down the infirmary straight away and see them".

Horace arrived at the infirmary and one of the nurses took a look at his eye.

"Yes, it definitely looks infected, Horace. Go into this cubicle and I'll get a doctor to come as soon as possible".

It wasn't long until the doctor arrived. He told Horace that they would have to take the stitches out and make sure the wound was clean. It was so painful and once they'd removed the stitches the blood started to trickle out. "Hold still, Horace" said the doctor "I can see something sticking out of the eye socket bone". He asked a nurse to fetch the x-ray from last night.

"You will have to lie down, there is something stuck deep in there".

He called for another doctor to come and help. Whilst keeping the cut open with his fingers the other doctor used some forceps to try to grab something that was inside the gash. After a few minutes of prodding around he pulled out a shard of metal. He looked at it through a magnifying glass

"What did the bloke hit you with?"

"He kicked me with his boot".

"Then he must have had a blade fixed into the toe cap of one of his boots". He looked at the x-ray, "Yes, you can just see it. Look, sticking into the supra-orbital ridge. I'm sorry it was so painful but it had to come out. I will get Sister Jones to clean the wound and stitch it up again. The police will want to see this".

"I can take it over to the police station if you want? I have to fetch my bike anyway, I left it there earlier. I had to leave in a hurry because the press were there demanding that I give them a story but I didn't want any fuss".

The sister cleaned the wound and stitched it up again but this time putting eleven stitches in, the full length of his eyebrow. She put a pad over his eye to protect the cut and told him to return in ten days to get it checked. She also gave him some penicillin tablets to get rid of the infection. He left and walked the half mile to the police station. He took the bit of metal to the front desk. Sergeant Simms was still there.

"Dear God! Horace, what happened to your eye? It looks a lot worse than it was earlier."

He showed Sergeant Simms the shard of metal that the doctors had extracted.

"Where did they pull it from?"

"From the bone above my eye socket".

"Did he stab you first then? I thought he just kicked you in the head, you never mentioned a knife, or did you?"

"No sergeant. He never stabbed me just kicked me in the head, but this is what they pulled out. They think it may be from the toe cap of one of his boots".

"Jenkins, go down to the exhibit room and brings me those boots, quickly now".

Jenkins brought the boots up and gave them to Sergeant Simms. He examined them carefully turning them this way and that. When he looked at the uppers he could just see a bit of metal embedded there.

"Well, I've not seen this before. Another eighth of an inch and it would have been straight through your eyeball, son. He must've really walloped you hard with that kick to break off metal in your face. Where will you be in the morning, Horace? I'm sure Inspector

Smart will want to talk to you about this".

"I'll be at work at Rush's Garage up at Henhurst, Sergeant. I started there full-time since being expelled from school yesterday morning".

"Expelled? Why were you expelled? You seem a good lad, very calm and of an exemplary nature".

Horace told him all about what had happened with Osborne and the school Principal not believing him and taking Osborne's side.

"Do you know, Horace, this isn't the first time I've heard about that school and that teacher. I will have a word with the inspector".

"It's OK Sergeant, I already told him".

"Well that's good, we can't let this happen to young people".

Horace said goodbye.

"By the way, Horace, before you go, the press didn't leave 'til about five minutes before you came back. They are really pissed off with you for not wanting to talk to them. They aren't used to that. They normally get a story before the person knows what's happening....well done, lad".

"Have you thought about being a copper when you're older? You're better than half the idiots we have here, isn't that right Jenkins? He's one of the worst, aren't you Jenkins".

"Yes sergeant, anything you say sergeant" and smiled at Horace.

"If you worked here with 'serge' you would get the same as us, Horace" and smiled again.

Horace got on his bike and rode home. He told his mum and dad what they'd taken out of his eye socket and they were both opened mouthed to think that someone walked the streets with a sort of knife hidden in a shoe. He bade them good night and went to bed.

Horace overslept, which was very unusual for him, and was woken by his dad shaking him.

"What's up dad?"

"Uncle Bill is here with the Morning Herald and your photo is on the front page. The headline says 'Does Anyone Know this Hero?'. You never told us it was you that intervened when that lady was attacked on Tuesday night".

"It's no big deal, dad. I didn't say because I knew mum would make a fuss and tell all the family and her friends that I'd saved the world from disaster. You know that, dad, you know I never want to make a fuss. I suppose she's down the street telling everyone about it now".

"No son. She wanted to but Uncle Bill and I stopped her from taking the paper down the row. You'd better come down and explain yourself though. It's seven o'clock and it's not like you to be in bed this time of the morning but understandable with what's happened to you in the last couple of days".

"Horace" said Eva glowing with pride, "you brave boy saving this lady's life, and she is a Lady. I know Lady Carpenter, she's a lovely down-to-earth woman".

Uncle Bill added, "Yes, and Stan is a nice chap too. That man deserves all that he has. A fearless fighter in the war, he ended up as Colonel in Chief of the British Lancers, now the King's Royal Lancers. He led his men into battle from the front, always the first one out of the trench. Not like some I've known that lead from the back. You had that in Ypres, George, in the first world war, didn't you?"

Ypres, the Belgian municipality in the province of West Flanders, has seen many battles. It was raided by the Romans in the first century B.C. and named in 1066 after the river Leperlee, on the banks of which the town was founded. Ypres played an important role in the textile industry during the middle ages. Its textiles could be found in markets all over Europe and further afield in the twelfth century.

It is said that Richard the Lionheart wore garments and used horse rugs made at the mills in Ypres when on his way to The Crusades. Ypres is famous for three major battles in The Great War, one of the biggest and most ferocious being The Battle of Passchendaele.

# CHAPTER THREE

Horace's dad told him that he'd better stay at home today. "Someone will be getting in touch with the paper, you can bank on that".

"This is exactly why I never said anything about what happened. I knew it would be like this, people making a fuss. Why can't some people just leave other people alone?"

Uncle Bill told Horace that the papers always like a good story. "I'm not doing down what you did, lad, but if it had happened to someone like Auntie Mavis or your mum there wouldn't have been so much fuss made. The secret is to ask the victim if she or her husband are famous or have friends that are government ministers. In this case it's friends with government ministers".

Horace's mum cooked a full breakfast for them all. George was happy as Larry. "My Eva, I'm glad Bill came round, you haven't cooked a breakfast like this for a year. Enjoy this, Horace, my hero. If it gets your mother out of bed to cook like this you can be a hero every day".

"You only came here for a fry-up didn't ya, Bill" Horace said, "you don't normally read the Morning Herald, you read the Express".

"I bought both. This one is for your mum to keep and treasure with her little boy's face on the front of the paper".

George joined Horace in ribbing Uncle Bill, "He's only jealous.

Horace is right, it's the breakfast you're here for".

"Well, it's a great excuse to get a free fry-up. Do you want a lift to work, Horace? You celebrities have to keep a low profile you know. You wait 'til I tell the boys what you've been up to, they won't believe it either".

After breakfast, Horace got on his bike and went to work.

"Morning Mr. Rush what am I doing today?"

"Good morning Horace, how's your eye this morning? Oh, sorry, hadn't seen your eye, it's completely covered....will you be alright working?"

"Yes Mr. Rush. I'd rather be working than staying at home all the time. Do you want me to service the Talbot?"

"Yes mate. Drop the axle and gear box oils first but make sure you don't get any muck in your bad eye. Just take your time and be careful. Christine said this morning that you've been through a hell of a lot in the last few days for someone so young. I don't know how you do it but you seem take it all in your stride".

"I don't want things to spoil my life, Mr. Rush. My dad said that you only get one shot at it and people like Osborne and that Ox Hay attacker will not stop me from doing what I want Mr. Rush".

Both Gordon and Horace worked on the cars until half past ten. Christine came in with a pot of tea and a bacon sandwich for each of them. "Tea up" she shouted. "Just been to the butcher's and everyone's talking about some lad in the morning paper that's from around here, so I bought one". She took the paper out and Horace tried to grab it from her to prevent Gordon from seeing it.

"My young lad, what's all this then? You said you were attacked on Tuesday night".

"Well, I was Mr. Rush. I didn't lie about it but didn't want to tell the full story either".

"Others would be shouting it from the rooftops" said Christine. "You are such a brave and lovely boy, Horace".

Gordon finished reading the article. "I don't believe this, Horace, you're the one in the paper. How and when did they get your photograph?"

"Must've been while I was at the police station yesterday afternoon making a statement. I wouldn't tell the press anything so they must've made most of it up".

"They say you saved this woman's life and knocked out the assailant....and they say your injuries were life threatening. Is that what the infirmary told you?"

"No, they never. Well, I don't think they did. It's all a bit of a haze if I'm honest Mr. Rush".

"They say you're a heroic kid and Mr. and Mrs. Norton told of how you swung into action without thinking of your own safety. They said it was like one of them early films with Buster Keaton doing his stunts, jumping off a horse".

"Sorry Mr. Rush but it was nothing like that. This is exactly why I didn't want to talk to them last night, I didn't want anyone to make a fuss".

"Well there is plenty doing it for you, Horace" said Christine, "now eat your sandwich before it goes cold".

"Yes, thank you Mrs. Rush. The bacon is nice and thick just how I like it, and with homemade bread".

"I'm glad Christine picked up a paper and went to the butchers we don't normally get the bacon this thick. Did you tell them that Horace worked for us?"

"Well, it might just have slipped out in conversation. Oh, by the way, I didn't even pay for it. They told me it was a treat for the hero. Let me tell you, Horace, you have lots of admirers in this town now. Your mum walked past like the cat that got the cream. She asked me to look after you so make sure to tell her I gave you a sandwich with extra thick bacon".

People waved to Horace as he went past on his bike on his way home after work. He hoped that this nonsense wouldn't last long. He muttered to himself "I don't want all this bloody attention".

At home it was even worse. People were in the house, some of whom he'd never met before. Dad was sitting there with a jug of ale courtesy of the brewery manager. Horace grabbed some food off the table. "This spread looks like a buffet at a funeral".

"Don't knock it, son. Good grub and a jug of ale....one each night for the whole week. Make sure to save someone else next week, I could get used to this malarkey".

Horace took some bread and a chicken leg and told his dad that he was going to see Kevin. "I don't want to stay and talk to all these strangers".

"Your mum will be disappointed, son. This spread is for you".

There was a knock on the back door. He looked out of the window and saw a group of reporters standing there. With only one door to the property Horace told his dad that he was going out via the front window.

"I'm not talking to those swine, dad. I don't see why I should".

"Well, I can't hear anyone at the door, not with my ears. Everyone knows I'm deaf". And that is why George was known as 'two-times' both at home and at work, because everyone had to tell him things at least twice.

Horace climbed out through the front room window, got his bicycle from the brewery shed and biked to see his mate. People were still waving to him but when he got to Winshill things changed. Kids from the local secondary modern started 'taking the mickey' and calling him names. Horace ignored them but they chased after him throwing stones all the way up to North Street. Kevin was on the street in front of his house. He'd just come back from his nan's and was talking to the neighbours. Seeing the lads running after Horace, he ran down to the bottom of the road. Now, Horace was big for his age but Kevin Mason was even bigger. Kevin called his older brothers on the way down the road and waded in to the fight without a second thought. Horace jumped of his bike and got stuck in too.

Pete, one of Kevin's brothers, told Horace to go up to the house "and watch your eye. These bastards will only try and open it up again. This is our territory and the Mason's fight, not yours".

Pete was sixteen and in his last month at the grammar school....until, that is, their dad stopped him going because of what had happened to Horace. Horace did what Pete said but in the long run it made no difference and he became a target for the secondary modern kids from that day.

But today it was the Masons that tasted victory. They went back home patting each other's backs congratulating themselves for a job well done.

"Sorry Mr. Mason. I didn't think they would run all the way here from Bearwood Hill Road. "Don't worry, Horace, those lads knew that if they came past the infant school it is our plot, our ground. Us Masons own these streets, and the new houses being built on the Manners Estate".

Horace never realized that the Masons carried that much weight in Winshill and said as much to Mr. Mason.

"There's a bit of a turf war going on, Horace. We go for a drink in the Anglesey Arms and they drink in the Elma, that's why there's always trouble in the Queens Arms, being in the middle there's always people there looking for a fight".

"Now, Horace, tell us what happened on Tuesday night. The Herald is full of this local hero business, that's probably why them bastards chased you. They wanted to beat up a grammar school hero, but we showed 'em eh?"

Horace thanked Kevin for helping out but asked him next time to please let him sort out his own problems.

"It's an unwritten rule mate. If there's agro up here and someone needs help, they come to us first".

"You sound like the old Mafia in 'Win'. I never realized that this was going on mate".

After a couple of hours with the Masons, Horace decided it was time to go home. After taking a beating he never imagined that those same lads would be waiting at Level Road once more. When he got to Bearwood Hill Road all four jumped out in front of him and dragged him off his bike. No choice this time but to fight them on his own. Getting clouted a couple of times woke him up a bit. He started to fight back using his fists, feet and bike. Swinging it around holding the back of the frame he managed to drop a couple of them. He got the ring leader on the ground hitting him with the heel of his hand, just like Uncle Bill had shown him. The one standing behind him was hitting him on the back of the neck so, having thumped the one on the ground sufficiently to remove him as a threat, he turned and grabbed the other by the bollocks and followed another piece of Uncle Bill's advice....he twisted them and pulled downwards. The boy managed to break free of his grip and fell to the ground in agony. Horace got up off the ring leader kicking him a few times in the stomach on the way. He turned his attention to the one whose bollocks he'd grabbed and for good measure kicked him in his knackers 'til his foot hurt. The fourth bloke ran off up Oxley Road. Horace got on his bike and rode home, but this time keeping to the roads giving the Ox Hay a wide berth.

Back home, Uncle Bill was there but this time with his sons and Horace's cousins, George and young Bill.

"How're feeling, young Horace? Over the weekend we're going shooting and fetching some old barracks huts from R.A.F. Fauld. They're making way for the United States Air Force to move in. I've had permission to take three huts up to Bladon Castle on Friday evening so try and finish work early on Friday night if you can. It'll take most of Saturday and Sunday to move them. We're borrowing one of the R.A.F.'s lorries and it could take two or three trips. The huts are degrading and these were the closest when the munitions dump went up in 1944 so they'll be a little the worse for wear".

"Why do you want three of them, Uncle Bill, won't one do? They're a good size".

"Son, they're free. They need to get shot of them and beings that the Ministry of Defence owns Bladon Castle we've been offered them, so we're taking them. These two have been whining all day about dismantling and re-erecting them. We'll put them up together as one unit for us and the Winshill scout group can have the rest of the space".

"I never knew the scouts had a Winshill group, Uncle Bill, although Kevin did mention something about joining a group last year".

"So, are you up for some shooting and building or are you going to whinge about your eye?"

"I think you know me better than that, Uncle Bill. You won't hear me whining about a little cut".

"There you go lads, the youngest member of the team isn't wimping out. So, that's settled then....four thirty on Friday. I told them we'd be there for five and we can load some and the rest on Saturday and Sunday if needed".

After they left, Eva, Horace's mum said "You little monkey, running off out the front room window earlier. I told the press that you're a shy lad....I didn't want people to think you ignorant so I told them some of what they wanted to know. They're just doing their job getting the story of that poor lady. She has taken a turn for the worse and the swelling's got bigger this afternoon. They think now she will be brain damaged. The doctors are draining the blood off her brain. Sir Stanley was a commander in the secret services. He told the paper that he owes it to you that she is still alive".

"I'll go and see her after work tomorrow. I should have gone tonight but had a bit of trouble in Winshill. A group of lads chased me up to Kev's from Level Road to North Street but Kev was out in the front and called his brothers. They sorted them out but they were waiting for me again at Level Road on the way back and dragged me off my bike".

"Well, you don't look any worse than you did earlier, son" said George. They couldn't have been very tough", he said in a friendly, mocking sort of way.

"They will know about it in the morning, dad, especially the one whose bollocks I pulled and twisted. That'll teach them to pick on a Gray".

"Horace, please don't use that talk in this house" said Eva.

"Our Eva, what do you want him to call them instead of bollocks, a piece of fruit? We're not in Victorian times now. You want to hear what they call me at work".

"What on earth do they call you, George?"

"Don't know Eva, I can't hear a word they say. You know I'm deaf as a post you silly old mare".

"You silly old fool. You get worse when you've had a few swigs of that damned filthy ale".

"Don't knock it woman, this dirty old filthy ale keeps a roof over your head and food on the table".

"Yes, but you don't after drinking the stuff do you? Why can't you just look at it as it's going past with the horse and cart?"

The next morning Horace went to work early.

"Horace, I want you to take the engine out of that old Prefect, it's been sitting there for two years and the chap's not been anywhere near to collect it. I can sell the engine. Let's see how far you get with it but don't struggle, give me a shout if you get stuck".

"Why are you only selling the engine when you can sell the

whole car?"

"The car wants a lot of work doing to it and I just haven't the time for that, Horace".

Horace got to work stripping the engine out. The car's bodywork was good apart from the front offside wing that was dented and rusted through. But it was a bolt-on so easy to change. He removed all the pipes, housing and mounting bolts then took off the bonnet.

He got the block and tackle out of the cupboard and attached it to a roof beam. In the meantime, Gordon was test driving a car that he'd been working on. It had been cutting out on occasion and did so again when Gordon was driving down Postern Road. Gordon kicked himself for not taking his tools with him. The Prefect's engine was out and hanging from the beam in mid air by the time he'd walked back to the garage.

"Well, son, it looks like you've had more luck than me with the Cowley. It's damn well cut out like he said and I can't get it started. I'll take the breakdown truck to drag it back, you might as well come with me, Horace".

While in the truck Gordon asked if Horace had any problems with the Prefect. "No Mr. Rush, it all went like clockwork. Do you mind me asking how much you will get for the engine out of the Prefect?"

"Well, I'm hoping to get about a fiver for it, why do you ask, son?"

"I don't want to be cheeky but could I buy the whole car and do it up? I haven't got a fiver but you could take it out of my wages over a few weeks".

"Why do you want it, Horace? It's in a bit of a state".

"I don't think it is Mr. Rush. The front wing wants changing, but that's a doddle being a bolt-on, I just want something to work on. I really want to strip the engine down. I will do it all in my spare time. What do you think it could sell for when it's all done?"

"Now that depends, Horace, on what sort of a job you do on it. With a half decent job you could get £20 but a great job you could get £50 to £60. If you want to go for it then we can go halves. I'll buy any parts that are needed and you do the car up. Any future projects we'll do the same but first you have to do a proper job on this one".

"Thanks Mr. Rush, I won't let you down, but I can't start it this weekend. Uncle Bill wants us to move some old barracks huts from Fauld Depot to Bladon Castle, plus going up to Sinai to do a bit of shooting".

"You have a busy weekend ahead. Moving those huts isn't child's play. Bladon Castle is a R.A.F. property, isn't it?"

"Yes, I believe it was acquired during the war Mr. Rush. We're putting the huts in the wood. It's a great place with lots of wildlife to shoot and catch and, as you know, the River Trent over the road with plenty of trout, bream and perch. You would never starve in the woods. It's great that the Ministry of Defence let us have the huts to put them there".

"How is Lady Carpenter now?"

"I heard last night that she has taken a turn for the worse so I want to see her tonight".

"Look, Horace, I'm not very busy today so when we get back you can have an early day".

"I would rather have a bit of time working on the Prefect if it's OK with you Mr. Rush".

"That's fine with me, just thought you'd need a bit of time to yourself in your first week".

When they got back, Gordon asked Horace what tasks he wanted to do first.

"The first thing to do, Mr. Rush, is to put the engine on the bench and strip it to the bare bones, clean polish and replace any parts that need replacing".

"Horace, you seem very keen to do it so you can have Martin's old bench in the corner. Take out all the crap that I have chucked there in the last few weeks so you have enough space".

Horace didn't need to be told twice. He got some hessian sacks and stuffed as much junk in them as he could. He couldn't understand why Gordon had saved so much of this old used stuff.

"Mr. Rush, why have you kept all this stuff....even old spark plugs and engine parts that have seen the best of their days?"

"Get rid of all of it all Horace. I've been a bit lazy over the last few weeks since Martin left".

"Do you want to check the bags before I sling them?"

"No, if we do that all the stuff will end up back in the corner for the next ten years. I just find it difficult to throw anything away".

When the bench was clear, Horace got started on the Prefect dropping the oil then taking the sump off. By the end of the day he'd got the cylinder head off, the pistons out and even the valves out of the cylinder head. Gordon kept looking over to see how Horace was progressing. He was really impressed that he had the car pretty much down to its bare bones.

Just before he finished, Brian Fisher walked in. He raised his voice at Gordon saying that he wanted a small package delivered to Duke Street. Mr. Rush was raising his voice too.

"You, kid get on your bike and take this package down to Brian Willoughby in Duke Street".

"I don't wish to be rude, Mr. Fisher, but I don't work for you so take it yourself".

Fisher gave the package to Gordon.

"Gordon, tell the little bastard to take this parcel down to Duke Street or I will shut and sell this garage and your sodding house".

Horace saw the worried look on Gordon's face. Horace went up and took the parcel off him, and that was the start of the dirty dealings Horace did for this horrible person. A man who threatened his own daughter, son-in-law and grandson with losing everything they had.

"I have never come across anyone like you before, thinking you can threaten everyone. Well, I will do this for Mr. Rush not you. One day I will get my own back". Then he left.

"Spunky little kid. I like that, we'll have to use him a lot more. Just make sure to let him know who's running this show, he thinks a lot of you and the other two".

"The other two?" Gordon shouted, "The other two? Don't you mean your daughter and grandson, you nasty old bastard. There is no love at all in your bones, not even for your wife and daughters. I wish I never got mixed up with you and all your shady dealings. Horace is right, you are the worst kind of person there is using your own daughter and grandson as bargaining chips. And I know you're using Martin down at Station Street. Just leave him alone, he left here to get away from you".

"Well he shouldn't have been a naughty boy, should he. And the same goes for you. If I go down again then you and others are going down with me. Get it straight, Gordon. I own you, Martin and that cheeky little sod that's just left".

"You don't know that lad do you. No one will ever own him, he's a young fighter. You can tell that even at his young age. Don't forget that the police think he's special, you ask any bobby around here. Oh, I forgot, they're not on your Christmas card list are they".

Horace dropped the package off at Duke Street and then went round to the Infirmary in New Street.

He asked a nurse if she knew where Lady Carpenter was and was pointed in the direction of the ward she was in. When he got there he was met by Sir Stanley.

"Horace my boy come in, you haven't met my wife properly yet have you".

He went in but she was asleep.

"She might wake up now that you're here. Edith, Horace is here to see you".

After a few seconds she opened her eyes. The shift nurse was very surprised. Lady Carpenter smiled then closed her eyes again. She kept opening and closing them for a few moments then, seeing her husband there, smiled at him. Tears were streaming down his cheeks. The nurse took her blood pressure which had been very high before, during and after surgery but had now returned to a more normal level. The Doctor came to see her and told Sir Stanley that he thinks she is out of danger. Stanley stood up, shook the doctor's hand then, with tears still rolling down his face, grabbed Horace by his shoulders and gave him a hug, just like a dad would his son.

"My boy, I think we have turned a corner now and if you hadn't done what you did I wouldn't have her here. Do you understand, son, you've saved both our lives. Edith this is the boy that saved your life".

She turned to Horace and lifted her hand. Sir Stanley cried even more when Horace put his hand in hers.

Sir Stanley's daughter walked in to see her dad blubbering, something she had never seen in her twenty four years.

"Dad what's the matter, is mum OK?"

She looked over to her mum, who was now awake, and saw Horace holding her hand.

"Helen, she's awake".

"Dad, I've only been away ten minutes". She hugged her dad and started crying then both took Edith's other hand.

Horace left them to be alone together. No one saw him leave as they were too busy talking to Edith.

Uncle Bill was at home with his two sons young Bill and George talking to Eva and drinking tea.

"We were talking about going to Fauld earlier tomorrow night, could you get done any earlier, Horace?" asked Uncle Bill.

"I'm hoping to finish a bit earlier but that's up to Mr Rush, so not sure yet. I have just been to see Sir Stanley and Lady Carpenter. She woke after a few minutes when I got there so Sir Stanley and his daughter were made up. I snuck out, didn't want to get in their way".

Uncle Bill and the boys left telling him they would be there at four o'clock. Bill's son George looked a bit 'mardy'.

Horace worked hard and fast to get his jobs done on Friday morning. He didn't want to go the entire weekend without seeing Lady Carpenter so left the garage at two o'clock then biked it down to the hospital. Both Sir Stanley and Helen were there so he explained that he had come again today to see Lady Carpenter because of the Fauld Depot work they were doing over the weekend.

"You're looking better Lady Carpenter, sitting up there".

"Horace, you don't have to explain, you can come anytime you want, can't he Edith".

She managed to muster a half smile but as yet was unable to speak. Stanley told Horace that when she can talk again there will be no stopping her. She has always been a chatter box, "Haven't you my love". The doctors came to check her over so Horace and Helen moved out to the corridor where she gave him a kiss on the cheek and held his hand.

"Horace, my dad is a hard man and has done great things for his country with valour and great courage but he feels guilty that he couldn't be there to help the one person that he loves so dearly. I had never seen him cry until yesterday and we both will be in your debt for as long as we live. Mum can't talk yet and we don't know if she ever will but she is going to get all the love and help we can give her".

"Helen, Horace, come here. She's trying to speak. I can't understand properly but I think she wants to see you".

They went back into the ward. Lady Carpenter extended her arm and with a lot of effort mumbled "Thank you". That started Sir Stanley off good and proper. He put his arm around Horace. "You must have special powers, Horace. She is trying like crazy to communicate with us".

Helen told Horace that he is the brother she never had, a special person. "Can I call you my brother, Horace?" Sir Stanley said "Yes, you came into our lives from nowhere and helped us as much as a son would, so, like it or not, you are part of our family and if there is anything you want just ask and it's yours. We will see you again in a few days, son".

Like Stanley, deep down Horace wasn't an emotional person but he did feel warm inside with pride, and love for the Stanleys.

"Where have you been?" said Uncle Bill, "We've been waiting for you. I went up to the garage but Gordon said you left on an errand an hour ago".

"Yes, it was to deliver something for that piece of shit, Fisher. He wants me to do his dirty work now. He's as bent has they come. He got me to take a package down to Brian Willoughby in Duke Street".

"Well there's two dodgy ones if I ever I saw them, you want to give them both a wide berth, Horace".

"I can't, Uncle Bill, not when Fisher threatens Mr. and Mrs. Rush with chucking them out of the garage and house. He actually told Mr. Rush that, and not for the first time. Mrs. Rush was there the first time he told them".

Dad chimed in "The best thing for Fisher would be a bullet in the head, the man's never been any good. He's got no scruples that bloke. I would hate to be related to him, he would have sold his mum for a farthing as a child. He saw her into an early grave with the things he did".

"Anyway, Uncle Bill, why are you all here, isn't Auntie Mavis coming home today, or is it tomorrow?"

"I did tell you on Tuesday, she's staying another week in Manchester, but I can forgive you that with all you've been through. It's been a damned week for you and that's for sure, young Horace. The reason we're here is that we're going to start dismantling the barracks huts tonight and I have permission of the Duchy of Lancaster to shoot on their land at Hanbury Woods so get your stuff together".

"You already told us we were making a start on them tonight, you've all just come for some free grub. Oh, I didn't tell you, I went to see Lady Carpenter after going to Duke Street. She woke up when we were talking. Sir Stanley got really emotional and started crying".

"It's exactly the same when Mavis doesn't get my tea on the table on time".

"That's a lie, our Bill, you would be straight round here" Eva told him, "You know what side your bread is buttered, you cheeky monkey. You haven't missed a dinner here since Mavis left for Manchester".

Young Bill said that his dad was always talking about going to the builders' shop every lunch time.

"Young Bill, you'll have to get your ears washed out. I said I'm going to build myself up for lunch time. Come on now, it's Friday and what does Friday mean?"

"Fish and chips, dad, and it's your turn to pay. You always say it's either my or Bill's turn to pay", said George.

They all got in Uncle Bill's Bedford van and set off to get their grub on the way to Fauld.

When they arrived, Uncle Bill was waved in, shown where to park and then taken to the huts they wanted.

Uncle Bill told them to get the tools out and to start taking the first hut down. "Horace, get the ladders off the van roof you can start with me. You two can start dismantling what's inside the huts. There's a wood stove in the first and last one so be careful you don't break anything on them".

Young Bill ran back out.

"Dad, there are beds and bunk beds in here, what shall we do with them there are far too many to dismantle".

"Leave four up 'til tomorrow, we need somewhere to rest our heads tonight".

Before it got dark Uncle Bill took the lads with a guide from the base to see the crater, known locally as the Hanbury Crater. They had to walk behind the guide because the area still wasn't fully secure and he told them it never will be.

Fauld was an R.A.F. bomb dismantling depot for the armed forces. On the 27th of November 1944 the underground munitions storage depot exploded and was the largest non-nuclear explosion to occur on U K soil. Between 3,500 to 4,000 tons of ordinance exploded. The munitions consisted of high explosive bombs and all types of weapon, including rifle ammunition and over 5 million artillery rounds. The crater that the explosion created was 300ft deep and 250ft across.

Hanbury Crater is still visible 76 years later and will be for some time to come as there are probably still unexploded munitions deep down within it. When the site went up it took out the local reservoir containing 450,000 cubic meters of water and obliterated a farm and several other properties. Over seventy people were killed in the disaster. With the base being short staffed the forces used 198 inexperienced Italian prisoners of war to help demobilize the shells and casings. The tragedy was blamed on one of the prisoners for removing a detonator from a live bomb using a brass chisel rather than a wooden mallet. People say they could feel the explosion in London, and hear it over fifty miles away.

Horace was eight years old and at school at the time of the explosion. Everyone thought that the Germans had dropped a massive bomb. The explosion was so severe it blew the windows out of his school building over five miles away.

"Stop complaining, time's getting on. They're wooden beds with metal frames".

Over the next two days they took down all the huts, with a bit more whinging from young Bill and George. Twelve servicemen arrived with three R.A.F. trucks to help them load up and take the cargo to Bladon Castle. This made young Bill's and George's day although George, not totally satisfied, reminded his dad that they hadn't been shooting yet.

"Well Lads, we won't have time to go back to Hanbury today but we can do some target practice here at Bladon when the servicemen have left. Get your heads together and decide what you want to shoot at, meanwhile get your backs under these pieces of wood. Uncle Bill thanked the servicemen for all their help once all the lorries were unloaded. Right lads, let's mark out where we're putting the huts then we can have a couple of hours shooting".

Horace had a thought of using Uncle Bill's tobacco tin as a target. Put some matches in, douse the wick in petrol and add some gun powder out of the shells for effect. It would be interesting to see who could get it to light first.

"How are you going to make sure the tin doesn't move on the first shot?" young Bill asked.

"You have to hit it first or it won't move, or at least get close enough for the wind to move it. Jesus! You're the builders in the family, just nail it to one of the tree trunks you thickets".

Uncle Bill came back from seeing the Lorries away and shutting the gate. Where had Horace and the boys gone?

Both the boys played ignorant so that when their dad found out about his tobacco tin it would be only Horace who would get the blame. "Where's me 'bacca' tin?" asked Uncle Bill. The boys lied and said they hadn't seen it.

Uncle Bill looked in the van but couldn't find it so opened a new pouch thinking he'd left it at Fauld. He lit his pipe just as Horace returned telling them that he'd set the target up.

"What's the target then, young Horace? It's not too big I hope".

"No Uncle Bill, it's just a small tin and from where I have put the guns it's three hundred yards away".

"Good lad, I knew we could rely on you to sort it out. Get my binoculars out of the van, George".

George asked Horace where the target was.

"It's just below the blue cloth in the row of oaks".

Uncle Bill looked through his binoculars moving the from side to side. "Where the hell is it?"

Horace ran to the tree and pointed to where it was. Uncle Bill shouted that the tin was on its side but Horace had placed it that way deliberately because he knew that Uncle Bill would have seen the words Old Holborn and cottoned on. He ran back to them. Bill hadn't noticed the petrol soaked wick that was poking from the blue cloth.

"Well, let's see if any of you can hit it then. You've all got three shots and I think it is an almost impossible target. Bill, you're the oldest, you go first".

Bill and George shot first, both missing the target by a mile and got some jip from their dad about how awful they were.

"Horace, I want to know how you are going to shoot when you are left handed and your left eye is covered".

"Never tried Uncle Bill but I will give it a go". He fired but was even worse than his cousins.

"Come on lads" Uncle Bill said, "Let's have another go".

Young Bill went first getting very close to the tin. Uncle Bill could see through his binoculars that he had only missed by a few inches. George's second shot was no improvement on his first. Horace went again but this time tried his right hand.

Uncle Bill asked him if he had shot right-handed before, "It looks a better fit on your right shoulder".

"No, Uncle Bill, you know I've always been left-handed but I can use a spanner in any hand".

Horace's next shot lit up the wick and a few seconds later the lid blew off. They ran over and when they got to the tree the whole tin was alight. "What the hell?" said Uncle Bill when he saw that it was his 'bacca' tin. "Did you two know anything about this?"

Both denied any involvement and blamed Horace, whilst just about managing to keep a straight face.

"You little liars, I know very well when you two are fibbing....your eyes give you away. Well, Horace, it was a clean shot and I can still use the tin but you all owe me three tins off 'bacca'. Well done Horace, we will have to practice more with your right-hand shooting".

# CHAPTER FOUR

Horace worked at Rush's garage during the next few months doing anything and everything on the vehicles that customers brought in. The Ford Prefect, his first project, went well. Horace did what he said and stripped it back to its bare bones taking all the seats and matting out and welding the floor panels where needed.

He put a new front wing on, rubbed down the body work, undercoated the floor and bulkhead with red oxide then sprayed the interior and exterior of the car black. In fact, Horace had rubbed down and re-sprayed the car a few times but never seemed satisfied with the results of his efforts. After six days of trying to get the paintwork right, Gordon took him down to Kennings Motors and had a word with his best friend, Tim Ball, the garage manager.

"Morning, Tim, this is my apprentice. He's been rubbing a car down and re-spraying it but is not happy with the end result so I wondered if he could work with you for a day or two to pick up some tips. What he's done is better than I could do but you know I'm not the best at bodywork".

"What's your name son?"

"Horace, sir".

"Less of the 'sir' now, Horace. My name is Tim Ball but everyone calls me Tim. Let's take you to see Jim Sutton, my foreman in the body shop. Horace you say, Gordon told me what you did saving that lady's life. Well done, son" then shook his hand. "Did the Herald ever manage to get you to talk to them?"

"Never. I kept out of their way for two weeks. They got their story from others".

"They got fed up chasing him, Tim. They were here, there and everywhere. They even spent a whole day up at my garage".

They walked over to the workshop. "Jim, this is Horace, he wants to see how we do the bodywork. He works for Gordon, you do remember him?"

"Yes boss. He plays crib with you in the Derby Inn. How are you, Gordon?"

"I'm fine thanks, Jim. I was hoping you can give Horace a few tips on bodywork. I've taught him all I know but it's not good enough for him".

"Well, Gordon, it's great to hear a mechanic that's not happy with what he's done, brings a tear to my eye. There are six in the shop and I have to be on their backs all the time because of their shoddy work. Boss, two will be going on Friday so get an advert out".

"It's Morgan and James that's going" said Jim. "We've given them a chance. They came with good references from Langley's but it's obvious they really only wanted to get shot of them".

"Gordon, Jim will work gladly with any man that wants to improve his skills and it's obvious from what you say that this young lad wants to do exactly that. You mentioned him being here for two days but I want him here for the whole week. I'm glad you brought him in on a Monday morning. You can have him back next Monday. If I keep him any longer you won't be getting him back again".

"How old are you, Horace?" asked Jim.

"Fourteen, Jim. I've been working full-time for Mr. Rush for three months but worked for him part-time since I was twelve".

"Well you look all of sixteen. What I'm going to do is to introduce you as a new starter and, if you're as good as what Gordon says you'll be a real asset to us. We will pay you accordingly for a week's work. Will you need him at all this week, Gordon?"

"I can just manage for a week but that's it Jim. We can put a few things off 'til next week, can't we, Horace".

"Yes, and thanks Mr. Rush. I will be there at five in the morning, just leave me a list of what you want me to do".

"Let's see how you get on today shall we, son. Come and see me later today after you're done here so we can chat about what you've learnt but there's no rush. They may need you to work late. Oh, and good luck".

Jim took Horace into the workshop to meet the other lads and show him the tools they work with. He introduced him to his best body fitter.

"Horace, this is Tony Whitehall, you can work with him this week. He's a new starter, Tony. His name is Horace Gray so look after him. What are the two twerps doing? Whatever you do don't let them near him, Tony".

"OK boss but I've not seen them since they logged in this morning. They're supposed to be working on the Jag but they've done nothing to it yet Jim".

"Leave it with me, Tony, I'll find the lazy bastards. Carry on with what you're doing and look after Horace".

Jim walked around the garage asking people if they had seen the two absentee body fitters. He asked the service manager if he had seen them.

"No Jim, I'll ask the lads".

Phil shouted back after a few moments, "They got in their car and went somewhere. I thought they'd been sacked, the lazy twats. Tony told me what they're like. They've gone off site somewhere, Jim, can't help you anymore than that I'm afraid".

Horace worked alongside Tony doing and learning things he wouldn't have been able to in Gordon's garage. But Tony was impressed with the lad's knowledge. Tony told him they'd been working on some really expensive cars like a Jaguar and Daimler DE36 in dark green.

"That Daimler Roadster isn't very old".

"Yes Horace, it's only done three hundred miles and hit a lamp post. There's a lot of damage and the front's all dented. That's the next car we'll be working on. We should finish this Roadster tonight. If you mask up the wheels and chrome for me I'll mix the paint, the paper and tape is in the big cupboard".

Horace did what he was told working really fast but doing a neat job. He'd nearly finished by the time Tony came back from mixing the paint. Tony went to Jim and said "Look at that lad work. Fast and neat, he really enjoys his work".

The two body fitters, Morgan and James, who'd got in their car earlier and driven off site walked in like they owned the garage. Jim came out of his office. "Where the hell have you two been? It's half ten and you haven't done a stroke of work this morning. Come on, where have you been?"

"We had to nip out".

"Nip out? You can't just nip out whenever you please. Just get on with that Jag. I'll talk to you two later".

As soon as Jim had gone they started taking the piss out of him. Then turned their attention to Tony and Horace "What are you looking at, moron?" and "Who are you, little boy? You must be the tea boy, go and get a brew on". Horace didn't answer Morgan he just went up to him and pushed him.

"Didn't you hear me? The youngest does the brews here, go and make a brew".

"You are not my gaffer and I am certainly not here to wait on you".

Morgan went over to the Roadster and ripped all the brown masking paper off the wheels and some off the chrome. Horace was furious. All that good work he'd done. He lunged at Morgan and punched him hard in the mouth then, doing what uncle Bill had shown him and his cousins, used his body weight and elbow to push a stunned Morgan to the floor. The others were amazed to see a young boy down a full-grown man so readily but they didn't have an Uncle Bill who'd been in the commandos. Horace pressed his knee into Morgan's throat to keep him on the floor. He picked up a panel hammer and asked Morgan whether he wanted to eat it.

Hearing all the commotion Jim and Tim Ball came running into the workshop. The other lads looked on with a wry smile on their faces. Morgan's pal, James, had been stunned by the speed of Horace's actions but started to move towards Horace to grab him and drag him off Morgan. Jim intervened and, anyway, there were too many others there for either Morgan or James to try anything else.

Jim asked Tony to take young Horace out for a cigarette and calm him down.

"You two, get your clobber and get out....you're both fired" Tim yelled at them.

"The young cunt attacked me" replied Morgan, "everyone saw it, didn't you lads?"

No one said anything except James who mumbled something in support of his mate.

Jim was not in the mood to take any crap from either of them. "I saw it all. I saw you rip the masking paper off the car. The lad's work is a lot better than your shoddy efforts so get out of my sight, I don't want to see either of you again....and what's more, neither of you will get any pay for the week. It's you that owes us because you damaged company property".

Tim and Jim walked out to Horace to see if he was alright.

"What property did Morgan damage?" Tim asked.

"The floor when his head hit it" replied Jim. They were both laughing when they got outside.

"Well that's as good a reason as any" said Tim. "We could have fired them anyway just for ripping the masking paper off the wheels, not to mention them always being late, their shoddy workmanship and disappearing without permission or telling anyone where they were going".

"Are you OK, Horace? I thought you were going to bury that hammer in Morgan's face. No one would have blamed you, son, if you had".

Tim shouted into the workshop "Higgins, get the brews going and come out for a break with the lads, I need to talk to you all".

They all came outside and gathered round, some sitting on the wall and others on the pallets smoking their fags.

"OK men, even before all the commotion this morning I was telling Jim that Morgan and James had to go today. Amongst other things, their disappearing for two and a half hours with no explanation and what they did to this young lad on his first day at work helped me to make my mind up".

Higgins brought the mugs of tea out on a tray. "I was just telling the rest, Ron, the reasons why I had to get shot of those two morons. That'll mean with the work we have on I will need you all to do a couple of hours overtime until we get replacements for them. Will that be a problem for any of you?"

They all told Mr. Ball that they would be pleased to earn a bit of extra cash especially as summer was approaching and there were holidays to pay for. "We'll do it gladly, Mr. Ball, and will be a much better team now that those two have gone".

"We'll have to employ two more because with the holidays coming up we can't manage with fewer men. Head office would chew my balls if we were short staffed in the summer holidays, so let me know if anyone knows of any decent body fitters".

After the meeting Horace got back to redoing the masking on the Roadster then went to help Ron with the Jag using a cutter to remove the front valance. Ron let Horace have a go. He'd never used one before and was very careful not to rush and cut too much off but Ron was there to give him pointers. Using a cutter made him feel really grown up.

Ron told Horace that he was doing extremely well. "Just take it steady at the bottom, the radiator and hoses are very close. That's it, well done. Now, let me have the cutter and I will finish it off".

"I enjoyed doing that, Ron. Will you cut the wing off the same way or do you break the weld with a chisel?"

"I do a bit of both but mainly breaking the weld. This isn't your first day in a body shop is it, Horace, not with the way you're working".

"It's my first day in a body shop but I have been working full-time for a few months at Rush's Garage and was part-time from the age of twelve before then but we don't have the tools you have. In fact, the only tools we have on the bodywork side is a hammer and a chisel but we don't do much of that type of work. Mr. Rush is a mechanic rather than bodywork specialist. I'm doing up a Prefect. I rebuilt the engine but it's still on the bench".

"So what have you both done to the engine then, mate?"

"Did it all myself, Ron. Stripped the lot down, ground the valves, fitted new shims, polished the head with emery cloth, and fitted new piston rings and big end bearings. Just can't wait to put it back in again but I want to spray the bulkhead the same colour as the rest of the car, that's why I'm here to learn more about the spaying. Just watching you do it this morning made me realise how far behind the times we are with the equipment we've got".

"What colour do you want to spray it? Prefects are nearly all black apart from the odd one or two".

"I would like a sort of turquoise, a colour that I've never seen on a Prefect before. If I mix green and blue it should be close to what I want. I would just love to mess about with different colours".

"Well, Tony is your man for mixing colours. Nearly all the other branches ask him to match colours for them".

With work slackening off in the afternoon Horace was told he could leave at four but had to be back at eight in the morning to help Tony spray the Roadster. He got on his bike and went to see Gordon to tell him all about his day and what he'd learnt about using the power tools and air guns.

"That's brilliant you had a good day, Horace. Tim phoned and told me what had happened with that Morgan chap and his pal James. He told me that you were like a rat down a drain pipe when he upset you but he also said what a good worker you are and that you are credit to me. I told him that you are invaluable to us. Have you got half an hour to spare, son, to help me with the exhaust on the Riley?"

"That's why I came back Mr. Rush, to see if you wanted me to do anything. I would like to go and see Sir Stanley and Lady Carpenter sometime tonight but I don't normally finish 'til half five anyway".

"How is Lady Carpenter?"

"She was a bit better last week, wasn't walking much then though".

"It's good to hear that she is on the mend, Horace. It must have been hard for them both in the last couple of months".

"She still can't walk far and has to use her stick wherever she goes. They say that the brain damage affected her motor movement. Sir Stanley is doing everything for her, with the help of their daughter when he's at work".

Horace went home after they'd finished working on the Riley. The doctor was there. Horace's dad, George, had taken a turn for the worse with pneumonia and was in bed. Poor George, he had these attacks five or six times a year. He often kept things to himself when he wasn't feeling well so as not to create a fuss. Eva was going frantic telling the doctor that one day he will just collapse and die, the silly old man but in reality he wasn't that old. He was only fifty five at the time but looked about seventy five with all that he'd been through in the war.

His chest often rattled like a pig grunting whilst rooting around for truffles.

Horace's mum asked him to fetch his eldest sister, Tara, to come and help. He biked down to Goodman Street. Vernon, Tara's husband, was there with the kids.

"Hello Vernon, is Tara here? Dad's bad again and mum needs some help".

"Horace, I haven't seen your sister for three days. I heard from next door that she's gone to Cannock with a bloke from the brewery, left me with our two kids to look after. Dorian from two doors down looks after them whilst I'm at work. It's better now that Jane has started school".

"Sorry Vernon, I'll have to get back. How do you put up with this all the time....her going off shagging every few weeks? Let us know if there's anything you need".

"Thanks, Horace. She's never satisfied, always wanting something or someone different but she always comes back in the end. One day I'm just going to tell her to piss off. No aspersions on your mum, Horace, but Tara can't be from the same litter as the rest of you. Your mum must have been handed the wrong baby when she was born. She's nothing more than a prostitute that girl".

Horace went back and told his Mum that Tara has gone off shagging again.

"Horace, don't use that sort of language in this house".

Horace's twin sister, Arlene, asked what a 'shagging' is.

"Never you mind, Arlene. Your brother shouldn't use those sorts of words".

"Will I go shagging when I get older, mum?"

"Do you see what you've started, our Horace? You know she isn't streetwise like you are".

Arlene was typical for a girl of her age in 1949. Most of the younger girls who hadn't been evacuated during the war stayed with their mums or spent time with female relatives helping with the chores around the house. They led pretty sheltered lives, unlike the older girls and women who worked bloody hard to support the war effort and were far from naive.

"No mum. I think you meant to say that she isn't the full ticket. I will explain it to you when you're thirty, Arlene".

"Will you stop teasing your sister, she is very vulnerable and naive. I have enough to do looking after your dad, please go and check on him while I get the tea going. Arlene you set the table please".

Horace went up to see his dad. He was asleep and his chest rattled as he breathed. Horace placed the palm of his hand on his dad's forehead to see how his temperature was....he was burning up. "That's not good", he said aloud and ran downstairs to get Jim from next door to help him take dad to the infirmary.

"No, Horace. If you're worried then go to Mable's and phone for Dr. Philips".

"Ma, there's no time for that. I have never seen him so bad, this isn't just pneumonia there's something else wrong with dad". He ran out of the house and, after a couple of minutes, came running back in with Jim and his brother, Ted. Ted was a big lad in his twenties, and very strong. Ted lifted George up like a rag doll.

"Just watch me down these stairs, Horace, they're bloody lethal. They're all the same in this row".

They got him to Jim's car. Horace got in the back with his dad and put his dad's head on his knees while Jim and Ted got in the front.

"I don't like the sound of your dad, Horace. I don't like to say it but I think he may be on the way out".

"I thought the same, Jim, that's why I wanted to take him straight to the infirmary. It would've taken the doctor about fifteen minutes to get to the house and we're only three minutes from the infirmary by car".

They pulled up by the Emergency entrance. Ted lifted George out and they ran in with him. A nurse spotted them and called a doctor. "Let's get him into a bed right away".

"It looks like you did the right thing" said Jim, "not waiting for a doctor to come to the house".

"Yes, mum would have just left it and phoned Dr. Philips, she thinks he can solve everything. One day, dad is going to die waiting for the doctor to come round, she just doesn't grasp the situation or reality, never has".

"Thanks both of you for bringing him it's really good of you. I'm going to stay here 'til I hear some news. Could you please drop in on the way back and tell my mum what's happening?"

Horace stayed there for a couple of hours before a doctor came back to see him and explain what was wrong with his dad.

"Hello son. We've had to put your dad into a negative pressure ventilator, an iron lung to you. We think he has double pneumonia and a collapsed left lung. It's a good job you got him here when you did or he wouldn't have lasted another hour. The nurse said you saved someone's life a few months ago, you seem to be making a habit of it".

"Will he be alright....he's not going to die is he?"

"We don't know to tell you the truth. The next twenty four hours will be make or break for him. If you want to bring your mum in we will let her see him anytime tonight, that's as much as I can tell you".

"Thanks doctor, I don't think she'll come. She doesn't like hospitals. The only time she's been to one is when my oldest sister was born. She had the rest of us at home after that. It's a pity my eldest sister wasn't born at home too".

"Why do you say that, son?"

"To tell you the truth, she is nothing like the rest of us. Some in the family say mum brought the wrong child home after she was born".

"Well it has happened in the past, but it happens very, very rarely".

Horace went home to tell his mum what the doctor had said but tried his best not to consider the possibility that his dad would not survive the next twenty four hours. Perhaps this is what mum had been doing all along; shutting out dark thoughts was her way of coping with the situation.

"I will take you to see him tonight, mum, just in case he doesn't make it through the night, he is very poorly".

"Don't be a silly little boy, exaggerating like that. Get off to bed. Go on, off to bed".

"Mum, he's in an Iron lung, he can't breathe without it. What did Jim tell you when he stopped by?"

"He said that dad would be home later after a check up. You should have asked Dr. Philips to come, he knows your dad better than anyone, there was no need to get those silly ideas and take him to that place".

"Mum, there is no telling you is there" said Horace and went upstairs.

Horace got up at five the next morning. Eva was still hiding in bed, something she always did when trying to avoid facing reality. He biked to the hospital hoping with every turn of the pedals that his dad was still alive. He saw a nurse when he arrived who told him that George had a restful night.

"Horace, the iron lung supports your dad so that he can breathe in a normal manner. The muscle control in his lungs is weak at the moment due to the collapsed lung and pneumonia. Do you want to see him?"

"Only if he's awake, no point if he's a sleep but then I do need to report back to mum so maybe I should see him anyway".

He went upstairs. The nurse followed him and showed him to the room his dad was in. There was a great big metal cylinder that looked like a submarine in the centre of the room. It shocked Horace. His mum would be devastated to see George inside this machine. His dad was awake but able only to speak very quietly and he couldn't hear Horace because his hearing box was on the dressing table at home. The nurse said that he wouldn't be able to wear it anyway because his head was only just protruding out of one end of the machine.

When he returned home Horace told his mum that dad would be there for at least a few more days then tried to describe the machine he was in. It was like pulling teeth trying to explain things to her. She was still hiding in bed and told him he had to take his twin sister to school.

"Ma, she's fourteen and hasn't been taken to school for five years. Anyway, I have to be at work in half an hour. Dad's sleeping most of the time. If he gets worse of course I will ask for time off. I'm going to have some toast before work, do you want anything before you go to see dad?"

"I can't go to those sorts of places, I just can't. I will see him when he comes home in a couple of days".

"Mum, I have to go now but please try to get into your head that he won't be coming home in two days, he is very poorly".

Horace was getting exasperated with his mum's inability to grasp what was happening. It was still on his mind when he got to Kennings.

"Morning, Tony".

"You're bright and early, Horace. Are you ready to put the first coat of paint on the Roadster? I mixed the paint last night and it looks really good, even if I say so myself. The customer wanted something different so that his motor would stand out. Go and have a look at the paint before we start, the chap's coming in around ten past seven to have a look at what we're planning to do. There's some paint in the gun, just start the compressor up mate".

Both Tony and Horace got a damp cloth and carefully wiped down the Roadster to make sure there was no dust.

"Go for it, Horace, but just do the back quarter first. That's it. You're doing fine but just go a tiny bit slower, you're not giving the paint time to land". It took just took ten minutes to do that bit of spraying.

The customer arrived bang on ten past seven.

"Yes, it's good but can it be a bit darker? I can live with it if it can't".

"It'll get a bit darker when it's dried" said Tony, "you can't mess about too much with this colour because it's very difficult to match but I'll mix another can of paint now and a slightly different one tomorrow so you can decide and we can get on and finish it".

"You might be right, Tony. Do the colour now anyway and if I'm not happy with it I'll pay for it to be done again".

So they sprayed the car with the colour that Tony had already mixed. The rest of the men had arrived at work and were laughing and joking when Tony and Horace came out of the spray shop.

"Morning lads, Tony shouted".

Ian asked Horace whether Tony had given him a chance to any spraying. "Tony's very particular about who he lets spray his cars".

"He's done quite a bit he just needed a few pointers that's all. He's very exigent for someone who's fourteen, more diligent than you, Ian".

Ian laughed and threw a rubbing down pad at them. That was it, the fun was contagious so everyone starting throwing things at each other.

"Horace, why weren't you happy with how you sprayed the car at Gordon's?" asked Tony.

"The paint always dried like orange peel, not smooth like this. It just didn't look right".

"Well it's not the way you're spraying, you're a natural. It must be the equipment you're using. Bring me the spray gun that you're using there and I'll have a look at it, I wouldn't mind betting that it's the culprit".

The week had gone by quickly for Horace. He took the spray gun in for Tony to look at and try out. He wasn't getting an even spray because some of the holes in the nozzle were blocked while others weren't.

Tony went to see Jim to ask if he could give Horace some of the old air tools they no longer used telling him that Horace had been doing whatever bodywork they did at Gordon's by hand. They don't do much bodywork so there were practically no tools for it.

"We haven't used those old tools for two years. I was going to throw them out six months ago but didn't have the heart".

"If you're sure we won't need them, Tony, then by all means give them to the lad. You can take him back to Gordon's in the van so he can put his bike in the back along with them. Give us a shout please before you leave with Horace, I want to have a word with him before he goes".

But before Tony had turned to get his van ready, Horace

walked into the office to thank Jim Sutton for all that he and the lads had done and taught him during the last week.

"Mr. Sutton, I would like to thank you and the lads for all that you have taught me this week, the things I've learnt will stay with me forever and I'm really going to miss using those spray tools, they showed me just how far behind we are at Mr. Rush's with our limited bodywork equipment".

"Well, son, it works both ways. You've taught us a lot too and I'm ever so sorry that you had such a bad start with those fellows Morgan and James". He shook Horace's hand and gave him his wage packet. "There's one more thing, you are welcome here anytime if you want a job. All the men have said how well you work. You're a fast learner and pick things up very quickly".

"I really enjoy doing everything on cars Mr. Sutton, whether it's mechanics or bodywork".

"There's one last thing" said Jim, "we're giving you some of our air tools, Tony will put them in the van with your bike when he takes you back to Gordon's" and shook Horace's hand once more.

They arrived at Rush's garage to shouting coming from the workshop.

"I think we ought to drop the things off here, it sounds a bit tense in there".

"Don't worry, Tony, it's just Gordon's stupid father-in-law throwing his dummy out of his pram again. He's just an idiot".

"Horace and Tony walked in carrying the tools and put them under his bench".

"What the hell is all that rubbish you're putting down there?" asked Fisher, "it looks like junk to me".

"Well whatever it is it's got nothing to do with you. Mr. Rush is my boss you're just a fat twerp throwing your weight around all the time and there's plenty of it, you fat bastard".

"Gordon, you get rid of this ungrateful sod, just get shot of him".

"This is my business and I'll employ whoever I want to. You can threaten me but boy, you won't threaten this young lad".

Tony told Gordon that Mr. Sutton had said he'd give Horace a job tomorrow but knew that the young man was loyal and that he wanted to continue working at Rush's Garage. "We don't know of, or have ever seen, a fourteen-year-old lad that knows so much already and is so willing to learn, so hang on to him if you want a top class bodywork specialist".

"Take the little bastard with you if he's that good" Brian Fisher said to Tony, "I don't want him around here, he is nothing more than a bloody nuisance. Take him and all that damn junk back where you came from".

"You're a very abrasive man. I don't know who you are, and really don't want to know but I do know Gordon very well, and I also know that it's his garage. Horace, is this the Prefect that you sprayed because you've done a good job on it. There's nothing wrong with your work it's the equipment that's at fault. Gordon how often do you clean out the spray gun?"

"Well, I can't really remember the last time I used it. Horace is the one that's done all the work taking the engine and the interior out, even the seats are looking good as new. Has he told you what he's done to the engine?"

"Maybe half a dozen times" Tony chortled, "he's really chuffed that you let him loose on the Prefect. We've brought over some air tools that we no longer need so you don't have to do the paintwork the hard way. I've even thrown in a spray line and gun. The boss was so pleased with the way Horace handled the situation with those two fitters".

Brian, annoyed that he was being ignored, re-iterated his earlier insult "Take him back with you if your boss likes him that much".

"Are you still here? Thought you'd gone" said Tony "and it's Gordon's decision what happens".

"That's where you're wrong, my friend. I own this garage along with half the road. I can throw out whoever I want".

Tony bade Horace and Gordon farewell and turned to leave. He glanced over at Brian and said "I thought Horace was exaggerating when he told us what you are like. "Sorry Horace, you were dead right about this man".

# CHAPTER FIVE

Fisher was still talking to Gordon after Tony left so Horace listened from behind the wall. Fisher wanted him to take the wrecking truck to fetch a Vauxhall Velox out of a pub car park at Branston and take it to the Old Bakery. Horace realized immediately that Fisher was up to no good. The pub in question was Uncle Doug's pub, The Gate Inn. Horace said good night to Mr. Rush, got on his bike and went to see how his dad was. The nurse told him that he'd been asleep most of the day but his breathing had improved quite a bit.

"Is your dad stone deaf, Horace, or is it his condition, he seems so vacant when he's awake?"

"He's partially deaf. He turns his hearing box off when my mum has a go at him for just about anything, and she does that quite regularly".

"We haven't seen your mum or anyone else for that matter".

"Well, my twin sister won't come because she thinks what dad has is catching, my mum is scared stiff of hospitals, my eldest brother has just started his National Service, one of my sisters has run off and left two kids with my brother-in-law and another of my sisters is getting married in two weeks....she's gone to tell my other sister so hopefully they will both come after work tonight".

Horace left and biked to Branston to see his Uncle Doug to ask about a car that's in the car park.

"Yes Horace, that car has been there over two weeks. I don't know who it belongs to or who left it here".

"No one has been to see you about it?"

"No son. I think it's just been dumped. I can't see why a nearly new car has been left here, we're off the beaten track down this end of this road but I did see that Brian Fisher bloke having a shifty look at it earlier".

"That's why I came, Uncle Doug, I heard him tell Mr. Rush to take the car to one of his lockups this afternoon. Would you mind if I take it away? It would make him so mad to discover that it isn't here any longer. That Rover is only about a year old so someone will miss it, there's something wrong if they don't".

Horace went outside to look over the car; it was backed up to the trees. When he looked around and underneath he spotted the ignition keys just inside the end of the exhaust pipe. He opened the driver's door and was hit by an awful smell, it stunk to high heaven. He went to the back and opened the boot. He staggered backwards when he saw the body of a man inside with a bullet hole in his head. Flies were crawling all over the body and maggots wriggled out of his ears and the wound in his head. He just about managed to beckon his Uncle Doug over to have a look.

His uncle's reaction was far more extreme than his. Uncle Doug gagged and threw up several times.

"How can you look at and smell that, Horace, without being sick, and who the fuck is it? Why the hell is it in my car park? We've got to get shot of it. We'll all be in the shit if the police find it".

"Horace told Doug that he would move the car after dark to the rear of the Ordnance Depot on Branston Road then come back later and drive it to Fisher's house and dump the body outside. Then I'll phone the police and tell them that something awful has happened there. Hopefully he'll get done for it....there is nothing I would love more".

"You can't drive the car, Horace, you're not old enough. What the hell shall we do? We can't tell anyone about this".

Horace composed himself, took a deep breath, jumped in, started the car and drove off. Doug didn't try to stop him. He was worried about Horace and in despair about the body but was grateful to see the back of it. Horace drove down Mellor Road and parked the car by the back wall of the Ordnance Depot. He walked over the fields back to The Gate Inn and told Doug that it was behind the depot as planned. Doug thanked Horace for getting shot of it.

"What are you going to do next, Horace?"

"At ten tonight I'm going to dump the body outside Fisher's front door. Give me a few minutes after ten to get away and phone the police".

"I can do better than that. I will see Bert Nolan when he comes in tonight, he lives across the road from Fisher. You can see his house over the fields. Look, you can even see Fisher's house from here and the garage he rents out to Bert. Bert hates Fisher's guts because he's always telling him what to do with the garage. I don't want to ask Bert to get involved directly but he can help us by being a lookout".

"Ah! Now I see Bert's garage, Mr. Fisher's is a few houses further down Henhurst Hill. Oh, by the way, my dad is in hospital with his chest".

Horace went home, got some tea and washed himself in the sink three times but could still detect traces of the stench from the car. His older sister, Iris, came home from Marston's Brewery where she worked in the canteen. Horace told her all about dad.

"Iris, I have something to do tonight after I've been to see dad, could you try to persuade mum to go and see him, and please take his box with you he can't hear a damn thing that the nurses or doctors are saying to him".

"What on earth have you got to do that can't wait, your only fourteen? Look at Arlene she still plays with dolls".

"You wouldn't believe me if I told you, Iris. I have to help Uncle Doug with a car that's stuck in his car park. It needs shifting so I said I would help him get it started, if that's OK with you sis?"

"Where is Mum anyway?" enquired Iris, "there's no tea cooking and I told Alan that he could come over tonight for tea".

"Good luck with that. Is he coming over before or after he's been to the pub because if it's after I need to be back".

"Why do you need to be back, I don't understand what you

mean Horace?"

"He's so rude to mum. They're like Buster and Flannigan when they get started, they should be on the radio".

Horace left to go back to the infirmary. Dad was awake and smiling at the nurses, albeit not hearing a word they said.

"How is he tonight?" asked Horace.

"A lot better than he was earlier, he just keeps laughing at us".

"He's like that without his hearing box he thinks you're talking to him". He sat down on a chair close to his dad's face.

"How are you, dad?" Horace said in a slightly louder than normal voice.

"A lot better thanks, son. The nurses are good to me. I didn't think I would need to be inside this wretched contraption again".

The nurse asked Horace how he managed to make his dad understand him. "We can't do it he just looks blank at us".

"I can always get through to him even when the rest of the family can't. I look at him straight in the face then open my mouth wide and talk slowly. All I can think of is that he reads my lips".

"I'll have to try that, Horace. He'll be a lot happier if we can communicate better with him".

She came over and stood as close to George as she could with her face directly in front of his. "Do you understand what is wrong with you, George, it's your lungs?"

"Those damn things again, nothing but a nuisance. It was the bloody Bosh that buggered them up. How did I get here anyway, I can't remember anything at all? All I can remember is waking up here".

"Horace brought you in with a couple of mates and it's a good job he did, you probably wouldn't have lasted the night".

"It's a good job it wasn't left to my misses, you mean. She would have waited for Dr. Philips to come over, thinks that man can work miracles. He is a good doctor mind. Thanks, son, you're a good lad. I don't think I'll be seeing your mother while I'm in here, you know how she hates these places".

Horace left the hospital just as the sun started to set and walked the mile to Mellor Road across the fields to the Ordnance Depot and got in the car without anyone noticing him. Loads of servicemen's houses were being built around the depot but the workmen had all gone home. The smell didn't seem too bad this time for some reason. Horace thought that he must be getting used to it. He looked at his watch, it said nine forty. "That should give me plenty of time to get there" he thought but he wasn't sure which house Fisher lived in. Doug had told him that it was next to Barton Autos so he drove in that direction. When he got there he looked up the drive. "Yes! That's Fisher's Bentley". He got out by the garage and had a look round. No one was in sight so he got an old blanket and put it on the floor then heaved the corpse out of the boot onto it.

The corpse made squelching noises as he manipulated it but was surprisingly lighter than he'd imagined it would be. Flies tickled his arms as they buzzed around and landed on him as he worked. He dragged the blanket next door and dumped it behind some trees in Fisher's front garden then crept as fast he could down the drive and got in the car. He left it in the car park at Marston's Brewery and phoned Doug from the phone box outside the church hall. "Doug" he whispered into the mouthpiece, "I've dumped the body in Fisher's front garden".

"OK Horace. You've been spending too much time with that Uncle Bill of yours. I went to see him earlier today to tell him about the car and body in the boot, and what you were planning to do. He said not to do it but if you did that you would need someone to cover your back".

Suddenly there was a knock on the window behind him. Horace's whole body jerked with the shock, he let out a stifled yell and spun around. It was Uncle Bill.

"Christ! Doug, Uncle Bill is outside the phone box".

Bill opened the door "You should have seen your bloody face, Horace, it was a picture. I wish I had my camera".

"Uncle Bill, where the hell did you come from, I thought it was the police following me? You scared the shit out of me".

"Who's that on the phone my boy?"

"It's Uncle Doug. I was just letting him know that I'd done the job and how things went".

"I followed you from when you left your house. You went to

see George, how is your dad?"

"He was a lot better tonight, chatting to the nurses, smiling. But I don't think he will be home soon".

"Then you left there, crossed the fields to Mellor Road and got into the car and drove to Barton Turns".

"How did you follow me over the fields when you were in your van?"

"You pudding. I crossed the fields then drove down Branston Road, jumped over the fence into Mellor Road then followed you here. Saw it all, Horace, you did well, I'm proud of you. Doug and me have got people watching Fisher's from Bert's house to see what happens. Let's hope the police do him and throw away the key. We would love to find out who the poor bloke was in the boot, it's obvious that fisher had something to do with it and leaving the car at our Doug's is unforgivable....he could have got done".

They drove to The Gate Inn to see Doug. "This is what family is all about" said Bill, "looking out for one another". Gordon Rush drove up with his wrecker soon after they'd met Doug in the car park. Bill went over to him.

"Evening, Gordon. How're you doing?"

"Fine thanks Bill. There's supposed to be a Vauxhall Velox to pick up, a customer phoned me earlier".

Doug told him that it had already gone. He lied that a mechanic had been that afternoon to mend it and that it only took a couple of minutes to sort out.

"How are you, Horace?" asked Gordon, "I didn't know you came here, I'll see you in the morning".

"Not bad Mr. Rush. This is my Uncle Doug, he's the landlord here. Yes, I come here a lot to ride Peg in the field over there. She's a four-year-old mare, we ride down by the Trent, I just love it".

Next day at work both Gordon and Horace were working when Christine came into the workshop. "Gordon, can I speak to you a moment?" They went outside to talk. Horace could see them from the door. Christine looked so happy and put her arms around Gordon. When Gordon returned he went over to Horace to have a word.

"Horace, you were here the other day when Brian Fisher came in. You know, when he was being rude to you and Tony".

"Yes, Mr. Rush, he told you he could chuck you out of here and your house. I don't know how he could think of doing such a thing, he's a horrible swine is Fisher, that's why I went to tidy up my bench and put all the new spray tools away".

"Yes, well done, I noticed first thing this morning. We did well sending you to Kennings for a week. I want to ask you and I want you to tell me truth, did you hear Fisher talking about a Velox being at The Gate Inn last night because it's very strange that you were there".

"Yes Mr. Rush, it's why I went to Uncle Doug's, I told him Fisher wanted a car moving. The keys were in the exhaust so I opened the boot. There was a dead body in it with a bullet hole in the head. It was awful I've never seen or smelled anything like it. Must've been there for a while, the body had flies and maggots all over it. I had the idea of dumping the body in Fisher's front garden, I didn't want you to get into any trouble because I reckon that's what Fisher wanted by sending you up there to get the car".

"Who knows about this Horace?"

"Just me and my two uncles, no one else needs to know about it, Mr. Rush, but it set me thinking all night. I wonder who it was in the boot and who and why someone shot him. It's pretty obvious that Brian Fisher has something to do with it but is he capable of shooting someone, Mr. Rush?"

"To that, son, I have no answers. One thing we do know, though, is that the pathetic man has been arrested for the man's murder. Christine's mother phoned just now to say the police found the body in his front garden last night around the time we were all at The Gate Inn. They want someone from the family to go and identify the body. The man's wallet was in his pocket with his driving licence in it. They didn't say anymore than that. Christine and her mother want me to go to the morgue to see if I know who it is. Will you be OK for a while? If all the jobs are done when I get back you can spend some time working on the Prefect".

Gordon told Christine before he left for the morgue that she shouldn't worry, it was hardly likely to be a family member.

He arrived at the morgue about twenty minutes later and waited for a policeman to accompany him to the cool room where they stored the bodies.

"Good morning, I'm Inspector Smart, and you are, sir?"

"My Name is Gordon Rush, Christine Rush's husband. You wanted someone to come to identify a body...."

"Let's get the paper work out the way first, your address please?"

"It's 360 Henhurst Hill....and I run Rush's Garage".

"Rush's Garage, isn't that where Horace Gray works? What a nice lad he is, and so confident even though he's still only a child".

"The lad is no child, inspector, I can tell you. He's taught me a few things. He's only fourteen but it feels like somehow he's acquired the experience of a much older man. But he is certainly someone you can rely on in a crisis. I have no doubt that he will go far in life".

"Yes Mr. Rush, I too think him to be honest and reliable. If you tell Horace that I would like to see him, I've got some news about a problem he has".

"Yes, inspector, I will tell him when I get back. I presume it's that business at the school, he said you were looking into it for him. It's unbelievable that these things happen at a school in this day and age".

"Nothing surprises me these days Mr. Rush. The world is getting more unfathomable by the day. Can we go in? Just a warning, although his features are still recognisable the man has a bullet wound to the head and he's been dead for a number of days so it will be quite unpleasant and disturbing. If you're ready we'll go in".

"I don't think I will know who it is, inspector but, yes, let's get it over with".

The room was cold and bare. A white sheet covered the body which lay on a metal trolley in the middle of a smooth cement floor.

"OK Frank, if you can lift the sheet".

Gordon jerked his head back when the man's face was revealed. He breathed in and out heavily for a few moments to steady himself then leant forward slightly so that he could study the face properly.

"Ya, yeah, yes....I know this man, it's Simon. Simon Green, my wife's sister's husband. He's supposed to be in Scotland. He's in....was in....the army. He came on leave two weeks ago....I gave him a lift to the railway station myself. My God! What am I going to tell Ruth and the kids....this is terrible?"

"Well, I can tell you that he never went AWOL or they would've been to his house, and us. What regiment was he in?"

"He was in the First Battalion of the British Fusiliers and going to India in two weeks time, I don't know when he was supposed to come back home again. What on earth did he get himself into? Could you tell me where they found him, inspector?" Gordon asked already knowing the answer.

"We found him in the front garden of 212 Lichfield Road, Barton-under- Needwood".

"My God! That's my wife's parents' home. Why was he there....he was supposed to be in India by now?"

"Did you see him get on a train when you took him to the station?"

"Well, no, I took him in the car, dropped him off and another soldier met him to go with him, he called him Charles, I think. Seemed to know him well, they were both smiling and laughing. Charles even put his arm around Simon as they walked to the stairs".

"Well, we now know his real name and the address".

"He lives at Clays Lane in Branston. He and his wife, Ruth, have lived there for over five years".

"That's very strange. The name on the driving licence is David Parker and the address is Luton Road, Derby".

"Derby? He wouldn't have known anyone from Derby, to the best of my knowledge".

"If you don't mind, Gordon, I will accompany you to Clays Lane to give his wife the sad news and to try to find out whether she can tell us anything, if she's willing and able to talk to us that is. This will be a terrible shock for her".

"Would you mind if I fetch my wife first, inspector? She's the best one to comfort Ruth, they're very close".

"I will meet you outside the house at half past twelve I just need to nip back to the station to get the lads to contact his unit. Do you know where in Scotland it is, Gordon?"

"He said Aberdeen, I think, I'm sure that Ruth will know. Dear God! She will be beside herself".

Gordon went home, but first stopped by the garage to see Horace.

"I have a favour to ask you, son. Could you please babysit Chris for about an hour, we both need to nip out to see Christine's sister? The body they found was Ruth's husband, Simon. We have to meet Inspector Smart there in half an hour. Oh, before I forget, Inspector Smart wants to see you about the school incident".

"You had me worried when you said he wanted to see me, Mr. Rush. I will just wash my hands then take Chris to our house. I've finished that pedal car I was working on, he will love that".

Gordon went in to see Christine.

"Did you sort it out, love? Thanks for going it must have been very unsettling to say the least. I told mum on the phone that there's no way we would know who it was....".

Christine stopped talking when she saw the blank expression on Gordon's face. She walked over and lowered herself slowly onto the chair.

"Christine, we have to go and see Ruth immediately. Horace will look after Chris for an hour or so. It's Simon's body they found on your dad's front lawn".

Christine's expression changed from sudden surprise to total incomprehension. Lines appeared in her forehead and she knotted her eyebrows. Her eyes began to water. "Don't be silly, Gordon, Simon's in Scotland you took him to the train station yourself".

"Christine, it is Simon who is lying in the morgue. I don't know how or why but it's him. The fact that they found him on your father's lawn raises a million questions that I can't even begin to try to answer".

Gordon made no mention of the fact that only yesterday her dad had asked him to move a car that turned out to have Simon's body in it.

The tears started to flow....Christine wept.

"My poor sister, she sobbed, what the hell did my dad get him into? I said this morning that I hoped they'd lock him up for good. Mum should never have let him back into her life when he came out last year".

Horace took young Chris for a walk down to his house, thought they could get some lunch while there. Uncle Bill and Doug were already there eating some hock wrapped in buttered, homemade bread.

"Not you as well, Uncle Doug, we already feed Uncle Bill. It's a good job dad's not here he would be tearing his hair out for having to feed you as well, but I'm glad you're here.... I have some news for the both of you".

Doug called out to Horace's mum "Eva, your son is here causing trouble again, and he's brought a kid with him".

Eva came into the dining room.

"Horace, how did you get in here without me seeing you and little Christopher? Come on, Chris, let's go and play in the front room until these two lumps go, I can see they make you nervous. Shall we take a meat sandwich with us?"

When they left the room Horace told his uncles that the bloke in the boot was Simon, the husband of Ruth, Christine Rush's sister.

"Simon?" asked Doug both shocked and surprised "in the boot? He was a regular at the pub when on leave from the army".

"You didn't recognize him then when you looked in the boot yesterday?" asked Bill.

"Bill, I couldn't focus, I couldn't concentrate. All I saw were maggots coming out of the side of someone's head....then I threw up....several times. Horace will tell you, I froze".

Bill had set things up beautifully. Doug picked up his sandwich to take a bite "Mind them maggots coming out of the meat" he chortled. Doug jumped up causing the cups on the table to rattle and threw the sandwich on the floor.

"You bastard! You sodding bastard! I won't be able to eat meat again now, that's done me that has".

Encourage by Doug's reaction, Horace went to the scullery and bought back some gorgonzola, his dad's favourite cheese. With his dad having been in hospital for a few days the cheese was rife with maggots feasting on the spoils. He put it on the table. "Here, Uncle Doug, try this". Well, Bill was practically on the floor laughing and clutching his stomach. Doug just shot up and ran outside shouting the foulest obscenities he could muster. Bill turned to Horace "Doug's vocabulary is broader than I thought, I didn't realise he knew all those words".

Horace gave Chris a push in the pedal car then took him back to the garage. Gordon's car was on the forecourt so he knocked and walked in. Christine came out looking exhausted, her eyes red.

"Thank you, Horace, I don't know what we would do without you. I couldn't have done what we had to do this morning with little Chris being there. It's the worst thing I have ever had to do but the inspector was as nice as he could be. She took Chris in the living room and Gordon came in. He and Horace went outside to talk.

"I am so sorry Mr. Rush, if I knew it was Mrs. Rush's brother-in-law I wouldn't have done it, I mean, dumped the body where I did. Should've just left it in the boot. This whole thing has been terrible for you all".

"Horace, you wanted what we all want....to get that man locked up. I wonder whether he was trying to set me up when I collected the car. At least now he's the one that will have to answer the questions, which will be tough with his record of robbery and violence. Both his daughters want him locked up too but I bet anything that he will still get away with it. No, if you'd never found the body I don't know what would've happened to it, we would probably have never known. At least Ruth has some closure. You don't have to but if you do want to stay this afternoon you can work on your Prefect".

"No Mr. Rush, our Prefect".

"Horace, if last night was the set-up I think it was I would have nothing left.... nothing. He wanted me out of the way. He told me that if I didn't move the car he would chuck us all out of the house and garage".

"It doesn't bare thinking about it Mr. Rush. Knowing what he's like it is very possible, even likely, that he planned to stitch you up".

"Yes, not long after you went he said that if I didn't move the car he would see me in hell. Prison would have been my hell. The whole of the family despises him now and he has no real friends to call upon. We are going to stay at least one night with Jean, she's understandably distraught that the body was dumped there, right outside the house".

"Sorry again, Mr. Rush, for putting the body there. I never really considered the consequences. I just wanted to get him into trouble and was fed up with how he was treating you and Mrs. Rush".

"Don't beat yourself up about it, son, you did what you thought best at the time, it's done now. We will find a way to deal with it. There are three cars booked in tomorrow. One is a service which shouldn't be a problem for you the other two have faults with their engines. Just let me know if you can't do them for whatever reason and I will look at them on Thursday".

"OK Mr. Rush, I will do my best. Like you say, the service won't be a problem and please don't worry about the garage I will do my best, it's your family that's the most important now".

"Take the garage keys with you I will phone sometime tomorrow to tell you what's happening. When we return we want Jean to stay here with us for a while, maybe until he's locked up for good....hopefully. Then, Horace, and only then will this all have been worth it and soon to become a distant memory".

Horace went into the workshop and had a look at the booking-in book. He sat himself down and thought that one day maybe he would have his own garage, but it would have lots of cars for sale on the forecourt.

He started to work on the Prefect. He got the air line and spray gun out and moved it from side to side practicing how he would go about spraying the car. He started up the air sander and began sanding off the paintwork. When the last coat was off he pushed the Prefect outside and washed it down. The time was getting on but it was still before four in the afternoon so he sat in the kiosk with Monica.

There were two lasses who worked for Gordon, Monica and Sheila. They each worked on different days, three days a week from ten in the morning to three in the afternoon serving customers and filling them up with petrol or diesel.

Monica told Horace that there was a car parked across the road with two men in it who'd been looking over this way. "Been there for over an hour, they look a bit shifty to me just staring at us".

"What time are you supposed to finish Monica?"

"Christine takes me off at half three normally but they've all gone out somewhere. Don't suppose you know where they've gone? With me being pregnant I really need to get home and have a rest".

"Look, you get off, there's nothing for me to do in the garage except working on the Prefect".

"Are you sure, Horace? It would be good to get away if I could and it's my day off tomorrow anyway".

"It's fine. I'll lock the pumps at six and then be off myself, I have the keys to the garage and safe".

Monica gave him a kiss on the cheek then left. Horace was keeping an eye on the car discretely. He locked the kiosk door and went into the garage to see what paint there was left. Seeing how Tony mixed colours at Kennings he thought he would have a go at some mixing himself but most of the paint had been there for years by the look of it. He decided to phone the spray shop at Kennings to ask Tony about whether it was likely to still be alright.

"Tony, I have some old paint here. The tins are rusty and I don't know how long it keeps for, what do you think?"

"Does it look like it's got any discolouration on the top of the paint?"

"It looks fine. I've stirred it up and it looks OK but I didn't want to have to rub it down again if it doesn't turn out well".

"Mate, the best thing to do is spray the bulkhead first, that will tell you but I've never known any to go off if it's been sealed properly and remember what I told you about cleaning up the spray gun and hose when you've finished".

Horace starting mixing the paint, a kind of Ford Blue, Rover green with white from what he thought had been used on an Austin. "I put in too much white it looks too light and a bit boring to me" he thought when he'd finished. He looked around to see whether there was any other paint that might make it a bit more different and interesting but there was just red. "Ah well, let's give it a go". He poured the red in and the mix started to turn purple. "Well, that's better than the yucky light blue I had before".

The bell rang outside at the pumps. Horace went outside, it was a regular.

"Good afternoon, Mr. Martin, how much would you like? It's a nice afternoon. How're Mrs. Martin and Rob?"

"We're all fine, thanks. Fill it up please, Horace. Are you short staffed today?"

"Monica had to go home and Mr. and Mrs. Rush went to stay with Mrs. Rush's mother. They've had a bit of family trouble I'm afraid.

"I bet it has something to do with Fisher" said Mr. Martin, "that man always lives on the edge".

"That'll be £1 1/- 6d please Mr. Martin. I don't know what the problem is but I think it may well have something to do with Mr. Fisher".

Horace went into the kiosk to put the money in the till, he looked across the road and the car with the two men in it was still there. Horace was getting worried. Why were they looking at the garage all that time? He pretended not to notice and went back inside the workshop thinking about what he could use if they came over and caused any trouble. He put an iron bar next to his bench just in case. He went outside to push the Perfect back inside before he locked up and saw that one of the blokes was out of the car and walking across the road towards him.

"Excuse me young lad, where is the owner of this garage?"

"Mr. Rush is out for the rest of the day, he's taken Mrs. Rush to the doctor's then out for tea".

"It's not Mr. Rush we're looking for. We were told that Mr. Fisher owns the garage".

"I'm not sure but as far as I know he rents it to Mr. Rush and has done for a few years".

"We've been to Fisher's office but he's not there and hasn't been for a while. We have someone watching it".

Not knowing that Fisher had an office, Horace thought on his feet and asked if they had the right place.

"32 Park Street isn't it?" asked the chap.

"Oh, I thought it was around the corner in Uxbridge Street, number 190" said Horace lying and hoping that would be enough to make them go away and keep them busy for a while.

Wherever his office is, number 190 is one of the places Fisher stashes stuff along with the Old Bakery, he knows that for sure. The bloke didn't say anything, not a thank you or kiss my arse, and left. Horace locked the pumps, kiosk and garage, got on his bike and biked home. His mum asked if he'd a nice day at work.

"He told her that Fisher has been arrested".

"I know, son, Bill told me at lunch. Found a body, he said, but that doesn't surprise me, Fisher's just like his dad. He was a wrong 'un he was. When all the men went off to war in 1914 he did a runner to Ireland and never come back, that's why fisher is over there a lot. People say he does a roaring trade there selling whatever they can get their hands on, and Fisher has another family over there too. It wouldn't surprise me if that's where he'll go....when and if he gets out".

"Have you heard how dad is today, mum? I don't think I'll get a chance to see him tonight I want to go to see Sir Stanley and Lady Carpenter".

"Arlene went this afternoon and Iris is going to see him tonight. They think he'll will be out of that lung thing tomorrow and be home at the weekend or early next week but I just can't see it".

Horace had a wash and changed, had his tea then went out.

# CHAPTER SIX

Horace knocked on the door of Oak House. Sir Stanley's daughter, Helen, opened it. Horace thought that she was lovely the first time he saw her but she looked even prettier to him now.

"Mum and dad will be so pleased to see you, Horace, not that I'm not. How are you?"

"I'm OK thanks. I didn't come round before because my dad is still in hospital with chest problems".

"I'm so sorry to hear that, come in and see my mum. She's a lot better now and starting to walk without her stick. Her speech isn't quite right yet but the doctors say it will get better in good time. Mum, dad, look who's here".

"Horace, my boy, come in what a lovely surprise. Edith, look who it is".

Edith's face looked blank to start with so Sir Stanley explained to her again who Horace was.

"She is still a bit slow on the uptake but the doctors say she will improve gradually over time. They told us that her injury was a bit like having a stroke. One way or the other the damage was done but it doesn't matter now how it was caused, we just want her to get better".

Edith's face lit up suddenly as her recognition of Horace returned. "Oh yes, Horace. My, you are bigger than I remember but I was very poorly then wasn't I dear?"

Horace had a job to understand her because her voice was slightly slurred but he got the drift of what she was saying. Horace got down on one knee to talk to her at her sitting height.

"Lady Carpenter, you look so much better than the last time I saw you, the progress is amazing. I hear that you're walking better too, please keep it up won't you".

"Stanley and Helen keep telling me what you did for me, a stranger you didn't know. We are so very grateful and much indebted to you".

Horace noticed out of the corner of his eye that Sir Stanley and Helen were both crying.

"Horace, you're the first person to get down on one knee to talk and listen to her, others have simply looked down and talked 'at' rather than 'to' her. We are so proud and lucky to have met you and I would like to introduce you to my best friend Sir Humphrey Cartwright. Humphrey and I served in the Royal Air Force together and he was recently knighted".

"I'm very pleased to meet you Sir Humphrey. I read in the Radio Times magazine that there was an Air Commodore who led the 617 Squadron to blow up German dams in 1943, was that you sir?"

"No son, that was another Air Commodore. I was on the ground involved behind the scenes in the planning of some of the operations. The crews who went on the missions were the real heroes and the great Vickers Aviation engineer and designer Barnes Wallis was the mastermind of the bouncing bomb. His superiors at the time thought he was crazy to even contemplate getting anything to bounce on water let alone a bomb. The concept was that, launched at the right angle with enough speed and momentum, the bomb would bounce along on the water avoiding torpedo nets or other obstacles below the surface making it much more likely to hit its targets, such as dams or ships. He started the project in 1942 by skimming marbles across a water tank in his garden."

Sir Humphrey continued, "Previously, Wallis worked on the Vickers Wellesley Wellington bomber and designed and developed an air ship called the R80, the first of its kind in Britain. It was when he was seconded to the Admiralty that he was able to talk to the right people about his ambitions to develop a bouncing bomb.

Wherever he went and whoever he met he promoted the concept and benefits of such a bomb. But it was too unconventional for many and they all took a step backwards until the then Prime Minister, Winston Churchill, stepped forwards and supported Wallis. Churchill had firsthand experience of some of the projects with which Barnes had been associated. Churchill joked that he would bang his head against the Barnes door to bring this project to fruition. A Wellington bomber dropped a prototype of the bomb at Chesil Beach in Dorset in January 1943 but, good as the Wellington was, it wasn't capable of delivering an operational bomb. They needed something that could carry a bomb of the size and weight required to damage or destroy sturdy dams. The R.A.F. adapted the AVRO Lancaster for the job and set up the secret 617 Squadron, most commonly known as the Dam Busters, to fly the missions from Scampton, Lincolnshire. Like much of the R.A.F. the squadron consisted of Commonwealth pilots from Britain, Australia, New Zealand and Canada".

"Sir Stanley and I both started in the Royal Navy working our way up through the ranks from shipmen to midshipmen. We were both air boatmen and, in 1920, were commissioned into the R.A.F., along with Barnes Wallis and Leonard Cheshire who himself was a wing commander and a big part of Operation Chastise, the code name of the Dam Buster raid".

"Sir Humphrey, you both started the Royal Air Force? Wow!"

"No Horace, we were two of many that made the R.A.F. what it is today".

"Come on Humphrey, you were with Winston when you met King George VI during preparations for Operation Chastise. Don't do yourself down, we won't will we Horace?"

"No Sir Stanley" said Horace, "no one should ever forget the blowing up of the German dams but meeting the King....there can't be many who've met the King in person and been able to discuss such a great operation with His Majesty".

Sir Stanley added, "In later years we were posted to the same air base but in charge of different units. Humphrey was the Commander of the Eighth Squadron and I was also a commander but of a different type of squadron".

"Now come on, Stan" said Sir Humphrey "tell the lad the full story. You were attached to this new unit now known as the S.A.S.".

"But you, Sir Humphrey, flew up through the ranks to become Air Commodore and you still work for the service, you are still flying high. I don't know why he's even talking to me, Horace".

"Horace burst out laughing. I'm sorry for laughing but you said he flew up through the ranks....you were both flying up....through the ranks and through the clouds in....planes".

Lady Edith and Helen laughed too. Helen was delighted to see her mum laughing and put her arms around Horace.

"Horace, this is the first time she has laughed since she was attacked. She was always jovial before the incident and it looks as if her joviality is returning. I'm so glad you came tonight, you're a tonic for my mum and for us".

"Sir Stanley's eyes were watering. Another milestone, Edith, that's another milestone, my love, and yet again it's down to our very good friend, Horace. Please come to see us more often, Horace, I will even pay you to keep us company".

A maid brought in tea and a plate piled high with a variety of sandwiches and pastries and put them on the table.

"Sorry, I didn't know you were eating" said Horace, "I will go and come back tomorrow if that's alright?"

"I won't hear of it, young Horace" Sir Stanley said in a mock stern voice, "there's plenty of food for us all, so let's all tuck in".

"I'm very pleased to meet you, Horace" said Sir Humphrey "I have heard a lot about you and you sound like a strong, solid lad, and you're only fourteen. The forces could do with more people like you. What would you like to do if National Service carries on over the next four years? I really hope that it does because that's where men are made, apart from Stanley here" he added mischievously.

"Ha!" Sir Stanley retaliated "I will always be more of a man than you, squeaking your way up to be Air Vice".

"Well I love coming here. It's a lovely well placed house overlooking the river, just what I want. I'm looking at a few properties around here that's the reason I came this week. There's a nice place that's just come on the market, an R.A.F. property. I don't know if you know it, Horace, it's a castle".

"A castle, Humphrey? Who do you think you are mixing with? Royalty has gone to your head my aristocratic friend. Where is this castle....Windsor?"

"No Stan, I am being serious, I wouldn't have thought of a castle but it's owned by the R.A.F., it's called Bladon Castle and...."

"Bladon Castle" Horace interjected "The R.A.F. gave us permission to put up three huts there. We fetched them from Fauld at the depot they're closing. Well, not closing, the US Air Force is taking it over".

"What are you using the huts for, Horace?"

"My Uncle Bill was in the army in the war and is training my two cousins and I in the art of shooting, self-defence and survival. We're also trying to help get Winshill Scout Group set up by sharing the space. We started erecting them three months ago but with my Uncle Bill being so busy they're not quite finished yet. Hopefully we'll be able to do a bit more this weekend".

"Shooting?" asked Sir Humphrey "what do you shoot, Horace, and where do you do it because I haven't been shooting for years? Is it at Bladon Castle?"

"No sir, we just do target practice in the castle woods. For the time being the ministry doesn't want anyone shooting there, we go either to a place two miles from here, called Sinai, or to Kedleston Estate in Derby. The one in Derby is a great shoot we have beaters and around twenty guns during the shooting season. I went for the first time last year to beat for them and only started shooting towards the end when Uncle Bill said he thought I was ready. If either of you wants to come I will have a word with him for you but this time of year it'll be just rabbits, pigeons and vermin and, with permission, the occasional roe deer".

"I will consider several properties" said Sir Humphrey "but think we will look at the castle first. After that might be a good time for you to have a word with your Uncle Bill about the shoot. You know where the castle is, Horace, would you mind coming with me to show me where it is, say, sometime tomorrow, if you're not too busy".

"Yes, of course, I can spare an hour around lunch time if that's convenient. I'm on my own in the garage tomorrow, Mr. Rush has family problems so won't be there but I can get most of the jobs done in the morning. You can call me on 3645 it links through to the workshop. I will be there by half past six in the morning. I'm spraying a car first thing and hope to get two coats on by ten then I've got a service to do plus a couple of small jobs. I can bike down there when you are ready".

"Bike down?" asked Sir Humphrey, "I wouldn't hear of it. I will pick you up from your place or work, as long as it's easy to find".

"You can't go wrong Sir Humphrey. As you come out of here follow the street in front and keep going down until you see the Benzole sign. It's the only one on that road".

"Talking of bikes Horace" said Sir Stanley, "I heard from the police you turned fourteen a few weeks ago, I would like to give you a late birthday present. Helen wheeled in a brand new push bike. Horace, this is from us for your heroic intervention saving Edith and our family".

"Wow! A brand new Raleigh, and this is for me? But you can't give me a brand new one I don't deserve that".

Helen gave him a kiss on his cheek "You most certainly do deserve it. It's only a bike, a bike for life".

Horace knelt to thank and say goodbye to Lady Edith. She grabbed his hand and squeezed it. He shook both Sir Stanley's and Sir Humphrey's hands and returned Helen's kiss on the cheek. "Would it be OK if I leave my old bike here until I find someone to give it to?" then left and rode home on his shiny, new bicycle. His hormones were raging thinking about how nice Helen is and the pecks on the cheeks that she had given him. He started to sing and whistle, it's the first time he'd felt like that for ages but Horace was a realist and the fact that she was five years older than him put things into perspective.

He got home and showed his mum and two sisters the new bike. His twin sister Arlene was jealous, as normal. If Horace had anything she wanted the same.

Horace was up at five the next morning. He put the kettle on the stove, warmed up the frying pan and went outside and lit a fag. After a hearty breakfast of bacon and sausage meat washed down with a cup of tea he cycled to the garage, it was six thirty when he arrived.

He checked that the air hose and paint gun were securely connected and turned on the compressor. He'd been dying for two days to repaint the Prefect. He did what Tony had told him and started with the bulkhead in the engine compartment. In just over fifteen minutes the bulkhead was done. In just under an hour the first coat was on the rest of the car, which was now a gleaming, bright magenta object that stood out in the corner of the workshop. It was a one-of-a-kind colour, no one else would possess a Prefect that looked like it and its individuality would make it very desirable thought Horace.

The first job of the day was just arriving for its service so he got on with that and by half eight it was finished. He'd even realigned the brakes. He went to the Prefect and touched the paint gingerly. It felt dry so he'd do another coat in an hour or so he thought to himself and went outside to unlock the pumps for Sheila who would be on duty in the kiosk that morning. No sooner had he done the pumps than the two blokes from the day before turned up again.

"Oi! Have you seen Brian Fisher, we can't find him anywhere? Tell him to give Jake a call if you see him".

"Have you tried the police station? His sort's always getting locked up. I'm being serious, that's where he is".

"What do you mean the police station, and what do you know about him being there?"

"Look, I have work to do so I can't stay here chatting to you. Good day to you both".

"One last thing, does he live on the A 38 because the rozzers are all over it there?"

"The reason they're there is because I think he killed someone, but you will have to ask the police about that" knowing full well that they wouldn't go anywhere near the police let alone the police station. Just then a policeman came up the hill on his bike. "I will ask PC Gibbs if he can help you".

"Morning, Dan, how are you this morning? I've just put the kettle on if you want one".

The two blokes got in their car and disappeared faster than they had materialised.

"They're in a hurry aren't they, Horace, is it me, I don't smell do I?"

"Well, Dan, they're after Brian Fisher. They've been here twice now and said they have been keeping lookout outside his office".

"Brian Fisher's got an office? Our guv'nor will want to know about that. Yes, son, let's have a cuppa. I should have got their reg number to check them out, if they're after 'Fishy' they can't be legit and they both looked dodgy too".

"The reg is M F 432 it's a dark blue Ford V8 Pilot, this year's model. Here's your tea officer".

PC Gibbs used Gordon's phone to tell HQ that two suspicious blokes had been at the garage asking about Brian Fisher, he gave them the details that Horace had memorised.

"Horace, there's a lovely smell in here what is it?"

"Well Dan, I've just put the first coat of paint on that Prefect I'm working on, you saw it when I took the engine out a few weeks ago. Do you want to look at it but bear in mind I still need it to give the final coat".

They walked around the corner to see the bright magenta object. PC Gibbs fell in love with it straight away.

"Horace, what colour is that, will you be selling it? If so, put my name on it. I can just see that parked outside Burton Police Station, they'll all be so envious, where's the engine and interior?"

"The interior is under these sheets and the engine is on the bench waiting to go back in when I've finished spraying the interior".

"These seats and panels look brand new, and so does the engine with that red paint".

"I stripped down every nut and bolt in that engine and fitted new piston rings and shims. It didn't need them but I wanted to do a good job reconditioning it. The car has only done seven thousand miles, that's why the interior is like new because only the driver's seat was used".

"Do you know who owned it, Horace? The car has been here ever since I took this patch over".

"Yes Dan, it was, and still is, owned by the Managing Director of the Marmite Factory in Cross Street. He dumped it here after bumping the front wing and it's been sitting here neglected for the last two years".

"Well, Horace, he's running about in a Jaguar now so I doubt he'll be back to claim it. Leave it with me, I will get the owners book off him. I'm going to tell him that you need it out the way and, if it's OK with Gordon, I will buy it off him".

"Actually, Dan, Mr. Rush told me that it's mine now seeing as I've done all the work on it. I can do whatever I want with it."

"You put it all back together then we'll come to an agreement on the price, what have you spent on it so far?"

"No more than seven pounds, I don't think it's even that much so it's mainly just my time".

PC Dan Gibbs spat on his hand then shook Horace's.

"Don't worry, son, you will be paid handsomely for it".

Mr Hollis brought in his Comer van because it was misfiring all the time.

"Morning, Mr Hollis. You don't have to tell me what the problem is you can hear it from Winshill. Are you waiting, it should only take half an hour, it's either a blocked carb or the points want replacing".

"Well I better be going, Horace" said PC Gibbs. "How are you, Reg? I hope that the fruit and veg side is going well".

"It would be better, Dan, if I had a van that worked right, it won't do over twenty miles an hour".

"I 'm sure Horace will sort it out for you. See you both soon, I better get my skates on or the sergeant will think I'm out skiving. I'm going to check on those two in that Pilot, Horace. Good day to you both".

Horace first checked the points in Mr. Hollis' van but they were OK so he stripped the carb.

"Dear me, Mr. Hollis, the carb's full of crap. When did it start playing up and where did you last fill up?"

"John Jones at Alrewas gave me a ten gallon jerry can that'd been in his garage for about five years, he's not had a car since then. I exchanged some fruit and veg for the fuel, why is that the problem?"

"Sounds like Mr. Jones got the better deal, Mr. Hollis. You got a jerry can and some fuel but half of the can is in your fuel tank, the can must have been rusty inside. Problem is, I don't know how much is in there".

"You're joking, Horace. How can you get it out if it's in the tank?"

"I'll drop the tank and see if I can force it all out somehow but that'll take the rest of the day and probably some of tomorrow too. I've never done it before but it's not a hard job to get the tank off, the problem is getting the rust out".

"Damn! I have all the deliveries to do and not having a van is a nightmare. Where can I get some other transport?"

"I can ask my Uncle Bill, he's got two vans that he normally takes to different jobs, they mostly stand all day". He Phoned Bill but got no answer. "I thought he might have nipped home because my Auntie Mavis is coming back today. Tell you what, there's that Ford Pop on the forecourt you can use that. I don't think Mr. Rush will mind just give me ten minutes to take the seats out, don't worry I'll leave the driver's seat in".

"Are you sure, son? It'll really help me out. I have lots to do today, Fridays are always busy days".

Once the seats were out there was plenty of room in the van. He shouted to Reg to come and have a look.

"You wouldn't think it, Horace, there's more room in here than in my van. I don't know how to thank you. I'll square it with Gordon when I see him. By the way, does his not being here have anything to do with the police cars outside Brian Fisher's house yesterday, they were all over Fisher's front garden"?

"I really don't know, Gordon and the family rushed off last night saying they wouldn't be here today, that's all I know".

Reg went to load the van and the last car to be worked on came in, it belonged to a Mr. Percival.

"Hello, Horace, Gordon not around this morning he said he would look at my car?"

"No, he had to go somewhere in a hurry last night but said you'd be coming in. He told me that there's something wrong with your engine".

"I'm not sure what it is, it seems to judder and pull to the right all the time".

Horace started the engine but that seemed alright, at least it wasn't missing. He jacked the front up and the wheels went around OK so they weren't binding but then he noticed that one wheel was buckled.

"Have you gone down a hole or hit a curb, Mr. Percival, because one of your wheels is buckled?"

"I did hit a rut when I went fishing at Newton but didn't notice the problem straight away. So that's all it is then, Horace, just the bloody wheel. I suppose I'll have to get one then".

"We've got a second hand wheel with a good tyre on it you can sort out the price with Mr. Rush when he's back".

"Thanks, Horace, if you wouldn't mind doing it that would be great".

It had just gone half past eleven and all the booked in jobs were done. Horace thought he'd give the Prefect another coat before getting ready to meet Sir Humphrey. He'd just started spraying when the two shifty blokes who'd been there earlier turned up again, this time with Shelia in front of them. Jake had a gun in his hand".

"You tell me where Brian Fisher is or I will shoot her. You've had us running about for two days".

"How should I know where he is? We have nothing to do with him he only comes here to see his daughter, Mrs. Rush".

Sheila started to cry so the other bloke backhanded her. The distraction gave Horace the fraction of a second he needed. He let loose with the spray gun spraying them both in the eyes blinding them temporarily. Sheila ran towards Horace but he ran past her and went for Jake knocking him to the ground. He grabbed the gun, pointed it at Jake's leg and pulled the trigger. He went over to the other who bloke who was bent over rubbing his eyes and cursing and did the same. He ran over to the phone, picked it up and rang the police. Horace made sure Sheila was OK then told her to lock the pumps and put the closed sign out. Both men still couldn't see anything and were writhing on the floor in agony. Horace dragged them together by their jacket collars, got some rope and bound them up as tight as he could. He calmly went over to the Prefect and started spraying it with a second coat. The police didn't take long to arrive, their cars screeched to a halt outside. Horace finished spraying leaving just the bulkhead needing a second going over.

Sir Humphrey arrived at the garage at the same time as Inspector Smart and his men. The police ran into the workshop followed closely by Sir Humphrey.

Sheila was in hysterics yelling and sobbing but managed to compose herself sufficiently to tell the inspector that the two men had held a gun to her head and hit her and that Horace had saved her life.

Sir Humphrey was incredulous. Why would two men bring a gun to a backwater garage to threaten the staff and who the hell were they anyway?

"What is this all about, inspector? The poor lad had already been through enough a few months ago when he saved my best friend's wife, Lady Carpenter".

"Sir Humphrey, at the moment I know about as much as you do. I'm sure that Horace will put us all in the picture".

The police were attending as best they could to the men's leg wounds. Horace was on the phone to his next door neighbour asking him to tell Uncle Bill to come up to the garage as soon as possible. He knew that his uncle would be at home with his mum having lunch.

Sir Humphrey looked at the two men who were sitting hunched on the ground and groaning with pain. It looked like they had deliberately painted their faces with magenta war paint before embarking on their mission. He remarked to Inspector Smart that the men had clearly not realised they were coming to the wrong place today.

"Constable" said Inspector Smart with urgency "put that gun in my handkerchief. Take it to Stafford for a ballistics check to see if they can match it with the Fisher incident. We will send the two bullets to them when they've been dug out of the legs of these two fine gentlemen. We won't be able to interview them today so make sure that you send a PC with them when the ambulance arrives, I want round the clock surveillance".

"Now then, Horace, tell me what happened here. You have certainly been getting an unfair share of attention from the riff raff in recent weeks. Do you know these two men?"

"All I can tell you, inspector, is that they came looking for Brian Fisher yesterday, I told them that I didn't know where he was. They kept asking but I couldn't tell them anything. They returned this morning and I gave PC Gibbs their details but they came back yet again half an hour ago but this time holding a gun to Sheila's head. I was petrified. Luckily I had a spray gun in my hand. The one wearing the red top slapped Sheila across the face and the distraction gave me just enough time to launch myself at them and give their faces a coat of magenta. I don't know what they would have done because I couldn't tell them something I didn't know".

"Well, thank goodness that you and Sheila are in one piece" said Sir Humphrey "you seem to have done it again. Were they robbing the place, the young lady seems very upset, understandably?"

"No, Sir Humphrey, they were looking for Mr. Rush's father-in-law. They seemed very insistent and wouldn't believe when I told them I didn't know where he was. I called Uncle Bill to take you to the castle and he can show you around better than me anyway. I think I will be needed here for a while".

Uncle Bill walked in.

"What the hell is going on, Horace, are you OK? Who on earth are these people and what are they doing here?"

"Thanks for coming, Uncle Bill. This is Sir Humphrey Cartwright he wants to have a look at Bladon Castle, it's up for sale".

"Bladon up for sale? We've only just been given permission to use the woods, although admittedly we don't have a contract to do so".

"Bill, you don't mind me calling you bill do you?" said Sir Humphrey.

"Not at all, Sir Humphrey, my name is Bill Reese. Pleased to meet you, I'm the uncle of that poor lad and would be delighted to take you to Bladon Castle".

"If the R.A.F. has given you permission I can assure that it will stand if I buy the property. I hear that you're using it for the local scout group".

"That was my intention once we get the huts finished. We were going to do that this weekend. Would you mind if I drive, Sir Humphrey, I know where we are going but you will have to rough it in my van".

"Not at all, Bill. Just because I have a title doesn't mean I've always been privileged. You want to see some of the motor cars I have driven and, please, call me Humphrey".

They bade farewell to Horace, Sheila, Inspector Smart and the other policemen and got into Bill's van. Bill started to drive.

"You strike me as a leader, Bill, and a tough one at that you must have been at least a sergeant in the army".

"Yes, Humphrey, I was a Sergeant Major in the Marines. We need to go straight on until the traffic lights then turn left, it's quite easy to find once you know where you're going and a bugger if you don't. I didn't know that the R.A.F. wanted to get shot of the castle but it will make a lovely house again. What do you do for a living now the war is over?"

"I'm still in the services but work in Whitehall now, I do the work when I want to".

"When we met did you say that your surname was Cartwright, because Air Commodore Humphrey Cartwright helped to plan the bouncing bomb raids, can it be you, a man of that calibre and distinction in my van?" Bill took his eye off the road momentarily to shake Sir Humphrey's hand and hit the curb. "Sorry, Humphrey but a hero in my van, well, my two boys won't believe it. We cross that bridge over the River Trent then turn left, the castle is just over half a mile on the right".

Bill pulled into the driveway at the castle and a guard came to see what they wanted. Sir Humphrey told him who he was and he opened the driveway entrance gate. They went about half way up the drive when Bill stopped and said "Let's get out a second, Humphrey, and have a look at the view. I'll show you now and again when we get to the top".

"Who lives in these cottages?"

"I think it's the services staff that work at the castle".

"So this all comes with the castle? It never said that when I saw it on the board in Whitehall. Well, you're certainly the right man to show me around with all your local knowledge".

"Horace would have been able to do the same, he's knows a lot for a lad his age. I can't wait to find out who put a bullet in those two at the garage but I do know who put on their magenta makeup".

"Well, Bill, I heard the girl talking to the police. She told them that Horace saved her life by spraying them, disarming and pointing the gun at them and then pulling the trigger, and also that the noise was so loud in that enclosed space that it deafened her".

"Humphrey, what I can't understand is why people were there with a gun in the first place. I didn't see Gordon Rush there. Gordon is the garage proprietor".

They walked the rest of the way up the hill taking in the views.

"I can see the river from here, what a wonderful place to live and I think I can see my friend's house as well".

"Can I ask you, Humphrey, how you came to know Horace? It's not like him to keep things from me he tells me everything normally. He's like one of my own and, just between us, the brightest out of all of them. You tell him something once and you don't have to tell him again. My two boys are two and four years older than Horace and, if I am honest, I'm a little disappointed that they won't be taking the same path I did by going into the services. But it's not their fault, they both have asthma from their mother's side of the family and it can get really bad in the summer".

"Of course, Bill. I only met Horace last night at Sir Stanley and Lady Edith's".

Humphrey and Bill walked up to the main gate. They stopped to wait for someone to open it and were greeted by a military guard. When he saw it was Bill he opened it immediately without the need for any formal exchanges with the visitors.

"How are you Bill, we haven't seen you for a couple of weeks?"

"Hello Steve, we've all been busy. This is Air Commodore Humphrey Cartwright he's here to look at the castle".

"Yes, we have him on our visitor's list. Good day to you, sir" and saluted Sir Humphrey.

"Never ever thought I would find a place like this, it's stunning".

First he wanted to look around the outside. I am sure that my wife and three children will love this place as much as I do. It's such a beautiful garden, superb for the children to play and for Hermione and me to relax in".

They walked into the castle and admired the skilfully crafted fixtures and fittings. Every room they went into still had the original period decor but it was difficult to picture the downstairs rooms as domestic living space because they were currently being used as offices and work rooms. Then they went to look at the upstairs rooms. The old oak beds were still there and being used.

"This is much more like it, Bill. This would be Hermione's and my bedroom, the one to the right would be Ann's and the one down the corridor would be John's and Malcolm's, and there are still a couple of rooms to spare".

Bill was pointing out a few things that needed doing as they walked around. Just before heading back downstairs Bill stopped suddenly and to Humphrey's surprise opened 'an invisible door', a secret door that had been made to look as if it were part of the surrounding wall.

"Bill, how did you know that was there?"

"Aha! Trick of the trade, Humphrey. When you've worked on these period properties for as long as I have you can spot them a mile off. Stand against the wall and look along it. Can you see the line of the wall?" He shut the door "Can you see it now?"

"All I can see is a wall, Bill, the workmanship is outstanding. You say you have worked on period properties, what is your job?"

Bill reopened the door and they both walked into the room. He felt for a switch and turned on the light. The room was like a treasure trove. There were dust covered piles of old furniture and other items. Paintings, ornaments, desks, dining tables, chairs....all looked to be Queen Anne period. It was too much to absorb in such a short space of time but this all made Sir Humphrey fall even more in love with the place.

"The castle reminds me of the place I grew up, Bill, but this one is on a slightly smaller scale. Yes, I used to live in a castle in Scotland, Cranford Priory".

"You asked what I did. I run my own building company, which I started before going into the army. When I was young I worked in my granddad's building firm and with my dad in the joinery workshop. The company continues to this day and still carries out work on old properties. We have one contract with the Bass and Radcliffe Brewery to do up all their old buildings and another five-year contract with the Town Council to build council houses. We've just employed another ten men to work on them. The council wants eight thousand houses to be built over the five years".

"Well, Bill, if I do buy this property, would you have time to fit any repair work that is needed into your busy schedule? You are an honourable man so I won't insult you by asking for a price upfront. I will try to bring the family this weekend to have a look. I would like to take a decision as soon as possible so that we can get the ball rolling".

"Humphrey, if I do a job I insist that the customer knows the price before I begin the work and, if you do choose us, then it would be me, my two boys and my father that would do it for you. My dad is still a better joiner than me but please don't let him know that I said that", Bill chuckled.

"Well I think I have seen enough for today, thank you Bill. I cannot wait to show this place to my family".

Bill and Humphrey headed back to the garage. Gordon was back and the police were still there when they arrived.

"Gordon, how are you with all this going on? It's pretty serious with armed people turning up, what's the story?"

"I am so sorry, Bill. I can't take it to be honest but it must all be to do with Brian Fisher by the sound of it".

Sir Humphrey asked how Horace was. "The lad's only fourteen and had a gun pointed at him and, by the sound of it, with intent. Sorry, Gordon, I didn't introduce myself, I am Commodore Humphrey Cartwright, my wife and I are friends of Sir Stanley and Lady Carpenter and I think I can safely say with Horace and Bill. Would you please tell me who this Brian Fisher chap is and why you think it was he that caused people with firearms to threaten a young boy?"

"Commodore, Brian Fisher is my father-in-law. These men were after him for reasons that I do not yet know".

"That man has lots of reasons why people would want to kill him and now I'm on that list, where is he?" asked Bill.

"Haven't you heard, Bill? He's been arrested and locked up, hopefully for good, but the bastard has more lives than a tom cat".

Bill asked the sergeant if they could see Horace then went in the workshop. Horace was still there with Inspector Smart.

"How are you son? It's a lot to take in. Do you know these people are, Inspector, coming armed to a garage to threaten to kill a child and young girl?"

"Mr Reese, we have no idea who they are, they had no identification or anything else on them to indicate where they are from but it almost certainly has something to do with the body we found on Mr. Fisher's property, it would be too much of a coincidence not to be".

Gordon came into the workshop.

"Bill, do you want to see the colour that Horace has painted the Prefect? The result is fantastic, such a professional job but it's a colour I have never seen before. He mixed the paint himself and sprayed it without any help. In fact, I wasn't even here and the best thing is that he already has a buyer when he puts it put it back together".

"That does look good, Gordon, you can see your face in the paintwork it's so shiny. Well done, lad, it is a great job but who in their right mind has bought it?"

PC Gibbs was standing behind Bill "I bought it, Bill, but don't tell any of the lads I want this to be a surprise when I pull up in front of the station next week".

"Well, Dan, people will surely see you coming. I wasn't sure to begin with but I must say it does grow on you the more you look at it".

"So, Horace, how are you....really?"

"I'm fine, Uncle Bill, it was a good job I had the spray gun in my hand at the time".

"But you shot them afterwards in the leg that takes a lot to do. Shooting birds and vermin is one thing but shooting a person is very different".

"Not when someone has a gun pointing at a girl's head. I shot them because I didn't want them to get up again Uncle Bill".

Inspector Smart came over to see them.

"Horace if you come to the station in the morning we can go through the events again, no rush, in your own time".

# CHAPTER SEVEN

Horace arrived at the police station early. He gave the desk sergeant his name and told him who he'd come to see. He didn't have to wait long before being shown to Inspector Smart's office.

"Morning Horace, you're very early but I'm glad you are. We have a lot to discuss today, not just one case but three. One second, I'll ask Chief Inspector Walters to come over, he wants to ask you a few questions as he's the one leading the investigations on all three cases and it's only right he tells you what he has found out".

"In the meantime, how are you today after that traumatic incident yesterday? You must have been frightened to death when you saw those men come into the workshop with one of them holding a gun. Poor Miss Roe is still in hospital, she collapsed after you left and it will take her a while to get over this mentally. She told me last night that she really thought she was going to die. I visited her again this morning before coming to the station, the doctors said she kept having flashbacks when she closed her eyes. How did you sleep, Horace?"

"I slept soundly last night, thank you inspector. The thing I kept thinking of again and again was Shelia with a gun to her head and the tears rolling down her cheeks. What I did was on the spur of the moment, it was an instinctive reaction when one of the blokes slapped her across the face. I was frightened and worried because I had no idea what they intended to do".

The door swung open suddenly and in walked a giant of a man. Horace was five foot eight inches so not small for a fourteen year-old, but this chap was almost a foot taller than him. Horace looked up at him.

"Wow! You're a tall man. My Uncle Bill would say, did your mum feed you horse fodder instead of rusks when you were a baby?"

"I am Chief Inspector Walters" he said with a grin on his face. "Well, you say what you think, son, hopefully you will make a good witness when this comes to trial because we are charging those two men at the garage yesterday with the murder of Simon Green. We sent the gun and bullet that we fished out of Simon Green to forensics to do finger print and ballistics checks. The gun had partial finger prints on it of both men who we now know to be Arthur Grimes and Walter Hognut, it obviously also had your prints on it but I think we can rule you out of this one. This same gun was used to kill three other people as well as Mr. Green. They are also wanted for armed robbery in four counties. Let's talk about the first time they came".

"It was yesterday morning about half eight. I went to open the pumps for when Sheila arrived but Monica told me the day before that they'd already been there watching the garage from their car across the road. They must have been there for at least a couple of hours. It was only when I locked the pumps yesterday afternoon and was pushing the Prefect into the workshop that they first approached me".

Horace paused a while to think and try to remember the details.

You were saying, Horace, that you were pushing the Prefect into the workshop when these men came up to you. What exactly did they say, from the start if you can remember?"

"Yes it's as clear to me now as it was last night. They walked over and asked where Brian Fisher was. I told them that he doesn't have anything to do with the garage but they said that he owned it; I replied that Mr. Rush must rent it off him then. One of the blokes told me that they had been down to his office in Park Street so I got rid of them by telling them there was a place at 190 Uxbridge Street that could be his. I knew the place was a fire damaged shell but just wanted them to leave. I never thought that they would come back again, how wrong I was."

"Thank you, Horace" said Chief Inspector Walters, you are helping tremendously with your account.

"Let's turn to the grammar school now, Horace. We've spoken to the other boys whose names you mentioned when you first met Inspector Smart. They and their parents all told us similar stories to yours, which is that one of the teachers, a Mr. Osborne, takes kids out off class into his office and tries to interfere with them. However, all but one said they didn't think that they had ever met you. The Meers boy confirmed that you did go to his house and ask him in front of his mum and dad whether Osborne had done the same to him. But Ray Wilkinson said he can't remember talking to you".

"That's right, Chief Inspector, I have never spoken to Ray Wilkinson but I've seen him working for my uncle. Uncle Bill said that Ray had told him in his job interview that Mr. Osborne had interfered with him at that school. I also got the names of the other boys from Uncle Bill when he mentioned them to the Principal, Mr. Reynolds".

"Well, I can tell you that Mr. Osborne is going to court and will be charged with indecent assault on minors, along with two allegations of male rape. After all the accusations that you and these other boys have made and the investigations that we've carried out to confirm them, the Principal, Mr. Reynolds, is being charged for withholding evidence. Thank you for that, Horace".

"Last but not least, the attack on Lady Carpenter. Nowak Fryderyk has been taken to Wormwood Scrubs Prison in Birmingham and is awaiting trial".

"Erm, Horace, back to the incident yesterday at the garage, would you tell me one thing, why did you shoot them in the leg and how did you feel afterwards?"

"I shot them, inspector, mainly because I was frightened and didn't want them to get up again but I didn't want to kill them either. My Uncle Bill told me that in the army they say that if you shoot to kill you can't ask any questions but if you shoot to maim you can find things out".

They thanked Horace for coming in and said that they would be back in touch.

The sun was shining and Horace's mood had lifted a little after meeting Walters. He got on his new bike and went just over a mile to Bladon to meet Uncle Bill and his two cousins in the woods.

"Where did you get that new shiny bike Horace, did the nice policeman give it to you or is it a getaway bike? Sorry, son. How are you feeling now?"

"Better now that the interview with the police is over, uncle".

"Come on, get stuck in with the lads, we have to get these last two hut sections on today so we can put the roof on tomorrow. I'll get the coach bolts from the van".

Bill and George childishly took the mickey out of Horace pretending to be shot and falling to the ground.

"You two can stop that. If you had been there instead you would have shit yourselves, Horace did a good job giving those blokes a re-spray. Are you sure the colour suited them, Horace? People will see them coming in the dark and that on its own would scare the living daylights out of you two".

They worked hard the rest of the day putting up the sides of the huts using a winch and rope because the sections were far too heavy to lift by hand. Uncle Bill manned the winch to make sure that the sections were lifted straight and that they aligned properly before being bolted together. Bill and George were whinging again. They seemed to spend a good deal of their time complaining.

"If you two worked for anyone else you would have been sacked by now. Just get on with it, Horace isn't moaning".

"Dad, that's probably because he doesn't work for you day in, day out being told George do this, Bill do that every five minutes".

"Horace, shimmy up to where the sections meet and put these coach bolts in, you'll need a hammer to belt them through. Be careful up there, the sections aren't secure yet".

"OK, will do, Uncle Bill".

"See, boys, that's how it's supposed to work, I give the orders and you carry them out. It's a good job you two aren't going to do your National Service, you would stick a foot in the door and say sorry Sergeant I can't go out because it's too cold or because my mum hasn't wiped my arse yet. Horace, jump down here a moment".

He jumped down immediately and without saying a word

knowing full well that this would wind his cousins up. He'd always enjoyed winding them up and had started doing so at an early age.

"Horace, do twenty press-ups" bellowed Bill, so he dropped down and did twenty. "Horace, run and take this hammer to my van". Horace sniggered and did what he was told at the double and ran back.

"Horace, where's my bloody hammer?"

"It's in the back of the van Uncle Bill, you just told me to take it there".

"Oh yes, silly me. Bill, go and fetch my hammer please".

"What's the matter with you, dad? You get Horace to take a hammer to your van now you want me to fetch it back. You're losing it you know that don't you? It's Horace do this and he jumps and Horace do that and he jumps. I don't understand what's going on, do you George?"

George remained silent.

"It's a wind-up" said Uncle Bill. "You would get this all the time if you worked anywhere else....and worse. I've known workmen in some places send a new starter to the store to ask for a 'long weight'. The storeman, used to new starters asking him for 'long weights', would tell the lad to stand over there for a bit. After a while, the chap who sent him would go to the store and ask the lad what he was doing. When the reply was 'I haven't got the weight yet' or 'I'm still waiting for it' he'd be told to bloody well get back to work because the wait was already long enough".

Bill said that he didn't get the weight thing and George just stood there flummoxed.

"Lads, I'm sorry but you both need to go and work with someone else for six months. You're in a bubble working for the family business and not getting any real-life experience, it would really do you some good".

"So what does the long weight thing mean, dad?" asked George. "Do you get it, Horace?"

"Yep, Horace replied".

The penny finally dropped for Bill and he roared with laughter.

"OK" said Horace. "George, there isn't anything called a long w-e-i-g-h-t but there is something called a long w-a-i-t, you know, if you wait a long time for something. So the poor lad would stand in the stores waiting for something that would never come, until his gaffer went to collect him. Get it?"

"You berk" Uncle Bill said to George. "If Horace hadn't explained it you'd still be waiting there if you were that new starter. On second thoughts, if you went to work for someone else they would realize what drips you both were and that would reflect badly on me and the business. One day you will have to be able to work things out for yourselves so starting on Monday things will change. I suppose it's my fault that you are as you are but I'm partly blaming your mum for mollycoddling you both. That reminds me, I have to pick your mum up from the station later on".

They finished the huts in the woods and Sir Humphrey bought Bladon Castle two months after Bill had showed him around it. Sir Humphrey asked Bill and his two boys to carry out full repairs to the property. Bill's dad did all the joinery work. The house was restored to its former glory and Sir Humphrey and his family moved in just over a year later.

Sir Humphrey and Bill became good friends and Bill introduced him to the local shooting fraternity. Sir Humphrey loved shooting and went most weekends with Bill and the lads. Horace's shooting improved each time he went and by the time he was sixteen he became an excellent marksman and was much better at it than his cousins, not to mention most of the Kedleston Hall shooters. The only two that were better than him were Uncle Bill and a chap called Richard, who was a friend of Ambrose the game keeper.

Sir Humphrey loved talking to and meeting people from all backgrounds but aristocrats tend to stick together. It was the Viscount of Scarsdale, Richard Curzon of Kedleston Hall, who became Humphrey's best friend in the region. Kedleston Hall was the seat of the family since 1297. The family originated in Notre-Dame-de-Courson in the Normandy region of Northwest France. In medieval times, Notre-Dame-de-Courson became a part of the barony of the Ferrers family, from nearby Ferrières-Saint-Hilaire, who took part in the Norman Conquest of England.

Sir Humphrey enjoyed talking to Viscount Curzon about their heritages. Sir Humphrey was the youngest son of Theodore Cartwright, 1st Baron Cartwright [Deputy Lieutenant, Justice of the

Peace] who was a Scottish soldier and politician who served during Arthur Balfour's administration between 1902 and 1905. He became a peer and the Baron Cartwright in 1919 shortly after The Great War.

Three months after moving to Bladon, Sir Humphrey took both Viscount Richard and Bill to his family seat in Scotland for a week of shooting, fishing and going to one or two 'cèilidh', which were social gatherings at which there was much dancing to Gaelic folk music and, no doubt, the consumption of vast quantities of alcohol. He then took them to the Highland Games at which Bill had a go at tossing the caber. To cut a long story short, they had a whale of time. Bill told Humphrey that it had been the best trip he had ever been on.

When Uncle Bill returned he raved to everyone, particularly George and Eva, about his having stayed in a castle for a week and had the most wonderful time. In the meantime, Bill's wife, Mavis, had returned to Manchester to stay with her mother.

During the two years that passed, Horace had been to court to testify against Fryderyk Nowak for his attack on Lady Carpenter and Mr. Osborne for his abuse of the young boys at the school.

Nowak was found guilty of attempted murder and jailed for ten years and would be deported at the end of his sentence. Osborne was found guilty of sexual misdemeanours and jailed for three years, and the Principal, Mr. Reynolds, was sacked.

Horace finished the Ford Prefect. PC Dan Gibbs had bought it for £55 10/- with the proviso that maintenance work on the car would be free of charge for four years from the purchase date, which was good for Horace because that really meant that he only had to service it once each year.

PC Gibbs had become notorious driving around in his magenta Prefect and it actually generated a reasonable amount of extra business for the garage. Some of those who saw the Prefect in town either asked Horace to find a car and spray it the same or an equally garish colour or to do the same to the car they already owned. Anyway, the bodywork business at Rush's Garage increased sufficiently for Gordon to hire another mechanic who, due to the machinations and meddling of Brian Fisher, would leave after two years.

The charges against Brian Fisher for the murder of Simon Green were dropped on the basis that there was insufficient evidence to prosecute him but the evidence against the two men whom Horace had shot in the garage was overwhelming, so they were the only ones to be found guilty.

This only exacerbated the situation as far as Fisher was concerned. He thought that he had become untouchable and this amplified his antics of deception and manipulation. Horace saw him from time to time and the verbal exchanges between them had become even more hostile than they were before.

Gordon and Christine's hatred of Fisher grew with a passion. Fisher's threats to evict them and constant meddling in their affairs led to them keeping an eye open for another house and business premises, just in case. They were interested in a detached house further down Henhurst Hill and some new units suitable for the garage were being built in Shobnall Road, a stone's throw from Christopher's school and the new house.

Fisher's wife, Jean, stayed with Ruth whenever she could to look after the children. Ruth told her dad that she would knife him if he ever came anywhere near her or the children.

Horace put the Velox, the car in which Simon's body had been hidden, on the garage forecourt.

"If that doesn't upset the bastard nothing will Mr. Rush. I can't wait to see his face when he notices it".

"It will probably go over his head, Horace. It was a long time ago now but it's worth it even if he only deems it to be an act of defiance. Where did you keep it all this time?"

"It's been in the brewery car park since the night I took Simon's body to Fisher's house. I asked the brewery manager first if I could take it, of course. I told him that it belonged to a friend who had joined the army and that I'd promised him I would look after it for him".

Lady Carpenter had almost recovered fully and was even going out by herself again for walks along the river bank. Sir Stanley was able to travel to London more frequently to his work in Whitehall now that he did not have to rely so heavily on Helen to look after her mum. The Carpenters bought presents for Horace on his birthdays, the best being a brand new B.S.A. motorbike. He used it to visit the Carpenters at least once every week and enjoyed travelling further afield on it whenever he had some free time.

# CHAPTER EIGHT

Horace loved to walk along the canal which was only about two hundred yards from where he lived. The boaters were an intriguing people, similar in many ways to the gypsies but living on boats rather than in horse drawn vans. One of the things they had in common was that their living space was small and somewhat confined. The boaters were basically good people but, as with any group, or society as a whole for that matter, there were bound to be the odd rogue individuals.

Horace spotted something half submerged in the canal water so went over to try to drag it out. It was quite large and seemed to be cylindrical in shape. He got down on his stomach, found a hand hold and was pulling as hard as he could but it was either stuck or heavy, or both, when a boater came up and asked what he was doing.

"I'm trying to get this thing out. I don't know what it is but it looks interesting. I can get hold of it but it doesn't budge".

"Hang on a bit there, I'll fetch a rope".

He came back with a rope accompanied by a pretty young girl who looked to be about the same age as Horace. Horace thought she was beautiful, which she was, with long blond hair and pale blue eyes that could hypnotise any young man.

"Here lad, put the noose around the top then we can drag it up the towpath to the winch on the boat". All three pulled as hard as they could. It rocked a little but the canal would not give up its treasure that easily.

"Lizzy!" the man shouted "come and help here". A woman in her early thirties, and also very pretty, appeared from the only boat that was moored just a few yards further down the towpath. They tried again but still couldn't budge the object. "I'll fetch Hercules" said Lizzy. Horace wondered who the heck 'Hercules' was.

"What's your name then?" the young girl asked Horace. "Mine is Charmaine Hackett and these are my mum and dad".

"I'm Horace Gray, I live in one of those cottages in that row over there and work at a garage up the road".

"How old are you Horace?"

"Sixteen and looking forward to being seventeen so I can drive a car, how old are you?"

"I'm fifteen and I'm looking forward to going out with you because you're a good looking one. Do you fancy me Horace because I fancy you a lot? Have you got a girlfriend and what do you do when you're not working?"

Wow, thought Horace, this girl was very direct and didn't waste any time.

"I work on cars mostly and in my spare time go up to Bladon woods to do woodland activities".

"What sort of activities do you do there, and would you take me there with you one day?"

"Yes, if it's OK with your parents, I will take you there on my motorbike".

"Dad, can I go with Horace on his motorbike? You know I've always wanted to go on one....please dad".

"Chamy, we don't even know the lad so let's take things slowly. You're always at full pelt aren't you lass".

Lizzy returned leading a huge, dark brown horse with massive hooves that left deep imprints in the towpath clay and gravel. "Here you are son, this is Hercules, he's the one that gets us up and down the canal". She put the rope around his yoke and he pulled the mysterious object all the way to the winch that was on the stern of their boat. When most of it was winched out of the water they could see that it was a sidecar off a motorbike.

"That'll be a good project for me to do" said Horace, "refurbish a sidecar".

Horace rode back to the garage to ask Gordon if he would help him move the sidecar to the garage, Gordon agreed but wanted to take a look at it first.

Gordon met the Hackett family beside their boat but all Charmaine did was to keep asking Gordon questions about Horace. She wanted to know everything about him. Lizzy told her to stop asking so many questions, "You're embarrassing the poor lad" she said.

They got the sidecar across the tow path and into a van and took it up to the garage where they left it outside to drain. Horace thanked Gordon and said he would see him on Monday.

Horace became good friends with the Hacketts. The family travelled along the canal three times a week taking cargo between the BTR factory in Burton, which made wellington boots, and Byrne Brothers in Birmingham. This regular contract work made them the envy of the other local working boaters. In fact, they had done so well that they planned to buy a new boat and a 'butty', which is a smaller canal boat towed behind and used either for cargo or additional living space.

James and Lizzy Hackett had four children, none of which went to school but Lizzy Hackett did her best to teach them what she could. The children's ages ranged from one to fifteen years, the oldest being Charmaine who was an impulsive but otherwise sensible girl. Having got to know Horace a bit better, James and Lizzy consented for their daughter to ride with him on his motorbike. She fell in love with him and couldn't wait to get back to Burton after their boat trips to see him.

The Hackett's soon got their new boat and butty. The new boat had a powerful diesel engine to propel both the boat and butty easily along the waterways. This meant that they no longer needed the services of Hercules so sold him to another boating family. It also meant that Lizzy or Charmaine could spend more time with the kids because it was no longer necessary for one of them to walk along the towpath minding the horse.

When Horace finished work and the Hacketts were moored back in Burton, he would ride his motorbike down the towpath to see them, which really pissed off the lock keeper at Barton Gate Lock, especially when there was a lot of boat traffic and the tow path was crowded. If it was busy it sometimes took a couple of hours for the boats to get through to Horninglow basin where the BTR factory was. The children would always shout and wave excitedly at Horace when he arrived on his bike.

The Hacketts were originally from Ireland and being very religious often went to the Catholic churches that were not too far away from the canal between Burton and Birmingham. Alongside this devotion, they were wise to the ways of the world and followed their own instincts as well as observing the boating people's customs and laws.

On one trip to see Charmaine, Lizzy took Horace to one side and had a word with him. "Horace, are you a virgin?"

"No Mrs. Hackett, Charmaine and I just go around and spend time together".

"Horace, I didn't mean to suggest that you'd had sex with Charmaine".

"Well no, Mrs. Hackett, I've never had sex before".

"Do you play with yourself then lad, do you do that? Be truthful now, I just want to know because our Charmaine thinks she is in love with you and wants to make love to you....she told me this".

Horace saw Charmaine peeping out from the butty.

"No, of course not" replied Horace.

"Well, have you feelings for my Charmaine, the same that she does for you? If you do, go to the butty now. The fire is on and it's nice and cosy. I have spoken to Charmaine about sex. Before you make love to her she will wank you off to get rid of the first ejaculation, then you will be safe to have sex as many times as you want tonight, the first sperm is the one that does the damage. I'm being honest and trying to help you, son, so don't just shag her and go home, you must stay with her tonight and make her feel like a woman. I am not asking you to marry her, just to make her happy. James wasn't my first love and I wasn't his, but this is what living together is all about....making sure you are right for each other and James and I will be together forever. So, if you want my Charmaine go and tell her that her mum and dad are staying on the boat tonight, and please be kind to my little girl, you must promise me this".

"Mrs. Hackett....I mean Lizzy, of course I will be kind to Chamy and, yes, of course I have dreamt about making love to her. I never said or did anything because I respect her and your family. First I will take my bike home. Do you think she will want to come with me? I can't tell my mum anything about what we discussed, though, she isn't as broad minded as you Lizzy, she just wouldn't understand. Won't it be a bit cramped if you all stay on the boat tonight?"

"No more than it used to be before we had the butty, lad".

Horace rode his bike home and told his mum and dad he was going to stay on the canal boat for the night, but left out the details of his discussion with Lizzy. Eva wouldn't have stopped him but she was judgemental about the boaters. She never understood 'those sorts of people' saying that they were worse than gypsies.

Horace got back to the butty and knocked on the roof. Charmaine came to the door crying.

"What's the matter, sweetheart?" he asked, "have you changed your mind because we don't have to do anything if you have".

"Don't be a silly boy. I thought you'd run off after my mom spoke to you....I want this more than anything".

She put more wood on the fire. "I'm sorry Chamy, I thought your mum would tell you that I was taking my bike home, I couldn't leave it here all night I just can't trust all you water 'gypos' you know".

She grabbed hold of him and pretended to fight him, then tickled him, and soon they were kissing.

"You will be gentle with me, Horace, this is my first time, as my mum told you".

"Yes Chamy, and I told her that it's my first time too, so you'd better be gentle with me".

Chamy put a clean rug by the fire and lay Horace down on it then knelt down beside him and kissed him on the lips. She undid his shirt and took it off. To Chamy she seemed to be doing it in slow motion but in reality she was nervous and was hurrying. Seeing Horace's bare chest and the anticipation of what they were about to do sent her heart racing, Horace sat up and hugged her.

Her breasts were heaving up and down. Horace put his hand on them but that made it worse, she started hyperventilating to such a degree that Horace became worried and ran to the boat to call Lizzy.

"What's the matter, Horace, is Charmaine alright?"

"I don't know Lizzy, her chest is going up and down so fast I think she's unwell. Can you please come quickly?"

They both ran to the butty. Charmaine's chest was going up and down faster than before....Lizzy slapped her across the face".

"Lizzy!" shouted Horace, "that's unkind, she isn't well. I will go and get a car to take her to the infirmary".

"That's very kind, Horace, but it won't be necessary she'll be alright in a minute. Get the pot on the stove and pour yourselves both a cup of tea with lots of sugar in then sit down together and relax. She will be OK, she just needs to calm down it's nothing but a little panic attack".

Horace wasn't sure, he thought she was going to die.

Charmaine sat up and told both of them she was sorry for causing a fuss and started to cry and sob. Horace put his arm around her and lifted a cup to her lips for her to sup the tea. "Come on, love, drink this it will make you feel better".

Lizzy got up and kissed them both on the forehead. "Horace, if you want to go home we will both understand, you must be very shocked yourself".

"No Lizzy, I am staying here, if Chamy still wants me to. I don't want to leave her like this. Can I just hold and cuddle you tonight Chamy? That's all I want tonight my love, nothing more".

Chamy looked up and smiled. "We both want more than that but you are a sweet boy".

Lizzy knew they would be alright so went back to Jim and told him all about it, they both laughed but were touched with the young couple's innocence and love for each other.

"Do you remember our first time?" asked Jim, "that was a night, Lizzy, that will stay with me forever".

"I bet it will but you were like a dog in heat, you were. That's why I asked Horace to be gentle with our Charmaine".

Horace held Chamy as they lay by the fire. She stood up and

unbuttoned the front of her dress and let it fall to the floor, she was completely naked wearing nothing but a smile. Horace's eyes and mouth were wide open as he examined the contours her body and marvelled at her beautiful smooth skin. He could see the goose pimples on her arms and neck, and the tiny hairs on her shoulders standing on end. Never having seen a girl naked before he thought that her breasts were enormous but in reality they were firm and perfectly in proportion to the rest of her body. Horace jumped up without saying a word and squeezed her tightly.

Charmaine knelt down to take his trousers off. He was ready for her. She had never seen a man's erect penis before but took hold of it and started pulling, perhaps a little too vigorously.

"Chamy, my love, you're not milking a cow, do it more slowly, let me show you".

That night they both experienced something together that neither had before. They stayed in each other's arms all night. The next morning was a beautiful, sunny Sunday morning, Charmaine was up first. She put the pan on the stove and by the time Horace stirred the smell of cooking bacon filled the butty. Charmaine stood there naked by the cooker. The sunlight reflected off the water through the windows and danced around her body making it glow first here, then there. Horace got up. That's my favourite breakfast you know, but he took the pan off the cooker, grabbed her hand and led her back to bed. They were relaxed and very much in love, they took their time and climaxed together. Charmaine said that she would love him forever no matter what happened.

About an hour passed and there was an abrupt knock on the roof startling Horace and Charmaine. Lizzy walked in within a second of knocking "That's so lovely to see. Two love birds sitting by the fire eating bacon sandwiches together with nothing on but love".

"Mum! You can't just barge in, Horace has no clothes on and neither have I, what are you doing?"

"Well, I came to see if you wanted to go to church but I don't think The Lord will want you there today and, if I may say so, how very nice you look, Horace, very nice indeed. Jim will have to watch it because if Charmaine gets fed up with you then I will be round to see you", Lizzy teased him and chuckled.

"Mum, you're embarrassing Horace....and yourself. Get off with you and take the young 'ns to church. Horace and I have got other things planned for the rest of the day. Don't hurry back, we will come and see you later".

They stayed in the butty all day, apart from when Horace put his trousers on to fetch some more wood for the fire. It was pure heaven just being together talking, cuddling and making love.

Charmaine was the first to get dressed later in the afternoon. "Come on lazy, let's go and see mum and dad otherwise she will be barging back in here again without warning". They went over and squeezed into the boat with Jim, Lizzy and the kids. Horace was surprised they could all fit in there at the same time.

Lizzy asked them if they'd both had a good night and day. "You must have, we haven't seen anything of you".

"Well, mum, what did you expect, I mean, dad, she came in while we had nothing on, I mean whatever next?"

"So the lad looked after you properly did he my girl?" James asked. "Hope he treated you like a woman".

"Dad, he treated me like a lady, no, a princess, and he was a very gallant knight".

"Are you staying tonight Horace because you're quite welcome? We don't load up 'til eight in the morning at Horninglow and then we'll be away for about three weeks. BTR wants me to take a load of boots to a different supplier the other side of Northampton. But we have to start getting ready at five in the morning to be able to get to Horninglow on time".

"Yes, Jim, I will stay if that's OK, I can go straight to work from here. I must go to tell mum and dad that I'm staying here for another night, are you coming with me Charmaine?"

"OK but I'll have to go back to the butty to get changed, I can't go like this, not to see your mum and dad for the first time I can't".

"You look lovely like that Chamy".

"But Horace, for one thing I don't have any draws or a bra on".

When they got back to the butty Horace lifted up her dress up and started to kiss and caress her once more.

"Horace, we've got to go to your mum's" but she didn't resist him.

Half an hour later Charmaine put on the poshest frock she could find trying to "Make myself look decent for your parents". Horace teased her that she will never be decent "Not now that a Gray's been inside you".

"Horace, don't be mean. OK, I'm ready. Do you think they will like me with me being a boater's daughter?"

"No, Chamy" Horace deliberately put on an accent "they will 'ate you for spoiling their lovely son, making 'im lose 'is virginity to a boating 'moll', forcing 'im to 'ave sex with an ugly, dirty gal".

Charmaine giggled and retaliated "Dunna forget I'm not yet of age, you horrible molester. What if I tells 'em that you 'orrible barbarian".

They walked the two hundred yards to the row of houses. Chamy remarked on how nice and quaint they looked. "I've walked down here lots of times since I was a child, so which one do you live in?"

"Just here, love, number 303. We have to walk round to the back there's only one entrance".

Chamy was amazed that the brewery had its own cottages for the brewery workers.

"Do you have to be a top dog to have one of these lovely cottages?"

"No, you'll know that when you see my dad. He's just an ordinary bloke that looks older than his age because of everything he's been through".

Horace and Charmaine walked in the back door through the scullery and Horace kissed the backside of half a pig that was hanging there.

"What're you doing you silly young fool kissing a dead pig's arse, that's awful you know it is".

"How do you think I practice my technique? Didn't you think I was a good kisser last night?" He went over to a cupboard, opened it and kissed a dead badger on its lips. "She is my first love" Charmaine, "Madge the badge".

"Horace you're disgusting, you will wash your mouth and clean your teeth before you kiss me again".

"And now you know where my lips have been, where do you

think my penis has been too? I love you Madge" and then he stroked the animal's underside.

"Now I know you're teasing me, you horrible man".

Horace opened the door to the sitting room. His dad was in a tin bath in front of the fire singing and sponging around his private parts, his mum was knitting with curlers in her hair and drinking tea.

Eva dropped her knitting and jumped a foot off the chair when he opened the door. "Horace!" she screamed, what the dickens are you doing here and with a young lady as well? George, cover yourself man. Horace, you knew your dad would be taking a bath this afternoon. He didn't get a chance Friday night what with our Bill and the boys here".

George lifted the cap he was wearing and doffed it at Charmaine, he always wore his cap in the bath. "Very pleased to meet you young lady. My, you are pretty, young lady, what's your name?"

"Charmaine Mr. Gray, Charmaine Hackett. My family are off the cut, we have a working boat".

"Don't do yourself down, Charmaine" said Horace, "don't forget to mention that you have a butty too, and a big contract with BTR".

"Horace" said Eva, "take Charmaine into the front room and I will bring a pot of tea, George, cover you up".

"Dad, how many more times does mum have to tell you?" then threw a banana at him from the fruit bowl on the sideboard.

"You silly young twerp" said George "go on, do what your mother said and let me get out of this bath".

They went into the front room. Charmaine looked around the room avoiding Horace's gaze.

"What's the matter, love, you look embarrassed?" he sat down at the piano and started playing a tune.

"I can't believe you brought me here knowing your dad would be in the bath. Why don't they bath in this room, it's much cosier than the other room? I love all the space you have here. The boating life is all I know and have ever known but to look around your house I want what you have. This is the first time I've been inside a house and I love it. I could get a job and we could live like a proper family does".

"You say that, Chamy, but I loved the time we spent in the butty last night. I loved how cosy it was, that little room, just you and me making love and sitting around with no clothes on. That's all I want, just you and me together in that small space, I couldn't share it with anyone else but you".

"You want to try it with five other people, and that's what we did before we got the new boat and butty a few weeks ago, now I want a house".

Eva walked in with a broad smile.

"Horace, go and get the tray with everything on it. Now, Charmaine, it's nice to meet you. So, you're off the canal then, how do you like life on the water, is it just you and your parents on the boat?"

"No Mrs. Gray, I have three younger brothers, I help to look after them and work the butty, I do a lot more of that now".

"What on earth is a butty dear? I have never heard of one before aside from the one you eat and you will have one too eventually if and when Horace brings it in" she joked.

"A butty is a boat without an engine that's tied to the back of ours and we tow it along. It gives us more space for living and storage. Before we got our new boat with a motor our Suffolk Punch, Hercules, would walk along the tow path and pull us along".

Horace came in with the tray followed closely by his dad. Horace poured out the tea and passed the cups and sandwiches around. "Do you want ham or cheese Chamy? There, dad, cheese for you, I know you like your cheese".

"Silly young fool, pass the ham as well, that cut of ham looks delicious". He took out his teeth very discreetly, which wasn't like George, he put a hanky to his mouth and spat them into it gave them a rub and put them back in. Everyone saw what he did but Eva didn't say anything, she just gave him a stern look.

"Ma, I'm staying on the boat again tonight with Chamy and her family. I will go straight to work from there in the morning but will come home to get changed and fetch my motorbike".

"What do you do for sleeping arrangements?" George asked. "How many are there in your family?"

"There are six of us, Mr. Gray, my mum, dad and three younger brothers".

"That's a bit cosy on a small boat isn't it? Have you got room for our Horace on there? It would be a bit like Eva getting into that bath in the other room with me, how about it my sweet?"

She glared at him but said nothing, not a word.

"Well, Mr. Gray, it's easy really, me and Horace sleep on the butty together".

Eva was just taking a sip of tea and nearly choked on it.

"Sorry, Charmaine, did I hear you right? You slept together on the boat and your parents agreed to it?"

"Yes Mrs. Gray, I told them that I wanted Horace more than anything in the world so my mum asked him if he wanted to sleep with me, and he said yes. Please don't worry, though, we will be very careful".

"You say your mum agreed to it but you're not old enough to make a decision like that are you? How old are you anyway? You might look older than Horace but I don't think you are my girl".

"You're right, I'm only fifteen but in the boating community some girls my age already have babies, sorry to disappoint you both".

"You don't disappoint us, my dear" said George "if that's what they want, Eva, then it's alright with us and that's an end to it".

They bade Horace's mum and dad farewell and went back to the butty. Horace made the fire up with more logs.

"What was that big hole in your dad's back, Horace? Your mum was a bit frosty with me when I said I wanted to shag you. Why are you still standing there, fed up with me already are you? Come, let's get your things off and try something new, things I've heard other girls say".

"The hole in dad's back is where he was shot in The Great War. So, what else can we try sweetheart, I've only got one.....".

She started to undress him before he could finish speaking, knelt down and put his semi erect penis in her mouth, it didn't stay semi erect for long. She was so rough with him that she actually drew blood, "You nearly bit it off" yelped Horace. She stuttered a quick "I'm so sorry", put her dress on and ran outside to the boat to fetch her mother.

"What on earth is the matter, Chamy?"

She told her mum what she'd just done. They both returned to the butty and Charmaine rushed in with Lizzy right behind her. Horace was still standing there, as was his penis.

Charmaine pointed at Horace's member "Look at it mum, it's bleeding I nearly bit it off".

"Chamy why did you bring your mum in here when I've got nothing on and I'm standing here, well......like this?"

"To show my mum....to make sure it's alright. I didn't mean to hurt you, Horace".

Lizzy had a wry smile on her face.

Horace covered himself up with his shirt and told Charmaine that he was fine and that there was really no need to get her mum.

"While I'm here let's have a look, Horace" said Lizzy. "Now, don't be shy" then grabbed the shirt he was covering himself with, pulled it away and took a good look at and around his penis.

"Look at those bloody teeth marks, Charmaine, you don't bite it you suck it like a dummy and, my, you have a lot of dummy to be going on with there".

After she had gone, Horace told Chamy that she mustn't call her mum every time there was a problem and went out to get some more wood. A few yards further down the towpath he did a double take....it was Fisher shouting at two boaters. He couldn't make out what Fisher or the boaters were saying so hurried back to Chamy and stuck his head through the door "Hey, love, come here a second". They both peeked out over the roof and he asked her if she knew who the boaters were.

"Yes, they're no good, they're just crooks on boats. That sort will move anything for anyone if it makes a bit of money".

"Well, the bastard they are talking to will be worse than they are for sure, I wish I knew what they are talking about".

"Chamy jumped off the boat and ran down the tow path towards them. Horace didn't follow because he didn't want Fisher to see him. It was ten minutes before she came back, but via the road rather than towpath.

"You shouldn't have done that, Chamy, he's a nasty bloke is Fisher and very dangerous".

"Horace, you're scared of him?"

"No, love, not scared at all, I need more ammunition to go the police. I just know he had his own son-in-law killed but I need more proof. The main reason I want him nicked is that he keeps approaching my boss, his other son-in-law, to do his dirty work".

"Fisher was discussing moving parts up north to Gateshead. The boaters he was talking to are not easy to deal with, they were saying that they want a lot more than he paid them on the last trip. Bonze, the big bloke, told him that they won't do it for less than thirty pounds. He said that if the stuff is hot they want their fair share of the profits. Your friend Fisher has two blokes standing by the road and another in a car, and I think they have guns in their jackets".

"I wonder what they are taking and from where, I would love to find out".

"I can help you there, my love. It sounds like they were talking about the tyre factory right by the cut. Fisher has two blokes in the factory ready to load some tyres tonight at midnight".

Horace grabbed her by the face and kissed her.

"Chamy, I will be half an hour. Let's try to get this piece of shit out of Mr. and Mrs. Rush's way then when I return you can have another go at trying to suck the dummy properly, or we could just carry on doing what we've been doing for the last couple of days".

Horace snuck out and ran down to the police station where he saw Sergeant Trevor Brake at the desk. He told him what knew about Fisher talking to these canal boaters and that his girlfriend Chamy had gone down the towpath to hear what they were saying.

"With it being Sunday late in the afternoon no one's here, Horace. Hang on I will phone Inspector Smart at home".

Smart said that he would be there in five minutes. Five minutes later Inspector Smart rushed in through the door. Horace told him everything that had transpired near the Hackett's boat that afternoon.

"Well, this girl friend of yours is as brave as you by the sounds of it".

"Trevor, get the others in, if I'm here they damn well should be".

"Now, you're sure it's the Pirelli place are you?"

"Yes, the canal runs by the side of the factory, it's the only tyre factory around here".

Horace got back to the butty to find Chamy cooking, it smelled delicious and he was ravenous.

"That rabbit stew you're cooking smells fantastic and it's one of my favourites".

"It'll take a while to cook properly" she said. "What did the police tell you then?" she asked, not really caring whether he answered her or not. She undid her dress and once more during those two delirious days it dropped around her ankles.

"Never mind" said Horace. He picked her up and kissed her on the lips then on her breasts teasing the nipples with his tongue. He laid her gently on the rug kissing her all over. When he reached her vagina she grabbed his hair with both hands and pushed his head firmly between her legs. She breathed heavily. Her nipples became even more erect than they already were as she squirmed this way and that letting out the occasional squeal. She shuddered and came time and time again as Horace explored her vagina with his tongue. Then she turned him around slowly and took his hard penis in her mouth, grasping the base with her hand and moving her hand and lips up and down the glistening shaft rhythmically until Horace arched his back, shuddered, let out a groan and sank onto the rug sweating.

They both slept for about half an hour.

Horace awoke and jumped up, "Rabbit stew coming up" he exclaimed but first he put his underpants on and went outside to get some more wood to put on the stove.

"Horace you went outside with practically no clothes on, your mum would say that it's me leading you astray. Did you notice if Bonze's boat has gone? They may have already left if they want to be at the tyre factory on time".

"My mind was on other things, Chamy, it never entered my head to look. I'd better have a look now".

They got dressed and wandered a little way down the tow path. They looked down the cut. Bonze's boat was still there.

They talked as they ate the rabbit stew, it was indeed very delicious. Chamy told Horace that the time they had spent together over the past twenty four hours was much better than she could ever have imagined.

"I am burning inside, Horace, I feel complete now".

"What do you mean burning, do you mean it hurts?"

"No, I mean that my body is glowing inside, although, yes it does sting a little 'down there' but my mum warned me that it would because it's my first time. This will be the last time we make love for a few weeks I don't know how I'm going to cope without you, Horace".

After eating their stew they talked for while longer but it was getting late. It would be an early start the next morning so they went to bed early, cuddled and fell asleep. They were both tired from their exertions over the weekend and slept for the best part of six hours although it felt as if they had only slept for a couple of hours when Lizzy came in the morning, slapped Horace on his bare arse and shook Charmaine out of her slumber.

"Come on you love birds".

They got up and got dressed then went to the boat. James shook Horace's hand. Me and Lizzy are having the butty tonight, it sounds a great place to go to sleep, if you know what I mean Horace" and winked at him.

"Good day to you young Horace, we will see you in a few weeks I hope. Charmaine will be ready for you again by then". Lizzy gave him a big kiss on the lips and Chamy cried when Horace kissed her goodbye.

"Come with me Horace please, come with me" she said.

"I can't, love, you know I have to work".

She was really upset and followed Horace up to the tow path, pleading with him to go with them on the canal. He told her that he loved her and would see her when they got back to Burton Wharf. She stopped and waved him off tearfully until he turned at the brewery entrance and disappeared.

When Horace got home his brother Ron was up with the pan

on the stove, a cup of tea in one hand and a fag in the other.

"You're up early, Ron, you don't usually get up 'til half six".

"Hey, you dirty sod, I've heard all about you from mum. She's distraught with you being molested by a 'trogger'. Dad didn't mind, he was smiling when she told me that the young girl must be a trollop, talking about having sex at her age. So, did you make her a woman then, brother?"

Horace went out, cut a piece of bacon off and chucked it in the pan. "I saw Fisher down the cut yesterday afternoon talking to some boaters. Chamy walked past them and heard him tell them that he wanted them to take some tyres up to Gateshead".

# CHAPTER NINE

Horace ate his sandwich and, having had enough lip off his brother, decided to go to the Pirelli factory to see whether anything had happened the night before. The police were milling around the towpath and inside the factory. He hoped they'd arrested Fisher.

He decided to go to work early so that he could tell Mr. Rush what had happened, if he was around.

It was only seven so he went straight into the workshop and started working on the sidecar they'd pulled out of the canal on Friday. He stripped it all down first taking out the seat then removing the two wheels and axel pretty much leaving just the chassis to tackle. Gordon came in at eight.

"You're getting on well with the sidecar, Horace, what do you plan to do with it?"

"What I'd like to do, Mr. Rush, is to extend the chassis by twelve inches and make it wider by the same and higher by two feet. I could fit that seat that was left over from the Cowley you scrapped to make it more luxurious".

He told Gordon all about the previous afternoon and night....seeing Fisher talking to the boaters, Chamy going down the towpath to hear what they were saying, and him going to the police to report everything to Inspector Smart.

Gordon shook Horace's hand and slapped him on the back.

"Well, son, you both did well managing to find out what they were up to. Let's hope that we get shot of him for a few years, that'd do me. I'm going to tell Christine, she'll be interested in this news".

Horace carried on working on the sidecar.

After hearing the news from Gordon, Christine phoned her mum. Jean told her that the police had taken Fisher in for questioning and that she hoped they would stick him in jail and throw away the key. Ruth was still distressed about Simon's murder and wanted answers about why he'd been killed in such a horrific way.

Gordon and Horace had been working all day when Inspector Smart walked in.

"How are you both? Thought I'd stop by to give you an update. It's been a good day all round, we arrested four people at the Pirelli factory last night, caught them in the act....a father and son, and two boaters".

But Gordon was more interested to hear about Fisher.

"Did you get you-know-who? He would be the ringleader, he usually is. He got away with Simon's murder....I just know he had something to do with it and so do you inspector. That man has ruined people's lives with his antics".

"Mr. Rush, if you know something you must tell us. There's nothing I would like more than to see him banged up to pay for all the crimes he's committed over the last four years, but I need information. That's the only way he will go down but no one is willing to come forward with specifics".

"Over the last two years" piped up Horace "Fisher forced me to take packages to three people in the Burton area....Brian Willoughby, Bill Platt and Colin Rushden, plus you know I saw him last night at the canal talking to those two off the boat, Bonze being one of them. I don't want Mr. Rush's name to be mentioned just mine".

"Thanks for the tip offs, Horace, not to mention what you told us about last night. Based on the information you gave us and the arrests we made last night we'll be doing some surveillance, keeping an eye on him to see where he goes and who he speaks to. We need to get enough evidence to make things stick, like a fly to fly paper".

When Inspector Smart had left, Gordon advised Horace to think carefully about what he is doing.

"I don't want you to go the same way as Simon did, Horace. I would never forgive myself".

"It's fine Mr. Rush, I have Uncle Bill, he knows what Fisher's like. I'm going to have a word with him later he always knows what to do. He's already giving me self-defence lessons when we go up to the woods".

Horace finished work and said good night to Gordon. He rode his motorbike home and took Bess, their dog, over to Shobnall fields for a run, it was dusk. He was throwing a stick for her to fetch when he thought he saw something moving in the bushes by a tree. He walked over to the boundary hedge and followed its line to the tree getting as close as he possibly could being careful not be spotted or heard. There were two people in amongst the tangle of branches and foliage, one was groaning the other said "that's it, just relax". He crouched down and squinted so that he could see better in the half light. It was that bloody Osborne with his cock up a lad's arse. The lad couldn't have been any more than twelve. He dove into the bush, grabbed the kid's arm and pulled him away from Osborne and out of the bush. Osborne came scrabbling out on his hands and knees. Horace saw red. He shouted to the kid to stay where he was, grabbed Osborne by his shirt collar, lifted him to his feet and started knocking his head against the tree. Osborne fell to ground. Horace kicked him several times as hard as he could, in the face, stomach and especially the groin. The kid was cowering by the bush, dishevelled and terrified. Horace went over and reassured him that he wasn't going to hurt him. In the meantime, Bess had run over and was standing beside them panting with the stick in her mouth. Once Horace had persuaded the child to tell him his name and where he lived he told him to run off back home. The whole episode had taken no more than five or six minutes. He left Osborne face down on the ground groaning, called Bess and went home.

When Horace got home he was hyperventilating. He put his head under the cold water tap. If anything, the cold water shock treatment made him breathe more quickly and heavily so he used a technique that Uncle Bill had learned from a US gunnery sergeant in Korea, he got a paper bag held it to his mouth and breathed into it. The theory behind it is that by re-breathing your own exhaled breath you reduce the amount of oxygen in your blood and increase the amount of carbon dioxide thereby rebalancing the levels of both and calming you down. Whether or not it is effective is up for debate but in this case it seemed to help Horace as he managed to calm down somewhat.

Eva had just come into the room.

"What on earth you are doing, have you caught something off that canal girl? You can't trust that sort to be clean, I mean, where do they wash and go to the toilet? You must stay away from her, son, they're not like us doing an honest day's work and being hygienic".

"Ma, they're as clean as we are. They go to the public baths three times a week when they're in Burton and do the same in Birmingham whereas we only have a bath once a week in a tin can. Chamy couldn't believe that dad was in the bath in the main room, she was horrified, so please stop saying that they are not as good as us. The reason I'm in a bit of a state is that I saw Osborne in the fields messing around in the bushes with a young boy. I hit him and kicked him until I was exhausted. I hope he's dead I really do".

"What was he doing with this young boy, Horace, to make so mad and get you into this state?"

"Ma, I didn't want to tell you but, OK, I will. Osborne was shagging him up the arse, that's what."

She didn't say anything, other than "What do you want for your tea, Horace?" This was typical of the way she reacted to things that she couldn't comprehend or that weren't to her liking. She just blanked them out as if they'd never happened. She had been like this all her life so there was no way that she was going to change now.

Horace said that he didn't want any tea and that he was going up to Kevin's. He got on his bike and went up Bearwood Hill Road. All was quiet this time, no trouble like there was two years before. He pulled up at Kevin's house and went in. Kevin was sitting there still in his work clothes.

"Hey Kev, you look knackered, mate, what's up?"

"Your bloody Uncle Bill, that's what. We worked our arses off up Kimberly Drive digging out foundations then at three we had to go to some waste land at Rosliston Road. Bill's just bought it and wanted us to move loads of soil that's been there for forty years, he's thinking of building a bungalow on the land. Mate, it's all clay, the ground is harder than these floor slabs. What you been up to this weekend? We haven't seen anything of you and neither has your Uncle Bill, it must have been something good whatever it was".

"Kev, you won't believe me but it's all true, I promise. I went down to the canal to see if the Hackett's were back from Birmingham, did you know they have a new boat with an engine?"

"What about the poor old horse, it's walked miles for that family over the years?"

"They sold it. Forget the sodding horse Kev, I stayed there the weekend with Chamy....all weekend mate".

"What made you want to stay on a boat with six others? There's no privacy. How did you get to sleep?"

"It was just me and Chamy on our own in the Butty, a weekend of never ending shagging".

"Piss off! You shagged her all weekend while her parents were on the other boat, they wouldn't let you".

"Yes she did. Chamy asked her mum if she could sleep with me, the boaters are like the 'gipos', they have their own rules on things. Neither of us had sex before, it didn't start off too well but got better as the weekend went on. Mate, it was amazing, I can't wait for her to get back again".

"Tell me what happened then....give me all the details".

"There is more important stuff to tell you. We were on the boat and I went outside to get some wood, I saw Brian Fisher further down the tow path arguing with two blokes on a working boat. Chamy put her dress on and walked down the tow path slowly right past them, she even said 'afternoon to them. To cut a long story short, Fisher wanted them to pick up tyres from the factory that night and to take them up north. I went to the police station to tell them what we knew. The police waited for them and arrested two people from the factory and the two boaters that Fisher had been talking to. The best thing is, they picked up Fisher too but Inspector Smart doesn't think they have enough on him to keep him in custody. I told him I would be a witness to what I saw on the canal. Chamy even thinks that Fisher's men had guns hidden in their jackets".

"Horace, mate, you have to be careful with that one. You know your Uncle Bill is scared of nothing, what with everything he's seen and done in the war, even he said to give that man a wide berth. Everyone in the town knows somebody that's been duped by Fisher. Look, it's all very interesting, pal, but get back to the story of sweet Charmaine. She's such a pretty girl. Those eyes would make any man weak at the knees so God knows what her body would do".

"When we first had sex on Saturday she dropped my trousers and sucked my cock, well, she meant to suck it but bit it instead and drew blood. She panicked and ran to her mum in the other boat to tell her that she'd taken a chunk out of it. They both came back straight away and Lizzy took hold of my semi erect cock and rubbed it. She said she was checking it. I did everything I could to stop it getting harder, luckily I was too embarrassed so got away with it. She told Chamy not to be a silly girl and to suck it like a dummy".

"Bloody hell, Horace. Lizzy had your cock in her hand, now that's a thought I will take to bed with me tonight. She is one tasty lady is Lizzy and she doesn't look much older than twenty three".

"You're not too far off, Kev, she's about thirty I think. It was really embarrassing, though, Chamy looking at me with her deep blue eyes over her mum's shoulder".

"But did you actually shag Charmaine, or did she get her mum again to help out?"

"Mate, we had sex all that night and spent all of Sunday shagging, I honestly can't remember how many times. She had another go at sucking my dummy and this time got it right".

After all the excitement of discussing Horace's brush with Fisher and his sexual exploits with Charmaine, they tried to return to talking about more mundane matters, but it didn't last for long. Kevin told Horace that he really loved his work with Uncle Bill and his lads.

"We've had three more starts today" said Kevin "and Bill's nephew started today as well".

"Is that Geoff Reece, Kev? Ma made my sister Iris call one of her kids after him. She thinks the sun shines out of cousin Geoff's arse. We get on well, me and Geoff, but he's a very avid church goer, he's in the choir at Winshill".

"There's one more thing I really need to tell you, Kev. After work I took Bess for a run in Shobnall Fields and walked towards the foot bridge over the railway track. There were two people in the bushes so I went to see what was going on. Just as I got near one of them groaned in pain, I parted the bushes and saw Osborne with his cock up a young lad's arse. I lost it, Kev, I went berserk thumping and kicking him, I didn't care if I killed him. I never looked round to see if he was alright when I left".

Horace got on his bike and rode home. His mum was still upset with him for being on the boat with that girl but dad just ribbed him about it "When's the wedding, son? It's bound to be a good do with plenty of ale, lots of shagging and some bloody good fighting. Go and fetch me some ale, lad".

Eva scolded George "How can you joke about something so terrible. That would kill me you know I'm not well. I'll probably be dead by Christmas. How can I face my friends if Horace carries on with this 'flossy'?"

"Friends, Eva? You don't have any bloody friends just people you meet so that you can gossip about one another. When you're with Francis you bitch about Rebecca, when you're with Rebecca you bitch about Francis, when you're with Margery and Pam you bitch about Francis and Rebecca. Take my word for it, they know what you're like you spiteful woman. Oh yes, and when you're with any of them you moan about me. The lad's got a girlfriend, he's happy, she's happy, and she seems like a great little girl, our Eva, so that will be the end of it."

Eva hurried out of the room passing Horace just as he was coming back with a jug of ale to give to his dad.

"Get two glasses, son, if you're old enough for a fag and shag you are old enough for a pint of ale".

"Where's mum? I don't mean to upset her but Chamy is such a lively young girl and so much fun to be around. I don't know whether it'll last but we want to enjoy it while it does, her mum's not daft, she knows that as well".

"Then son, I'll tell your mum that she doesn't need to die

before Christmas. Cheers! Looks like I have a new drinking partner".

Horace and his dad continued to chat about their day and to make other small talk. Horace mentioned what had happened at the tyre factory and his dad was pleased that Fisher might go back to prison again although, like everybody else, he thought that Fisher had impenetrable armour that nothing could pierce. Horace said good night and went down the garden to the toilet. They'd never had a toilet in the house, not many places like theirs did. The only house in the row that had a bathroom was the old manager's house at the end of the row."

The next morning Horace was the first up followed by his dad.

"My word you're up early, son, what's the matter did you shit the bed? Six is your normal time".

"I need to do something before I go to work, dad. That Osborne should have upped sticks and gone to a different area but he was in Shobnall Fields last night doing awful things with a lad in the bushes. I lost it and beat him up, so I'm going to the police station before work to tell them what I did".

"Well good for you knocking the shit out of him but I wouldn't bother going to the police about it, I doubt he will".

"No dad, I'm going to own up to what I've done. Osborne must've just got out of prison, he should have learnt his lesson but clearly hasn't. He's still a danger to young people and someone has to stop him".

PC Gibbs pulled up in the Prefect just as Horace arrived at the station.

"Horace, my boy, I'm so glad I bumped into you. Can you give the car a service? It's still running well and that's how I want to keep it, and it still looks as good as the day you sold it me. Anyway, why are you here?"

"I want to report myself for beating up Osborne".

He told PC Gibbs all about his encounter with Osborne in Shobnall and what Osborne had being doing to the young lad.

"The dirty bleeder! I didn't even know that he'd been let out but I wouldn't bother yourself about it. He definitely won't be making a complaint, not with what he was doing".

"Probably not, PC Gibbs, but he could be doing it to some other young 'un, the lad was no more than twelve, possibly younger. The man wants locking up again. The poor boy actually screamed in pain. I just lost it, beat up Osborne and told the kid to go home".

"Come on in then, Horace, let's have a word with the new desk sergeant".

PC Gibbs told the sergeant about what had happened three years before and how Horace had punched Osborne and been expelled and that Osborne had eventually been jailed for molesting youngsters. Horace had come across Osborne last night committing a lewd act against a minor and, outraged, had beaten up Osborne. "Could you find out when Osborne was freed, please sergeant?"

"Right, Horace, we will confirm what prison Osborne was sent to and when he was let out. They will have his address and I will run it past Inspector Smart".

It was still only seven o'clock when Horace arrived at the garage. He opened the pumps and workshop before Gordon had even got up and started work. He got on with his favourite job of stripping an engine down. He loved working on his own bench and put all the items that he removed from the engine in order ready for when he did the reassembly. He glimpsed through the door a car pulling up at the pumps so went out to serve the customer.

"Morning Mr Simnett, how are you today?"

"Top of the morning to you, Horace, I'm just grand. How are you this bright and beautiful morning? Fill her up please".

"Are you going far this Morning, how's the photography going?"

"Yes, as you mentioned it I am. I'm going to a photography competition in Portsmouth and I'm hoping to be there for three o'clock. Photographers from all over the country will be there".

"Well good luck to you Mr Simnett, you'll get there on time alright with this Mark IX, it'll stick at sixty all day but it all depends on the A38. You have to go through a few towns to get to Portsmouth but I'm sure you won't be late".

"It's not imperative that I get there bang on time today we are only setting up really, the competition doesn't start till tomorrow. Thanks. See you when I come back".

Gordon came out of the house just as Mr. Simnett was leaving and waved to him.

"Morning Horace, Leslie is out early this morning. Thanks for opening the pumps, Monica's back this morning so if we help her a bit to start with it would be a nice gesture".

"How is little baby Malcolm he must be two months old now?"

"I think he's more like three months now. Her mother is looking after the baby for a couple of hours while Monica's here, she and her husband, Albert, are still living with her mum and dad. I don't think they will ever move out of there, it's a six bedroom house down Calais Road, too big for Monica's parents, Archie and Meg, to live in on their own".

"What does Albert think about living with his in-laws, he works regular nights on the railway doesn't he, getting them trains ready for the next trip? Now that seems like a good Job. Mr. Rush, has Fisher said nothing about the Velox yet?"

"No son, he hasn't been here for a few days, Christine thinks he's gone to London and that can't be legit. We think he's doing more and more up there, don't know what but I suppose that we will never know and, to be truthful, we don't want to".

"Shall I crack on with the Oxford engine or do something else Mr. Rush? Oh, look, here's Monica....how are you, Monica?"

"I'm fine, thanks Horace. Nice to see you again, you are keeping out of trouble I hope. Thanks for having me back Gordon I've missed it here over the last two years, but with getting married and then having little Malcolm it's been quite chaotic. I need to work again because Albert has lost his overtime and we need the extra money. To make matters worse my father-in-law had a stroke a month ago".

"No, Monica, it's you that is doing us a favour. I want Christine to have more time with her mum and Christopher. Horace, if you can service the Hillman I will go and get some parts for the Victor".

Horace was servicing the Hillman when Inspector Smart came into the workshop with PC Green.

"Morning Horace, I hear you bumped into an old friend yesterday, he was only released on Friday and it looks like he's up to his filthy tricks again. Would you recognize the young boy again because we think we know who it is? We have some PCs out there looking for him. Osborne will go down for a long stretch this time".

"I did get the lad's name, he told me he was Trevor Bayles and comes from the children's home in Calais Road".

"Don't worry yourself about the kicking you gave Osborne it was self defence, if you get my meaning, but we do have to find the degenerate. We've been to the address of the lodgings we were given but all his belongings have gone".

"Do you think he's scarpered then Inspector? Good riddance if he has gone".

Inspector Smart and PC Green left. Horace thought that if Osborne does leave town and avoids capture it would be his fault. It would be unforgivable if other young children suffered at his hands. Maybe he should have dragged Osborne and the boy to the police station instead. He couldn't get it out of his mind.

When Gordon returned he told him all about what happened and how guilty he was feeling. Gordon told him not to beat himself up about it and that he had done the right thing to stop him.

"Doesn't want locking up" said Gordon, "what he wants is a bullet in his head. That sort will never be any good in our society".

"Well I hope they catch him soon before he does any more damage. I've finished the service, Mr. Rush, what's next?"

"Right then Horace, I know you haven't done this type of work before. John Dean's Comer van needs a new leaf spring on the driver's side, I'll let you work out how to get it off. It shouldn't be difficult but needs thinking about and I know you're good at thinking things through and working them out".

Arthur Alwyn Dean, John's father, started up Deans the Chemist in 1927 in Horninglow Road. After World War II, John married a young pharmacist called Joan Smedley. Joan had previously been one of John's apprentices and went on to run her own pharmacy in Derby. When they married the two companies joined and in 1946 became Dean and Smedley, the pharmacy that is still going to this very day over seventy years later.

Horace had partially jacked up the van but was standing beside it scratching his head. I have to jack the van up as high as it will go, he thought. The next thing is to chock the front and back wheels to stop any movement and put axle stands under the chassis. If I lower the van slowly onto the stands it will take the pressure off the springs so that I can get the bolts out more easily. He got a hammer and started trying to knock one of the bolts out.

"How's it going?" asked Gordon.

"Fine thanks but these bolts are pigs to get out, I think I'll put some paraffin around them".

"Sorry, Horace, were waiting for a delivery of paraffin just try some oil instead".

"I don't think that will work Mr. Rush the oil's to thick to seep in around the bolts. I'll put some oil in this can and heat it up until it gets really hot so the paraffin rises to the top and I can separate it. Is it OK if I use your old spray gun to spray it round the bolts? It'll get into the joints a lot easier if it's thin."

"Well I haven't heard of that one before but give it a go if you think it will work and the old spray gun is buggered for spray painting anyway so, yes, you can use that".

Horace heated the can of oil with a blow lamp 'til the can started to glow. He put on some asbestos gloves and carefully poured the paraffin liquid off the top into a separate container. He sprayed the paraffin around the bushes and left them to soak for ten minutes while he put the kettle on and went outside for a cigarette, he took Gordon a cup of tea and had a chat.

"You're doing well with that van Horace. I thought I'd leave you to figure how to get the tension off the springs and that trick with the oil is great, we can do that again if we're ever out of paraffin".

"That thing with Osborne is really bothering you, isn't it, Horace?"

"Yes, it keeps me awake at night, especially after what he tried with me three years ago. The worst thing was to see him getting enjoyment out of what he was doing to that child. I promise that next time I see that man I will kill him and I don't care if I'm sent down for it".

Horace went over to the van. "Well, let's see if the paraffin's done any good". He got out his hammer and bar and gave the first bolt a good clout, the thing shot out like a bullet out of a gun. The others took a bit of persuading but came out after a few clouts. He took the leaf spring off and saw that the mounting was knackered.

"Mr. Rush, the leaf mounting has rusted through and the chassis around it is in bad shape too. I don't know what's been holding the thing to the chassis, it must just be will".

Gordon came over to have a look at it. "That's bad for a van that's only five years old. I'll have to phone John because the chassis around the mounting has seen better days and is going too. Put the wheel on and we'll drag it over the pit to have a better look at it".

They supported the offside and after quite a struggle manage to manoeuvre the van over the inspection pit. Once it was in place they jumped into the pit and saw that the chassis was rotten pretty well down all of one side. Gordon phoned John Dean to tell him the bad news. He told Gordon that he would come up and have a look.

Horace worked on the sidecar over the next two weeks. He told Gordon what he planned to do to make it longer, wider and taller. He welded on a roof to make it an enclosed, weatherproof vehicle and fitted a door that he'd made onto the side. When the structure was complete he sprayed it a dark red colour, fitted the seat from the Cowley and affixed matting to the floor.

Gordon told him that he should make a living out of doing these projects. The sidecar looked so comfortable.

"Go on, Horace, put it on the bike and give me a ride in it, let's see if it rides as well as it looks".

# CHAPTER TEN

Horace finished work at the garage and rode his motorbike up to Bladon woods. The R.A.F. had left behind a sizeable quantity of RAF-blue paint when they moved, just before Sir Humphrey bought the property, there was no point in wasting it so they put it to good use on the huts.

A young girl called Angelica lived with Sir Humphrey and Lady Hermione Cartwright. She became Sir Humphrey's ward after her parents had been killed in a car crash when she was younger. She was returning to the castle from a walk in the woods when she spied Horace busy stirring paint.

"Hello, Horace, you look busy with that paint brush, how are you? I've not seen you for a few weeks".

"Hello, Angelica, nice to see you again. I've been busy at the garage for the last few weeks so I promised Uncle Bill that I would come tonight and do some painting. Why aren't you at boarding school? I thought that's where you'd be which is why I haven't been round more often". Horace felt a little guilty about this blatant attempt at flattery.

"I've changed schools, I now go to a day boarding school at Abbots Bromley and like it a lot better there. How's your motorbike, you haven't let me have a ride on it yet and you know I so want to?" she said with a glint in her eyes. "I will ask Uncle Humphrey to see if he will let me".

Just then Uncle Bill turned up with his lads. "You've made a good start on this, Horace. Good evening, Angelica, how are you today, are you on your own tonight? You're normally with the commodore."

"Yes, we went for a walk and he's behind me with Penny, she's been chasing rabbits all over the woods. And how are you, Bill and George, you're very quiet".

Both Bill and George were older than Angelica but were both very shy so they just replied "hello" and fell silent. They both liked her a lot but the prospect of speaking to a girl for any length of time put the fear of God into them.

Sir Humphrey and his Golden Retriever, Penny, appeared through the trees. "Good evening, commodore, lovely to see you this fine night, hello Penny what have you been up to?"

"She's been chasing rabbits, Bill, and what do you want being so formal, you haven't called me that for over two years" he said pulling Bill's leg.

"I don't want anything, Humphrey, I'm just setting these kids a good example on the importance of being polite. Well, come on Bill, George, say 'good evening commodore' to Sir Humphrey".

Horace mischievously took a bow and laying it on really thick said "Er, good evening Commodore, Sir Humphrey Cartwright, how the devil are you this fine day, sir, my liege?"

Angelica burst out laughing "You're so funny Horace, I'm glad I changed schools so that I will be able to see more of you".

"Uncle Humphrey, could I have a ride on the back of Horace's motorbike, you know I really want to?"

"Well, if it was anyone but Horace I would say no but I know he will look after you so go on both of you but don't go far please Horace".

"No Sir, we'll just go around the block into Newton Solney up to Bretby Lane and back through Winshill".

He put the footrest pegs down got on and helped Angelica onto the rear seat. She put her arms around his waist and they set off down the track through the woods. If Bill and George were jealous of their cousin before, this made them even more so. Horace drove down the lane and onto the road. Angelica held him tight as they rode and by the time they got to Bretby Lane she put her cheek on his back and squeezed him even tighter. Horace felt a little embarrassed with her being so intimate and although they'd been close for over a year he would never think of encouraging her because Sir Humphrey trusted him implicitly and would never break that trust.

"Go faster Horace, go faster".

Horace turned his head and said "Sorry, I can't, I promised to look after you and that's what I'm going to do".

They got back to the huts about thirty minutes later. Angelica dismounted, kissed Horace on the cheek then gave Uncle Humphrey a hug and thanked him.

"Before you go Humphrey" said Bill "we've got permission for a shoot at the Kedleston Estate on Saturday, we're going to cull some deer. Richard has got a customer for them plus we can have two that we shoot".

"That's a date then, Bill, I will put it in my diary. What time? If it's the five of us I will pick you up".

"That's very kind of you, Humphrey, we will see you here at seven on Saturday".

The sound of loud coughing emerged from inside the huts. It was Bill and George, they were both wheezing and coughing and had gone red in the face. Bill rushed into the huts "Are you two alright?" When he saw their faces he told them to go outside immediately. "You bloody idiots! I said to come out if the fumes made you unwell. The paint fumes have started your asthma off again, have you brought your Aminophylline tablets with you?"

"They're in the van dad" George managed to splutter.

Horace ran to the Van and got their tablet tin. "These bloody fools don't listen to a word I say" grumbled Bill.

Horace got back with the tin and gave it to his cousins. "Here you are, take two of these".

Bill looked a lot better after just ten minutes but George hadn't improved at all and started to hyperventilate. Uncle Bill laid him on the floor, undid his trousers buttons, extracted his penis and pissed straight in the lad's eye. George stopped hyperventilating almost immediately. Horace and young Bill just stood there and gawped at each other. George's erratic breathing had subsided. He rubbed the urine from his eye and the rest of his face, and spat out what he hadn't swallowed, just in time to catch sight of his dad re-holstering his manhood in his trousers.

"Dad! What did you do that for, you dirty fucker? That's a disgusting thing to do, pissing on my face".

"Well son, it worked didn't it? We used to do that in the war when young soldiers became scared and started to hyperventilate. It worked....mostly. Well, only one of them died when I did it. The last time I tried it was when I got back into the building trade after the war. I was working with a bloke on a building site who was sawing wood and cut his bloody finger off. It did the trick then too. I was only a year older than you, young Bill, when I went to war. A WW I hero taught me the trick, old Fillmore, he was a great chap. His family originated from Germany, but he fought for us and killed plenty of them".

"You're having a laugh" said young Bill "there is no one called Fillmore and to piss on someone who's lost a finger, well, it's a joke, dad, how would that help?"

"Worked on your brother, you saw how quick he got up when I did it".

Uncle Bill told them to pack the paint away and put the brushes in the van, "We'll clean them when we get home".

"What's the most important commodity in survival even before food, shelter and warmth?" Uncle Bill asked Horace and the lads. But it was a rhetorical question so he answered it himself "Next up we must find a water source. There's a bloody big hill behind us leading up to the castle so next time it rains we'll be able to see which route the water takes as it flows down. If we dig a big hole at the bottom to capture and store the water we'll have a natural clean-water storage tank right on our doorstep. Who could ask for more than that, boys....fresh water, shelter, warmth, a river across the road that's teeming with fish and game aplenty here in the woods?"

George asked his dad what size hole they needed....how wide, how deep.

"Why on earth do you want to know that, lad? We aren't going to dig it today".

George was mightily relieved. Digging was the thing that he hated more than anything. I don t think that his dad ever noticed that George would have a go at most of the other jobs but made himself scarce when digging holes was on the agenda.

But young Bill had noticed and piped up "George, our kid, you're never around when there are holes to be dug".

Horace met them all up at Bladon Castle over the next ten days to finish off the huts. With him starting at the garage at seven every morning he usually finished at half four so was there before anyone else. Three days after his cousins' asthma attack it rained continuously for two days. Horace went to Bladon to see if Uncle Bill was right about the flow of water down the hill from the castle. He walked around the bottom of the hill surveying it but there was no flow at all so he climbed up it and walked round trying to figure out why. After half an hour he spotted a small plateau only a few yards up just before the hill dropped down again. That was where the water was accumulating and pooling, the water that the earth wasn't absorbing that is. He slid down the hill, but not on purpose, getting really shit up. When he was at the bottom he fetched the spade and climbed back up to the plateau to start digging.

It had become a bit boggy up there so he decided to make the hole a bit larger, around three foot square should do it. He spent an hour digging and when he was about three feet down decided, wisely, that he'd better do something about being able to get out when it got deeper. He clambered out and fetched a rope from outside the huts, tied it to a tree and jumped back in to continue digging. He stopped when the hole was about six feet deep. He was completely drenched in a combination of water, sweat and mud. He pulled himself up using the rope, climbed out and looked at the results of his labour. It's a bit dangerous, he thought, a bloody big hole right there. "Maybe I should have asked permission first".

He went up to the Castle to tell Sir. Humphrey what he'd done and to warn them so that they could avoid falling in the thing. He pulled the door chain and Smithers came to the door.

"Horace, what a state you are in. If you go to the garden outhouse there is a sink in there, I will bring you some hot water and some spare clothes that Sir Humphrey wanted to throw out. He gave them to me a few months ago but I don't like throwing perfectly good things away".

"Thanks Mr. Smithers, that's very kind of you. He found the outhouse. It looked small from the outside but when he opened the door it was bigger than the scullery at home, a fire was still burning in the grate. Hang on, he thought, he never saw a chimney when he came in, so went outside to have a look and spotted the small chimney at the back. He looked up at the castle and saw Angelica at an upstairs window so waved to her then went back inside. Smithers brought in two kettles of boiling water, some soap and a large towel. He tipped the water into the enormous sink that was three times the size of the butler sink they had at home and big enough to sit in, even larger than the tin thing they bathed in at home.

"Thank you again Mr. Smithers this sink is big enough to bathe in".

"Well, Horace, that was the intention what with you being in such a state. How did you get so muddy?"

"With it raining I decided to dig a hole to make a well for the huts and got carried away. I didn't realize I was so dirty 'til you mentioned it. Would you please tell Sir Humphrey about the hole for me? I came to warn him about it, I'll get Uncle Bill to make a cover for it but it won't be tonight".

"I will tell him directly and fetch your clothes, I won't be long, Horace".

He added some cold water to the boiling water in the sink got undressed and climbed in. He'd just started soaping himself and was whistling when someone knocked on the door".

"It's OK Mr. Smithers, come in, I'm in the bath....I mean sink".

The door opened and in walked Angelica. Horace was so surprised that he thrust his hands down to cover himself up as quickly as possible. Soapy water splashed onto the floor.

"You shouldn't be in here, Angelica, I haven't got anything on you will get into trouble, that's for sure".

"Well Horace, I would have been in here much sooner if I'd known this was your bathroom".

"You must go, love, or we we'll both be in trouble. Mr. Smithers will be back in a few moments".

She did as she was told and a couple of minutes later Smithers returned with the clothes, all freshly pressed. He'd even brought some size ten shoes, one size larger than Horace normally wore.

"Horace, Sir Humphrey and Lady Cartwright asked if you would like to join them for dinner at seven o'clock".

"Thank you, Mr. Smithers, tell them I'd be delighted to join them and thank you again for the clothes, the ironed shirt and pressed trousers, I'm being really spoiled. If I can do anything for you, Mr. Smithers, please don't hesitate to ask me....this sink is better than our tin bath at home".

"You only have a tin bath? I thought that all houses would have bathrooms by now but working in service most of my life hasn't really equipped me with a good understanding of the normal world, although I do have vague memories of bathing in a tin bath as a child. I am sure Sir Humphrey wouldn't mind if you bathe here whenever you want. Don't forget, Horace, dinner is at seven o'clock".

Horace got out and stood in front of the fire. He dried himself and got dressed, the clothes smelt new. He felt like a real gent. There was even a tie so he put that on as well wanting to look as smart as possible when he went to dinner in the castle. He sat down in a small armchair by the fire and lit up a cigarette, this is the life he thought. He looked around for the muddy clothes he'd taken off but they were nowhere to be seen. Smithers must have taken them but he soon forgot about them, he had much better clothes on now. He walked over to the front door of the castle he didn't want to keep Sir Humphrey and Lady Hermione waiting.

"Come in Horace" said Smithers "I will show you through to the sitting room, Miss Angelica is already there waiting for you".

"Thank you, Mr. Smithers, by the way I couldn't find my old clothes".

"Sorry Horace, I forgot to mention I gave them to Val to wash for you, no point taking them home dirty".

"Hello again uncle" said Angelica teasing him "Oops! Sorry, it's Horace. Why have you got his clothes on? You do look suave and sexy in them, I could actually fancy you....well you know I do anyway".

Hermione came in. "Good evening, young Horace, my, those clothes suit you better than they did Humphrey he just didn't look right in them. I think perhaps they are supposed to be for the younger man. It's lovely to see you again and thank you for coming to dine with us".

"No, Lady Hermione, thank you for inviting me you're really kind, and thanks for these clothes they fit very well. Did you really mean to throw these shoes out? They're so comfortable even though they're a size bigger than I normally wear".

"Yes we did, Horace, they pinched Humphrey's feet like blazes. What would like to drink before dinner?"

"Could I have a cup of tea please, Lady Hermione".

"Don't you want a brandy or a whiskey, or you could try what Angelica is drinking, it's punch. Mrs. Bell makes some every night for her it's a nice fruity drink and I'm sure you will love it".

"Here, Horace, try mine it's yummy it really is. We all drink it at our age, honestly you will love it".

He had a sip. It was fruity and sweet so he said he would have a glass. Sir Humphrey came in and apologised for being late, telling them that he had a phone call from Whitehall.

"I'm needed there first thing in the morning on some new project. Smithers will to take you to school in the morning, Angelica, I have to leave here at five in the morning. Hermione, dear, could you and ask Smithers to take her please. Horace, those clothes really do suit you, they made me look like a cad".

"What's a cad sir? I've never heard of one of those before, I hope it's not a bad thing".

"Well, yes and no, son, it's someone who pretends to be what they're not that's all".

Dinner was served. The starter was whitebait on a bed of lemongrass, not one of Angelica's favourites, in fact she can't bear to see people even eat it so she asked if she could leave the table until the next course arrived.

"Whilst you're eating those disgusting little fishes I will go and ask Mr. Smithers if he can take me to school tomorrow, if that's alright with your uncle?"

"Of course dear but why did you call him Mr. Smithers, we've always called him Smithers".

"It's because Horace likes to be respectful to him and I agree with him. Just because he waits on us does not mean that we shouldn't show him the respect he deserves. We don't call the cook and bottle washer Bell, we call her Mrs. Bell so Smithers....I mean Mr. Smithers should be treated the same".

Angelica went to see Smithers, a.k.a Mr. Smithers, and asked him whether he could come in early to take her to school because he normally started work at ten. He apologised and told Angelica that he'd already spoken to Lady Cartwright about the jury service he was starting tomorrow.

"I have a replacement coming in" he told Angelica "but he can't drive, and why did you call me Mr. Smithers?"

"It was Horace that brought it to my attention Smithers....Mr. Smithers. We don't give you the respect you deserve for doing everything for us".

"Well, thank you, Miss Angelica, but there's really no need. Smithers is less formal than Mr. Smithers and I don't really mind it at all, and please give my apologies to Sir Humphrey and Lady Cartwright, I told her Ladyship last week that I would be unavailable for at least three days this week".

The "disgusting little fishes" had been cleared away by the time Angelica got back to the dining room. She told them what Smithers had said about the jury service and Lady Cartwright apologised for forgetting all about it.

Sir Humphrey couldn't think of anyone who could take Angelica to school at such short notice.

"Well, Angelica, it seems you may be having a day off school tomorrow" until it dawned on him that there was a simple solution staring him in the face, quite literally.

"Horace, my boy, if the weather is fine in the morning could you do me a favour and take Angelica to Abbots Bromley? It's alright if you can't I should be able to arrange alternative transport but it'll be challenging to do so in time for tomorrow morning".

"It will be fine for me to take her irrespective of the weather. I have a sidecar that I've just finished renovating I'll go and bolt it on after dinner. I can be here for seven o'clock take her to school and still be back in time for work at eight".

"I was going to suggest that you stay the night, you could always phone your parents and tell them".

"It's fine, Sir, we don't have a phone anyway".

"Uncle Humphrey, they don't even have a bath in the house, just a tin bath they put in front of the fire, that's why Horace found it so luxurious to bathe in the big trough in the outhouse. He told me when I went there that the sink was even bigger than the tin thing they use at home".

"Sorry, Horace, I'm sure that Angelica didn't mean to embarrass you. You are always welcome to take a bath in this house any time you wish. Angelica what do you mean when you went into the outhouse while Horace was bathing?"

"I saw Horace go there from my bedroom window and was curious to find out why he'd got into such a muddy state, but he was a gentleman and covered himself up immediately, he does have some lovely broad shoulders, though".

"I apologise, Horace, Angelica is being rather silly today. You should ask Smithy....Smithers, I mean Mr. Smithers....dash it all, Angelica, any time you wish to bathe in the outhouse or in the house for that matter".

"Well, I loved the outhouse, Sir. It was so cosy with the fire going. It's self sufficient you can even warm the water in there".

"Well, as I say, you are welcome to bathe anytime you want, and that side car sounds a fine idea, thank you".

When Horace got home his sister was there with an older bloke.

## CHAPTER ELEVEN

"Hello Horace, I'm glad you're back" said Arlene "I want you to meet Frederick, we are walking out together".

"Walking out together? That sounds like something a courting couple would've said in Victorian times. What you mean is, this old bloke is your boyfriend. He's old enough to be your dad. Come on, sis".

Eva told him not to be so cheeky and to apologise to Mr. Fordham.

"Mum, what about the way you reacted when I brought a girl home two weeks ago, you called her all the names under the sun?"

"Yes, our Horace, but she had a filthy tongue on her the things she was saying, things that no grown woman would say".

"Ma, she was only being honest, you might not like the boaters but they wouldn't tell untruths. The boaters are hard working and many are more religious than us, and cleaner. Like I told you, they bath three times a week. Mr. Fordham....Frederick....must be about twenty years older than our Arlene, you call that normal, ma?"

"Look, I can see that I have caused some upset" said Frederick "I will go now, Arlene, and see you tomorrow".

"No, please don't go, Fred" said Horace "I was simply making the point that you are quite a bit older than our Arlene, that's all".

"Horace, he's not twenty years older, just nineteen years older. I'm happy with the age difference and want my family to be happy for me. You're quiet, dad, you haven't said what you think yet".

"Apart from him working for the opposition, and the fact that it's me that's twenty years older than him, there's not much to say. Other than to add that Everards beer is shit. Pleased to meet you, Frederick, by the way".

"Horace, will you go and get two jugs of ale? I want to show Fred what good beer tastes like, get some crackling too".

Horace went to the brewery shop just around the corner to get the jugs of ale and was confronted by one of the shop's neighbours".

"Horace, who's that chap with your Arlene, he seems quite a lot older than her?"

"Mrs. Brook, our poor Bess died and that chap is the taxidermist. Dad can't bear to be without her, he wants her stuffed and put in the front window. He likes stuffed things no matter what their age but he prefers it when they're young because the skin pulls over them tighter, looks much nicer that way don't you think?"

He returned with the jugs of beer to a telling off from his dad for taking such a long time.

"Sorry, dad, I was talking to Mrs. Brook. You know what she's like, won't let you go past without wanting to have a chat".

"Yes, what did the woman want with you, or was she gossiping about someone?"

"She just wanted to know who Fred is so I told her he's the taxidermist come to do our Bess, I told her that you wanted her stuffed and put it in the front window".

Everyone laughed, even Frederick and Arlene, but not Eva. "I've got to face that woman tomorrow and what am I supposed to say when she asks about Bess?"

"Tell her you're too distressed to talk about it and walk away, you don't like her anyway".

The men drank the beer while Arlene and her mum had coco and biscuits.

"There you go, Fred" said Horace mischievously but not

maliciously "this is what you've turned a sixteen year old into, an old lady with her coco and biscuits. Do you smoke Fred?"

"Yes, Horace but I didn't want to light up on my own. It's not very polite to smoke in someone else's house anyway".

"Dad what's a matter with you, not smoking today? Unusual when you have a pint in your hand".

"It's your mother's fault, told me not to light a fag while Arlene brings her gentleman friend".

"Right! Fred, would you like a cigarette?"

"Yes please, Horace, that's very kind of you. Arlene told me you're a mechanic, that's a good trade to be in".

"Er, trainee mechanic. Do you have a car, Fred, I can do a cheap service for you if you do?"

"No, never even tried to drive and not really had the money what with bringing up a family".

That made my Eva sit bolt upright in her chair.

"Um, did you say you have a family Frederick, what family would that be, Arlene never mentioned a family?"

"Yes, I have two girls, Polly and Anna, eleven and nine, they took the break up badly but you have to move on in life, no good staying together just for the kids, is there Mrs. Gray?"

"That's nice, sis, two more little girls to play with how lovely for you. This is so meant to be, I'm sure you will have a lot of fun".

"Horace! They are very nice girls and so grown up for their ages too. We had a lovely time together when we went out for tea, well, we didn't just go out for tea we took the train to Derby and went around the shops first".

"Did you go to any toy shops in Derby, did each of you buy a toy?"

"No, just the Girls Horace, I'm far too big for toys now you know....now that Frederick and I are walking out together".

"Sis, will you stop saying 'walking out together', just say 'we are taking a turn in the garden'....".

Horace couldn't help himself laughing out loud.

"You're just talking like a child, Horace, why do you make fun of and laugh at everything?"

Fred thought it might be best to beat a retreat, said good night and thanked them for their hospitality. He took Arlene's hand and they went outside to talk in private. Horace saw him lean forward and kiss her.

"That shouldn't be allowed, kissing a girl of her age. He must be thirty five if he's a day, ma, and he's got kids that are only a couple of years younger than she is. You gave me a right lecture about a girl that's only a few months younger than me. How long have you known about this Frederick? This is the first time I've heard of him. What do you think, dad, you're very quiet?"

"To tell you the truth, son, I am shell shocked, lost for words. Eva, what do you think of it, someone to look after his kids for him that's all it is".

"Let's just see how it goes shall we? It might just fizzle out as soon as it started, but of course I'm not happy about it either. The same as you going off with that floozy of yours, I'm shocked at the both of you".

"Well, I'm going to bed. It's been a busy day with going up to the castle".

"Yes, and you never came home for any dinner tonight" protested Eva.

"I grabbed some meat on the way home. I'll make a breakfast that'll keep me going all day so you can join in if you're both up early enough. I'll be up for half five".

"You can count me in" said George "the full works. I even got some black pudding from Terry tonight. Son, are you OK to give me a hand tomorrow evening at the small holding, the pigs need shifting?"

"Yes, of course dad, I will give you a lift on my motorbike, save you walking over the fields. What about the sheep?"

"It only takes fifteen minutes to walk to Kitling Greaves Lane, I finish before you at the garage and I'll do what has to be done with the sheep in no time so if you can just give me a hand with the pigs. We'll kill one of the lambs next week we've got plenty still hanging in the scullery. Don't you want to finish this beer off? There's too much for me because Fred only had half a pint".

"Go on then, dad, and where did you hide that crackling, you kept that to yourself didn't you?"

"Well I wasn't giving him any he pulled a face at the beer, he's only used to that piss they make at Everards and, no, I don't think much of him for wanting to be with a girl nearly twenty years younger. You're quiet, Eva, you must have something to say about it".

"Be quiet, our George, I'm trying to listen to what he's saying to her. Of course I'm not happy about it, we will be a laughing stock to all our neighbours and friends, and that's not to mention the family".

Horace went to bed before Arlene came back in and it didn't take long before he was oblivious to the world. The next morning he was up before half five getting the pans on the stove and chucking lots of dripping into them. He and his dad just love a fry up dripping in fat. The smell wafted upstairs, George jumped out of bed, well, swung his legs out and lowered himself gingerly onto the floor, and followed the scent downstairs almost as if it had put him in a trance. Horace came in from the scullery with four large cuts of bacon and chucked them into the pan.

"With it being thick cuts I'm going to cook them slow" said Horace "that'll give me a chance to get some eggs from up the garden and bracket mushrooms from the brewery trees".

"I'll do the brew then, lad, got to make myself useful".

Horace timed his return perfectly. The bacon and black pudding was almost done so they cooked the eggs and mushrooms and served up a magnificent feast.

George panicked "Where's the fried bread, son?"

"In the pan, dad, it'll be ready in a few seconds".

"Well come on, son, don't do half a job".

Horace got to work for dead on six. He fixed the sidecar securely to the bike and got in to try it out for size and comfort. "Nice and cosy" he said to himself. "She will love it, this chauffeur driven bike".

Horace was at the Castle for six thirty and walked around the back to the kitchens. Mrs. Bell was in there lighting the fires.

"Morning, Mrs, Bell, you're bright and early this morning".

"Good morning, Horace, come and sits you down, I'll put the kettle on in a second, I must fetch some more wood first though".

"No, Mrs. Bell, I will fetch you the wood if you're making the tea".

"I can't let you do that, Horace, it's our job to get the wood in, Mr. Young the gardener isn't here yet".

"I insist Mrs. Bell. I'm a worker like you not a guest. I'm the chauffeur this morning while Mr. Smithers is on jury service. Oh, have you seen my limousine? It's at the front of the house all new and shiny".

"Well I must go and look at it whilst you're getting the wood in for me".

Horace went with a basket to fetch the logs from the store beside the outhouse that he'd bathed in the previous day. He decided to have a quick look inside. It was still nice and warm and a few embers in the grate were doing their utmost not to go out. Horace fetched some kindling to get it going again and when the flames took hold he put some logs on then went back to the kitchen to take the logs to Mrs. Bell.

"That's a fine sidecar" said Mrs. Bell "it must've set you back a bit buying it, and the colour is so regal".

"It cost me nothing, I fetched it out of the canal two weeks ago. It had just been dumped in there. I got some help from a working boat family to pull it out then me and my boss took it to the garage where I work. I modified it to make it bigger and more comfortable so that it would be suitable for anyone to sit in and enjoy, even you Mrs. Bell, and there is room for your shopping in the boot. I just wish I had a chauffeur's hat for a joke to make Angelica laugh".

"You drink your tea, Horace, while I take this tray of tea to the dining room, can you watch the toast for me please?"

Mr. Young came in.

"Good morning, son, are you new here? There is a fine bike and sidecar at the front and someone lit my fire in the garden shed".

"It was me, Mr. Young, because I was in the woods yesterday digging a well for the huts at the bottom of the hill and got so dirty Mr. Smithers said I could use your shed to get cleaned up. I wanted to make sure that the shed was clean and tidy so had a look inside this morning. The fire was still just about alight so I stoked it up, and put some kindling and logs on.

"Well that's very kind of you, son, but you haven't said who you are yet".

Mrs. Bell walked in. "This is Horace, young Angelica's friend. Lady Hermione asked if you would join them in the dining room, Horace, I told her you've been helping me in the kitchen. Here you are, there's a full chauffeur's uniform in this bag, I mentioned to Lady Hermione you wanted this to play a joke on Angelica".

Horace took the uniform out of the bag.

"It's all size 'large', Horace, so it should fit you".

Horace tried pulling the trousers over his own but they were too tight so he went in the pantry to change properly. He came out looking every bit the chauffeur, Mrs. Bell and Mr. Young couldn't believe how good he looked.

"I will put the bag and my clothes in the boot of my sidecar then go and see Lady Hermione".

He knocked on the door to the dining room and walked in. Angelica looked at him with her mouth open.

"Horace you so look the part in that uniform, where did you get it from, you cheeky thing?"

She got up, ran over to him and gave him a wet kiss on the cheek. "The girls at school are going to go wild when you drop me off".

Lady Hermione told him that the uniform made him look smarter than any chauffeur she had ever seen. "You managed to bring your sidecar then, what is your surname?"

"Gray, Lady Hermione, Horace Gray at your service. If you are ready your ladyship I will take you to school".

Angelica rushed to get her things. Horace held her coat for her while she put it on, he then went to the front door, opened it and bowed.

Angelica saw the sidecar. "Wow! This is such a wonderful machine".

Lady Hermione had a look "That is a fine thing, Horace. I certainly haven't seen a sidecar this big before and such a beautiful colour too. Did you buy it for any specific purpose, Horace?"

"Not really, Lady Hermione, I made it myself. It was an old one that someone had dumped in the canal, I fished it out to work on it. I altered it to make it bigger, then sprayed it dark red. I mixed the colour myself as well".

"Why, you clever boy. The other girls will be jealous of you, Angelica, turning up in this beautiful thing. Have a good day, darling, and I will see you soon, Horace".

"Lady Hermione, I will take Angelica in the mornings until Sir Humphrey comes back to save him having to find someone. It'll be fine as long as I'm at work for eight".

"Well, if you are sure. We will, of course, pay you, Horace, for taking her every morning we cannot expect you to do it for nothing".

"There's no need, Lady Hermione, it will be my pleasure to take my friend to school".

"Come on, Gray, I haven't all day to waste so hurry up now. I don't know where you get the staff from these days, aunty".

They all laughed and Gray, the chauffeur, led her to the sidecar. She couldn't believe how spacious and comfortable it was when she got in and sat down. Horace started the bike, revved the engine and they set off down the hill towards the road leaving a wispy trail of white smoke behind them. Everyone looked at them and the marvellous machine as they drove slowly through Burton. Horace opened up when they approached Rush's garage speeding past it and overtaking a line of cars in the process. When they pulled up outside the school he dismounted and Angelica, knowing that Horace was still in character, waited for him to come around and open the door for her. She took her time to get out, she wanted to make absolutely sure that everyone saw her, and they did. Well, most of the staff and a large group of girls who had gathered near the entrance. She said "Thank you, Gray" as loud as she could and held her hand out for him to kiss it.

"I will see you at five o'clock, Gray, and don't be late my good man".

Horace laughed all the way back to the garage. Even Gordon chuckled when he saw Gray, Horace's alter ego.

"Not sure why you're dressed like that, son, but you look the part".

"Sir Humphrey asked me to take Angelica to Abbots Bromley this morning because he had to go to Whitehall and Mr. Smithers wasn't available".

"Horace, that sidecar looks fantastic. Do me a favour and leave it on the grass in front so that people can see it".

Horace got changed into his work clothes knowing that he had a number of car jobs to do but decided to clean the workshop first. It hadn't been cleaned properly for weeks. He opened the doors to let the air circulate and get the dust out. The floor was covered with patches of oil, grime and muck. He couldn't make it spotless but he could improve things considerably and tried to do so during the next hour or so.

As he was finishing he looked up and saw a silhouette in the doorway. It was none other than his old friend, Fisher. He walked in out of the sun's glare and Horace could now see his features. He looked as miserable as the last time Horace had seen him, perhaps a little more miserable than normal this time because he'd seen the Velox on the forecourt when he arrived.

"You're still here then. I was hoping he'd got rid of you. Where the hell did that Velox come from?"

Horace was delighted he'd asked "Why? does it bring back bad memories? I bought it two days ago off a bloke with a cockney accent. He asked me to remember him to you, said he's been looking for you for two years".

"What the hell are you on about, no one's looking for me, so I'm going to ask you one more time, where did it come from, you little twat, who brought that car here?"

"I told you, I bought it last week how many more times?"

He brushed past Fisher and walked outside so that the Velox would be in full view, Fisher followed him.

"And, Fisher" Horace added, "I'm not scared of you. The bloke said the boot needed cleaning, told me there had been a mishap and it was a bit messy in there".

Just then, Gordon came out and told Horace that there was a call for him and that he'd put it through to the workshop. Horace went back inside and picked up the receiver.

"Hello, can I help you?"

"Horace, this is Lizzy. Charmaine went out last night and never came home. The police aren't doing anything because we're boaters. They treat us like gypsies and think we're all up to no good anyway".

"Where are you, Lizzy?"

"Near Luton, Horace, and with not coming this way very often we don't know any of the other boaters. This girl came talking to Charmaine and asked her if she wanted to go to a dance with her, she seemed like a nice, polite girl"

Lizzy told him the number of the bridge near where they'd moored.

"Lizzy, I'll have a word with Mr. Rush and tell him the circumstances. I will see you in a couple of hours".

Gordon was still talking to Fisher, well, Fisher was doing most of the talking, as normal.

"Mr. Rush" interrupted Horace "can I have a word please".

"Yes, of course, Horace".

He told him what the call was about and wanted to go and help if he could. He suspected that Charmaine had been kidnapped and with the police not being interested to get involved he just wanted to do something, anything to help.

"Yes, of course, Horace, go immediately, but be very careful, son. If she's been kidnapped near London you can bet it's for prostitution. Look, I know that Fisher has a gun under his dashboard. I'll take him into the house he wants to talk about family business anyway. You'll know how to get into his car, see what you can find in there. Call me if you need anything and let me know how you get on. I won't mention anything to Fisher, especially not about canals he will put two and two together about his arrest over the weekend".

Gordon disappeared inside with Fisher. It didn't take Horace long to get in the car. He could hear his own breathing and heartbeat and was sweating. He bent to look under the dashboard, there was a compartment down there so he put his hand in it and felt around. There was no gun just a cloth bag, which he pulled out. He undid it and found loads of fivers inside. He put the bag on the floor and continued searching frantically for the gun, he couldn't find it but did find a dagger under a seam of the carpet in the passenger foot well. He concluded that if the gun wasn't in the car then Fisher must have it on him. He could by a gun with all that money but thought about what Uncle Bill would do in those circumstances so decided against it.

Horace jumped on his motorbike and rode up to the New Manners Estate looking for Uncle Bill's van. Uncle Bill was there talking to someone.

"Horace, you will be out of your league" said Bill when they'd managed to find somewhere private to talk.

"Going up against people from the London area on your own is extremely unwise and dangerous. I know a sergeant major from shooting at Kedleston, he's in the Royal Marines and attached to the Home Office, I will try to contact him through Sir Stanley Carpenter. He owes you a lot so I'm sure he will want to help. We can call him from the phone box on Ashby Road".

They were at the phone box within five minutes. Bill phoned Sir Stanley and relayed to him everything that Horace had told him. Sir Stanley asked him to tell Horace to come straight to Oak House so that he could call the authorities in London.

Horace pulled up outside Oak House, the door opened and Sir Stanley beckoned him inside. Sir Stanley told Horace in no uncertain terms, much as Uncle Bill had done, to go back to work and leave it to the people who knew what they were doing and had been trained to deal with these types of incident.

Fisher was still at the garage when Horace returned giving Gordon some grief about something or other. He pulled up on the grass verge and Fisher walked over.

"And where have you been?"

Gordon told Fisher that Horace had been on an errand for him. Fisher opened the boot of the sidecar.

"You have loads of space in there" He went to his Jaguar took out a box from the boot, walked over and put it in the sidecar boot. "Yes, excellent, you could get eight to ten of these in there".

"Take this one to Derby for me, it won't take you long".

"Get fucked you old bastard, I'm not doing any more of your dodgy stuff again".

"Well, if you don't I'll shut this place down right now and sell it along with the house".

Horace didn't have anything to lose, although he was conscious that Gordon and his family did. Nevertheless, he decided to call Fisher's bluff.

"As I said before, get fucked! There are plenty of other places Mr. Rush could work from, he doesn't need you".

"Well, that's where you're wrong you little twat. If he leaves here he leaves with nothing because he signed a contract that would put all his money into my bank account".

"I have done no such thing" Gordon shouted "when did I do that and why would I do it, give you all I have, rubbish!"

"Well, it don't matter what you think, it's all done, signed and sealed. See, I knew you'd give me trouble, especially after Simon made his final farewell. I own you all and don't forget it. I mean, I don't want to lose another son-in-law now do I....but?"

"You're threatening me? Your own daughter's husband, someone you have known all these years. Well, there's no end to how low you will sink is there".

Fisher ignored him and turned his attention to Horace.

"Anyway, young 'un, this parcel is going to Derby Scrap Yard, you know where it is so get going....go on, off you go delivery boy. If you don't do what I say, I will kill you one day, and that's a promise. Oh, silly me, I almost forgot, if you want to see your little canal girl again you will do a few jobs for me. Do you know, those boats can only do in a day what a car can do in an hour, so it wasn't difficult to track the boat. The hard part was to get someone to befriend the girl".

Horace launched himself at Fisher and punched him on the chin. "You bastard! I will cut your insides out if you harm her, Fisher".

Fisher recovered from the blow that had sent him backpedalling a few yards. He stepped forward tentatively, rubbing his jaw.

"Do these few jobs for me and she will come back just as she was, pretty and untouched. But if you ever hit me again or go to the police like you did a couple of weeks ago, she will come back ugly and very much touched, if you get my meaning. Do you think I'm stupid? She's the only one who could have heard the conversation I was having with those men on the tow path".

Horace snatched the parcel and left, but first went to Oak house to tell Sir Stanley about his encounter with Fisher and what he had said.

"Who is this man and why has he done this? I need to know something about him that I can convey to my colleagues in London to set the hare coursing, as it were. So how do you know this man, Horace?"

"He's Mr. Rush's father-in-law and a local criminal, although his operations extend further afield. He has spent time in jail before and was arrested as a suspect for the murder of one of his sons-in-law, a Simon Green, but there was insufficient evidence to convict. He was also arrested last week as a suspect in a theft at a local tyre factory but got away with it again. I've got to do a job for him now, to take a package to the Derby Scrap Yard otherwise he will throw Mr. Rush out of his garage and he and his family out of their house. He is also behind the kidnapping of the girl my Uncle Bill told you about when we phoned earlier".

"Excuse me one moment please, Horace".

He picked up the phone and dialled, what seemed to Horace, an extraordinarily long number. Horace heard a ring tone followed by a click and "Hello?"

"Hello, this is Sir Stanley here. I want you to look into someone for me, his name is Brian Fisher. Yes, that's right, he lives in Staffordshire and is a small time villain that has ideas above his station but is not to be underestimated. I need to know everything about him, is that clear? Thank you".

The phone clicked again and purred. Sir Stanley put the receiver down.

"Where is this package now?"

"It's in the boot of my sidecar."

Sir Stanley went out to look at the motorbike and sidecar.

"My, this is a smart thing, never ever seen one like it. Don't open the boot and don't look round, you've been followed here. There are two men over the road in a blue Rover P2, just shake hands and go. Take your time to Derby and just treat this as a normal ride out, those men will undoubtedly follow you there".

Horace kick started the bike and turned it around passing the Rover. He wondered whether it might be the blokes at the canal, but there were three of those and there were only two in the car. He carried on to the drop off place, handed the package over and was given an envelope to take back to Fisher. He came out of the gate and the car that was following him was parked nearby partially visible behind a building.

He got back to the garage but there was no sign of Fisher's car. He took the envelope to Gordon.

"Horace I'm so sorry you're involved in all this mess, I wouldn't blame you if you left to find another job. This is my mess not yours".

"I wouldn't give him the satisfaction of thinking that he'd driven me away from here. By the way, he had me followed. I went to see Sir Stanley first to give him some more details about Fisher and to reinforce what Uncle Bill had told him about Charmaine when we phoned earlier. It was Sir Stanley who noticed the car that was following me, I wouldn't have seen it. They followed me to Derby but I never saw them on the way back".

"He had you followed to see if you went to the police, he will probably have you followed all week".

"Mr. Rush, I can't let him know about Angelica, I would never forgive myself if anything happened".

"Horace, I'm going to phone Sir Stanley to tell him that Angelica needs picking up from Sir Humphrey's to be taken to school. You are right, we can't take any risks. Sir Stanley will want to help so don't worry, Horace. I should have put a stop to all of this nonsense four years ago when Fisher came out of prison. But I lost my bottle when Simon was murdered".

Gordon phoned Sir Stanley to explain that Horace had been taking Angelica to school in the morning and relayed Horace's worry about her and the Cartwrights becoming involved because Fisher's men were following him.

"That's fine, Gordon, tell the lad not to worry. I will phone the Mayor to see if we can use his driver and car but, one way or the other, we will get her picked up. We will tell her the white lie that Horace's dad is not well so she doesn't get worried or upset about why Horace isn't going there. It'll also be good for me to put

Humphrey in the picture about all this".

Gordon went to tell Horace about everything he'd discussed with Sir Stanley. When he entered the workshop he saw that Horace was sharpening the dagger he'd taken out of Fisher's car.

"What are you doing, Horace?"

"I'm going to try to get those two that Fisher sent to follow me. Uncle Bill told me to always do the unexpected when you're up against a wall. They don't know this area like I do. We'll be going on a little trip up to Sinai but first I have to get a rifle off Uncle Bill".

"Horace, I know I can't stop you and that all I can do is to beg you to be careful. I have a Gewehr 43 semi-automatic rifle from the war that I can give you but it hasn't been fired since then".

# CHAPTER TWELVE

Horace was on the garage forecourt sweeping up. Having been followed the day before he was nervous and kept a constant watch for vehicles that went past repeatedly or that parked outside with people sitting in them for long periods. He looked up and down the road and saw a car with what he thought were three men in it but wasn't too sure because it was about thirty yards away. He went to see Monica in the kiosk.

"Did you notice that blue car by the post office, Monica?"

"Yes, it's driven past a few times during the last two hours and I saw another car stop beside it, a man leant out of each car and they talked to each other. There isn't going to be any trouble is there, Horace, like with Sheila? Because I'm going home if there is".

"You live just down the road don't you, Monica? Does your dad have a car, because if he does I need a favour?"

"Yes, he does, Horace".

"Could you please ask him drive to the new estate they're building in Winshill and look for Bill Reese, everyone will know him up there. When he finds him get him to call me. I will ask Mr. Rush's permission but think it's better if you stay away for a day or two, Monica".

She phoned her dad from the kiosk and he agreed gladly to do drive to Winshill as Horace had requested.

"Is this about Christine's dad again, Horace?" asked Monica "He was here all day yesterday throwing his weight around. My dad told me that he's no good and I should stay away from him".

Horace talked to Gordon about Monica staying away for a while and he agreed to let her go early.

"I've also asked her to get her dad to drive up to Winshill to get Uncle Bill to call me, I think we may need his help sooner than we anticipated".

"What are you planning, Horace? Be very careful we both know that Fisher isn't stupid. God only knows where he's getting his henchmen from but he must be paying them well because there's a few of them about. He seems to be able to find things out and I've no doubt they play a big part in that. With everything that your Uncle Bill has seen and done he's definitely the best man to help but I worry that something may get back to Fisher and that will not be good".

Uncle Bill phoned the garage and told Horace to wait there till seven o'clock to see if the men leave. He told Horace that he was leaving to get a team of former service people together and asked Horace what his plan was.

"What I want, Uncle Bill, is to get Fisher's men up to Sinai to interrogate about Charmaine and find out where they're holding her".

"OK, don't do anything yet, Horace, wait 'til I phone you back. We'll get the bastards up to Sinai and use some tried and tested techniques that will get them to tell us what we need to know".

Horace relayed the plan to Gordon and asked him to act as normally as possible. They carried on as best they could with their usual daily routine of serving customers at the kiosk and servicing and repairing the vehicles that had been booked in.

"If you're still here at seven, Horace, you may as well have dinner with us. I'll go and tell Christine".

"By the way, Mr. Rush, did you buy Mr. Dean's van off him or do you want me to strip it down before you take the chassis to Moors scrap yard?"

"May as well, he told me to get rid of it, said it cost him a lot of money for little more than a couple of years driving".

Later that evening just before seven, Gordon told Horace to go into the house while he locked up. Horace greeted Christine and played with Christopher while talking to her about her father, careful not to mention any details to her about his plans so as not to upset her. Gordon came in and Christine dished up a sizeable meal of sausages, chips and beans.

Just as they were finishing there was a loud knock on the door and it burst open. Fisher walked in as if he owned the place which, according to him, he practically did.

"What the hell is he doing here he should have finished work two hours ago?"

"It's got nothing to do with you who we have in our house" Christine yelled at him.

Fisher started to say "When I have...." but stopped himself when the phone rang. Gordon went to answer it.

Bill told Gordon to tell Horace that he and his former servicemen mates would be up at Sinai and ready within half an hour. "Tell Horace that when he gets here he should go to the back of the building and park up. I have a small army of people here with me". Gordon thanked him and put the phone down.

"Who was on the phone?" Fisher demanded to know.

"Christine, take Christopher into the sitting room for a minute while I have a word with your dad".

Fisher tweaked little Chris' cheek and told him he'd see his grandson soon but Chris pulled away from him, even he, a mere child, had grown to mistrust the large, loud, bombastic man that was his grandfather.

"I would hate to be you, Fisher" Horace said when Christine and Chris had gone "even your grandson thinks that you're a twat and a waste of space".

"Let me tell you something, lad, your time is nearly up here and don't forget that little whore of yours we have in our company".

"You hurt her and I will kill you myself" Horace retorted.

"Taking a person's life isn't as easy as you think, you little squirt....".

Gordon cut him off before he could say anything else "By the way, Horace, that was your uncle on the phone. He wants a hand tonight, said he would meet you at the back of the house he's working on, said it won't take long because he's got an army of people to help".

"Thanks, Mr. Rush. I'll just say goodbye to Mrs. Rush and Chris before I leave".

Fisher told Gordon he would see him in the morning. "I have something to discuss with you about your future, Gordon. How you respond will determine not just your future but that of my daughter and grandson too".

Horace went outside, kick started his bike and rode up to Sinai.

Sinai is a hill in an area to the west of the Burton-on-Trent called Shobnall, which gets its name from the Scobenhal Family who owned the land in the early thirteenth century. The name Sinai was ascribed to the hill at the end of the 18th century as a biblical reference but is believed to derive from one of its former names, Seney Hall, which itself may have derived from 'seney' (blood), which in medieval times was a place of blood-letting that was often performed by monks at monasteries. Due to its elevation, the hill is believed to have been used as a strategic position as far back as Roman times.

In the early 14th century the Scobenhals donated their fortified house to Burton Abbey to use as a monastery, which persisted until the 1530s when Henry VIII started his disbandment campaign of all the monasteries, priories, convents and friaries in England.

Henry VIII gave the former monastery to his then Knight of the Shire and adviser William Paget the first Baron of Beaudesert. The Pagets were given a substantial portion of Staffordshire including Cannock Chase and Burton Abbey and they owned Sinai for almost four hundred years. During their tenure the Pagets entertained nobles from all over Europe and used Sinai as a place for hunting as well as renting out some of the land to tenant farmers.

Leading up to the war the land was used as a co-operative farm until the R.A.F. acquired it to use as a billet for personnel from R.A.F. Tatenhill. After the war, the house had become dilapidated but was still habitable as a shelter and Uncle Bill used the grounds to keep pigs and chickens. He also used the location for shooting and combat training.

*Author's Note: There used to be plenty of deer and other wildlife within the boundaries of the surrounding park. In the late fifties and early sixties I went there myself to shoot with Horace and his friends.*

Horace noticed that he was being followed on his way to Sinai. The sun had just set and it was dusk. When he arrived he turned up the track and went half way up it. He dismounted and hid behind some trees to see how many men had followed him. Despite the track being more than wide enough to drive up they parked their car at the foot of the hill and turned the lights off. Four men got out. They had clearly decided to walk up to surprise Horace at the top.

Horace got on his motorbike and rode up the rest of the track to the back of the mansion house, as instructed, to tell Bill. It was dark save for the light that the passing clouds occasionally permitted the moon to cast over the house and surrounding forest.

"They're walking up. The car's at the bottom still on the road" said Horace.

Bill told Horace to take the bike and sidecar to the front of the building and just sit there and wait. Bill was using Horace as a kind of lure to attract Fisher's men deeper into the trap. They would almost certainly be observing the place with binoculars as best as they could in the darkness before making their move.

"Don't worry, we will have you covered".

When he got to the front Horace turned to look behind him. He saw half a dozen men including Bill hiding just out of sight in the shadows, but thought to himself that there must be more. There were. Three more of Bill's men had secreted themselves in the bushes at either side in front of him. His heart was racing. He was anxious but not afraid and looked forward to Fisher's men finding out that they had walked into a trap. Horace got off his bike and lit a cigarette, something that Fisher's men were bound to see.

A camouflaged Uncle Bill crawled up in the grass not far from Horace's feet.

"Don't look down" Bill said "go and sit on those bales near the entrance and talk to Gringe".

Horace walked over to the bales of hay where Gringe was

sitting wearing a policeman's uniform. They sat together nervously for two to three minutes squinting and peering into the gloom trying to spot any signs of movement. Suddenly, there was a commotion and the sound of shoes crunching on gravel slightly to the left in front of them. Three men rushed towards them out of the semi darkness and stood in front of them menacingly. It was Fisher's men.

"The boss was right" said one of them "you were meeting a rozzer. That's you and your girlfriend out of his way now".

Shane, the man who spoke, was pleased. He was going to get a lot of money for this, catching Horace with a copper and helping to dispose of him.

"Norm, go down to the car to bring Mr. Fisher here, he wants to do this one himself".

Before Norm could turn around there was a loud crack and he dropped to the ground with a thud. He'd been shot in the leg below the knee. The other three swung around. There were nine camouflaged men in combat gear pointing machine guns at them.

Letts, one of Fisher's other men, was the only one to go for his gun but Bill shot him in the right ankle. Letts cried out and dropped to the ground to join Norm.

"Who the hell are you" bellowed Shane "the police? You'd better let us go or that girl will be killed if we're not back tonight".

"You're not going anywhere" Bill told them. "If the girl is still alive we will get her back but if she's dead you will all be fed to the pigs....bit by bit. You'll be able to watch them eat the first few bits because you'll still be alive, albeit with various parts missing, but you can all go if you tell us where she is".

"We can't tell you where she is because our boss will have us killed if we do, and that's for sure".

One of Bill's other men spoke "We don't care who your boss is. See, we are much more dangerous than anyone you've ever worked for, and there are many more like us we can call upon. Fisher doesn't have a monopoly in the vicious bastard business".

"It's not just Fisher that we deal with. He's the main one in these parts but there are others elsewhere who are higher up, bigger fish than he is, so you'd better let us go".

Bill told his men to hang them up by their feet.

"It's getting late so if it's OK with the rest of you we'll hang them up now and leave them that way 'til the morning. Just make sure that their heads are an inch off the ground so the rats can have a good, close look. You chaps might be more talkative by then. Horace you get off home and we'll see you tomorrow. We will get her back".

"You can't leave us here, the girl will die if we don't get back tonight" one shouted.

"I doubt that" said Bill "you may have been planning a rendezvous tomorrow but we will find out what we need to know before then. We'll all sleep upstairs but don't worry, Piglet will stay with you for a couple of hours to keep you company. What's that you've got there Piglet?"

"Just a bit of bamboo sergeant major, I need something to play with at night when I'm on my own".

"And how exactly do you intend to play with it, Piglet?"

He laughed and snorted a bit like a pig.

"I just like to swing it around a bit. Do you want me to show you, sir?"

The bamboo cane swished catching Shane and the other man who was still standing across the face. They cried out in pain and cursed him. He repeated this move a couple more times until the men's cheeks were bright red and they were grimacing with their lips pulled back so tight that they bared their nicotine stained teeth.

"Piglet" said Bill, "they're making far too much noise we'll never sleep tonight. Gag all four of the noisy bastards and tie their hands, you're getting sloppy, men".

"Sorry, sir, one of them piped up, we don't get much practice these days. Shall we let them know we're still here, sir?"

"Of course soldier, you can pay them a visit during the night and get to know them better if you wish".

Horace went home much happier than when he'd set out to Sinai. He didn't think that Bill would have so many men there. He got home just after ten and went to the end house beside the brewery shop to see if his dad had been to collect his beer. The lady told him that no one had been so he borrowed a jug. Horace asked if he could use the phone and rang Bladon Castle to tell Lady Hermione that he would be there for quarter to seven in the morning.

"Then you must have some breakfast with us, Horace. It's the least we can do, and how is your father now?"

"Er, I'm just taking his medicine to him now" Horace lied but didn't feel too guilty, after all, beer did act as a kind of medicine to perk his dad up "I will see you in the morning, Lady Hermione".

He got in and his dad shouted at him "You're late, son, where have you been?"

"Sorry dad, I've been working on something at the garage and didn't realise what time it was".

His dad saw the jug of ale in his hand. "Get two glasses, lad, and let's get stuck in, your mum's gone to bed with another of her headaches".

They had a few glasses and a chat and Horace went to bed exhausted. It had been a long and stressful day to say the least.

He was up bright and early and pulled up at Bladon at six thirty just in time to help Mrs. Bell with the fire.

"I will do this, Mrs. Bell, you have other things to do" then fetched some wood.

After he'd helped Mrs. Bell with the chores he took the tea tray through to Lady Hermione and Angelica. He apologised for not having been there the previous afternoon but Angelica told him that it didn't matter because the Mayor's car was amazing. She couldn't believe it when it turned up, a limousine with a crest on the front.

"It even had a drinks cabinet in the back so I had to try some gin". Lady Hermione raised her eyebrows.

"What did the chauffeur say?" asked Horace "I bet he wasn't too impressed with that".

"I expect he didn't mind, it was only very little and anyway I smiled at him and chatted. I asked whether he liked his job".

"And does he?" asked Horace.

"He didn't say but he did ask about the school. He said he would mention it to the Mayor because his two girls would be old enough to go next year. I told him that it's the best girl school in the area".

Mrs. Bell brought them their fried breakfasts which were delicious, although Horace thought that the bacon was a little on the thin side for his liking. Horace chatted to Angelica and Lady Hermione politely, as usual, but he had other things on his mind and was keen to get away as soon as he could. After breakfast, Horace took Angelica to school.

On his way back, Horace rode up the track at Sinai. There had been lots of activity over night. One of Bill's men, who he later found out was called Soloman Saltzman, Sol for short, greeted him. Soloman was an English Jew and one of the best fighters, not to mention accomplished torturers, who had served in Bill's company in the Far East. He was reliable and most definitely not someone you should cross. He was only thirty two, the youngest of Bill's men at Sinai.

Horace walked into the house. The four men were still hanging there upside down and looked a lot more the worse for wear than the night before. The two who'd been shot in the leg and ankle were in a particularly bad state. They'd lost quite a bit of blood, much of which had run down their bodies onto their necks and faces and into their matted hair where it had coagulated. Spots of dried blood were on the floor beneath their heads.

Horace greeted Fisher's men.

"Morning, lads, you're still hanging around here I see. I've just had a nice fried breakfast and lots of tea, have they fed you your breakfast yet?"

Sol came in with a bucket and Petra, his Alsatian. He put the bucket down next to the dangling men.

"Morning again boys" he said with a strong accent that Fisher's men couldn't place. "I've brought Petra to say hello to you. I heard Horace ask whether you'd had any breakfast".

Sol put his hand into the bucket and brought out a handful of worms, snails and the odd woodlouse. He pinched Shane's nose forcing him to open his mouth to breathe and stuffed the contents of his hand into it. Shane spat out it spluttering.

"You ungrateful turd. Corporal, undo the rope".

Shane fell to the floor. Sol picked him up, slammed him down on a wooden dining chair and tied him to it.

"You will eat for me".

He scooped another handful out of the bucket and rammed it in Shane's mouth but this time held his hand over it firmly. Shane was gagging and couldn't eject the sickly mix out of his mouth so bits of worm, snail and woodlouse appeared out of his nose along with copious amounts of snot.

"Come on you bleeder, eat!" then slapped him hard across his face.

"Eat or I will cut off your toes one by one and give them to Petra".

Sol took his hand away to give Shane a chance to speak. He gasped for air, coughed and spat out what he could. His voice made a wheezing sound as he spoke.

"How much are you getting paid for this? I will treble whatever it is to let me go, you can have the other three".

"Did you hear that boy's?" Sol asked the others who were still upside down and swinging from the rafters like out-of-synch pendulums that had just about but not quite come to rest. The ropes creaked as they did so.

"How much will you give me, let's see now, five big ones? Have you got that sort of money on you Shane, my friend?"

"I will get it for you if you let me go and bring it to you within the hour".

Sol stood up and went over to one of the inverted rag dolls, untied the gag, and enquired "Can I trust him to bring me the money? Or will he let me down? What do you think?"

"Yes, you can trust him he will bring your money".

Sol beckoned Horace to come over.

"Horace, do you think I can trust Shane to bring me the money?"

"If he was happy for you to let him go and leave his friends here I expect he'd scarper and you wouldn't see him again".

"Well, Horace you could be right there, but then again he might come back but not alone. Maybe bring more of his friends here to play with us".

Sol got his knife out "Here, lad, take this knife and cut this cunt's ear off. Start as you mean to go on is what I always say. If they have your girl then they will tell us. Come on, Horace, cut the bloody thing off" he screamed.

"Never done it before, Sol"

"It's OK. Just cut it like you cut a piece of bacon off for your Uncle Bill when you have breakfast".

Horace took the knife. Grasped the chap's ear lobe and stretched his ear outwards. He placed the knife between the ear lobe and side of the head just above the jaw line and pressed down, sawing slightly as he did to get through the gristle. The man's scream was blood curdling but the ear came off quite easily, much to Horace's surprise. He thought he might be sick but it didn't really bother him at all. The blood dripped onto the floor making the same plopping noise as a leaking tap over an empty sink.

Sol asked Horace to pass him the ear, which he fed to Petra. The dog turned it around in its mouth a couple of times and swallowed it whole.

"That's bad manners, Petra, you must chew your food properly".

"So, Shane, Horace doesn't trust you to bring me the money but then again, I'm not doing this for money. I do this for my own pleasure and enjoyment. You should have seen what I did for enjoyment to our enemies in the war. You may still get a chance to, if you don't tell us where the girl is".

"Where are the rest of the lads" asked Horace "only three of you here?"

"They will all be back soon, they're in the parkland getting breakfast".

He opened Shane's mouth once more and fed him another handful of the garden creature potpourri but this time with the point of his knife pressed into and making a dimple in Shane's throat.

Bill and the other's came back from the woods with a deer around Piglet's shoulders. Bill asked one of the men, Ming, to get the fire going while they skinned the deer. Bill asked Horace what time he should be at work.

"Eight, Uncle Bill, but not sure if I will go with these being here. I want to find out where Charmaine is".

"Son, you have to act normal if you don't want Fisher to smell a rat. I will be going to work myself after breakfast. Sol and Piglet will find out what we want to know, there is no doubt about that".

Horace did what he was told and arrived at the garage before Gordon was about. He'd just opened the pumps when the first customer pulled up. He served him then another arrived straight after, and another. By the time Gordon came out he'd served nine or ten customers.

"You've been a busy lad, I kept hearing the bell going. Any news? My esteemed father-in-law stayed for an hour or so after you left just after seven last night and was pestering me to find out where you'd gone. I told him that you'd gone to help your Uncle Bill as per the phone call and that you'd probably gone straight home afterwards. The bad news is that he's coming back again today for a meeting with me and Christine but I don't know when he'll turn up. Any news on Charmaine, did that car follow you last night?"

Horace told Gordon that the car had followed him but he couldn't tell him anything more about it just yet and that there was no further news on Charmaine but they were working on it. He promised to update him later when he knew more himself.

"OK, son" said Gordon. "By the way, can you please take the exhaust off the Morgan, I'll go and get a new one when Fisher leaves after our meeting, oh, and while I'm away there is the Morris to service".

Gordon left Horace to get on with his work but went back and popped his head around the workshop door.

"Sorry, I forgot to tell you, Monica isn't coming in today. She's still scared to death after what happened to Sheila, not to mention us being jumpy all the time about what cars are passing by and parking in the road".

Horace carried on his work flitting between the workshop and the forecourt when customers came in for fuel. It was on one of his trips back from the kiosk that Fisher pulled up, glanced over at Horace and went into Gordon's house.

Horace worked on the cars until lunch time then went and sat in the kiosk to have a smoke and cup of tea. Uncle Bill drew up outside to put petrol in the van and ask Horace how things were. He said that he saw Fisher going to the garage in the morning.

"I want to play Fisher at his own game so I'm keeping tabs on him. I have two motorbike riders and a council van tailing him and following his every move. He may twig that he's being followed but he won't know who they are".

"How are things at Sinai Uncle Bill? Sol was giving Shane his breakfast when I left".

"I won't tell you the details of what Sol did after you left but let's just say that it was something that he specialises in and enjoys. Keep away from Sinai tonight, with those men going missing Fisher will be on edge and will probably have more people watching you. Just be on guard, he could even use a woman or a girl to approach us to find out what's going on. Don't forget that it was a young girl that persuaded Charmaine to go with her....and we all know how susceptible you are to the charms of a pretty young girl, Horace."

"Thanks Uncle Bill. Didn't those men at Sinai say anything at all about Charmaine?"

"Don't expect this to be a quick operation, Horace. If these are professional hit men it could take days to break them down but, I assure you, Sol and Piglet will do it. They're experts in their line of business".

"Are you paying them to do this, Uncle Bill?"

"Horace, these men work for free, they're old mates. But they will take some of the spoils, such as the new car parked at Sinai that those men followed you in. They'll flog it to pay for their expenses plus there was money in the men's pockets not to mention the arms in the boot. Well, I'm off to work now I don't know what state the building site's in with me not having been there for hours. I'll come and talk to you later".

Horace carried on serving fuel to customers who seemed to be turning up in greater numbers today for some reason. Fisher came out of the house with Gordon and walked towards the kiosk.

"Oi! I want a word with you" said Fisher. "The bust at the tyre factory last time cost us a lot of money, so tonight you're going with three of my men to take the tyres we should have had two weeks ago. There will be only one security guard on duty tonight and a lorry is loaded ready for the morning....and you're the one who's going to take it. At least we'll know exactly where you are this time. You'd better do a good job for the sake of your girlfriend and this pillock son-in-law of mine. If your girlfriend isn't enough to persuade you to do it then perhaps this will. I have some stolen bank notes with Gordon's finger prints on it would be a real shame if they were to get into the police's hands somehow".

Horace flew at him with his left fist but this time it was Gordon who stepped in between them and stopped him from hitting Fisher.

"Horace, calm down, son. He's got me by the bollocks. I know the money he's talking about and that would see me go down for a long time. That's why this bastard wanted me to move the Velox with Simon's body in the boot, so he could incriminate me".

"Well, son, if you don't want your little girlfriend to end up in the boot of a car then you will do what I want".

"How do I know you haven't killed her already? If you can do it to your own son-in-law you wouldn't have any problems doing it to a stranger".

"Well, you little piece of shit, you don't know do you, and if this goes wrong tonight you won't know anyway because you'll be at the bottom of the river. Tell your parents you won't be home tonight. That reminds me, your dad isn't too well is he, if you were to bugger things up or try to make a run for it then your old man is another that might go to an early grave".

"Fisher, my dad was a hero not a zero like you. You know what, I don't believe you have the guts to kill someone yourself. We can see you have guts alright, you fat bastard, but not the sort to pull a trigger".

"Keep this lad in order, Gordon, and make sure he's here tonight, and this time it better go well".

Once Fisher had left Gordon placed his hands on Horace's shoulders.

"I'm so sorry, son. I sometime wish that I'd never set eyes on you, I never wanted you to get involved in all of this, you don't want or need it".

Christine came out with young Chris on her hip.

"Has he gone? That man definitely knows what happened to Simon but the one thing he doesn't know is who put the body on his lawn, that's got him frightened. He doesn't suspect you, Horace, and it could have been anyone, that's what's troubling him. Poor Ruth will never recover from this. I'm glad at least that mum is staying with her. As well as the shock of losing a husband to murder there are so many unanswered questions. Why was Simon leading a double life? What was that address that he had in his wallet? How was he earning all the money?

# CHAPTER THIRTEEN

Horace was filling in for Monica in the kiosk when a customer came in for some fuel, a young woman he hadn't seen before. She asked him to fill the car up, a handsome green two-seater 1949 MG TC.

"Could you check the oil please and clean the windshield for me?"

Horace said he would and asked her if she wanted the hood putting up as it looked as if rain was coming. She declined but began to flirt with him and ask him lots of questions about where he came from, what he did, whether he enjoyed his job. She got out and accompanied him to the kiosk to pay.

"My you are self sufficient in here with a stove and a kettle, how about a cup of tea then? I don't know your name, I'm Veronica".

"Pleased to meet you, I'm Horace. If you'd like a drink could you please move your car so as not to block the pumps?"

Horace went to the house whilst she moved her car to tell Gordon that he thought one of Fisher's stooges was outside. They'd never seen the girl or the car before and although it was perfectly possible that she was simply passing through the present circumstances made them extremely wary of people they hadn't seen before.

"I'll be out in a minute" said Gordon "keep her talking for a few minutes while I make a phone call to Kennings".

A few minutes after he got back to the kiosk and was making tea for the girl, another car pulled up.

"Morning, Horace, where is Sheila or Monica today one of them is normally here?"

"Morning, Mrs. Hampton. Sheila is ill and Monica has gone to the doctors with baby Malcolm, and her father is getting worse too. Monica and her mum are really worried about him".

"Is that a new girl in the kiosk, looks a bit too well healed to work at a garage?"

"Can you please help me Mrs. Hampton....perhaps come into the kiosk and ask her a few questions? She just pulled up for fuel but now she wants a cup of tea and it doesn't look as if she's planning to leave. Gordon and I think she may be a confidence trickster" Horace fibbed, "and we want to find out what her real motives are".

"Of course I will, Horace. You know me I can be very direct and personal if you want me to. Is that the car she came in?"

"Yes, it's a nice MG one of the top cars at the moment, although I suppose you knew that with Mr. Hampton being the sales manager at Kennings". Horace smiled at her. "He was good to me two years ago when I worked there".

"Yes, it was unfortunate that you had that trouble with those two louts when you started, you would like it much better now".

They both went into the kiosk and the girl was sitting on the counter. Mrs. Hampton thought to herself straight away that she looked a bit like a tart.

"You're not from around here are you, are you Horace's girlfriend? He told me that he was going out with a canal girl".

"A canal girl? I hope you don't think that I'm a canal girl. I have that car over there. How could a canal girl afford that may I ask?"

"I don't know, but by the same token how can a young lady like you afford a nearly new MG TC soft top car? I know I can't afford one. What do you do for a living, young lady, or does your daddy keep you?"

Gordon saw Mrs. Hampton and walked across the yard and

into the kiosk to join them.

"Morning, Mrs. Hampton, how's Don doing, I've not seen him for a while? Horace, how many times do I have to tell you not to have your girlfriends drape themselves across the kiosk".

He turned and winked at Mrs. Hampton. They made a good double act and continued to press the girl. Horace and Gordon knew instinctively that her motives for being there were not as genuine as she wanted them to believe.

Veronica was starting to get riled and snapped back at them.

"I am neither his girlfriend nor a canal girl I am a self made woman, that's why I have a car that you can't afford old lady" Veronica said brusquely.

"Self made girl?" Mrs. Hampton retorted "prostitutes are self made girls aren't they? Horace I am surprised that you need a prostitute, what with that lovely girlfriend of yours".

The ruse worked, the girl's demeanour changed from cross to furious. She produced a knife from the back of her slacks and held it out in front of her menacingly. But she stuck it out too far. Horace knocked it out of her hand and then hit her across the head with a swipe of his fist stunning her. His and Gordon's instincts about who she really was turned out to be right.

"Thanks for coming, Marge" said Gordon, "I knew if anyone could get her going you would".

Horace pulled her out of the kiosk by the arm and put her in her car to take to the others, she was still groggy.

"Did you plan this, Mr. Rush?" asked Horace, "Mrs. Hampton coming, I couldn't believe the way you bounced off each other".

"When you told me one of Fisher's mob was here I had to think quick so I phoned Marge, she is Christine's best friend and Don was with me in the army. I didn't give her all the details, of course, but this won't go any further than Marge anyway. Now quick, get her out of here, I will fetch you back when I can".

"No need to fetch me, Mr. Rush, it's just ten minutes over the field".

Horace drove up to Sinai and stopped the car. The girl was leaning forward with her head in her hands not yet knowing what was going on. It was eerily quiet save for the wind rustling the leaves in the trees. There was no sign of anyone. Horace got the girl out of the car, she started to protest and tried to wriggle free from his grip. Piglet's face appeared as he peeked out from behind the front door that was partially open.

"Who the hell have you brought us now Horace, this wasn't on the agenda"?

"She's one of Fisher's lot, came to the garage earlier. She got a bit heated and pulled a knife out, bit of an overreaction to being called a prostitute wouldn't you say? If you can get her to talk she might be able to tell you where Charmaine is. By the way, Fisher wants me to do a job with some of his lads tonight".

"We'll see what we can do Horace, bring her in".

They stripped all her clothes off, tied her hands together and stood her in the corner. Sol got a large butcher's knife and went over to the chap who'd already had an ear cut off.... and cut the other one off. He screamed but not quite as loud as yesterday, his energy, and perhaps even will to live, having waned considerably after the ordeal of the last twenty four hours. Sol went over to the girl and put his face close to hers. He slid the blade of the knife between her legs and lifted it slightly exerting enough pressure to part her labia. In a hoarse, loud whisper he said "Tell me everything I need to know or I will cut you from your fanny to your chin".

He slid the knife out from between her legs went over to the chap with no ears and ran it across his stomach slitting it open. The wound opened as the knife moved, not dissimilar to a tightly packed bag that is being unzipped. There was no blood to begin with but then it started to appear, slowly at first and then in rivulets that gushed out rhythmically as his heart pumped. Mercifully for him, the man passed out.

The girl screamed "That's my dad, that's my dad, don't kill him, please don't kill him".

"Now, young lady, I haven't even asked him any questions yet, it's just that I never liked him really".

Sol slid the knife slowly into the open wound and started to jiggle it around, it squelched as he did so. The girl tried to look away but couldn't because Piglet had clasped the sides of her head from behind and forced her head round holding her eyelids open with his index and middle fingers. She started to weep.

Sol told her that he didn't think she was much of a gangster's moll behaving like that, then teased some intestine forwards with the tip of the knife and cut a small chunk out. The girl vomited and vomited again until there was no more liquid left for her body to expel.

"Don't leave him like that" she yelled. "Cut him down and let me take him to the hospital to try to save him".

Sol went over and slid the knife between her legs once more.

"Let him go?" bellowed Sol, "while your gangster friends are holding an innocent girl hostage and doing God knows what to her? If you tell us where she is we may be able to free her too. You didn't consider the consequences when you got her to go with you to those crooks, did you? You better start talking young lady".

"Yes anything, anything at all".

"Then tell me your name".

She was sobbing. "Please don't hurt him anymore he's had enough....my name is Veronica Clay".

"Now tell me where the canal girl is otherwise I will make a start on you".

"I can't or they will kill me, just like the others...."

"What others?"

"They kill anyone who double crosses them".

"I just want you to tell me where the girl is and who is holding her".

"Save yourself" her father managed to whisper, "tell them what they want to know. Please don't hurt her". He exhaled sharply and fell silent. His eyes were open but the light inside them had extinguished. For a brief moment the only sound that could be heard was the wind gusting outside and the sound of a rope creaking. The silence was interrupted abruptly by a shrill cry.

"No! No! You bastards you killed my father, I'm telling you nothing".

"My girl" said Sol, "you will when I've finished with you. I have something special planned for tomorrow. Leave her here all night, Piglet, you do the first couple of hours, and leave her with no clothes on".

Horace had remained silent throughout. Despite his loathing of Fisher and rage that his girlfriend had been kidnapped he was more surprised than anything else at what he'd witnessed. He had never seen anything like it before. He said that he would go back to the garage over the fields.

"Sol" he said, "there is another car outside for you and your men".

As he left the house to walk back over the fields he saw the others in Uncle Bill's team each of whom had chosen a strategic position around the property to conceal themselves. They reminded him of snipers, watching and waiting but ready at a moment's notice to open fire.

"See you tomorrow, men" Horace shouted. They all put a clenched fist up in response.

Horace sat with Gordon and Christine when he got back to the garage. He ate a sausage cob and drank a cup of tea. It was the first opportunity he'd had to give them the detail about everything that had happened to him during the last twenty four hours. He told them about his arrival at Sinai, the appearance of Fisher's men, how they'd been captured, strung up and tortured and what had happened to the girl that had showed up at the garage earlier, including the cutting open and death of her father. His recounting of the events seemed so matter of fact, as did Gordon and Christine's reaction to them, but then, so many extraordinary things had happened to them all over the last few years that the word shock had all but disappeared from their vocabularies.

Horace and Gordon went outside to start their work in the garage. Horace asked Gordon whether it would OK for him to fetch Angelica from school at four.

"Of course, Horace, but make sure you're back here for ten tonight. Fisher has me over a barrel with that set-up money of his but I can't risk him going to the police with it".

"Can you imagine him going to the police?" asked Horace, "and who would they believe, you or a known crook?"

"You are wiser than your years, Horace. I wasn't thinking straight. Christine doesn't know about the money but I'm going to tell her, then I will phone Fisher".

"But that doesn't help Charmaine, Mr. Rush, that's why I've got to go. I don't want you to be involved, you have too much to lose Mr. Rush".

Horace finished work then went to school to fetch Angelica and waited outside. Lots of girls walked past smiling knowingly at him. Angelica came out, put her arms around his neck and kissed him on the lips.

"Horace, kiss me back, I told Joanne that you're my boyfriend so please make it look like you are".

"Horace kissed her passionately but felt guilty because it was Charmaine who was occupying all of his thoughts.

"Wow! Horace, you're such a good kisser, I feel strange, all warm inside and alive. When we get back will you come to my bedroom to carry this on?"

"Sorry, Angelica, I promised Sir Humphrey that I would look after you and I would never take advantage of you".

Horace opened the sidecar door to let Angelica clamber in. Angelica was really pretty and he really did like her but felt more affection than love for her.

"Angelica, you can and will do better than me. You go to boarding school and mix with people of a different class than mine and will continue to do so throughout your life. I really like you but we're friends, Angelica, and I hope always will be".

"Oh Horace, I know deep down that you're right but we get on so well together, we are more than just friends aren't we? I know that you would do anything for me".

"Angelica, yes, we are more than just friends but I respect you and my love for you is more like the love of a family member than a lover. My life is complicated at the moment. There are things that I cannot tell you and my being with you may even be placing you in danger, I would not forgive myself if anything happened to you".

Angelica sat in silence. Horace knew that she would be upset but also that in time she would come to understand the wisdom of his words and that she would find the true love of her life.

They drove back to Bladon Castle a different way via Draycott in the Clay, Fauld and Tutbury and when in Burton they avoided going down Henhurst Hill and past the garage. Sir Humphrey was back from London and in a good mood, his work there must have gone well. He thanked Horace for all he'd done for them. Angelica looked at him tearfully but with admiration as he left and they waved him goodbye.

Horace went home and told his mum and dad that he would be out late that night helping Mr. Rush fetch a car from Nottingham and that he hoped to be back around midnight. He knew that he wouldn't but, of course, couldn't tell them the reason why. He had something to eat and went to get his dad his beer then left to go to Sinai to find out whether there was any news about Charmaine's whereabouts.

He walked behind the brewery and over the fields, not wanting Fisher to see him should he be at or near the garage. It only took fifteen minutes. He raised his hand as a signal as he approached, he didn't want to be shot by mistake. He couldn't see them all but nevertheless shouted a greeting to them when he was near the house. Those that he could see responded as they had earlier by putting a clenched fist up but not saying a word.

"Hello, Horace" Piglet said "we didn't think you were coming tonight".

"I'm in a dilemma, Piglet. Fisher wants me to do a robbery with him tonight from the tyre factory but if I knew where Charmaine was I would go to get her instead".

Sol heard Horace tell Piglet about the robbery.

"You must go along with it, Horace. Tell me where the factory is, we will follow them to see where they go with the load. Tyres are an easy commodity to get rid of".

"Have you found anymore out yet, Sol?"

"Yes, Horace. I have found out what a foul mouth Veronica has. She hasn't stopped cursing since you left, come and see if she will talk to you".

"The girl was still naked and looked cold. Despite his state of mind, Horace felt pity and covered her up. Do you want a drink?"

"Fuck off! I've been drinking his piss all day, why not shit in my mouth while you're at it. My dad is still hanging there, cut him down for pity's sake, have you no mercy. If I get out of this I will kill you myself".

Sol told her that they had lost the ability to be merciful years ago.

"I'm no soldier of mercy, lady, but I may cut you some slack if you tell us what we need to know. They will tell me by tomorrow, Horace, we've worn them down a lot. Tomorrow won't be a picnic for them either. These things can take time but everyone breaks in the end".

"Sol, I've written down the directions to the tyre factory from here. I will see you later then, just before midnight".

He walked back to the garage after going to the pub for a pint and stopping at the chip shop for something to eat. Fisher was talking to two men when he got to the garage. It was hard to hear everything but he got the gist of this conversation. Fisher was telling them that five of his team had gone missing, four men and a girl.

"Just be careful tonight" Fisher said "something's going on but I don't know what, or who's behind it, but I will find out soon enough. I'm getting more men from up north tomorrow and these won't be as easy to get rid of...."

He stopped talking when he saw Horace approaching and ordered him to get in the car. The two men jumped in after him, one in the passenger seat and one in the back. Fisher got in the driver's seat.

"I'm going to drop you off on Main Street. You just need to sort out the watchman, his keys are in his hut. The lorry's already loaded and its registration number is FA 490 Make sure you keep your eye on this lad here. I will see you when you get back on Saturday".

All three got out at Main Street. Horace looked around discretely to see if he could spot Sol but there was no sign of him. Maybe he'd changed his mind about coming.

When they got to the gates, the watchman was leaning on the fence facing away from them smoking a fag. One of Fisher's men snuck up to cosh him over the back of the head but as he got close the watchman spun round and punched him in the face. There was a crack, which Horace assumed was the man's jaw breaking. He fell to the floor clutching his chin. At the same time that all this was happening, someone snuck up behind the second of Fisher's men and looped a piece of rope around his neck pulling tight until the man fell to the floor gasping. Sol and another of Bill's men tied their wrists behind their backs.

Just then, the lorry pulled up. Sol, the other chap and Horace bundled the men into the back of the lorry, put the tailgate up, fastened it and pulled the sheeting down. They drove up to Sinai where they bound Fisher's men tightly and put them in a corner of the room where the others were being held.

They cut Veronica's dad down because he had gone gaunt, grey and stiff. Piglet and another man took him outside to bury him in the parkland. Horace went upstairs to bed down for the night. Sol turned to him "We will start early in the morning, we will find out where your girl is".

"You won't get anything out of us" hissed Veronica, "these aren't easy to break. We are professionals not amateurs like you".

Piglet pulled off the blanket that Horace had put over her earlier and started to caress her body. She smiled at him then, without warning, kicked him as hard as she could in the balls.

"You little scrubber! He undid her hands and pushed her backwards onto the floor putting his right forearm across her throat. He used his left hand to bring her right hand up until he could grab her wrist with his right hand and hold it there. She tried to wriggle but was immobilised because he was lying on top of her. He got his knife out with his left hand and cut her right thumb off. She opened her mouth to scream but nothing came out other than gasps. He put her thumb in his mouth and chewed it a couple of times. "Not salty enough" he mumbled. He took the thumb out of his mouth, forced her legs apart with his thighs, reached down and inserted her severed thumb into her vagina.

He eased himself off her and pulled her into a sitting position, she started to sob.

"When will you start to realise that we are not playing games here? Did seeing your dad die in front of you not convince you? If you don't tell us what we want to know you will all die".

Shane, who hadn't spoken for a long while, said "There's nothing you can do that we haven't seen or done ourselves, you morons don't know who you're messing with so for your sakes you better let us go".

Sol, Piglet and Horace looked at each other for a few moments and then roared with laughter.

"In the morning" said Sol, "you will see what we do and I can assure you it won't be anything that you have seen before".

They were all up early the next morning, apart from those who'd been on the last lookout shift. Sol opened the back of the lorry. It was completely full apart from the two foot deep space near the tailgate they'd used as temporary storage for Fisher's men.

"Well, lads, this job is starting to be lucrative for us; two cars, some weapons, a lorry and now a load of tyres. Let's have some breakfast".

More meat was cut off the carcass of the hanging deer and thrown into the sizzling pan. Horace went to fetch some bracket mushrooms from the trees and eggs from the hens that were roosting in one of the cottages. Horace was surprised at the number of pigs that Uncle Bill had there now. He made a mental note to tell him that it was time to slaughter some of them.

After they had eaten, Sol went to the main room to fetch a bit of wire out of his bag, a thin piece of galvanised wire that was a part of his 'specialist kit'. He went over to Shane and removed his belt then cut the buttons on his fly.

"What are you going to do?" Shane shouted, "What's that wire for?"

Sol pulled Shane's underpants down, or rather up as he was hanging upside down, grasped his penis and extended it outwards. A bit like threading a needle, Sol inserted the wire into Shane's urethra stopping every now and then as the wire met resistance to readjust the angle of the wire and push it in deeper, wiggling it as he did so. Words cannot begin to describe Shane's agony. He screamed and wailed in equal measure. After a few seconds blood emerged from urethra opening. The wire had passed the ejaculatory duct and prostate gland and pierced Shane's bladder.

"Is that the best you can do?" Shane managed to utter through gritted teeth, saliva running up his cheeks.

Sol withdrew the wire with rather less care than he'd taken when inserting it, went over to the fireplace in the adjacent room where they'd cooked breakfast and heated the tip of the wire until it glowed yellow, almost white. He returned to Shane. Smoke was coming off the end of the wire that was charred black about half way along its length but the end had cooled and was now glowing red. He repeated the procedure of inserting the wire except this time it hissed as it entered Shane's penis producing wisps of smoke and the smell of burnt flesh. Shane arched his back and screamed.

"I don't know where she is, Veronica and her dad knew her whereabouts".

The hot wire had seared the flesh so less blood came out than before. Sol persisted until Shane passed out with the pain. Sol told Piglet and Ray, another of Bill's men, to cut Shane down and bury him somewhere outside.

One of Fisher's men shouted "He's not dead, he's not dead you can't bury him".

"OK" said Sol, "so tell me where the girl is, that's all we want to know".

"We don't know where she is. The girl, Veronica, she's the only who knows where the girl is".

"Good luck with that bit of wire" mocked Veronica "my hole is bigger than his, and there's a thumb stuck in it".

"My dear I have something else planned for you. They don't call me the surgeon for nothing. Shane knows nothing, bury him as he is with his bleeding dick".

Shane had regained consciousness....

"You can't do that, kill me first, please don't bury me alive, I would tell you if I knew where she was".

"Ray, take these bastards out and bury them, leave their hands tied. Right, young lady, let's find out where Charmaine is".

Sol knelt in front of her and grasped her right breast. She tried to wriggle free but Piglet held her still. Sol inserted the sharp pointed wire through her right nipple making her cry out in pain, but still she wouldn't tell them where Charmaine was. He withdrew the wire and then pushed it straight through the front of her breast perpendicular to her body until a small bulge appeared in the skin on her back. The wire pierced the skin and the tip appeared. He had skewered her front to back.

Horace watched it all. What occurred at Sinai and the events leading up to it had a profound affect on him, an affect that changed him irrevocably in ways that he did not yet comprehend or could have imagined just a few short years before. The change was akin to that experienced by those who witness the horrors of war and become inured and desensitised over time to the pain and suffering of others; much as many of Uncle Bill's men had during their campaigns in the armed forces.

*Author's note: It was not easy to put in writing the description of the events that took place at Sinai. Doing so was even more difficult than listening to them being recalled and recounted. Before starting to write this book I decided that it was essential not to leave out or try to moderate integral parts of the story and to tell it in full, warts and all. Suffice to say that Uncle Bill's men got the information they wanted....eventually.*

Charmaine was being kept at the dog track on Skimpot Road in Luton in a hut on the far side of the track where they trained the dogs. The hut had been used to house dogs until 1946 when a new kennel block was built but the hut persisted as a storage area and, with the kidnapping of Charmaine, was the place where Arthur and Sid Lawrence kept and tormented her.

Sol asked Horace to phone Bill to tell them what they had found out and that he and Piglet were on their way to the dog track. Sol left the task of burying Fisher's men and the girl to the others who interred them in the parkland woods before leaving to reassume their roles, for now at least, in everyday life.

Sol and Piglet drove to Luton in the car that Fisher's men had arrived in on the first day, Horace travelled with his motorbike and sidecar. It was just over two hours to the dog track; they arrived at twenty past ten without stopping for food or drink.

The track and building was surrounded by a high fence and the gate was locked but it didn't take much for them to get in because much of the fence was in a poor state of repair. They walked round the track until they saw the lone hut in the gloom on the far side. The hut wasn't locked. Sol opened the door just a little to peek inside. A man was asleep in a chair snoring with his head thrown back and mouth wide open. A single bare, dim light bulb hung from a chord in the centre of the hut which was messy and cluttered with dog racing paraphernalia and other junk. A makeshift ashtray beside the chair was overflowing with cigarette ends and ash.

Sol opened the door wider, it creaked slightly. The man snorted but remained deep in slumber. Sol picked up a piece of rope that was lying on the floor and wound each end around his hands. He crept up, looped the rope around the man's neck and crossed his hands behind his head and jerked him out of the chair.

Horace looked around frantically for Charmaine and found her bound and gagged in the corner partially hidden by an old advertising sign. He undid the rope and gag.

She squealed with delight and hugged him tightly.

"How did you find me Horace?"

"It's a long story Chamy but I couldn't have done it without these great lads and my Uncle Bill".

Sol pulled the rope around his captive's neck upwards lifting the man onto his tiptoes.

"Are you one of the Lawrence's" Sol barked into the man's reddening face.

"He isn't" interjected Charmaine, "but he had his way with me twice in the last three nights you can see the scratches and bruises on his face and teeth marks on the side of his neck".

Horace lunged forward and grabbed the man taking him out of Sol's grip and punched him around the hut stumbling over items as he pursued his prey. He grabbed the man by his shirt collar and pulled him forward.

"Where are the Lawrences?" Horace spat the question into the man's glaring eyes.

"You defiled my girlfriend you bastard" and hit him again. Horace reached out and grabbed a rusty knife that was on the edge of a bench beside him and pressed the point into the man's throat.

"Where are the Lawrences?"

The man remained silent but Charmaine told them that the man was their watchman and that they always came early in the morning to take him with them.

Horace applied pressure and the knife slid into the man's throat about an inch. Blood splattered out.

"Look at me, my face is the last thing you're going to see" screamed Horace then pushed the knife in a little further. The man spluttered and tried to cough but all that came out was a rattling sound. Horace's biceps flexed and he thrust the knife in up to the hilt. The man's eyes glazed over and he went limp.

Sol got hold of Horace's arm, tugged him off the man and got him to stand up.

"You can do no more here, son, we've got to get rid of his body. We'll carry him to the car and put him in the boot. We'll dispose of him and the others tomorrow when we've done with them".

"Horace, you take Charmaine back to her family, I'm told that they're in the same place outside Luton moored where they were three days ago. We will wait for the other bastards to come in the morning and give them a surprise welcome".

Horace kissed Charmaine as if the world were about to end and took her to the motorbike.

"You are so brave, my knight in shining armour. You killed a man, Horace, it was horrible....what did you feel?"

"I can't remember most of it, Chamy, I was so mad that he'd taken advantage of you and everything happened so quickly. But I'm glad I killed him, I feel nothing but hate for him even now that he is dead".

He helped her gently into the sidecar, kick started the bike and drove her back to the canal to look for her parents' boat. Horace pulled up when they arrived at the canal and they sat there with the motor ticking over.

"Look for the railway line then I will point you in the right direction, Horace, don't worry you won't get lost".

They drove around for a few minutes until they found a way onto the towpath and drove down it, it wasn't long before they came alongside the Hackett's boat. Charmaine got out and shouted to her mum and dad. There was a commotion inside the boat and the sound of things being knocked over as her parents rushed to the door. It swung open with a loud bang and her parents emerged and stood there dismayed. They jumped onto the towpath and ran towards Charmaine picking her up, twirling her around and hugging and kissing her.

"You found her, Horace, you found our little girl. Where was she, what happened?"

"Charmaine will tell you over a cup of tea" said Horace, "there is much more that needs to be done so I must get going, my friends need my help".

Charmaine didn't wait to be taken into the boat and be given a cup of tea. She poured out the story of how she'd gone off with the girl, been kidnapped and imprisoned in the hut at the dog racing track. She sobbed as she told them about her ordeal and how she had been violated repeatedly. He mother hugged and tried to comfort her.

"How will you ever want to be with me again, Horace" Charmaine sobbed, "will you ever forgive me?"

"There is nothing to forgive, Charmaine, none of this was your fault. You are as dear to me now as you ever were, dearer in fact, I love you".

Charmaine wept uncontrollably. The terror of being in captivity and not knowing her fate, the sudden joy at seeing Horace, the relief of escaping and the overwhelming love she felt when she saw her parents had allowed her to block out some of her darker thoughts. But now that she knew she was safe back in the bosom of her family the feelings of shame and guilt that she had hitherto held in abeyance flooded over her. She realised at that moment that she could never be the same again. How could any man love her, how could she even be with a man again? She was two days away from her sixteenth birthday.

Horace took her in his arms and told her that he loved her but that what she needed now was to be with her mum and dad. He kissed her and told her that he would return soon. He rode up the tow path without a backward glance and some twenty minutes later was parked not far away from the dog track. He clambered into the sidecar and tried to get some sleep. It wasn't easy, all he could see was Charmain's tearful face and the pain etched onto it that her young beauty was attempting but failing to conceal.

He awoke at five o'clock and walked over to the fence, wedged apart two wooden panels and squeezed between them back onto the track. He walked over to the hut. The patches of grass around the hut were wet with dew and there was a thin carpet of mist surrounding its base. He called out to let Sol and Piglet know that it was him returning, opened the door and walked in.

He told Sol and Piglet about his trip back with Charmaine and what happened when she was reunited with her parents.

"I want these bastards to pay for what they have done to that sweet young girl" said Horace.

"What do you want us to do with them, Horace? This is your choice" said Sol. "We will gladly oblige with whatever you ask us to do".

They made some tea on a small gas stove and, as there was no milk or sugar, drank it black while they waited. Horace picked up a hessian bag from the floor and held it up.

"I've thought about it" he said. "What I would like is take the Lawrence's heads back to Fisher in this".

He planned to maximise the shock to Fisher and leave the heads somewhere where he would find them unexpectedly. Just then, Piglet whispered that someone was coming. Piglet and Horace hid in a closet in the corner while Sol sat in the chair facing the door.

The Lawrence brothers were dismayed when they walked in.

"Who the hell are you?" Arthur Lawrence demanded to know.

"I'm your worst nightmare, that's who. From your appearance I would guess that you are Arthur, the main man in this operation, but I'm only going by Veronica's description of you. It was the last thing she said to me, in fact, it was the last thing she said, full stop".

"Von wouldn't tell you anything, I helped her dad to bring her up better than that".

"Funny you should mention her dad, Arthur, sadly he too is no longer with us".

"What do you mean....last thing she said?" Arthur was moving his hand slowly towards the inside of his coat.

Sol already had a gun hidden under the jacket on his lap. He took it out and pointed it at them.

"You move your hand another inch and I'll blow your bollocks out your arse. As far as your Von is concerned, people will tell you anything when you cut out one of their eyes and, more often than not, it's the last thing they manage to do".

"Well, how do you manage to do all this on your own in this neighbourhood? We've got people all over the shop, some just a few yards away. And where's that slag of a girl we all fucked?"

"Oh dear" said Sol "I'm not sure that was such a good idea, saying what you just said".

Horace and Piglet kicked open the closet door and burst out. They walked over to Arthur and Sid and removed all of the weapons they could find frisking them to make sure they hadn't missed anything.

"Who the hell are you people?" said Sid, "you're not local and you'll be sorry you came to our neck of the woods".

Horace swung and hit Sid hard in the mouth. Some teeth, not all of them his original ones, flew out and he dropped to the floor backwards like a 100lb sack of grain falling over. He parted his blood spattered lips in a grimace exposing the voids in the places where his teeth had once been.

"Like that slag, Von, who came into our neck of the woods?" Horace asked sarcastically.

Horace knelt down between his outstretched legs, leant forward and put a gun to Sid's head.

"You say you fucked my girl".

Horace brought his knee forwards with some force into Sid's testicles causing him to gasp and hunch forwards. He then lifted his hand and brought the butt of the gun down on the side of Sid's head with a thump.

He looked up at Horace blinking the blood and sweat out of his eyes.

"She's your girl? Well you'll need a bigger dick now, lad" then he laughed, although it was more like a wheeze that turned into a cough. His tongue protruded as he coughed convulsively.

Horace had secreted in a compartment in the boot of the sidecar the knife he'd taken out of Fisher's car. He'd brought it to the hut this morning as this was a special occasion and it might come in handy, and there was no time like the present to put it to good use.

He grabbed Sid's protruding tongue and pulled it out as far as he could. Sid gagged and tried to shake his head from side to side. Horace thrust the knife into the mouth and sawed this way and that cutting the ligaments and muscles until he extracted the tongue and held it aloft before throwing onto a tarpaulin that was covering some tins of paint. Sid gurgled as the blood gushed out.

"What were you saying about needing a bigger dick?" asked Horace in a measured and calm tone.

He cut through Sid's belt and ripped open the front of his trousers, the buttons flew off and pinged across the floor. His large, baggy underwear wasn't too difficult to pull down even though Sid was still sitting on the floor. Horace grabbed the end of Sid's penis with his left hand and stretched it out as far as he could then stabbed the base with the knife in his right hand and sawed through the tissue. The penis came away half torn and half sliced. Sid was already semi unconscious with his head slumped backwards and mouth wide open, all that remained was for Horace to push the severed penis into the gaping cavern and to prod it with his finger to make sure that he got it all in, a bit like stuffing wadding into the bolt hole of a sump to prevent the oil from pouring out, thought Horace.

"You bastard!" screamed Arthur "I'm going to kill you before you have the chance to grow up into a man".

"The lad's already more of a man than you" said Sol.

Piglet asked Horace what he wanted to do with them, did he want them to suffer some more or should they just finish them off.

"I want their heads in this bag to take back to their friend Fisher but I want them alive while we do it. I want them to have what's left of their time to reflect upon the anguish and distress they caused Charmaine".

He looked around the junk that was scattered all over the hut floor and picked up just what he was looking for, a rusty old saw.

"This will do it, lads, that's if you wouldn't mind helping me with it, it's not very sharp".

"That's why we are here Horace".

They went through the Lawrence's pockets and a holdall that was slung over Arthur's shoulder when they came in. They found a considerable amount of cash and some car keys and house keys.

Arthur, whom Piglet had been holding against the side of the hut, tried to push forward and wriggle free from Piglet's grasp but he wasn't strong or fit enough and Piglet knocked him to the floor.

"Try that again and I'll cut your fucking arms off" Piglet yelled at him.

Arthur, somewhat belatedly, began to realise the severity of the situation that he was now in. His brother had already arrived at that conclusion some time before.

"Let us go and we can make you rich. You don't know the extent of what we have, you can all be a part of it, just let me and my brother go. Can't you see that he's suffered enough? If we can stop him bleeding there might still be a chance to save him".

"It's too late to plead" said Horace. "My mates will show me the best way to take off your brother's head with this rusty saw and you will watch us do it".

"Horace" said Sol, "we'll deal with that one first but this one over here still has a lot more to tell us. There's a Rover out there somewhere, go and find it for us these keys are bound to be for it".

Horace shut the hut door behind him and walked around the dog track. The sun had now risen fully and he could see the surroundings in all their glory, although much of the track and buildings were far from glorious and were in need of urgent repair. He saw two young girls walking some greyhounds and asked them if they were their dogs.

"No" one of them replied "these belong to the Lawrence family".

"That's who I'm waiting to see....Arthur....Arthur Lawrence" said Horace. "I'm not sure what time he gets here but he asked me to stop by to pick something up for him".

The other girl advised Horace to keep well away from the Lawrences.

"We both work at the dog track. Our boss, the manager, Mr. Saunders, told the Lawrence's to get off the land and take their dogs with them but they refuse to take the dogs. They rarely come in to walk them so we take pity on them and walk them ourselves from time to time. Mr. Saunders is a nice chap and he dislikes the Lawrences. There is a young girl who hangs around with them. She's a nasty piece of work often throwing her weight around. We saw her the other day hitting a young girl over there by the hut. Mr. Saunders went over but they threatened him so he left them alone. They use the hut as if it belonged to them but it really belongs to the farm behind it.

"Well, I work for a chap who I think may be as bad as the Lawrences, I'm trying to find another job. Do you know where the Lawrence's will be if they're not here, I can't wait for them all day?"

"They have a car lot a couple of streets away. The best way to get to it is over that field, it's just a few minutes' walk but it's a bit early for them to be there. What time were you supposed to meet Arthur?"

"Well, Mr. Fisher told me to get here first thing, so I left at half five to get here. Do they live near here do you know? By the way, I'm Horace, thanks for your help".

"Hello, Horace, I'm Betty and this is Shirley. Yes, they live in Foxworthy Hall on the outer Bedford Road. It's a big sprawling place with wrought iron gates at the front, they all live together. I don't know why they leave the dogs here what with all the land and big stable block they have there".

"Do they win a lot then these dogs?" asked Horace.

Shirley laughed. "Winalot? Like the dog biscuits. Your accent is funny, you're not from these parts, where are you from?"

"I'm from the Midlands that's why I'm early, didn't know how long it would take to get here".

"You said your boss is like the Lawrences, does he come here then?"

"I don't know but you couldn't mistake him, he's the same shape and height as Burl Ives."

"That fat American singer? I saw him at the Gaumont picture house. There is someone a bit like that who comes here about once a month. I think he sells them something, always brings a few packages with him".

"Thanks for telling me where they live. The Bedford Road, whereabouts can I find that then?"

"Go back to the main road" said Betty "turn left and keep going 'til you see the mansion".

The girls said goodbye and walked off in the opposite direction. Horace went back to the hut.

"Did you find anything out, Sol, Piglet?" asked Horace.

"Not yet, might be a longer job than we thought, we'll have to bring some of our expertise to bear".

"OK, this is what I've find out. They have a car lot across the fields and live at Foxworthy Hall on Bedford Road. The whole family lives there. The manager of the track, a Mr. Saunders, wants the Lawrences off the land and to leave this hut, although the hut actually belongs to the farm behind them".

Sol told the Lawrence brothers that it felt as if he and Piglet had just won the pools. All the brothers had to do was die and he and Piglet would possess not only a new car but also a mansion and considerable amount of land.

Horace went to the cob shop to bring back some breakfast. He wouldn't admit it to Sol or Piglet but he felt a little shaky. Despite everything that he'd witnessed over the last few days, and after killing the watchman and turning himself into a makeshift surgeon and removing Sid's tongue and penis, he was still only a young lad after all.

# CHAPTER FOURTEEN

Horace arrived back in Burton mid morning and went straight to the garage. Christine came running out of the house when she heard his motorbike and Gordon emerged from the workshop, both dying to hear the news.

He told them that they had found Charmaine in Luton. She was physically well but suffering emotionally because of the trauma she had been through, all down to Fisher. Fisher had paid three men to capture and abuse her just to spite him and to force him to do his dirty work so as to incriminate and own him just as he'd done to so many others. Christine hugged Horace and apologised for her father being the bastard that he was.

"It's not your fault, Mrs. Rush, you didn't choose your father and you and Gordon are kind and have been very good to me. When we found Charmaine she appeared alright at first but broke down when I returned her to her mum and dad".

"How did you find out that Charmaine had been abused, Horace, was she able to tell you herself?"

"Yes, but she was distraught. Me and two of Uncle Bills' men waited at the dog track where they'd held her and one of the men that turned up bragged about it. They didn't expect to find us there and they certainly didn't bank on how ruthless Uncle Bill's men could be....or me for that matter. I flew into such a rage that I cut his tongue out".

Christine gasped. Horace decided not mention the rest of what he'd done to Sid so as not to embarrass her.

"You did well to get her back, lad" said Gordon. "We were both very worried about you. We knew how much danger you were putting yourself in to save the girl. You are very brave and we are very proud of you. Let's just hope that Charmaine can get over this in the fullness of time".

Christine asked Horace to be patient with her and to not expect her to get over this quickly. She explained that it could take years for Charmaine to come to terms with what had happened and even then it is probably something that will be with her forever.

"Yes, thank you, Mrs. Rush, I know. I could tell when I left her with her parents that she was broken, that she no longer had the look on her face of a happy-go-lucky innocent young girl. I am heartbroken for her".

Christine gave him a kiss and left Horace and Gordon to talk. She knew that Horace adored her but there were probably things that he might be more comfortable discussing alone with Gordon.

"Horace, you can have the day off if you want I expect that you are exhausted mentally and physically after what you've been through".

"I would rather work, thanks, Mr. Rush. It might help to take my mind of things a little. But there is one thing that I must do....I have a present for Mr. Fisher and would like him to receive it as soon as possible".

"What exactly do you mean by 'a present', Horace?"

"I will show you, Mr. Rush. I hope you're not very squeamish and that once I've shown you it will remain just between you and me".

"I'm intrigued, Horace, if a little apprehensive. If you can stand to see this....whatever it is....then I'm sure I'll be fine too".

They walked over to the motorbike. Horace opened the boot of his sidecar and dragged the blood-stained sack forwards then opened it.

Gordon stepped backwards, his eyes wide open and mouth agape.

"What the bloody hell! Horace, who the hell do....did....those belong to?"

"The two Lawrence brothers".

"What do you propose to do with them?"

"Give Fisher the shock of his bloody life. Put them somewhere so only he can find them".

"The only place I can think of is the garage at his house no one but he goes in there, probably because that's one of the places he stores his stuff. But I don't know how you'd get in, it's double locked and he keeps the keys on him. Hang on, it's Chris' birthday today so Fisher will be coming here for tea tonight. That would give you the time you need to do it".

They worked on the bookings the rest of the day. Horace arrived home having gone to Woolworths in Burton on the way to get a present for Chris. When he walked in, Tara, his sister was there with the three kids.

She was asking Eva and George to look after the children, most probably while she went on another shagging spree. Dad told her to "bugger off home" and look after her own kids, not mention husband, Vernon.

"Vernon is always drunk and never pays me any attention. I've met this lovely man, Steve. He's a salesman in Scotland and I'm going with him, he loves me like no other man has".

"What about the others in the last six years of your marriage, did they all love you like no other man? Your legs open and close more times than the Bass rail crossing, you've had more affairs than Lloyd George, you're just a bloody tart. Why don't you start charging you might get enough to buy a meal after a month".

Harsh, thought Horace, but put in such a way that made him laugh inwardly. Tara stormed out taking her poor children with her.

"Aye, our Eva, I don't know which kid you brought home when she was born but I'm glad you had the rest at home, at least I know they're mine. Somewhere in Burton there is a sweet girl that should be here instead".

That upset Eva who thought the world of her first born but was probably the only one in the family that did.

Horace sat next to his dad to have something to eat while his mum trudged upstairs wearily to have a lie down. She usually did that when George was angry about something, especially if he implied wittingly or otherwise that she'd had a part in it.

"Right, son, tell me the truth. Where have you been the last couple of nights because it's nothing to do with work? I'm not as stupid as your mother".

"Well, dad, it's a long story but I will do my best to keep it short. Just before Charmaine and her parents went on one of their BTR trips we saw Fisher talking to two boaters. Charmaine walked past them on the tow path to listen to what they were saying. She overheard them talking about a job at the tyre factory so I went to Inspector Smart. He caught them in the act and arrested them. Fisher put two and two together and kidnapped Charmaine. He got some of his criminal mates in Luton to hold her there. I was desperate and didn't know what to do so went to see Uncle Bill. He got some of his ex-army mates and they waited up at Sinai. Fisher's men followed me there and it didn't end well for them but they told Uncle Bill's men where Charmaine was. I went to Luton with two of his men and got her back. Oh, I forgot, there was also a young girl that came to the garage, one of Fisher's stooges. She ended up at Sinai too where she will stay for the rest of eternity with the others".

"What happened when you found Charmaine, son?"

"We found her at the dog track in a big hut where they'd raped her repeatedly. Dad, I can't tell you what we did to the men that did this to her, and never will because I don't want you to think the worse of me. All I can say is that it was an ordeal for the poor, innocent girl and she will never be the same again. When I took her back to her mum and dad she broke down and wept uncontrollably. They've ruined her life".

"Son, I will never think the worse of you and after all that you've been through you had to come home and listen to that sister of yours banging on about her boyfriend. Bill is the best of the bunch, that's why I asked him to take you and Ron under his wing. With my ill health I knew that I wouldn't be able to spend time with you doing the things that you enjoy the most, shooting, fishing and being in the great outdoors. And to think, we spent four years, well, three and a bit in my case, during The Great War wishing that we were safe and sound, indoors. It brings tears to my eyes when I think of the four uncles you never knew. Not a mark on them, until they all went in the same week to the battle of Amiens on the 8th of August 1918. That was the start of the one hundred day campaign. That was an outing I wouldn't wish anyone to go on, Horace, it was hell".

*Author's Note: The Great War, or First World War as it came to be known after WWII, was triggered by a series of events following the assassination of Archduke Franz-Ferdinand of Austria and his pregnant wife Sophie in Sarajevo on 28th June 1914. The Bosnian Serb, Gavrilo Princip, a member of the revolutionary group Young Bosnia, carried out the assassination. But the geopolitical situation in Europe was extremely complex and there were many factors that led to the start of The Great War. Historians still debate the predominant causes to this day.*

*Great Britain, France and Russia were part of the Triple Entente which itself resulted from different alliances – The Franco-Russian Alliance and the Entente Cordiale between Great Britain and France – which primary aim was the peaceful resolution of colonial disputes. However, the Triple Entente did not mandate that member nations were obliged to defend any of the others in the event of conflict.*

*Austria-Hungary, known at the time as the Austro-Hungarian Empire, was a great power in Central Europe and part of the Triple Alliance with Germany and Italy. One month after the assassination (a month that became known as the July Crisis) and backed by Germany, Austria-Hungary declared war on Serbia on 28th July 1914. But Austria-Hungary was nervous about the reaction of the Russian Empire, which supported the Serbian cause. Germany too feared that a conflict between Austria-Hungary and Russia would lead to Russian troops amassing on or near its borders.*

*Great Britain and Germany had friendly diplomatic relations but attempts at mediation to reduce the tensions failed. The German military strategy in a conflict with Russia was to attack and defeat France through Belgium in the west before turning to face Russia in the east. Germany declared war on France on 3rd August 1914 and invaded Belgium the day after. Feeling that it had a moral responsibility to defend its allies, Great Britain declared war on Germany on 4th August 1914. But some say that the decision to go to war was influenced in part by the increase in size and power of the German navy, which Great Britain regarded as a potential threat to its empire.*

Fisher's car was at the garage when Horace arrived to give Chris his present. He knocked on the door and handed it to Gordon saying that he would see him the next day. Gordon stepped outside so that he was out of earshot and asked Horace whether he was still planning to go to Fisher's that evening with his 'present'.

"Yes, Mr. Rush, I'm going there now. I thought I'd park by the side of Barton Autos and go over the back field".

"OK, I'll ply him with whiskey to keep him distracted. He won't leave 'til the bottle's empty".

Horace drove to Barton Autos, took the macabre sack out of the boot and walked over the fields to Fisher's house. He put the sack down by the side of the garage and went to garage's back door, but it was padlocked. It would be far too risky to try to enter through the double doors at the front in case anyone saw him and besides, the doors were chained and padlocked.

He had a look around but couldn't find another way in. He wondered whether Fisher might keep a set of spare keys in the house. The doors to the house were all locked so he tried the windows but the only one that was open was the upstairs bathroom window at the rear of the house, which conveniently had a cast iron drain pipe that ran up beside it. He climbed up it, managed to reach over and grab the window ledge and haul himself head first through the opening, knocking over a number of toiletries in the process. He rearranged everything on the window sill and had a scout around the bedrooms but found nothing. He rifled through the books and bric-a-brac in an antique oak cupboard on the landing, being careful to leave everything tidy and in order afterwards, but there was nothing there either.

He decided to head downstairs and went into the kitchen. He spied a toby jug sitting on top of one of the cabinets, the perfect place to leave the odd loose items. He tipped it over gently into the cupped palm of his hand and out came some tacks, coins and a key ring with a number of old keys threaded onto it. He wedged the back door open so that he could get back in to return the keys to the jug and went to the back door of the garage to try them out.

This will take a while, he thought to himself. Starting from one side of the ring he tried in sequence the ones that looked likely to fit and was getting dispirited when the last but one key clicked and the padlock sprung open. He almost did a little dance. He crept around to retrieve that sack and took it into the garage.

Now, he thought, where best to leave these for maximum

effect? A tool rack hung on the back wall with, amongst many other things, a neat row of long hook picks. He selected one of the appropriate length took Arthur's head out of the sack and placed it on a bench. Horace wasn't a specialist in anatomy and more by luck than judgement inserted the pick just below and slightly in front of the ear. It found its way through the hole just above the back of the jaw in front of the occipital bone. He pushed and wriggled the pick until it tore through muscle and tissue to emerge at the other side of the head, along with some pieces of mucous covered human meat. There was no blood, it had already drained out. It was hard work and he was sweating. He tied some string to the bent end of the pick and pulled it back through, much more easily than it had gone in.

He repeated the procedure with Sid's head, the whole process had taken about half an hour, and stood back to figure out the best place to hang them. He decided on a joist above the double doors. Yes, that would certainly give Fisher a nice surprise when he opened the garage.

He had a quick look around and underneath the tool rack was a desk with some files and a phone on it. There was a small safe beside the desk underneath some shelving. He tried to move it but it was too heavy, he wouldn't have been able to get it in the sidecar anyway.

He picked up the sack to burn later, locked the padlock on the garage backdoor, went into the kitchen through the backdoor and dropped the keys in the toby jug, which he put back on top of the cabinet. He pulled the door shut hearing it click as it locked, walked back to his motorbike and rode home feeling very pleased with himself.

Horace arrived at the garage bright and early the next morning. Fisher's car was still there, which upset him because it meant that he wouldn't yet have discovered what was in his garage. Gordon had either taken him home or he'd stayed the night. Horace carried on and did the usual opening the workshop and the pumps and then started work on a car that was waiting to be serviced. He worked for a couple of hours flitting between the pumps and workshop 'til Monica arrived and manned the kiosk. They chatted for a few minutes, smoked a cigarette and had a brew. It was half ten when the door of the house opened and Gordon emerged. He blinked in the daylight and shaded his eyes with his hand. He looked grey and pretty unwell.

"Are you alright, Mr. Rush?" Horace shouted across to him "you look dreadful".

"I did my bit, Horace, and kept him drinking all night".

"Did you drive Fisher back in that state Mr. Rush?"

"No, Horace, he and Jean stayed the night. Jean is up but the fat man is still snoring. As soon as he wakes up he'll want a fried breakfast so could you do me a favour and nip down to Dewies to get some bacon, sausage and eggs? We have some but Jean said that he will want a pan-full just for himself. Have you done the Minx, what about the Pullman?"

"It's just the air filter still to do on the Pullman. I've got to go down to Routs for one so I'll call in at Dewies on the way back. What shall I do when I get back, come over and provide the entertainment?"

"Very funny. Job wise I think that's the lot, but you can clean all my mess up if you want. I don't know how you keep your area so clean all the time. Anyway, thanks for all you've done this morning. By the way, how did you get on last night?"

"I broke in through the bathroom window. It took me over an hour to find the keys to the back door of the garage. They were in a toby jug on top of a kitchen cabinet. I left the heads dangling at just the right high for him to kiss them when he opens the double doors. He'll get the shock of his life when he sees them".

"Well done, Horace. He was drawling on after a skin full last night about two of his men coming back today and that they'd be rolling in money".

"Good luck to him with that then, Mr. Rush. The two he was on about are from the tyre factory job and they are both resting up at Sinai, if you know what I mean. The lorry's probably hundreds of miles away by now, minus the tyres".

"You are joking, Horace. How many are buried up there, it sounds like that old fashioned western Shoot Out at the OK Corral. Oh, and thanks for the Meccano set you bought Chris, you shouldn't have spent so much money".

"It's the least I can do. Don't forget you gave me a job at

fourteen and with decent money too. Engineering is the future now so when Chris leaves school there will be jobs in abundance for him to choose from. Look how it's all come on in your lifetime, Mr. Rush. Just look at the brewery industry around here, bigger and better equipment all the time".

"You're right there, Horace, and that's probably the route I will steer him down when the time comes".

Horace got on his bike and went down to Burton to get the air filter and ingredients for Fisher's mammoth breakfast. Fisher was up by the time he got back, you could hear him above the noise of Horace's BSA as he pulled in.

"Your friend is on top form this morning" said Monica "he's been barking orders and shouting for the last ten minutes".

Hearing Horace's bike, Fisher stuck his head round the door.

"Hey! You, have you got the provisions for us, bring them here now, can't you see the time?"

Horace walked over to Gordon's front door and held out the bag.

"You miserable old bastard, I know what time it is I've been up for five hours. I bet your neighbours are pleased you're here this morning it gives them a break but keep your voice down, you're upsetting our customers and the local residents. Look, Mrs. Jackson over the road is waving a white flag, she's had enough already. I pity Mrs. Fisher but she'll be alright soon won't she, you're due another stretch in the clink".

"One day you're going to push me too far and then you will be sorry".

Fisher snatched the bag and stepped back to slam the door but not before he heard Horace say....

"By the way, you old fart, Veronica and her dad asked to be remembered to you but said they won't be seeing you again, not in this world. But they'll be waiting for you in the next, in hell that is".

Horace walked back to the kiosk chuckling to himself and shaking his head.

Monica was horrified. "Horace, how do you dare you talk to him like that, even Gordon is scared stiff of him. Christine told me that last week when he was here throwing his weight about".

"Monica, if I go missing you'll know who did it. But he doesn't bother me, not at all. I've known nastier people than him".

While they were talking, Jean brought out a plate of bacon and egg sandwiches for them both.

"Horace, I don't know what you said to him but it got him worried, I've never seen him so quiet".

## CHAPTER FIFTEEN

Horace was at home eating dinner with his mum and dad. He told them that after dinner he was going to Bladon Woods to help Uncle Bill for the weekend and that he would see them on Monday.

At the woods Bill asked him how he got on in Luton.

"I've not seen Sol and Piglet since you went to Luton, did you find Charmaine?"

"Yes, Uncle Bill, we found her in a hut at the dog track".

He proceeded to explain the events in detail as they had unfolded from the time he arrived to the time he departed, including the state that Charmaine was in when he dropped her off at her parent's boat and that she should be back in Burton in a week or two.

"You haven't told me about Sol and Piglet, Horace, where they are, what they're up to. You left together and I thought that you would return together".

"I think that they're both still up in Luton. The Lawrences owned a car lot and mansion with loads of land. They ran quite an operation up there. The opportunity was too good for Sol and Piglet to miss. They, shall we say, persuaded the Lawrences to sign a statement saying that they had lost everything to them in a card game".

"Bill, George, you carry on with what you're doing on the hut, I'm going for a trip to Luton with Horace. Call in on the way home to get some plasterboard for Monday, and be careful with the van you've only just passed your test. Come on, Horace, I'll try out that sidecar of yours, I hope it's as comfortable as Angelica said it is".

Uncle Bill got in and lit his pipe and all but disappeared from view. Horace opened the vent that he'd fitted to the top of the sidecar and a small mushroom cloud of smoke billowed out, followed by smaller pulsating bursts each time his uncle sucked on the pipe and exhaled.

"Thanks Horace. I've always told Sol and Piglet to keep a low profile but do they listen to a word I say? It's like those bloody tyres, I told them to leave them up there".

Horace kick started the bike and they set off. Bill was impressed. He could stretch out and almost lie down fully but the seat was reclined at just the right angle for him to relax but be able to see out. Horace had tried to fit a ratchet system to the base of the seat to make it adjustable but hadn't had the time. Adjustable, reclining seats was something he felt would become standard in all vehicles in the not too distant future.

After about an hour and a half they stopped at Northampton Railway Station for a cup of tea and a fag before driving the rest of the way to Luton to the car lot just around the corner from the dog track.

"This can't be it, Horace, there must be fifty cars or more here".

They both wandered around looking at the cars and were impressed not only with the size of the place but also the cars that were on display. A gentleman who must have been in his late fifties or early sixties came out of the prefab office and approached them.

"Can I help you two gents? We have some lovely motors here".

"Yes, you do indeed have some very good cars here. Is this your place?" Uncle Bill asked him.

"No sir, I just work here, first day actually. The place is under new management, the last owners lost it together with their house in a card game and I understand that the legal side of things has all been signed and sealed".

"I bet they're pissed off about it aren't they?" asked Horace, "I don't know what I would do if that happened to me. Where are the losers now?"

"Nobody knows, sir. They disappeared, probably because they were devastated and embarrassed. Not even the rest of the family knows where they are".

"So who won everything?" asked Uncle Bill.

"It's two out-of-town gentlemen, and very nice they are too. If nothing here takes your fancy there's another lot three blocks away, that's where the new owners are".

"I like the look of this Daimler" said Uncle Bill, "can I have a test drive?"

"Of course, sir, I will just lock up and we'll go for a ride".

They got in and Bill drove the car around the outskirts of town.

"This handles very nicely, how much is it?"

"It's on that label in the corner of the windscreen, passenger side".

"What is your name?" asked Uncle Bill.

"Bert Lawrence, cousin of the previous owners".

"Aren't you pissed off that your family lost their business on a card game?"

"Not me, sir, my cousins stole it from me in the first place. The gentlemen that bought it....won it I should say....told me that I will be a partner so it's win-win for me".

Horace asked how they had taken the business off him in the first place.

"They must have forged my dad's will when he died. The family never really got on. My dad's brother, their father, was a villain and so were they. They've had me in their grip for four years".

Uncle Bill drove into the second car lot a few blocks away from where they'd picked up the Daimler and pulled up outside the office. Bert got out and walked over to it looking every part of the salesman. He turned and said to Bill....

"I will go and ask their best price for you, sir".

Sol and Piglet were grinning when they peered through office window at the two sitting in the car but wondered why they hadn't come in themselves. Sol thanked Bert and asked him to tell the two gentlemen to come in and for him to take the Daimler back to the other car lot.

"We'll have a chat about it when we walk back over there, Bert" said Sol.

Bert took the car keys from Uncle Bill and both he and Horace walked into the office.

"What the hell are you doing here?" barked Uncle Bill, "didn't I say to keep a low profile when you came up here? Not to get yourselves noticed. Now look at you, you've only gone and taken over the business of the ones who abducted Charmaine ".

"Sorry skip" said Sol, "this was too good an opportunity to turn down and with Bert up here taking care of things we won't have to spend all of our time up this way. You should hear Bert's story about the Lawrences and what a bunch of shysters they were".

Bill told them that Bert had already explained everything.

"So how did you meet Bert, very strange to find him the first day you took over?"

Piglet recounted the events.

"Horace found out a lot about the Lawrences so we decided to look into it, what with them having the dogs, the car lots and the big house. We got Arthur and Sid to sign a statement handing it all over, it wasn't difficult, and then finished them off. We cleaned up then went to the pub for a bite to eat. We met Bert at the bar, what are the chances. He'd had a few and started to tell us about his woes, that he'd lost his business to some crooked family members and would do anything to get rid of them. We got him to witness the statement and he got four other blokes to sign and witness it too. Bert agreed to be equal partners with us".

"What about the others who witnessed the statement, what do they get out of it?"

"They're Bert's good mates. He promised them that he would see them right. We're going to come up here once a month".

"What did you do with the Lawrence brothers, Sol?"

"Well, parts are buried deep behind the hut on farm land other parts at the end of the car lot just inside the wire fence, but we don't know what happened to the heads. Horace what happened to the heads?"

"What does he mean by 'what happened to the heads', Horace? Why the hell did you want the heads and what did you do with them?"

"Uncle Bill....I hung them up just inside Fisher's garage door so he'll get one hell of a shock when he opens up, he'll find them there staring at him. Maybe enough to give him a heart attack and finish him off".

"You're a sick little bastard, Horace. How'd you hang them up?"

"Threaded string through their ears, Uncle Bill".

"Horace, I've done some things in my time but that takes the biscuit. You can't thread string through a human skull, it's too thick".

"You can if you ram a sharp hook pick through first, well, just below the ear above the jaw. Tie the string to the bent pointed side and pull it back though again. Takes a few minutes and it's a bit messy. I kept thinking about what they'd done to poor Charmaine, it gave me the strength to do it".

"So, who cut the Heads off? I hope it wasn't you, son, because that would mean I'd gone too far with you. Your dad wanted me to teach you about life and train you to be tough enough to survive if there was another war. Many soldiers die because they aren't well enough mentally prepared and hesitate at those split second life and death moments. We've seen it time and again, son. There may never be another war but the world has seen two in the last thirty five years or so. Those wars shaped our outlook and attitudes, for better or for worse".

"No, Uncle Bill, it was Sol and Piglet who sawed the heads off, but I asked them to. I was so angry about what they did to Charmaine and I have no doubt I would be capable of doing it myself next time. I killed the Lawrence's watchman and looked him in the eyes as I did it".

"Horace, son, you've been through more than a sixteen year old should ever go through and it's all to do with Brian Fisher. You've become mixed up in something that is outside your control through no fault of your own but I want you to promise me that you won't start to believe that this type of thing is normal. If you do, you will take a path that leads to nothing but destruction. I was in Japan with Sol and Piglet. We saw and did some terrible things and it takes very strong personalities to keep a balance and to separate the two types of existence".

"Yes, skip" Sol chimed in, "the war will stay in Japan. We did everything we could in the last couple of weeks to help good friends to stand up to some very bad and dangerous people. But this is England in peacetime, how about trying to lighten things up a bit tonight by watching our dogs race then going to the pub afterwards? I will book some rooms at the Horse and Jockey, we can get legless and stagger upstairs afterwards".

"Well, Sol, that sounds like a great idea. I haven't been to the dogs for years".

Piglet told him he thought that Bill had gone to the dog's years ago. Bill grabbed him and they punched each other and wrestled playfully, some papers fluttered off the desk onto the floor and tea cups went flying. Horace and Sol watched and laughed out loud encouraging one and then the other.

They arrived at the Horse and Jockey and went to their rooms to freshen up and have a rest. When they met downstairs an hour or two later Bill told Horace that what happens in Luton stays in Luton. Horace wasn't quite sure what he meant but smiled and agreed anyway. They ate some grub, had a few beers and went to the dog track. Sol and Piglet's newly acquired greyhounds looked in fine fettle. Beth recognised Horace and came up to him.

"What are you doing here, Horace? I didn't know that you knew these two. What a welcome change they are to the Lawrences. Mr. Saunders nearly did a little dance when they showed him the statement proving that they were the new owners. The Lawrences were trying to get a controlling share of the track but Mr. Salzman [Sol] and Mr. Squiller [Piglet] said they would transfer all of their shares to Mr. Saunders in exchange for lifetime memberships".

Beth advised Horace to put all of his money 'to win' on the dog she'd been looking after, Baltray Prince. He'd broken the track record in the last couple of days.

"There are only three of us who know that, Horace, well, four now that I've told you. He's in great form. We've been feeding him foxglove flowers and seeds. There's a trainer in Ireland who swears by them. He goes like shit off a hot shovel....the dog that is, not the trainer" she added giggling. "Come and buy me a drink and meet my friends before the race starts".

"How many girls work here?"

"There are around twenty girls working here as kennel lasses, and they all like a nice boy" she winked at Horace. "It's really strange, though, since you were here yesterday the Lawrences have disappeared. No one knows where they are, as if anyone cares, the rest of the family were quite glad to see the back of them. Up until a few years ago, Bert and his father owned the car lots, the big house and a bookmaker's down Solway Road".

"Well, Beth, my uncle and his friends have a way of persuading villains to behave properly. They were in the Royal Marines and fought in Japan during the war so not many can resist their charms. What do you think of old Bert? The saying goes that the apple doesn't fall far from the tree, especially a well established tree".

"Horace, Bert is the sweetest and most honest man I've ever known, he wouldn't do a bad turn to anyone. Even after he'd lost everything he had he picked himself up and started again. He did odd jobs for people then started his own building company and when he had some success and had built a few houses his cousins took that off him as well. Now they're gone, and I hope for good".

"What I can tell you, Beth, is that they definitely won't be coming back again".

"That will certainly please Dorothy over there. Arthur took her".

"What do you mean 'took' her, Beth?"

"Arthur and his brother forced her into that hut and, well, took her virginity. She said that they both carried on until she couldn't take anymore. When Mr. Saunders found out about it a few days later he told them to get out and never come back but Arthur threatened him with a gun. Poor Mr. Saunders, and Dorothy, the Lawrences were just too mean and powerful for anyone to do anything without putting their lives at risk".

"Beth, I lied to you when I first met you and Shirley on the track the other day. The fat man I told you about, Fisher, is not my boss. He got the Lawrences together with a girl called Veronica to kidnap my girlfriend. She must have been the one you saw being hit and forced into the shed. The Lawrences and another man raped her repeatedly".

"She is your girlfriend, Horace? How terrible for you both, where is she now?"

"On a canal boat back with her family, they are boaters. I don't know if or when I will see her again. I wonder sometimes whether it would be best not to, I'm not sure what I could say to her to make things better".

"You will when the time comes. Take Dot, she still hasn't got over her ordeal with the Lawrences and says that it will be with her for the rest of her life but there has to be someone, another man, who can help to restore her confidence and let her lead a normal life".

Dot saw Horace and Beth talking and came over to meet them. Beth told her about what had happened to Horace's girlfriend and how he and his uncle and friends had come to be in Luton. Dot took Horace's arm.

"Swear I will never see them again, Horace. It will help me to come to terms with happened to me, I still have nightmares every night".

She clung tightly to Horace's arm.

"Dot, I swear. The only place that you will ever see them is in your nightmares and I hope that means that you probably see them less and less now you know that they've gone".

She kissed him on the cheek affectionately and thanked him for his reassurance and kind words.

Bert shouted over to them that the first race was about to start. He invited them all to join Mr. Saunders in his office at the top of the stadium. Mr. Saunders shook their hands and asked whether they were staying at the Horse and Jockey, which they confirmed.

"Then your stay is on me" said Saunders, "you can rely on that any time you are in Luton, you won't pay a penny for lodgings, food or drink. Whatever happened to the Lawrences is a blessing, not only to me but to the whole community. And don't expect the police to ask any questions about them either".

Bill thanked him for his hospitality and asked why he'd said that the police weren't likely to pursue the matter.

"Well, Bill, two police officers went missing over the last three years, one was a sergeant and the other a constable. Superintendent Richards knew that the Lawrence brothers had something to do with it but they always had people to vouch for their whereabouts and he couldn't get sufficient evidence to prosecute them."

Bert added....

"Hear hear. I would also like to thank you all for getting my property back. When I have sorted out Foxworthy Hall you will always be welcome to stay there too whenever you come here. Unfortunately, the Lawrences made a mess of it inside, they led murky lives and lived in a correspondingly squalid home but I will put it right myself. So, let's drink to Foxworthy....Oh! I almost forgot, gentlemen and ladies, I also owned a bookies so if it's alright with you, Sol and Selwyn [Piglet] we will ask Mr. Saunders to have an equal share in it and manage the place".

Sol and Piglet both agreed to the proposition without any hesitation whatsoever.

"Splendid. Please call me Melvin" interjected Mr. Saunders, "now that we are business partners".

The dogs were waiting expectantly in the traps. The lure shot past them, the trap doors flew open and the dogs loped out with their backs arching and hind legs digging into the turf propelling them forwards at great speed. It didn't take long for them to accelerate and for the melee of blurred creatures at the start to extend out into a line as the faster dogs powered forward. Baltray Prince flew into the lead as if his 'arse was on fire'. Within twenty seconds he was ten lengths ahead of the rest and by the fourth lap was starting to overtake the rear dogs.

"What a one sided race" said Bert, "how can a dog win by so much, it's impossible."

Melvin explained that it was because Baltray would probably have to go up to the next class with the faster dogs but on that performance was likely to beat anything. Those that bet on Baltray Prince made a small but not inconsiderable amount of money.

After the last race, the guests and their hosts went back to the Horse and Jockey for some more refreshments. The two girls went with them.

Dorothy sidled up to and leant against Horace.

"Horace, I have something to ask you but please don't take this the wrong way. Can I stay with you tonight? I can't or won't be able to do anything but I need to start trusting another man. You are one of the most genuine and kind young men that I have met and I would love to just cuddle up to you".

"Dot, I would love for you to stay and be close to me. I can't do anything either because I don't want to be dishonourable to you or....well, Charmaine. She is in my thoughts all the time".

They both went upstairs and slept together fully clothed hugging each other. The next morning they went down for breakfast and Uncle Bill was there with a woman that he'd befriended at the dog track. Horace twigged what Uncle Bill had meant when he'd said what happens in Luton stays in Luton.

"Morning, Horace, Dorothy. We'll head back home after breakfast, son, nothing further we need to do up here now that we've met everyone and seen how well things are being handled. I hope that you two had a good night".

"Mr. Reece, he's been nothing but a gentleman. I had, shall we say, an unfortunate experience a few months ago and Horace was very kind, he respected and helped me".

"Well Dorothy, that's what I've tried to teach him, to have respect for and be a companion to those who deserve it".

Piglet and Sol came down with Bert Lawrence, Bert placed some keys on the table in front of Uncle Bill.

"We had a wonderful night at the stadium, a wonderful night all round" he said to them all.

Bill looked at the key fob, it was a Daimler key fob.

"What are these for Bert, it's the Daimler I test drove yesterday isn't it?"

"Yes, Bill, it's your car now. These boys told me that they wouldn't have come up here if it wasn't for you. Horace, when you're seventeen and driving I will have something special for you too. Don't be a stranger, young man, you will always have a place to stay and friends to be with when you come to Luton. Bill, I have to talk to you before you go, I have a proposition for you".

They finished their hearty breakfasts together and parted the best of friends. Horace went back to the track with Dorothy to bid them all farewell, and especially Beth and Shirley. Dorothy cuddled him and kissed him on the lips and Beth too gave him a smacker on the lips thanking him for helping her best friend.

Horace departed on his motorbike and Bill in his new Daimler. They stopped and met up at Northampton Railway Station for a rest and cup of tea, as they'd done on the way up.

"Horace, this is a fantastic car, a poor man's Rolls Royse. Your Aunt Mavis will be so surprised when I park it outside the house".

"What did Bert want to talk to you about, Uncle Bill, you both looked quite serious and businesslike?"

"Bert wanted some advice on submitting a tender for new council houses that are going to be built in Luton. He wanted me to go into partnership if he gets the work and I agreed. If he does get it, I'll have to come up here a couple of times a week but it'll be a doddle in this lovely, comfortable machine".

# CHAPTER SIXTEEN

Brian Fisher went out to his garage on Sunday morning after he and Jean had spent the evening with Gordon and Christine celebrating Christopher's birthday. He was still feeling a little delicate after polishing off a bottle of whisky with Gordon.

He unlocked the padlock and opened the double doors. It took about second for his eyes to adjust to the darkness inside and for the two objects that hung down at head height just behind the doors to come into sharp focus.

Brian screamed and staggered backwards falling over onto the paving stones of his drive. He scuttled backwards on his backside scrabbling with his hands in the dust and grit to push his not inconsiderable bulk away as quickly as he could from what he was looking at.

Jean came running out when she saw her husband's undignified backwards shuffle.

"What the hell is the matter, Brian?" she called out.

"Get away from here, Jean, get back into the fucking house".

But it was too late. She turned and saw the heads hanging there swinging slightly from side to side as the breeze caught them, they stared at her with half closed eyes and downturned mouths. She didn't register at first what exactly she was looking at but her perplexed expression soon turned to horror as her brain processed the images and informed the prefrontal cortex that it had better get on and do something.

That something was a scream. At first it was an undulating moan that grew in intensity and volume transforming itself into a scream of such volume and pitch that it's surprising the glass in the windows didn't shatter.

Dogs started to bark further down the street.

"Shut up you silly cow, go back in the house and don't do anything. Leave this to me" hissed Fisher.

He turned so that he could kneel and gradually picked himself up. He ran over to her and grabbed her by the arms.

"You're not telling me to do anything....ever again" she heard her voice scream into his face, which was now flecked with her spittle. "I am going to phone the police. I'm going to phone the police".

She shook her arms about until he lost his grip. She turned to run back into the house but he grabbed her hand as she did so pulled her back and hit her across the face so hard that she could only stand there blinking through the tears. She backed away from him a couple of paces, leant forward and started to run. She ran past him brushing his shoulder knocking him off balance and carried on running, to where not even she knew, she just ran and ran.

Fisher had more pressing things to do than run after her. He got a knife and cut the heads down letting them thud into a wheelbarrow that he'd placed underneath them. There was no way that he had the stomach to manhandle them.

He rushed into the garage and got a spade knocking over his other gardening implements in the process. He lay the spade on top of the wheelbarrow and pushed it up the path, through a gate and into the back of the adjacent field. He pushed until the sweat ran in rivulets down his face and his shirt was soaking wet at the back and under his armpits. The spade clanked as the wheelbarrow bumped over tufts of grass. He stopped half way across the field to catch his breath and glanced down. One of the heads had tipped sideways appearing to be whispering something into the other's ear but the other one stared up at him accusingly. He threw up. When sufficiently concealed by some bushes and small saplings at the top of the field, he dug a hole and tipped the heads in. He filled the hole as quickly as he could and stamped down the sods of earth with both feet.

He sat on the freshly created mound and put his head in his hands. Who the hell could have done this? No one from Luton apart from the Lawrence brothers knew where he came from except, that is, for the little tramp Veronica, she knew. It must be her he thought, not knowing why or even that Veronica had herself already met the same fate as the heads.

Meanwhile, Horace was returning from Luton and passing through Overseal just a few miles from Burton. He decided to cut through to Walton to see his other uncle, Uncle George. He had some lunch and after about an hour rode back through the lanes. As he was doing so a woman came towards him running and stumbling in equal measure down the centre of the road, possibly heading towards Stapenhill. He slowed down as she approached, he could hear she was wailing and sobbing.

He pulled up in front of her and dismounted. He hadn't yet recognised her because her face was very swollen, red and the tears had smudged her makeup. But she had recognised him and fell on her knees at his feet. He knelt down to lift her up and then he realised who it was.

"Mrs .Fisher! What happened to you? Are you alright?"

She sobbed but couldn't answer so he helped her into the sidecar and rushed her to the infirmary. When they got there he lifted Mrs. Fisher out of the sidecar and carried her into the building shouting to the nurses to come and help. Two nurses came and Horace helped them to take Mrs. Fisher into a curtained cubicle and lay her on a bed. She had trouble breathing, her face was swollen and perhaps her windpipe was constricted too. The sister called for a doctor immediately and one appeared almost straight away.

"Quick nurse" he said urgently "get a piece of tube, we're going to perform a tracheotomy".

After the procedure was complete the doctor went to Horace who was in the waiting room drinking a mug of tea.

"What happened, young man?"

"She was running down the road in distress, I saw her coming towards me as I rode my motorbike. I know who she is, doctor, her name is Mrs. Jean Fisher".

The doctor asked him whether he could get the family there as quickly as possible. In addition to the tracheotomy he said that further urgent treatment was going to be necessary. He suspected that her jaw was broken, hence the pronounced swelling on the left side of her face.

"We are waiting for the results of the x-ray to confirm how badly her jaw has been damaged. Her condition has stabilised a little but she is still in grave danger and she may not make it through the night".

Horace walked over to the nursing station and asked whether he could use the phone. He called Gordon. Not wishing to tell Christine he disguised his voice and asked to speak to Mr. Rush. Gordon came to the phone so Horace related to him what had happened.

"Please come to the infirmary as soon as possible, Mr. Rush, if you bring Chris I will look after him".

It wasn't long before Gordon, Christine and Christine's sister Ruth rushed through the door with Chris in tow. Horace took little Chris to the Gaumont picture house to see a Marx Brothers film, it lasted only an hour so, not long enough for the child to get bored. But Horace's mind was elsewhere. What had happened to her and why was she so distraught and running away? It didn't cross his mind then and there that it might be something to do with the heads that he'd hung in Fisher's garage although it must surely be something that Fisher had done.

Chris was laughing along with everyone else, not understanding the dialogue but appreciating the slapstick and japes. Better there than being in the hospital with Chris asking him questions all the time, most of which he wouldn't be able to answer even if he wanted to. After the film, Horace took Chris for a walk along the canal tow path mainly hoping to see whether Charmaine was there but he knew that Chris loved seeing the horses in the stables anyway. When they got to Horninglow Basin one of the boater's wives gave Chris a string dog that she'd made, he loved it and thanked the lady politely. The Hackett's boat was not there.

It started to drizzle so they rushed back to the hospital. Horace's bike was in the car park so he lifted Chris into the sidecar to use up some more time. Chris was delighted to be in his own special compartment and vibrated his lips to imitate the sound that Horace's bike made when he drove into his dad's garage. But it didn't take long for the boredom to set in with that particular game so Horace lifted him out and they went into the infirmary waiting room and sat down. Horace was immediately called upon to explain that they were there because grandma had fallen over and hurt her face and she needed a lot of rest.

Ruth was outside the cubicle and overheard Horace and Chris talking and went back to tell Christine and Gordon how patient and caring he was being with the child.

"Yes, they have a good relationship. Horace has been coming to the garage asking for a job ever since he was ten, around the time that Chris was born. Martin was really good with Horace too and he was really upset when Martin left a few years ago to find other work".

The doctors came into the cubicle and said that Mrs. Fisher would have to undergo surgery straight away. The tracheotomy was doing its job but her heart was irregular so they had to act quickly in case it weakened further but they needed the next of kin to consent to the operation.

Ruth leant forward over her mum and asked in a whisper where Brian was but her mum couldn't talk, she just raised a hand and made a shooing motion, her eyes stern and fixed on her daughter.

"The bastard doesn't even know she's here" Ruth turned and hissed to Gordon and Christine.

Mrs. Fisher then raised her hand and pointed to her face.

"Dad did this to you, mum, he hit you?"

She nodded gently then turned her gaze away.

Christine told the doctors that she and Ruth were Mrs. Fisher's daughters and that she consented for the operation to go ahead. Two nurses came in a few moments later and wheeled Mrs. Fisher, along with the drip feed and other paraphernalia to which she was attached, out of the cubicle and towards the operating theatre.

"I hate that man" said Ruth when they were alone, "he had something to do with Simon's death now he has done this to mum.

I will never call him 'dad' ever again. He is nothing to me....I never want to see him again".

A nurse returned and told them that the best place for them is at home. The surgery would take most of the night and they would call in the morning to let them know how things had gone. They all went back to Gordon and Christine's house, except Horace, who went home to tell his mum and dad about what had happened.

"It wouldn't surprise me one bit if that man kills someone, if he hasn't already" said Eva, "he's been a bad person all of his life. It's true that much of it has been troubled, even at school, and when it came for him to serve his country he claimed that he was a conscientious objector".

"Yes, Horace, your four uncles and many of my best friends were killed fighting for King and country and someone like Fisher walks around up to no good having shirked his duty and responsibility, the fucking coward".

"George, could you please stop using those words in this house, you should have left them behind on the battle field".

"Eva, people have been using words like that even before we were thought of and they will continue to use them long after we've gone, so don't come over all high and mighty. I'm just telling Horace that people like Fisher don't deserve to breathe the same air that we do, and I'm sticking to it".

The next morning, Horace went to work as usual. He opened the workshop and pumps and worked for two hours on the booked in cars when Mr. Simnett brought in his Jaguar.

"Morning, Horace, is Gordon about? I went to do a photo shoot at Warwick Castle yesterday and some clown reversed into my front right wing. The bugger took off and no one wrote down the registration number. I actually saw him do it but from where I was I couldn't see the number plate".

"Let me have a look for you, Mr. Simnett".

He felt the dent on the outside and rubbed his hand under the wing.

"Give me a couple of minutes while I take the wheel off".

He fetched the jack and wheel brace and removed the wheel. When it was off he brought over a foot long block of oak and a hammer, got underneath the car and hit the dent twice. It popped back out again without leaving a crack on the paintwork. If you looked down the line of the wing you could just about see where it was but it was barely noticeable, Mr. Simnett couldn't see a thing.

"Horace, my lad, how did you manage to do that? I can't even see where it is now. You've saved me a lot of money there, if I had gone anywhere else they would have fleeced me".

Horace had just finished putting the wheel back on when the bell rang outside, a car had pulled up alongside the pumps.

"How much do I owe you for that Horace?"

"Nothing Mr. Simnett, you're a good customer. Excuse me one moment, Mr. Simnett, I just need to serve this customer".

He went over to the pumps.

"Good morning, Jane, how're the horses these days, more important, how's your mum?"

"Mum is a lot better thanks, Horace, she will be out of hospital in a few days and it's about time you came riding again, you haven't been up for at least a couple of months".

"Yes, sorry, I've been so busy at weekends helping Uncle Bill, but I promise I will come over soon".

Gordon came out of the house to find Leslie Simnett standing in front of his car with his hands on his hips leaning sideways first to the right and then to the left.

"Morning Gordon, I was at a photo shoot yesterday and some arse reversed into my front wing, put a hell of a dent in it. Can you tell which one it is?"

Gordon stood beside Leslie and had a look. He knew which one it was because he'd seen Horace working on it from the landing window.

"I think it's this one" he said, "the driver's side".

Leslie was surprised but Gordon chuckled.

"Well, Leslie, the only reason I know is because I saw Horace do it from the house, he did a hell of a job didn't he".

"Yes, he did, Gordon, you had me going there. The lad said that there was no charge but I thought I should check with you before I go".

"How long did it take him to do it, and what parts did he use?"

"Ten minutes tops, a lump of wood and a hammer, no car parts".

"Then, Leslie" Gordon smiled broadly, "like Horace said....no charge. Don't worry, Leslie, we will get it back over time with your loyal custom".

"Well, thank you both, I will see you soon. Let me know if you want young Chris' photo taken, one good turn deserves another, and let me know if there is anything I can do for Horace".

Mr. Simnett drove off and waved.

"How is Mrs. Fisher?" asked Horace.

"From what the doctors said, if it wasn't for you getting her there when you did she would be dead. The swelling on the side of her face had extended to her neck and was starting to constrict her windpipe and with her being so distraught her breathing was getting more and more laboured. The tracheotomy was carried out just in time. I don't know how you do it. The number of lives you have saved in this town is incredible. Ruth is staying with us for the time being, she doesn't want to go home in case Fisher turns up, she can't bear to see the man, not to mention that she is scared of him too".

"Has Fisher been to see Jean yet?"

"Not as far as we know. From what Jean indicated last night before going into surgery it's pretty clear that it was her husband that walloped her and broke her jaw. I'm expecting Fisher to turn up at any moment. He probably thinks that Jean stayed here over night, I doubt he has an inkling of what happened to her or that he even cares".

"What shall I tell him if he comes when you're at the hospital?"

"Try to be your normal self, Horace, and tell him as little as possible, tell him that you don't know where we are".

Christine called Gordon over.

"Is everything alright, love, you sound worried?"

"The hospital phoned to say that they are taking mum to Birmingham to have her jaw wired".

They told Horace that Mrs. Fisher was going to Birmingham to have her jaw wired and that they were going to see her and drop

Chris off at a friend's house. Christine and Ruth thanked Horace for everything he had done to help their mum.

"I know he's hit her before" said Ruth, "but this time the blow must have been really hard to do this amount of damage to her. She can come and live with me when she's ready to go home, she will not stay in the same house as that monster".

Horace spent a good deal of the morning in the kiosk serving fuel to customers because neither of the girls was coming in. It was shortly after lunch that Fisher turned up and parked erratically on the road in front of the garage.

He opened the car door and nearly fell out. He'd clearly had a liquid lunch and was completely pissed. He shouted something indistinguishable at Horace and hauled himself out by supporting himself on the car door. He walked towards the house like a trainee tightrope walker on a very slack rope. He turned the handle of the front door expecting it to open so he could barge in but it didn't because it was locked so he slammed into it face first and fell over backwards on his arse. Horace was having the time of his life, this was better than the Marx Brothers film. Fisher flipped himself over, crawled a yard or so forward on his hands and knees and then got to his feet very slowly holding his arms out to steady himself. He closed one eye, lined himself up, grunted, and made a bee line for the workshop, the line that a very drunk bee would take. Propping himself up on the door post he looked inside and nearly fell inwards. He turned, squinted at Horace in the kiosk but was clearly unable to see straight so shuffled back to his car, dived in head first across the front seats and fell asleep.

Horace's imagination ran wild. What if, he thought, the handbrake was to release accidentally and the car roll down the hill and smash into the wall a hundred yards away at the bottom? He walked over to Fisher's car and looked around furtively. No one was around. Horace folded Fisher's legs onto the driver's seat and reached around and underneath his considerable girth and released the brake. Fisher grunted. Horace turned the steering wheel slightly to the left, lent on the car door with his shoulder until it clicked shut, went round to the back and gave it a push until it started to move. He returned to the kiosk and put his feet on the desk to watch the car disappear from view. About ten seconds later he heard a loud crump accompanied by the sound of breaking glass.

Horace saw people running past in the road. Pretty soon there was a crowd surrounding the car and the sound of a shrill police car bell approaching. The police dragged Fisher out of the car believing him to be injured but soon realised that he was drunk, plain and simple. Two officers propped him up and led him to their car to take him to the station, another walked up to the garage to ask Horace if he would fetch a car from down the road that had crashed.

"Yes, officer, I will do it straight away, what on earth happened?"

Horace got into the breakdown truck and retrieved the car unhooking it on the forecourt in front of the workshop. This was a golden opportunity. He went through the front and back of the car to see what he could find but was disappointed. He went around to the boot and found a compartment in the passenger side wing. The jolt of the crash had opened it partially otherwise it would have been hard to spot. Inside the compartment was a velvet sack that contained watches, bank notes and assorted precious stones. There were several small stones of different colours and one that was enormous and beautiful, it looked like it might be a large diamond. But being Fisher, Horace wondered whether they were all fake.

Horace put everything in Gordon's safe at the back of the workshop, locked Fisher's car and threw a brick through the driver's window. He locked the workshop and pumps and went home.

When Horace got home, Uncle Bill's new Daimler was sitting outside the brewery.

"Mr. Charles's, the Director's car, looks rather small and inadequate compared to your Daimler, Uncle Bill".

"Yes, Horace, I have just given your mum and dad a quick ride around Needwood. The gypsies are setting up for a bare knuckle fight tomorrow. We will have to see if we can go and watch, well I'm planning to anyway. Shye told me about it a couple of weeks ago, but you and the lads will be OK to go with me".

"Son" said Eva, "I don't know what the matter is with you....water gypsies and horse gypsies. Why you mix with that sort of person is beyond me they're just not the right sort".

Uncle Bill beat Horace to it.

"Our Eva, I agree that there are exceptions but the boaters and gypsies are good honest people. The Romanies have lived that way for centuries and it isn't fair to judge them because of their itinerant lifestyles. Sometimes, our Eva, I wish I could do that, live somewhere for a bit then just pick up my house and belongings and go and live somewhere else, they know a lot about nature and being self sufficient. Horace has learned a lot from them this last couple of years, and they've taught me a thing or two".

"Taught you, our Bill, who on earth could teach you anything, you know all there is to know".

"You're never too old to learn, Eva, the man who thinks he knows everything knows nothing. My travels during the war taught me a lot about different cultures and I learnt to respect them, whether they were those of our enemies or our friends. The furthest you've ever been is Manchester, and you moaned about that".

"You certainly picked up something in Luton didn't you, Uncle Bill, and quite tasty as well" Horace said mischievously and stifled a full on laugh.

"What are you on about Horace, what did Bill pick up there?"

"The Daimler, ma, what else would he pick up? What happens in Luton stays in Luton".

Bill looked daggers at Horace who knew that it was only be a question of time before he took his revenge.

"We will have to get you to the seaside, mum, before you're much older, you would love it".

"The seaside? With all that mud and sand? No thank you" said Eva, "the sand gets everywhere, between your toes, up your nose, in your mouth".

"Eva" said George, "who the hell have you been talking to, you've never experienced the seaside?"

Horace went up the road to fetch some ale. Bill shouted after him to get two jugs and added, "by the way, it's your round". Horace walked through the fence gate with the jugs when he returned. Uncle Bill grabbed him from behind startling him and causing some of the beer to slosh out.

"You little bugger, after all I've done for you. If Mavis was here she'd have twigged about that 'picking up' gibe you made".

"I know mum and dad, Uncle Bill, they wouldn't have had a clue what I was on about".

The next morning, Horace got to work bright and early and did the same tasks that he always did and loved in the mornings. He thought how wonderful it would be to have his own garage, bigger and better than Mr. Rush's.

Gordon was up early.

"Horace, I noticed Fisher's car when we came back last night, you never saw him did you? The car is in a right state, the front's a mess and the driver's window is smashed".

"How is Mrs. Fisher, Mr. Rush?" Horace said evasively, knowing that he would soon have to tell Gordon what had happened anyway.

"She hasn't improved much at all unfortunately. They spent the day trying to realign her jaw before they wired her mouth shut. She will probably spend the next three months with it wired. She isn't in the best of health and all this has affected her heart, they reckon she must have had an underlying heart problem all along".

"About Fisher's car, Mr. Rush. I'd finished all the repairs on the cars and with the girls not being here I spent two hours on the pumps 'til lunch time. By the way, Mr. Rush, you will need to order some more fuel, Marston's have got ten new Bedford SBs so that made a big hole in the stocks. They had one hundred and fifteen yesterday and when I dipped the tank afterwards there were just under four gallons left. Fisher never even saw me in the kiosk when he parked in the road outside, bumping the wheel up the curb. The lorries were all gone and I was finishing off the paper work when he turned up. He was completely plastered, stumbled all over the place before falling asleep in his car. I couldn't resist it, Mr. Rush, I checked that no one was looking and....um....took the handbrake off and gave the car a little nudge".

Horace had tried his best 'til now to keep a straight face but could no longer keep up the facade. A snort came out followed by a guffaw.

"The car went down Henhurst and straight into Wagg's wall....I heard the crunch and then police car bells. To cut a long story short, the police took him away and asked me to tow the car back up here. Er, one other thing....I put a brick through the window to make it look like a robbery and put everything that I found in the car in your safe. There are some interesting things in there if you want to have a look later".

"You had an eventful day, then, to say the least. But I've got to say, you are very good at thinking on your feet, Horace. I'm keen to see what you found but I'm also worried that this all could spell trouble for us further down the line, depending on what's in there".

Gordon went to tell Christine where her dad was and what had happened the previous day. He came back out with four bacon and egg sandwiches to share with Horace who was working on a car when PC Dan Gibbs turned up.

"It looks like it's my lucky day, Gordon. I hope there's more tea in that pot and I'm sure you can't eat all those bacon butties yourselves".

"Help yourself, PC Gibbs" said Horace.

"By the way, Horace, the Prefect is looking fantastic but it could do with a wash and brush up. That does come with the deal doesn't it?"

Horace knew when he was being ribbed.

"Well, you can do that when you clean Chief Superintendent Walters' and Inspector Smart's cars can't you?"

Christine came over with another plate of sandwiches.

"Daniel, I'm not letting you eat all of Horace's sandwiches, not after all he's done for us. Here, Horace, you have these. By the way, Daniel, I understand that my father has been availing himself of your hospitality since yesterday, I don't suppose you can throw away the key or give it to me and my sister and we'll do it".

"That's why I'm here Christine. Yes, he's still with us, he's being charged with assaulting a police constable and possessing a firearm, a Browning pistol. He says it's not his but it was in his jacket pocket. We tried to get hold of your mother last night, have you seen her?"

"Yes, Dan, we have. She's in Birmingham City Infirmary with a broken jaw, it was wired yesterday. She indicated that he did it. She's not able to talk at the moment though, of course".

"Did anyone witness the attack? We can't do much about it if not".

"But, Dan, if my mum says that he did it that's got to be good enough hasn't it."

"Not necessarily, Christine. It depends on whether you mum makes a statement, when she is able to that is, and doesn't retract it afterwards. Your mum has retracted them before when he's abused her. The best thing we can do for now is to pursue the firearm and assault offences, those could see him go down for two years".

After PC Gibbs had left, Gordon looked in the safe to examine the items that Horace had taken out of Fisher's car.

"Did you see these stones, Horace? They can't be real surely, if they are we could both retire. The money is most probably fake so the stones probably are as well. We'll keep them here for a while anyway".

They worked the rest of the day until a suited visitor came to the workshop door and enquired....

"Which one of you gentlemen is Gordon Rush?"

"I am, who wants to know?"

"My Name is Mr. Cedric Jones from Jones and Jones. We represent Mr. Brian Fisher, your father-in-law. We have the paperwork signed by Mr. Fisher and would like all of his belongings from his car".

Horace pointed him in the direction of Mr. Fisher's Jaguar.

"Help yourself, Mr. Jones. The car was broken into last night so don't be surprised if there is nothing in it".

"Broken into? But there are some valuables in there".

"We wouldn't know about any valuables, all I did was to tow the car up here after Mr. Fisher's crash and lock it. Someone put a brick through the window so if there was anything in there it's probably gone by now".

Cedric Jones went over the car with a fine toothcomb but left empty handed.

Horace finished work and rode his bike over to Needwood to see Shye and his friends at the gypsy camp. Uncle Bill was right, there was loads of activity and people were milling around. Whatever they were getting ready for looked like it was going to be a lot of fun.

# CHAPTER SEVENTEEN

"Good evening young Horace and Uncle Bill, we haven't seen you for a couple of months. Well, what a nice machine that is, is it one motorbike or is it made up of a combination of parts from different bikes?"

"No it's the same bike, I just made the sidecar. I fetched the frame out of the cut then rebuilt it. The chassis is extended both ways, you won't find another like this anywhere".

"Then I will buy it off you, young Horace, the whole lot, what do you say?"

"Sorry, I can't sell it, Shye. I was given the motorbike as a present".

"That means it's yours to do whatever you want, you don't have to keep it, Horace".

"No, Shye, it would be disrespectful to sell it, I will keep that bike for as long as I can".

"Then find me another bike and attach that magnificent thing onto it, have we a deal?"

Shye spat on his hand.

"Come on, son, I want that tube on wheels. I'm renowned for getting strange things for the Appleby show and selling them to the highest bidder. Or, you could make me another one that's bigger and better but there are only seven months 'til the show, it's always in the first week in June".

Horace took Shye to one side.

"I can always make you one, all I need is some axles. I can make the rest. It's a deal, Shye".

Horace spat on his hand and they shook, the deal was sealed.

"Did you hear that lads? Horace will make me one of these and deliver it to the Appleby show for me. I can't take it, not with my vardo [Romany wagon] and the horses I'm going to sell there. I buy yearlings, bring them on and take them to Appleby every year without fail and that keeps Mrs. Boswell in love with me forever, doesn't it, Ethelinda, my sweetness and life".

"You silly beggar, you're always up to something with that poor lad. Take no notice of him, Horace, take no notice of him whatsoever. He's full of that horse manure over there and be careful, mind, he might try to sell you something by telling you it's magical. He's done that before to others and that's no word of a lie".

"Are you staying to fight Uncle Bill and Horace?"

"No Ethy, we made a deal and he can come to the show in June, I will show him who the Gypsy King is then".

"Of course we have Shye, why do you think we're here, it's certainly not to admire your good looks but Ethy's, you can come with me anywhere, anytime, you gorgeous lady".

"Magnetta, put some extra meat on" said Shye, "we have guests for dinner. Come on lads let me show you some of the Italian boys but watch your pockets. You can't trust any of them, damned foreigners, aren't you Ravelino?"

"Be careful there, Shye, old love, don't forget I'm in the ring tonight so if you want to keep your looks I would hide in your vardo".

*Author's Note: Shye and his wife Ethelinda were descendents of the old Romany gypsies. Her grandfather, Django Gaskin, had heritage that went back to the Nomads of the Middle East and the Bedouin tribes of Saudi Arabia. The families had, and still have, their own laws, customs and royalty.*

*But some communities have changed from the days that I remember in the late nineteen fifties and during the sixties. They were a proud people, meticulously clean and never left a mess anywhere after they departed. In fact, they used to get gifts for managing the land at Tatenhill, which was owned by the Duchy of Lancaster, including crates of ale for the men, soaps and towels for the women and toys for the children. In the summer at the end of June, after returning from the Appleby show, they would invite the landlord and his staff from the Rangemore Estate to a damn good shindig. It was a great party with some of the estate guests even sleeping off their excesses in the vardos.*

Shye was the tallest of all the gypsy men standing at six feet four inches and was built like the side of a vardo. He was a gentle and kind person who would do anything for anyone but never turned his nose up at the prospect of some sort of monetary gain. He was the King of the Gypsies [a title that at time of writing is currently held by Tyson Fury].

The bare knuckle fights were just about to start. The only rule was that there were no rules, for the grownups anyway. If one of the fighters didn't get up the other was declared the victor. There was an adjudicator rather than a referee who tried to make sure that no one was killed but, unfortunately, that didn't always work out. In 1959 a chap called Melton died in a bare knuckle fight.

*Author's Note: I can't remember whether Melton was his Christian or surname.*

The fighting began. As you can imagine there was plenty of blood but Horace didn't bat an eyelid, especially after the last few days up in Luton and the preceding days at Sinai. The first few fights were between young lads and these were typically settled within a few minutes, largely because the adjudicator was a little more attentive due to their young age. But when the main bouts started all hell could, and often did, break loose. Even the spectators would start fighting amongst themselves although Shye would step in and stop them if things got too out of hand.

There was also plenty of gamesmanship because the betting was, shall we say, fluid. One fighter, Mel Copper, would play at being knocked down, money would change hands and he would bounce back up and knock the other fellow out.

The preliminary bouts went on for four hours and the eagerly awaited piece de resistance between Shye and Ravelino loomed large. The Italians were moving money around faster than dealers on the floor of the stock exchange. Both fighters agreed to delay the start of their fight for ten minutes to allow the frenetic monetary activities to settle down. While they waited, Shye and Ravelino went to a vardo to have a drink together, they were great friends even though they were about to knock seven bells out of one another.

*Author's Note: It is believed that the phrase 'knock seven bells out of someone' originates from the nautical practice of ringing a bell eight times to signal the end of a watch. The fact that seven is used means that the watch is due to end in half an hour or, in the case of a fight, that the recipient of a beating is nearing the end of his capacity to take any more, or even nearing the end of his life.*

Magnetta came and stood next to Horace. She had beautiful long flowing red hair. They had known each other for over two years from when he visited the camp on his push bike. She was probably the same age as Horace but no one was sure. Shye and Ethelinda had taken her into their care when her mother died of TB and all they knew was that she was about two years old, they didn't even know her name or whether she had even been given a name. They called her Magnetta simply because they did some research and believed it was similar to one of the historical family names on her mother's side. Names were often used to denote a family's origins or affiliations.

She took Horace's hand and whispered "Come with me, lubirica," the Romany word for sweetheart.

"Let's go and have some fun, you promised me that we would the next time you came to see me".

"Magnetta, please can we watch your dad fight first? Then I must get his blessing before we do, he is a great friend....plus I don't want to get on the wrong side of those fists".

There was a roar from the assembled spectators when Shye and Ravelino entered the ring for the last fight of the evening. Uncle Bill grabbed two hands full of horse meat and went over to the circle trying to get as close to the action as he possibly could. Both men circled each other gauging each other's likely tactics and trying to anticipate the first move, they stared fixedly into each other's eyes. Shye slapped Ravelino playfully a couple of times to rile him. Suddenly, the two men exploded into action like two stags competing for the affections of a harem of hinds, the ground shook. Muscles flexed, tendons strained and sweat poured off them as first one then the other struck resounding blows but neither of them was giving any quarter.

"Come on, Horace, these two will be here all night, I've seen my dad stand there for ages, he's like a dog gnawing a bone until he gets fed up, hungry or thirsty".

"Has he ever had a drink of ale while he's fighting?" Horace toyed with her.

"Not sure he's ever thought of trying that one, my lubirica, let's go and play. And don't think you're the first, I popped my cork at Appleby last year but these travelling boys are just there for their own pleasure. That was your fault, I told you I needed it before we went up there, so come on, I'm on the boil, that was nine months ago".

"Have a play?" Uncle Bill taunted them, "you sound like two kids".

"You shouldn't be listening to other people's conversations, old man, get away with you" Magnetta admonished Uncle Bill.

They both went to the other end of the camp and climbed into a beautifully painted vardo.

"Who's is this, Magnetta, it's just been done up by someone and it's really nice work?"

"Just get the fuck inside me you stupid boy. I'm giving myself to you and you're checking the decor. My dad and I did this ready for Appleby this year so don't scratch it with your shoes. Take them off....and all your clothes".

She slipped out of her shoes and unfastened her dress, it slid down her silky smooth skin to the floor.

"Close your mouth, haven't you seen a woman's body before?"

Horace felt guilty that he would have sex knowing that Charmaine was on her way back but he'd promised Magnetta last year that he would make love to her. He was a little suspicious that she'd lied to him about having had sex at Appleby because she seemed unsure about what to do but after some gentle foreplay and kissing he entered her, she shuddered and virtually came straight away. She lay back feeling warm inside and looked at him but he was still erect and entered her again. She thrust her pelvis upwards repeatedly as he thrust downwards and before long she moaned and exhaled, her vagina contracted around his penis and they both came together. It was all over in a little over ten minutes. Horace noticed there was some blood on his penis.

"Are you alright, Magnetta, have I hurt you?"

"I'm not hurt, my lubirica, that's what women do when we pop our cork".

Horace tried to remember whether the same had happened to Charmaine but the lovemaking was far more intense so perhaps it had but he simply hadn't noticed.

"Magnetta, you lied to me. You said you'd already had sex last year but this was your first time".

"Well, I thought you would like it better if I said that I'd done it before".

They got dressed and walked back to the ring, it was only about twenty minutes since they were last there. Shye and Ravelino were still fighting like men possessed although both were a little bloody now and somewhat slower than before. Horace and Magnetta stood beside Uncle Bill.

"That was a quick one, did you manage to get your trousers down, or was it just a peck on the cheek? Give me a cigarette, Horace, I've run out of 'baca' and I don't want to miss the end of this fight. I think your dad is still playing with him Magnetta but I wouldn't like to be on the end of that punch your dad just took, that was a 'brammer'...."

Horace walked over to the food table and picked up some meat. He loved horse meat, a lot like beef crossed with venison, a sweeter meat than beef but with a lot less fat on it. It was the main meat of the gypsies, they would buy a cheap horse that was lame or that the owners were going to put down anyway and slaughter it. They were frugal so nothing went to waste. They fed to their dogs whatever they didn't eat. The organs, the bones and even the skull were used or devoured one way or the other. They hung up the skin to dry for a few weeks then the women made trousers for the men or leather skirts for themselves. They also used it to cover the bow top vardos each of which had its own distinctive colour as a result.

The gypsies held their livestock in very high regard and never stole any to eat. When the time came they disposed of them humanely and with dignity. The 'vanner' [Irish cob] was venerated and when one died they held a funeral and cremated it on a pyre.

Horace thought he would be clever and grabbed a bottle of ale for Shye and another for Ravelino, they must be thirsty, surely. He pushed his way to the front of the crowd so the fighters could see him and held the bottles out in front of him. Both fighters stopped, shook hands and downed the ale. The crowd was stunned into silence, particularly the ones who didn't know Horace.

When they finished they threw the bottles to the ground and resumed where they'd left off but it seemed as if they had been reinvigorated hitting each other harder than before the unplanned break. Horace went back to stand with Uncle Bill and Magnetta to watch the rest of the fight. Blood was now streaming out of a cut above Ravelino's eye and his cheek bones looked swollen. Dark bruises adorned his face and his body, particularly around his ribs and sides where Shye had gone for his kidneys. Shye wasn't exactly unscathed but Ravelino looked as if the seventh bell had been rung for him. Shye spotted a gap in Ravelino's defences and struck him on the forehead, it sounded like someone slapping a flat surface with a wet towel. Ravelino staggered backwards a single step and then fell to the ground like a sack of spuds. Sixty five minutes all told it had taken.

All hell broke loose. The Italian and Romany gypsies piled into each other, including the women and, unwittingly Horace and Uncle Bill. A fist swung at Horace and he didn't see it coming, he was too busy watching Uncle Bill clobbering someone else. Horace felt the blow and saw what looked like fireflies dancing in front of his eyes, and fell to the ground. The perpetrator, an Italian lad, jumped onto his chest and pulled his arm back to strike as if drawing the string on a bow but he'd overestimated how stunned Horace was. Horace's fist shot upwards catching the lad in the chin and jerking his head backwards. As soon as his head had snapped back into its normal position it received another blow, this time in the nose and mouth. Horace pushed the lad off him and sat on him instead, the tables were turned. He proceeded to pummel the young man until Magnetta decided to intervene and pulled Horace off. He got up and stood there with blood coming out of his nose and mouth.

"That bastard started it, I was watching Uncle Bill, never even saw it coming".

"Yes, maybe he thought he'd have a go at a 'gorger' [non-

Romany person] thinking it would be easier".

Shye and Ravelino busied themselves running in and out of the mayhem trying to stop what had turned into a mini riot. Eventually, with plenty of shouting and pushing people away, they managed to restore order. The participants looked like battle weary soldiers nursing their wounds, muttering and wandering around aimlessly. But in the middle of this outbreak of peace, like an oasis of violence in a sea of calm, Uncle Bill was still pounding one of the Italians.

"I don't play by your rules, Shye, I haven't finished yet. This one wanted a fight and made the mistake of hitting an ex No. 2 commando".

He slapped the unfortunate chap into tomorrow and that brought an absolute end to all of the fighting.

"Come on Horace it's time to go, I think we've outstayed our welcome".

As they were leaving, Shye shouted "Horace, don't forget my new carriage you have seven weeks to do it".

"What's that all about, Horace, what are you going to do for him?"

"Don't you remember when we arrived? He wants a sidecar like this one but bigger. The frame isn't a problem but I'll need to find some thin metal sheets to do the bodywork".

"That shouldn't be a problem, your Uncle George is working on a project at Bass's he has lots of off cuts of thin gauge metal, I'll see him tomorrow for you. Bye, lad".

Horace arrived home to a dad who was slightly disappointed that his son hadn't been there to fetch his ale for him.

"Where have you been, son? I had to fetch my own ale tonight, and what's that mark on your cheek, it looks like you've been in a fight".

"I went up the gypsy camp with Uncle Bill there was a bare knuckle fight, well six actually, then afterwards a free for all. This lad hit me while I was watching Uncle Bill fight".

"Bill had a fight as well? I don't know what your mother is going to say about that, lad, she won't be pleased to find out that Bill had ago. He doesn't know when to stop".

"Goodnight, son, I will see you in the morning. I'll be awake at five we have to plant the rest of the autumn barley. Colin and I will be on it all day, we're starting at six".

Horace was up first the next morning. As per the usual routine, he put the kettle and pan on the stove and chucked in the bacon, and it had the usual affect of getting his dad out of bed when he smelled the irresistible aroma, telling Eva to stay where she was and to get some more sleep.

"Morning, Horace, that smell would wake the dead. Well almost, it didn't wake your mother, how are you feeling now after your beating?" he knowingly baited Horace for fun.

"I told you last night, dad, I didn't get a beating I wasn't looking when I was struck".

"Just playing with you, son" his dad chuckled, "I know what happened to you".

Horace finished his breakfast lit a fag and said cheerio to his dad.

"Take it steady in the fields, dad, you know your chest isn't quite right yet, you don't want to be bad again. You've only just got over that last bout. I thought you were going to take it easy from now on anyway, you had a cushy job in the malting".

"Yes I did, but you know I've always worked on the land, from when I was ten years old on your grandpa's farm in Horninglow. See you later, son".

Horace thought he would have a look in Moor's scrap yard, he knew that they had been decommissioning field guns so maybe he could get some axles if they weren't too big. When he got there the field gun axles turned out to be far too big, but they had some old wooden Eccles luggage trailers, their axles would be ideal and they weren't likely to be expensive. He decided to come back for them later.

He arrived at the garage at six thirty and started to work on the cars that had been booked in. There was nothing that Gordon wouldn't let him do now and very rarely, if ever, checked his work. He'd already completed work on a couple of cars by the time Gordon came into the workshop.

"Morning, Horace, did you go to the bare knuckle fight last night? I will have to go to the next one. What's that mark on your cheek you never had a go did you?"

"No Mr. Rush but there was a free-for-all afterwards. I was watching Uncle Bill pounding someone when this kid took me by surprise and hit me on the cheek. I'd like to see what he looks like this morning. I need to ask you a favour, Mr. Rush, Shye wants a motorbike and sidecar for the next time he goes to the Appleby Fair. There are half a dozen Eccles luggage trailers at Moors, if I can get some cheap I can convert them into another sidecar. Just the axles will do but they need fetching".

"Let me have a word with John. He owes me a favour, I never charged him for the last two cars I picked up for him".

"Thanks, Mr. Rush, those axles will be just right for the sidecar I am going to build. By the way, how was Mrs. Fisher yesterday?"

"She was a lot better thanks, Horace, but still won't give us an indication of what Fisher did to her. Christine hopes that she will tell all when she can actually talk. Ruth is there at the moment and we will go to visit later this afternoon. My mum and dad are looking after Christopher for the rest of this week, it's so handy them living in Shobnall Street".

"I've finished the service on Mr. Holt's car and nearly finished the wishbone on the Austin 90 then I will get the Morris Z van from the Co-Op bakery. Did you order the new clutch with all the hoo-hah over the last few days?"

"I'll go to Station Street after I've phoned John Moore about your trailers then I can pick it up on the way back. You still have your old motor bike in the spray shop, will you sell it with the sidecar when you have finished it?"

"That's my idea, Mr. Rush. I can't wait to start it. Uncle Bill told me that he will ask my Uncle George about some off cuts from the Bass workshop".

Horace finished Mr. Holt's Austin and then took the gearbox out of the van. He heard a car outside and saw a taxi pull up. It was Fisher. He got out and went into the house. An argument started within a few seconds of him going inside. Horace jumped out of the pit and rode his bike to Moors scrap yard to intercept Gordon before he got back to the garage. He didn't want him to turn up and be unpleasantly surprised.

He saw Gordon standing by the Eccles trailers shaking hands

with someone.

"Mr. Rush, I've something to tell you and you won't be very happy about it".

"What have you done, Horace, burnt the Garage down? We have a deal on the trailers for you, if you take the engines out of three Ford Pops for them then you can have the trailers".

"What time do you lock up tonight, I can do it then?" Horace asked the man from the scrap yard.

"We can have someone here 'til you finish, Horace, if you're sure you will be here".

"You can come over earlier, Horace, once the clutch is in the van" said Gordon. "That'll be the work done for today".

"Mr. Rush, I wanted to tell you that Fisher has turned up at the garage in a taxi, that's why I came down here. I didn't want you turning up and being surprised. He only been there for ten seconds and an argument between him and Mrs. Rush had already erupted".

"Thanks, Horace, let's get back. Why the hell have they let him go, what's wrong with them?"

They both rushed back to the garage and Gordon shot into the house before Horace arrived. Gordon asked Fisher why they had let him go.

"Just shut your mouth before I do it for you. They had to let me go because a kind policeman forgot to send my gun off soon enough to have the fingerprints lifted. That didn't cut the mustard with my brief, so they had no evidence on me".

"Now, where the hell is the stuff that was in my car? I've just been to look at it and I don't believe it was just broken into. The things in that car don't belong to me....yet....and you really don't want to mix it with the people who do own them. Did that little bastard out in the workshop nick them? You will never be able to sell them stones, they're specially cut".

"It's nothing to do with Horace. I put the brick through the window" Gordon lied, "to see what you had inside and put the stuff in the safe in my office".

"Well, don't just stand there, go and get it now and I'm borrowing your car 'til you repair mine. That'll teach you to put your nose in my business so, go on, fetch it....Now!"

"No! You're not bossing us around anymore" Christine barked, "we need the car to go to see your wife and my mum. You haven't even asked after her, what did you do to her?"

"It's nothing to do with you, we had a row that's all, nothing to do with you or anybody else and I am certainly not going to justify myself to anyone".

Ruth turned up at the house from her trip to Birmingham hospital. She was so shocked to see her dad standing there that she just flew at him picking Christine's rolling pin up on the way.

"You rotten bastard, why have they let you out? You should be rotting in prison for what you did to mum. You want to see the state of her, she's having to eat through a straw just like you will be doing".

Fisher just gave her a back hand like he did Jean, but not quite so hard. Christine screamed at him to get out of the house and never come back.

"You're not welcome near my family".

"Just sling your hook before I call the police" said Gordon, "I will get your stuff. Your car is drivable, we need ours to go and see your wife. You hurt her so badly that she won't be able to talk or eat properly for three months, and that's if she gets better".

"Listen to me you three. I slapped your mother once that's all. She has got to do what she is told, just like you two girls. I own everything you have and I can pull the plug on it anytime I want. You would all be on the streets if it wasn't for me, it's a pity Simon didn't realise that up in Scotland, which is why you are a young widow, Ruth, and your two kids have no father. Don't let the same happen to you, Gordon. There are more people involved in this than just me so you'd better all behave yourselves".

Horace had already fitted the clutch in the van and was tightening the bell housing bolts when Gordon came striding into the workshop. His face was red with rage as he moved things about on the bench making them clatter and bang about.

"Mr. Rush, this should be done in the next half hour. When I've tightened the housing bolts there is just the prop shaft to go on. Are you OK, you look very angry".

"Don't mind me, Horace. It's that damned Fisher again. I'm getting the stuff out the safe and giving it back to him. I don't want his ill gotten gains, I would be no better than him if I kept it. He just slapped Ruth across the face. I'm not a man, what man would just stand there and take that? I'm worse than a coward putting up with it in my house".

"Mr. Rush, you have your family to think about but I have no family. I'm not particularly proud of the things I've done in the last few weeks but I could kill Fisher with pleasure".

"Taking another's life isn't an easy thing to do, Horace, I know from the war. People have been left in pieces after killing other human beings, and some have even committed suicide".

"Mr. Rush, if I tell you something will you promise not to judge me? When I went to Luton to look for Charmaine, Sol and Piglet went with me. I killed the man that was holding her in captivity. Things got a bit out of hand when I saw her there and when I found out what he'd done to her. I lost control and stabbed him in the throat with the knife I took out of Fisher's car".

Horace continued....

"Believe me, I would do it to Fisher for you. I lost no sleep after I killed that man but I have lost lots just thinking what Charmaine must have gone through. I found out that it wasn't just the man I killed but there were two others as well, two brothers. Sol and Piglet saw to them, it was their heads that Fisher found hanging in his garage".

"Son, just let him go away from here, he's done enough damage for one day".

"Mr. Rush, why isn't he in a police cell? I thought he would be locked up for two years with what happened. Do you think he has someone in the force on his books because he is literally getting away with murder?"

"I don't know what to think anymore, Horace, he could very well have a stooge in there, that possibility just makes him all the more dangerous. We don't know what he will do next, and we can't risk it. When you finish the van you have the rest of the day to yourself, son, I know what you will be doing up at Moors".

Gordon went to the safe and took Fisher's things to him in the house then got in the car with Christine to collect Chris from his parents before heading off to see Jean in Birmingham.

# CHAPTER EIGHTEEN

Horace waved to Gordon, Christine and Chris as they headed to Birmingham to visit Jean and carried on with what he was doing in the workshop. After a few moments he saw Fisher emerge from the house carrying in his left hand the bag that had been in Gordon's safe. He jumped out of the pit, grabbed a metal bar that was on his bench and went over to Fisher. Fisher drew himself upright and they looked each other in the eye for a second, Horace stepped forward and struck Fisher's left hand hard with the bar. Fisher let out a yell, dropped the bag and gripped his left wrist with his right hand. The fingers of his injured hand were red and trembling, he'd bent them inwards making the shape of a claw.

"You bastard! I will kill you myself if you ever hurt any of your family again. Leave the bag on the ground and fuck off. You don't know what happened in Luton do you. Well, I can tell you that your associates up there will never do anything for you or anyone else again. By the way, do you know what happened to your tyre lorry and men? Do you know what happened to the four henchmen you sent to follow me? Let me tell you. Their body parts ended up as pig swill. Veronica turned out to be tougher than the hardest of your men but, unfortunately, things didn't end well for her either. You see, what you did to my girlfriend has made me very angry, Fisher, and I am going to kill you myself one of these days....slowly".

Fisher was still grasping his injured hand.

"Do you think you can scare me with your threats? You're just a dead kid walking but you don't see it do you?"

Horace lashed out and hit Fisher's right hand with the bar causing him to gasp and hunch forwards. Both hands looked broken.

"Who's going to wipe your arse over the next few days? Just piss off and leave your family alone".

Fisher got in his car and managed to wrap a handkerchief around his right hand and some paper around the other to try to help him grip the steering wheel. Splotches of blood appeared through the paper much like ink on blotting paper. He sat there grimacing and hoping that the pain would dissipate enough for him to get away. It was a full ten minutes before his car crept forward across the forecourt and pulled out onto the road.

Monica came running out of the kiosk. Horace had forgotten that she was there with everything that was going on.

"Horace, are you alright? I thought you were going to kill him with that bar, I've never seen anyone stand up to him before. Do you think he will be back with his friends?"

"He could well do Monica. If I were you I'd have an early day, I will watch the pumps for you".

"I was supposed to be going in half an hour anyway so I'll stay 'til then. Surely he won't return that quickly, he looked in a lot of pain. That was so brave of you, Horace, doing that for Gordon and Christine".

Horace worked on the trailers stripping the wood off two of them to expose the metal frames and axles then removed the axles completely. Welding two axles together would allow him to build the frame of the sidecar chassis around them. He got a tape measure. The sidecar would be three feet longer than his, Shye would be pleased with that. He welded the axles together and lay on them, perfect he thought. A car drove up to the pumps so he went outside and took the metal bar with him just in case but it was Kevin and his dad.

"Horace, mate, are you expecting trouble with that great big bar? Your Uncle George asked me if I could bring these sheet metal off-cuts for you. Looks like you're working on a new project".

"Yes, Mr. Mason, I'm keeping the bar with me in case Fisher or his men turn up again. I had another run in with the fat man this morning, he's going to have to give up his knitting for a while. I'm fed up with him running roughshod over people, everyone is shit scared of him so I decided to stand up to him. How're you doing Kev? Sorry I haven't been up to see you I've had quite a lot going on over the last few days".

"It's not a good sign if you need to have a bar at the ready" said Kevin, "shall I stay and help?"

"Horace's Uncle Bill will be more help than you, son".

"Yes, but no one takes the mickey out of us Masons, we're a force to be reckoned with in Winshill and have been for a while".

"Thank you, Kev, but your dad is right. Uncle Bill is the best person to help me if I need it".

Horace thanked them and took the metal sheets into the workshop. He started to build the sidecar's skeleton welding uprights onto the axles for the body and struts to support the floor. He cut out panels from the off-cuts that Uncle George had given him so that he could start to shape them for the sidecar's body. There was no further sign of Fisher or his men for the rest of the day. Horace chuckled thinking that Fisher probably couldn't use his hands to dial and call anyone. At five o'clock he went to the scrap yard and spent a couple of hours removing the engines from two of the Ford Pops telling the owner he'd be back in the morning to remove the third and last one.

Horace went to Bladon woods at around seven o'clock to see Bill and his cousins, checking behind him every so often to make sure that no one was following him. He'd promised the night before to take them a fish and chip supper so stopped off at the chip shop on the way over.

"Good evening you load of reprobates have you got the kettle on for a brew?"

"It's about time you were here, thought you'd got lost. Bring them fish and chips over, my stomach thinks my throat has been cut. George, get the brew out here".

"It's always me that has to get the brew, Horace the youngest he should do it. I'm doing it all day at work running around after you and the rest of the men, George this George that".

"Are you handing in your notice, son? Do you have another job? You've got a cushy number, someone always lends you a hand to carry and mix the cement, ask Bill".

"You're not wrong there, dad, that's why he looks so weak, never does the hard jobs".

"Right, starting from tomorrow you're going to be doing some back-breaking work, I'm hot having the lads think I favour you two. I'll have less time to keep an eye on things now that I have to be in Luton once or twice a week so I'll hire a foreman on Monday to do it for me, and it won't be one of you two".

They ate their fish and chip supper and started work on the well that Horace had dug a few weeks before. The foundation had already been completed over the weekend so all that was needed was for them to line the sides. Young Bill put some bricks from the van in a hod and carried them up the hill, George did the same and followed him up.

"Horace, could you get some bricks in the boot of your sidecar? If you go up the drive and cut across the top then you could roll the bricks down to us, the van would be too wide to do it".

Horace did what he was told. He piled just over thirty bricks in the boot of the sidecar and drove to the mound just above the well. From his vantage point Horace could sling the bricks down for them to cement in. The scheme worked well speeding up the whole process, they were finished in no time at all. The sun was still shining through the trees but was thinking about setting sometime soon. Uncle Bill went to the van and returned with a bucket full of bottles of ale. They stretched out on the grass to relax, have a drink and smoke a cigarette. It gave Horace a chance to tell them all about his day; the trailers for the sidecar, Fisher avoiding being sent down, the possibility of there being a bent copper, Fisher's bag of treasure and getting a wrap across the knuckles with an iron bar.

"I saw red to see him swaggering to his car. I jumped out of the pit, grabbed an iron bar and hit him over the hands with it. The bag that he dropped was in his car to begin with, I found it there after his accident and Gordon put it in his safe, but Fisher forced him to give it back".

"Where's the bag now then Horace?"

He fetched the bag from his sidecar.

"Have you looked through this yet Horace?"

"I know there's some money and stones in there".

Uncle Bill loosened the draw string and looked inside.

"Jesus! There's hundreds of pounds in here, it's not legit. Definitely counterfeit, you can see that the metal strip is just a painted line but these would probably pass in a lot of places, especially if it's busy. He examined some of the stones. I can't tell whether the stones are real, I'll have to take them up to Sinai, five of the men decided to stay up there in two of the cottages. They made them watertight and with the fires going in those grates the places are quite cosy. Three of them work for me on the Field Lane project and one of them is Sol's best mate, he knows more about jewellery than I do. Horace, If you get any trouble from Fisher about this tell him that you hid the bag at Sinai and get him to follow you up there. He and his men won't come back again if they do".

"What do you mean, dad" asked George, "won't come back again?"

"You just carry on enjoying your ale, lads. Fisher has been causing a lot of problems for Horace and all I'm saying is that it won't end well for him or his men if they go up to Sinai".

Horace was up at five the next morning. He hadn't slept well worrying about when and who Fisher would send next. He went to the scrap yard and took the last engine out of the Ford Pop and asked if he could have four suspension springs that he saw lying around. When he got back to the garage he left the workshop doors open so that he could keep an eye on the forecourt and kept an iron bar close by. He carried on welding bits to the frame of the sidecar but left a bit more space for a slightly larger door otherwise it would be a tight fit to get in, not a problem for Shye but Ethelinda was, shall we say, a bit on the large side. It was almost ready for him to weld the side panels on. It would only take him another week or so to fit the front and back suspension springs, tidy things up and paint it. Gordon came into the workshop at nine o'clock.

"Morning, Horace, how you are this morning? Bloody hell, you've certainly cracked on with this. Did you weld the trailers together and use them?"

"Yes, Mr. Rush, I couldn't believe how easily it all came together, but first I need to talk to you and Mrs. Rush urgently".

"That sounds ominous Horace, what's it about?"

"I would prefer to tell you both together if that's OK, Mr. Rush".

"Yes, of course. Come into the house then, son".

They went into the house and Gordon called Christine "Horace wants a word with us".

"What's the matter Horace? I hope you're not leaving us, you're like one of the family to us now".

"I'll come straight out with it and will understand if it's you that wants me to leave. When you left yesterday your father came swaggering out of the house with the bag that I took out of his car. I saw red. I couldn't forget that he'd threatened you, Mr. Rush, with meeting the same fate as Simon. I went over and hit him on his hand with an iron bar, he dropped the bag. He threatened to have me killed so I hit his other hand. Monica was here and saw it all, I hope I haven't upset her too much what with everything that's been going on and what happened to Sheila. I've given the bag to Uncle Bill, he's going to get some of his friends to check out the contents but we know that the notes are fake".

"Is that all it is, Horace? Thank you for telling us, and believe me we're not in the least bit upset that you hit my father, on the contrary in fact. He slapped Ruth yesterday and admitted to her face that he had something to do with her husband's death and, well, threatening Gordon was the last straw. Just sit yourself down and I'll make breakfast. Maybe your standing up to him will mean that we don't see him again for a while".

"Even better" said Horace, "not to see him for good. But I'm not sure, Mrs. Rush, he seems to get away with it every time, always has an alibi".

Gordon talked to Horace over breakfast about what they were doing for the day and told him that when he'd finished he could get on with the sidecar.

"What're you doing about the suspension, Horace, there weren't any springs on the trailers".

"I picked some up this morning from the scrap yard they should be easy enough to fit. I'll rub them down and paint them black along with the chassis, it'll look like new when it's finished".

Gordon and Horace went over to see Monica in the kiosk on their way to the workshop to make sure that she was OK after witnessing the altercation with Fisher the day before.

"I'm sorry to say it, Mr. Rush, but it was good to see someone stand up to that horrible man, he was in a bit of a state when he left".

As expected, it didn't take long. Fisher turned up with three men later that morning and marched straight over to the workshop where they stood just outside the door. Gordon came out and told him to get off the premises. Horace hid just inside the door gripping his iron bar. Christine came out of the house to warn them that she had already called the police.

"You stupid woman, we want the bag that young idiot took off me when he did this to my hands. He raised them to show her and grimaced as he did so, they were both red and wrapped in makeshift bandages with black and blue bruising just visible at the edges. I need that bag or others will be coming to see you and they won't be as nice as me, I'm just a small cog in a big wheel".

Horace stepped out of the workshop with the bar in his hand.

"Just clear off or I will bury this in your head this time. If you want your stuff I'll get it later, I've buried it somewhere. If you promise to leave your daughter and son-in-law alone I will fetch it tonight after work".

One of Fisher's men took a step forward.

"It doesn't work like that, son, we want it now".

A police car pulled up on the forecourt, PC Gibbs got out with a police sergeant and walked over to them.

"What's the problem, Mrs. Rush, you seemed quite upset when you called?"

"These men are bothering my husband and his mechanic and they won't leave".

"Good morning, Mr. Fisher" said PC Gibbs, "just leave now then there will be no bother. If you don't we will take you in for questioning".

Horace saw the sergeant glancing at Fisher and thought there was something strange about the way they looked at each other. Fisher told the sergeant that Horace had threatened them with an iron bar when they arrived this morning.

"PC Gibbs" said the sergeant, "take Horace in for questioning about the assault on Mr. Fisher. Go on, put him in the car".

"Hang on" said Horace, "what assault? Mrs. Rush only phoned this morning to tell you about these men coming here and bothering Mr. Rush".

"Yes, but I understand that you may also have some of Mr. Fisher's property".

"You seem to know a lot about this crook" said Horace, "are you the one at the station that keeps losing evidence against him? One of you must be because he seems to get away with an awful lot every time you take him in".

"Constable, put Horace Gray in the car, we will question him at the station. But first you must tell us the whereabouts of Mr. Fisher's belongings".

"I don't know anything about his belongings".

"I don't suppose you know anything about how is hands got injured either, how he was attacked yesterday?"

"All you need, sergeant, is proof....evidence, someone to confirm his story. What are they called? Oh, yes....witnesses".

"That girl in the kiosk was here smirking when he hit me yesterday. Ask her, she will tell you" said Fisher.

PC Gibbs led Horace to the car and they got in.

"Sorry about this, Horace, I don't know what he is doing taking you down to the nick".

"Dan, he's on the inside doing Fisher's dirty work for him. How does he know about Fisher's belongings, whatever they are? Do you honestly think that Fisher reported them missing? He wouldn't go near the police station. The keener he is to find them the more likely it is that they are not legit".

"Just keep what you think to yourself, Horace, you won't get anywhere accusing Miller".

Sergeant Miller came to the police car and leaned through the window.

"Where's Mr. Fisher's bag? That's all he wants then you can get on with your work, otherwise you will go to the station and be charged with theft".

"Bag, how do you know the belongings are in a bag? Did Fisher tell you that, did he tell you exactly what the belongings are, what's supposed to be inside this bag? What proof do you have to charge me with the theft of anything? Ask Monica, she was here all the time yesterday. If I do find anything that's not mine I will bring it to the station and give it to Inspector Smart, I know and trust him".

"No, Gray, I am the investigating officer not Inspector Smart, you will give the belongings to either me or Mr. Fisher".

"What, that Mr. Fisher, the one over there? That crook, wife beater and murderer, the one who owns the house where you found his son-in-law's body? If you search his garage I'm sure you will find lots of interesting 'belongings', Sergeant Miller".

"He's not the one I am accusing of theft, Gray, you are".

"Evidence, sergeant, I would have thought you needed some before you charge me with anything and you don't have any. I don't know anything about this bag of Fisher's".

Sergeant Miller told him to get out of the car.

"I will investigate this further, Gray, and I'm warning you that I will be keeping an eye on you".

Fisher ordered Gordon and Christine to tell him where the 'stuff' is by tomorrow and left with his henchmen. Sergeant Miller and PC Gibbs bade Mr. and Mrs. Rush good day and left too. Horace went back into the workshop with Gordon to finish what he was doing.

"Horace, please return Fisher's things to him. He won't back down and who knows the trouble he will cause for us all".

"OK, Mr. Rush, I will bring them in the morning but please don't expect or ask me to do anything for him again, I would rather leave here than do any more of his dirty work".

Horace finished the servicing and repair work that Gordon had asked him to do that day. He welded on the last of the sidecar panels and just had the door and roof to complete. He left for Sinai at half five to see if Uncle Bill was there but walked up the long way leaving his bike behind at the garage. It would be easier that way to spot anyone who might be following him. He hid in some bushes when he got to the top of the hill and scanned the forest and fields below to double check that no one was moving about.

Bill wasn't there yet so he spoke to Fred.

"Have you seen Uncle Bill today, Fred?"

"Yes, Horace, he came up last night and showed me the booty".

He gave Horace the bag that contained the cash and gems.

"The money's shit but the gems are real. If I were you I'd tell the bloke you got them off that you want to return them in person. Arrange to meet at, say, half ten under the town hall clock but make sure that he's alone. We can follow him to find out who else is involved. Some of the stones are diamonds and extremely valuable, it's hard to put a price on them but it's a lot, one hell of a lot. I sent Rocket to London with some of them to see an old mate of ours in the Jewish community, they know an awful lot more about these things than I do and they confirmed that they are genuine. Rocket returned from London this afternoon with two more men and plenty of ammunition. They won't know what hit them if things kick off tomorrow. Don't forget, ten thirty under the clock and try to act normal we don't want him to become suspicious".

Horace walked back a different way through Mace's farm yard and down the farm lane. He opened the workshop and hid the bag underneath some oily rags in the sidecar. He knocked on Gordon's front door and explained what the plan was and the time and place.

"Thanks, Horace, at least it will keep him off our backs for a few days. I will phone Fisher now".

Gordon phoned Fisher and told him to meet Horace under the town hall clock at ten thirty and to come on his own.

"He wants to talk to you, Horace, he wants to know why you don't just hand them over here at the Garage".

Horace took the receiver from Gordon.

"Mr. Rush told you what I wanted".

"What you want? Who the hell do you think you are dictating to me what should happen? Why not the garage?"

"Because people will be around in town and you're less likely to try anything in public. If you do try anything, you won't see your precious loot again, it's up to you".

"You little bastard".

The phone line clicked and burred. Horace took this to mean that Fisher had assented to meet him at the appointed time under the clock as Fred had proposed.

The next day Horace went to work, welded some hinges on the sidecar ready for the door he was making and kept an eye on the forecourt in case Fisher or his heavies showed up to try to force a change in the plans. Gordon came into the workshop.

"Are you OK for today, Horace?"

"It's OK, Mr. Rush, I've got the doors open because I don't trust that man. If he keeps to his side of the bargain I will keep to mine, but anything can happen. Simon must have thought he could trust him".

"Where have you hidden the things, Horace, don't leave it too late if you have to fetch them?"

Horace moved the rags in the sidecar to reveal the bag and Gordon wondered whether they had been there all the time, not realising that the experts in London had assessed the contents and that a whole host of other activities had taken place behind the scenes.

Horace got down to the town hall half an hour early. He looked around but couldn't see Fisher, there was nothing that struck him as suspicious....for now at least. Horace went and stood in St. Paul's Church yard because it gave him a good view of all of the angles of approach. Fisher pulled up outside St. Paul's Square at twenty to eleven, ten minutes late, and stood under the clock. Horace walked up and they exchanged insults under their breaths so that none of the people passing by would think that anything strange was going on. Horace produced the bag. Fisher wanted to snatch it off him but that would look odd so he glanced left and right and accepted it calmly. He loosened the draw string and peeked inside. It wasn't the right place to check all of the contents but everything seemed in order.

"Soon your days will be numbered you bastard" he spat out at Horace with as much venom in his voice as he could muster.

Horace looked around and waited a few minutes until Fisher

was out of sight. There was still no sign of Fred and his blokes. He began to wonder whether they'd let him down but there was nothing he could anyway so he went back to the garage and got on with the booked in jobs.

A regular customer came in and asked Gordon if he could tidy up the bodywork on his car.

"There are scratches and scrapes everywhere, my daughter is getting married in a month's time and she wants to travel in this car".

"Well, Alf, you can't get a more comfortable car than a Humber drop head. I've always wanted one of these, you know, nothing better than the roof down on a sunny afternoon. How come it's in such a mess, it looks like it's been through a desert sand storm?"

"Yes, Gordon, it's my fault I've been too lazy over the last year or so and have been parking it outside my office at the quarry. You can just imagine what's been blowing around there, plus some of the men lean on it while waiting for me. So, how much to tidy it up, and please be kind to me, I went to Willoughby's first but he's a robbing bastard is Brian".

"Well you might think that of me when I give you my price. It's lucky you have a cloth roof that'll make it cheaper. You probably won't get any change out of sixty five pounds, Alf".

"Ah ha! I told you he was robbing me, he wanted double that. When can you do it?"

"We'll need it for a week to do the job properly. Drop it in tomorrow and Horace will crack on with it. Do you still want the maroon or something different? You could have a greenish-yellowy-blue tinge but I think maroon is probably better, it's entirely up to you, Alf".

Horace overheard them.

"Maroon and black would look good Mr. Gilbert" Horace shouted to them from the inspection pit.

"Morning, Horace, I didn't see you hiding down that hole. Yes, maroon and black does sound majestic but would the price be the same or more?"

"Well, Horace, what do you think? Can we do it for the same price for a regular?"

"That depends, Mr. Rush, what was he doing going down at Willoughby's in the first place?"

"I didn't realise you sprayed cars 'til I spoke to your Uncle Bill, he came for a load of sand in his new tipper truck. He's doing well for himself these days with all these council houses going up".

"I didn't know he was thinking of getting a new truck, he didn't say anything".

"He wasn't 'til yesterday. Belleries has gone bust and the yard and equipment is all being sold. I'm told that they're moving back to America. He only came here after the US Air Force moved in at Fauld, that's when he met Iris. His family in the States are in the engineering business and he is joining them. Bill saw him yesterday and they came to an agreement over the sale of the business".

"Uncle Bill has bought the lot? With him going bust surely it can't be worth much".

"That's why it's too a good deal to turn down, Horace. Bill told me he can take sand and cement from here to Luton, the price they charge up there is out of this world. If he gets his way he will have a truck going there every day, but he said he will see how the land lies for a couple of weeks".

"Yes, Mr. Rush, we can do it for the same money. We only need to mask it off and the black paint's cheaper anyway. How are you going to get to work Mr. Gilbert while your car's here?"

"I hadn't thought of that yet, I could always bike there it's only five miles".

"There's a Vauxhall Velox doing nothing out the front, if you want to borrow it" said Gordon.

"Who does it belong to? I've seen it here for a few weeks now".

"It's Horace's. It's ready and waiting for him when he passes his test in a few weeks".

"Well, thank you Gordon, Horace for the kind offer. Can I leave my car with you now and borrow yours?"

"No problem, Mr. Gilbert".

Christine appeared in the workshop doorway.

"Horace, can you please pick up the phone in the office?"

"Who is it, Mrs. Rush?"

"It's Lizzy....Lizzy Hackett. She won't tell me what it's about".

Horace went into the office and picked up the phone.

"Hello Lizzy, how are you all, are you on the way back? I can't wait to see you all. I've been down to the canal the last few nights to see if you were there, I got as far as Fradley but there wasn't any sign of you. I was going to try again tonight after work, but it'll be a bit later than normal".

# CHAPTER NINETEEN

"Horace, I have something to tell you, something terrible. My Chamy is dead. She hanged herself sometime during last night. She left us a note and there is another one here waiting for you. In ours she said that she believed she was pregnant and I don't know why she thought that, it has only been three weeks since she went through that the terrible ordeal. She hadn't been the same since then. She became very depressed and aggressive, shouting at people, shutting herself in the butty, distancing herself from everyone and everything".

Horace cried, he wept bitterly.

Lizzy could hear him and waited a few moments for him to absorb the news, to compose himself. That was the last time ever that anyone would see or hear Horace crying. Something inside him changed that day, something that hardened his resolve to right the wrongs that people did to him or those that he loved, something that shortened his tolerance of those he knew to be abusing their positions, something that increased his inability to trust any but those who were able to demonstrate beyond doubt that they deserved it, fully and unreservedly.

Horace changed.

"Where are you Lizzy? I am coming to you now" he managed to say eventually.

She told him where they were moored in the cut in Kidderminster. He put the phone down and went into the workshop. Mr. Gilbert had gone but Gordon and Christine were still there. Horace wiped his eyes as he walked towards them.

"Horace, what is it?"

They knew that whatever it was must be serious if it had upset Horace to such an extent. He was still effectively a child, a strong-willed, determined and courageous one at that and his crying was the first demonstration of vulnerability that they had witnessed in him. They felt affection, love and sympathy for him all at the same time.

"Mrs. Rush, it's Charmaine. She hanged herself last night. She couldn't cope with what happened to her. Is it alright if I go to them, I want to see her for the last time?"

"Horace, son" said Gordon, "go immediately. Take as long as you need".

Horace went home to get some clothes. He told his mum what had happened and despite what she had said about the girl and her people, she was very upset to hear the news. The loss of life of a young person was sad at the best of times but for the poor girl to take her own life under those circumstances was a tragedy beyond words.

Horace found the bridge number that Lizzy had given him. He walked down the canal and there were still a number of police milling around. One stopped Horace to ask who he was but Lizzy saw them talking and ran down to him. She hugged him and cried as she did so but Horace was done crying, he had nothing left. He walked over to the tree where Charmaine had killed herself, the rope was still lying in the wet clay and grit beneath its branches. He knelt at the foot of the tree and vowed that he would avenge her, that he would see she got justice, that he would kill Fisher, the man who ultimately was responsible for her suffering and death.

Unbeknown to Horace, James had come over to see him and was standing just behind him, he heard Horace making his vow. Horace rose and hugged James.

"Horace, my son, the boaters have people who will take care of this. From Kidderminster to Burton-on-Trent boaters will be putting donations into a hat as we speak to pay for the man's execution".

"Please James, this is something that I must do. She was my sweetheart and I know that as her parents you must feel an even greater sense of loss and grievance but this man has caused pain to so many other people that I know, including his own family".

Horace placed his hands on James' shoulders.

"I know, James, that it is probably too early for you to have thought about it in detail but what are you planning to do for her funeral? I must and will be there".

"We are taking her to our hometown, the place where she was born. We have lots of family in Romford. We haven't been there for two years but it will always be home to us".

Horace stayed the rest of the day but decided to go home when they told him that they couldn't see Chamy until after the post-mortem.

"Where are the children?" Horace asked.

"When I found Charmaine this morning I wrapped them up and took them to the Gaskell's boat, they're going to be looking after the kids for the next few days. I didn't want them to see Charmaine hanging there and I couldn't cut her down until they were out of sight".

He kissed Lizzy and hugged James and they parted company.

"Before you go, Horace, this is Charmaine's letter to you. Go somewhere quiet to read it, if it's anything like ours it is best to be alone when you do".

Horace got on his bike and left without looking back. He returned to that spot every year to place a single rose under the tree. Horace didn't realise then that in a few short years he would become another person entirely. He would become violent and controlling and would be feared perhaps even more so than Fisher.

Horace stopped in Redditch to read Charmaine's letter.

She told him that he had been the best thing that happened to her but she couldn't live with herself after those men had taken advantage of her repeatedly. There was a surprise shock. Charmaine mentioned that it wasn't only the watchman and two brothers who had abused her but also a fourth man whom they referred to as 'Lefty', he was a dog breeder. They had ruined her and she would never be able to come to terms with what had happened to her over those three days. She wanted to die.

She wrote further:

"Horace, my love, I miss you with all my heart. Please understand that I could never be the same again. I know that I am bearing a child, a child that I could neither keep nor not keep. It is better that I go now to be at peace and that we meet again in the next life. There could never be any other for me, you are and always have been the one that I love".

Horace stared at the piece of paper in his hands, they were trembling. He was numb, he felt empty. He ran through the events in his mind leading up, during and just after her kidnapping. He prodded his mind with the question, who was this fourth person? He sat for what felt like an eternity but in reality was little more than thirty minutes. He folded the letter and put it in the top pocket of his jacket and rode back to Burton.

It was tea time when got home. His mum and dad were shocked to see him back so soon, he had told them that he would probably be a few days.

"How are you coping with it, son? It's a terrible tragedy. I too have seen much death and suffering so understand what you are going through. Whatever you do, I will be here to support you".

Horace had something to eat and told them that he was going to the garage to work on his sidecar, he just needed to be alone. He went into the workshop and put on his overalls. He finished the welding and fitted the door, all that was needed now was a coat of paint. Gordon saw the light in the workshop and popped his head round the door at ten o'clock.

"Sorry, Mr. Rush, I just needed to be on my own for a while, I've got to try to get my head around this".

"I understand. Be careful, son, and lock up after yourself but, please, go and get some sleep".

Horace worked day and night over the next two weeks, he couldn't sleep properly anyway. He would cat nap in between jobs to try to compensate but it didn't, he felt very tired. He had told Sol about this person called Lefty whom Charmaine had mentioned in her letter and waited anxiously to hear news of whether Sol had found out who it was, where he was. Every time the phone rang he wondered whether it was Sol. The other thing that bothered him was that he hadn't heard a thing from Fred after his meeting with Fisher under the clock tower and, strangely, he was upset that Fisher hadn't shown his face either, for no other reason than his absence confused him. Where was he, what was he up to? A tornado whirled around in his head picking up the fragments of his thoughts and flinging them around his mind with such speed and fury that he couldn't catch them let alone hang on to them.

Horace had been in shock, plain and simple. He was a young man who had been through so much in such a short space of time and Charmaine's death had tipped him over the edge. It had been building slowly all the while. But the human body is a wonderful machine. His body and mind fought with all their might and the tide of the battle was starting to turn, Horace was beginning to organise his thoughts and to start to think about the future once more.

On Thursday, January 8th 1952 at ten thirty in the morning, Lizzy phoned Horace to tell him that Charmaine's funeral would be on the Tuesday of the following week. The boaters would be giving Charmaine a traditional boater's funeral. Horace rushed to ask Gordon for time off so that he could go.

"Take as long as you want, Horace. You have worked so hard these last two weeks and for much longer hours than normal at your usual rate. I will pay you for however long you are away and that might go some way to redressing the balance".

*Author's Note: Paid leave was unheard of in those days, if you wanted any time off you would have to fund it yourself.*

Horace went to Bladon woods to see his uncle for the first time since returning from Kidderminster. Uncle Bill was there with Sir Humphrey Cartwright and Lady Hermione, Sir Stanley Carpenter and Lady Edith were also there.

"We were just talking about you" said Sir Humphrey, "you have helped so many people and now it is our turn to help you so please don't hesitate to let us know if you need anything".

"Thank you, Sir Humphrey, but this is something that I have to get through myself. Lady Edith, you are walking much better now".

"Horace, please don't call me Lady Edith, Edith will do. And yes, thank you, I am much better now, thanks to you. Come on Hermione, let's go for a walk around you beautiful garden".

Once the ladies had left the room, Horace spoke frankly to Sir Humphrey, Sir Stanley and Uncle Bill.

"The only thing I want is to see two people dead, Brian Fisher and Osborne, and I want to kill them myself, to look into their eyes when I do it".

"You have to be a particular type of person to kill someone in cold blood" said Uncle Bill. He didn't want to prompt Horace but he hoped that he would tell Sir Stanley about what had happened in Luton.

"Sir Stanley was in the secret service, Horace, he has seen and done things that many men, most men in fact, have not". He winked at Horace.

It took a while for the penny to drop.

"I have a confession to make" said Horace, "and I hope it stays just between us. I found Charmaine in Luton tied up and scared to death. When I discovered that the man who was paid to watch her had raped her repeatedly I was so angry that I killed him, I stabbed him and looked him in the eyes as I did it".

He took Charmaine's letter out of his pocket and handed it to Uncle Bill to read.

"This will help you all to understand why I did what I did".

"Are you sure that you want me to read this, Horace, it must be very personal".

"I want you all to know why I said what I did about Fisher and Osborne. Fisher was directly responsible for Charmaine's death and is the source of the pain and suffering of so many others. Osborne is similar in many ways although the method he uses for spreading the pain and suffering is different. I found him in the park interfering with a young boy. I wish that I'd killed him then and there because he is bound to be in another town or city as we speak doing exactly the same to some other poor child".

Uncle Bill gave the letter to Sir Humphrey to read and then to Sir Stanley.

"There are circumstances" said Sir Humphrey "in which taking another's life are justifiable, indeed necessary, but taking the law into your own hands is a crime and there are reasons why that is the case. How did you feel, Horace, after you had done it, most people would have nightmares after something like that?"

"To be truthful, sir, I would do it again. People like Fisher take the law into their own hands every day. The law isn't always available or able to reach some in society who need help the most, the help to stand up to scum like him. I understand, Sir Humphrey, that there must not be a free-for-all and that the law is there to protect the majority but there are those who slip through the net and they too must be helped. Mr. Rush's family are an example. They are being held to ransom by a wicked, cruel and manipulative man who gets away with murder, literally. The law seems unable to protect them from him. By the way, Uncle Bill, I haven't heard anything about those stones that I returned to Fisher".

"Well, Horace" said Sir Humphrey, "that's the real reason why we are meeting here today. We believe that the stones in Mr Fisher's possession were stolen from a collection".

"Bill described the large stone to us" Sir Stanley chimed in, "but we want to be sure that we are not mistaken. Can you describe it to us please, Horace?"

Horace picked up a newspaper that was lying on the coffee table and drew a pretty good diagram of the gem stone where there was some space underneath a report of a match between Preston North End and Blackpool.

Sir Stanley held the drawing close to his face then moved it away and back again scrutinising it.

"You should take up art, young man. This looks similar to the item that was stolen in June last year from the Victory Gallery in Portsmouth's Historic Dockyard. Your drawing looks uncannily like Admiral Lord Nelson's lost Chelengk".

*Authors Note: A chelengk is an ornamental brooch fashioned to a style that originated in Turkey. It consists of a decorative centre piece with spokes that radiate upwards simulating feathers. The chelengk was attached to a warrior's turban to denote bravery. This particular brooch was one that Admiral Nelson wore on his bicorn hat to commemorate the Battle of the Nile that took place in 1798.*

"How many small jewels were there, Horace, give or take, and were any mounted in anything?"

"They weren't mounted in anything. It's hard to say how many there were. The bag was half full with different items but I could run my hand through the stones and hold them in my cupped palm with plenty still sitting in the bottom. I thought they were fake because there were so many of them".

"Bill, I was telling you before the ladies left and Horace joined us that one of my men investigating the case came back yesterday from the Grand Hotel in the centre of Birmingham. One of the suspects has stayed there a number of times before and is back again. We were able to find out the room that he occupies but are still working on who the others are and what rooms they are in. I am assured that none of them is Fisher, we believe that he is just a mule for the real villains. We spoke to the hotel manager and he is assisting us incognito".

"Can you tell us who you think is behind it, Sir Stanley? It's intriguing that they were so bold to steal something so valuable and prestigious. What else did they steal from there?"

"That's the thing, Bill, nothing else was taken. This must have been stolen to order. We believe that whoever stole the Chelengk realised eventually that it would be impossible to sell because it is so unique and recognisable so they must have cut it down. Even so it is worth a small fortune. The hotel manager, Mr. Montrose, is going through the names of the guests and trying to identify anyone who looks out of place. They won't, of course, be using their real names and are probably just using the hotel as a meeting place until they figure out how and to whom they can sell the gems for the best return".

Sir Stanley continued....

"We need some men on the case who won't look out of place, two hotel workers, for example. What do you say, Bill, as you and Horace are already involved and in the picture, would you both be able to help us pull this off?"

"What if Fisher and his men are there at the hotel?"

"Fisher and his two men are at his house in Barton Turns, we know that much. We are carrying out surveillance on the place. What do you say, Horace? This would be entirely voluntary and for King and country but we will, of course, recompense you".

"Of course I will help, Sir Stanley. We have all weekend but I must be in Romford without fail on Tuesday for Charmaine's funeral".

"That's not a problem, Horace. If we don't find the men or the jewels in three days then we will have missed the opportunity anyway. We were going to set off tomorrow but may as well get going tonight, the more time we have the better. Don't call me Sir Stanley from now on, just call me Hill, not Mr. or Sir, just plain Hill. That's what I'm known as these days for security reasons, very few know my real name or where I come from. Someone followed me home once, we were living in London at the time, but I noticed. It's what we are trained to do in my profession. I changed course to protect my family and ended up leading him to Dover instead. I booked into a hotel and the not so clever sod booked into the room next door. I phoned the office to send some men down to help me find out who he was. We broke into his room that night and, shall we say, made him very uncomfortable until he told us who had sent him. It turned out to be one of the very men that my office had sent to Dover to help, a traitor, a double agent. As soon as his cover was blown he pulled out a gun but was shot immediately by one of the others. Unfortunately, it is not uncommon in my line of work for this type of thing to happen, especially if large amounts of money are involved".

"Sir Stanley....er....Hill, Mr. Rush already gave me time off to attend Charmaine's funeral and as we will be doing all of this over the weekend I am ready to go whenever you wish, I just need to let my mum and dad know that I will be away for a few days from tonight".

"Splendid. Be here for nine o 'clock so that we can be at the hotel well before midnight".

Horace went home to pack a few essentials and told his mum and dad that he would be away for the weekend plus a few days the following week to attend Charmaine's funeral. He got on his bike and rode back to Bladon. He parked his bike and sidecar in one of the garages and waited for Sir Stanley and Uncle Bill. They set off at nine o'clock sharp in a car that Sir Stanley had arranged to collect them.

On the way to Birmingham, Sir Stanley explained the plan and told them what they would be doing.

"Bill, you're in maintenance, you will go into all the rooms on the pretext that you are checking the water system because there has been a drop in pressure. Once inside you can carry out a cursory check to see whether there is anything within that looks suspicious. Horace, you will be a busboy. We need you to listen discretely to people's conversations in case they say anything that indicates their involvement in this clandestine group of thieves".

"Sir Stanley, what is a busboy and what does one do?"

"A busboy is a helper, a waiter's assistant in the restaurant and bars. He clears the tables and helps to set them up ready for the guests' meals. You will get a crash course in what to do when you get there but the basic duties are putting on the table cloths, folding the napkins, arranging the cutlery, setting out the condiments and waiting on the tables. You will be the first in the restaurant and the last to leave, particularly in the evening as you will be laying the tables for the next morning's breakfast. The only one in the hotel who knows what we are doing is Mr. Montrose. If any of the staff ask, tell them that you are temporary personnel. We will park around the corner and go to the hotel separately. Horace will go first because you will need some time to meet the restaurant staff and get some training. Go straight to Mr. Montrose's office when you arrive this evening and tell him that I sent you. Bill, you will go to see Mr. Montrose in the morning".

"Sir Stanley, are you able to tell me who exactly you work for?" asked Horace. "It's clearly not the police force".

"No, Horace, it's not the police. I can' tell you much but my work up to and during the war was focused mainly on foreign affairs that affected national security, there is a separate department that deals purely with domestic security. However, sometimes the two overlap, as seems very likely in this particular case".

"By the way, Uncle Bill, what's this about buying a new business and truck, you never said anything".

"The whole deal isn't signed and sealed just yet but I needed a tipper truck urgently with all the work that we're doing, not to mention the amount of material that we are transporting. Young Bill thinks he's the lord and master driving it, I just wish that George would put in for his test soon. The poor lad lacks confidence. It's painful to see sometimes".

# CHAPTER TWENTY

Sir Stanley and Uncle Bill dropped Horace off and he made his way to the Grand Hotel to see Mr. Montrose. The concierge showed him to the manager's office where he waited for Mr. Montrose to come down from a customer's room.

"Good evening, you must be Horace Gray. Sir Stanley has been in touch to put me in the picture as to why you are here. You'll be pleased to hear that I've narrowed down to six the number of rooms and tables that need to be watched. They guests sit at the same tables every day so it shouldn't be too difficult, you will soon get the hang of it. You will start at six o'clock and, as it's getting late, I will get someone to show you to your room straight away".

A maid showed him to his room, a small affair on the top floor at the back of the hotel with the rubbish bins and sacks directly below the window four floors down. Horace hoped that there wouldn't be too much clanging and banging during the night. The room was small with two single beds and two sets of drawers for clothes. He shut the door, opened the window, lit a cigarette and lay on the bed. He was just nodding off when the door creaked and opened and in walked a slight lad who must have been of a similar age to Horace, maybe slightly younger.

"Sorry if I disturbed you but I always work until midnight then I'm up at six. I'm Nigel Homes, I've been here for six months working mainly in the kitchen doing the fetching and carrying".

"Very pleased to meet you, Nigel. I'm Horace Gray, from Northampton. I'm the new busboy but I'm temporary so only here for a few days".

"I wanted the busboy job but they wouldn't give it to me because of my Black Country accent. They told me that they only want well spoken lads to service the guests because they probably wouldn't be able to understand me, plus they said that the guests would be nervous that I might pick their pockets....the bastards".

"That's a terrible thing to say to someone, who told you that? Whoever said it wants a cuff round the ear. There's nothing wrong with your accent, I can understand you perfectly".

"It was the kitchen manager, he's never liked me. He said it's my background that's the problem but he's Scottish and I can't understand a bloody word he says. Mind you, I think it's a posh Scottish accent".

Horace was up first the next morning. He washed, dressed and went to the reception desk.

"Good morning, I'm Horace Gray and I start today as a busboy. The manager told me to come here so that someone can fetch me a uniform".

"Hello, Horace, I'm Juliet, I'll take you to where they keep the uniforms. You can try them on to find one that fits the best. When you've found the right size come back here and I will show you who's in charge of waiter service".

Horace changed into his new uniform and nipped back to the room. He was surprised to see Nigel still fast asleep so woke him.

"Sorry to wake you, mate, but it's five forty five, I didn't want you to be late".

"Thank you, Horace, I would have been in the shit if I was late again".

They went down stairs together.

Horace was shown to the lead waiter's office and told to go with Graham to start getting things ready. It wasn't long before the dining room was almost full. Horace looked around and saw Sir Stanley, nodded discretely and carried on greeting the guests, pulling out their chairs for them and showing them the menus. But he was only interested in hearing what they were talking about so he hovered around each table before moving onto the next one. Most of the tables were occupied by couples or families but there was one that caught his eye, there were three men sitting at it. Horace went over to Sir Stanley, bowed and asked whether there was anything else that he needed. Sir Stanley lowered his paper and nodded almost imperceptibly towards the table with the three men.

"No thank you, lad" said Sir Stanley.

Horace walked over to a few other tables first so as not to arouse suspicion and then headed to the men's table. He asked them whether there was anything he could get them and spotted the room key on the table with the number on it. They thanked him but said that they were alright. Horace went around and collected a few empty plates and some dirty cutlery and went back to Sir Stanley's table to collect his cup. Sir Stanley was pretending to do the crossword.

"Room forty" Horace whispered as he collected the cup and brushed some crumbs off the table cloth with a shiny little copper dustpan and brush. Sir Stanley put his pen away and folded his paper, he rose and put his napkin on the table in front of him and departed. Horace noticed a piece of paper sticking out. He picked up the napkin and put the piece of paper in his pocket. After he'd collected some more items and taken them back to the kitchen he went to the corridor just outside the dining room. He took out and unfolded the paper, it was a note from Sir Stanley to give to maintenance saying that the basin tap in room forty wasn't working properly. Horace took the note to the lead waiter.

"Take it to maintenance please Horace" said the lead waiter and showed him where the workshop was.

The small maintenance workshop was on the ground floor near the back entrance to the hotel. Horace knocked and went in, two men were sitting inside one of which was Uncle Bill. There is a note from a Sir Stanley Carpenter, he has a problem with a tap.

"I'll get this one, Bert" said Uncle Bill thanking Horace and taking the note off him.

"If it's only a washer" said Bert, "you can go ahead and do it, if it's anything more involved we'll have to get a requisition form from the manager, but it's usually only a washer".

"OK, Bert, thanks, I'll be in room forty".

Bill took his toolbox and went to room forty. He knocked but no one was there so he opened the door with his skeleton key. He left the door ajar and his toolbox by the door so that if the occupant returned he would know that it was nothing but a routine maintenance visit.

Clothes were strewn over the chair and bits and bobs lay scattered on the desk but nothing of interest. There was a brown crocodile skin briefcase on the unmade bed but it was locked. Bill had no problems picking the locks with a pick and small screwdriver. Inside and on top of other items in the case was a letter from a jeweller whose premises were in the jewellery quarter. The letter said that the 'item' should be ready four days from the date on the letter, which was dated two days ago. It was possible but unlikely that the men would have yet had a chance to take to or collect anything from the jeweller.

Bill locked up, went to Sir Stanley's room and left a note of the jeweller's name and address and went downstairs. They carried on with their work for the rest of the morning. Horace finished at ten but had to be back in an hour and a half to get the dining room ready for lunchtime. Uncle Bill carried on his pretence of working as a maintenance man and hoped that he would not be called upon to do anything too demanding.

Sir Stanley went into the lobby and saw Horace by the tea trolleys in the seating area, he walked passed him and told him to meet outside as soon as he was ready. Sir Stanley sat down and started reading his paper to give Horace time to go to his room and get changed. Horace returned and walked past in his civilian clothes towards the front entrance, Sir Stanley followed him outside. He told Horace what Bill had found in the briefcase.

"I have no idea whether we are on the right track here, Horace, but it's a start. There is a jewellery shop about two blocks from here on the left called Zachary's. Make sure that it isn't obvious that you are watching the place in case any of the men who were at breakfast this morning turns up and recognises you. Make a note of everyone else who enters and leaves the shop, you don't have much time".

Horace walked as quickly as he could to Zachary's and stood across the road by a bus stop. Anyone seeing him there would assume that he was just waiting for a bus. Several people entered and left the shop, mainly young couples and older ladies. He had been there about forty minutes when a well dressed gentleman with a cane stopped outside the shop, it wasn't anyone he had seen in the hotel. Rather than going into the shop, the man stood with his back to the display window and waited, he kept looking up and down the street. Horace glanced away every time the man looked across the road.

About ten minutes later, two more men arrived. They spoke briefly to the man that Horace had been observing, all three turned and went into the shop and the door closed behind them. Almost immediately a hand appeared in the glass of the door and the open sign was flipped over to read closed and the curtains pulled shut behind it. Horace now had a dilemma. There were only thirty minutes before his lunchtime shift started but he wanted to see how long the men stayed inside. He decided to wait another fifteen minutes, which would give him just enough time to run back to the hotel, alert Sir Stanley and get changed to start work. A few minutes later the curtains in a window above the shop were also drawn and he could just see through the gap in the curtains that someone had switched on the light.

Horace ran back to the hotel and found Sir Stanley sitting near the tea trolleys where he'd been reading his paper earlier. Horace walked over to the trolleys pretending that he was contemplating having a cup of tea. Sir Stanley got out of his chair and stood about a yard or so next to him. Horace moved some cups around and without looking at Sir Stanley whispered that three men had gone into the shop, the shop had closed and they'd gone to a room upstairs where the curtains were drawn. Sir Stanley poured himself a cup of tea and turned to go and sit down. As he did so, and without look directly at Horace he spoke in a low voice.

"You get off and do what you have to do in the restaurant, but tell your Uncle Bill that I need him here in case we have to follow these people. I will get the car to park up outside the hotel, ask him to meet me out in front in five minutes, I'll be waiting in the car".

Horace rushed to the maintenance room and knocked on the workshop door, it was ajar. Uncle Bill was alone, Bert had obviously been called upon to work on something for one of the guests. Horace explained in detail everything that had happened and that Sir Stanley would be waiting for him in his car at the front of the hotel. Uncle Bill scrawled a note to Bert to the effect that Mr. Montrose had asked him to go urgently to pick up some supplies and that he would be back later that afternoon. He knew that this would be alright because Mr. Montrose was well aware of what he and Horace were doing so he would confirm anything that Bert or anyone else asked about him in his absence. Horace ran upstairs got changed and ran back downstairs to the dining room for the lunchtime shift, he was seven minutes late. The lead waiter was not amused.

Nothing of any note happened either at lunchtime or in the evening for that matter. No one else suspicious turned up, and neither did the men he'd seen at breakfast that morning. The restaurant had been quiet during the lunch period because it was a Saturday and people were out shopping, walking around town or strolling in the parks. Dinnertime was a different story, it was very busy with couples who wanted a meal before going to the theatre or groups who were going out on the town and wanted to line their stomachs before visiting the bars, cinemas or dance halls. The life of a busboy was hard work and long hours. Horace had done the breakfast shift followed by a break, then the lunchtime shift followed by a break and then the dinnertime shift. All in all he had worked for something like twelve hours. He hadn't been bored because there was a lot to do but he'd found the constant attentions of the lead waiter annoying, telling him that he'd done this or the other wrong, but Horace didn't mind too much, he knew it was all for a good cause and that it was only for a limited amount of time.

The last guests left the restaurant at about ten and Horace was able to finish preparing the tables for breakfast by about eleven o'clock. The cleaners came and all of the workers went to their rooms, or homes depending on where they lived. Horace stopped by at Uncle Bill's and Sir Stanley's rooms on the way upstairs but neither of them was there.

Horace woke up early the next morning and had a wander outside and smoked a cigarette. Sir Stanley's car wasn't in the car park.

"Where the hell are they?" Horace said to himself out loud.

He went inside, got dressed and made sure that Nigel didn't

oversleep again. His breakfast shift was as boring as the previous day.

But the previous day had been anything but boring for Sir Stanley and Uncle Bill. They had driven from the hotel, parked in a side street and watched Zachary's for about an hour and a half when the curtain in the upstairs window opened and the light went out. The closed sign was flipped back to open and the shop door opened. A car pulled up in front of the shop, the three men that Horace had seen earlier got into it and it drove off. Sir Stanley pulled out of the side street and followed them out of the city centre towards Coventry, they took the A45 to Banbury then to Oxford where the car slowed down and pulled into a driveway. It was about three thirty in the afternoon and slightly overcast.

Sir Stanley and Uncle Bill had been keeping their distance so as not be detected. They slowed down and drove past the entrance and saw the car they'd been following driving down a sweeping driveway towards a grandiose house. The sign on one of the gate pillars said "Mullion Hall".

"Shall I have a look around?" asked Bill.

"Yes, but be careful, Bill. There's a phone box a few yards back down the road and we need reinforcements. I will get some of the lads to join us, but it will take them a couple of hours to get here. The best place for you to start is probably around the back. Take this with you".

Sir Stanley reached back behind Bill's seat and lifted the carpet underneath which was a trapdoor with a handle. He pulled it open and took out an impressive looking weapon.

"What the hell is that?" asked Bill. "I've seen some weapons in my time but nothing like that".

"It's based on a Sten gun but with a two inch barrel and 6.8 calibre bullets, twenty five of them to be precise, slightly fewer than the thirty two of a regular Sten. The telescopic sights were an afterthought to be used for, shall we say, engagement at a distance".

He dropped Bill off then turned around and went to the phone box to call HQ. He told them that they would be at Mullion Hall just off the A40 down Wychwood Lane. He left his car at the top of the lane to act as a marker and walked back towards the house with two revolvers. As he was walking a silver Wraith Rolls Royce sped past him and turned into the driveway of Mullion Hall. Although in his fifties, Sir Stanley had been well trained physically, he'd always kept fit and was very agile. He found a small gap in the hedge, looked both ways then jumped up and grabbed the top of a seven foot wooden fence. He pulled himself up using the hedge on either side as footholds and scrambled up until his waist was level with the top then swung his body around and dropped to the ground on the other side and crouched down. When he was satisfied that he hadn't been spotted he crept down the left hand edge of a field keeping close to the fence until he was at the rear of the house. There was a six foot stone wall between him and the sweeping back lawn with plenty of bush cover on either side. He found a reasonable foothold in the wall pushed himself up, grabbed the top of the wall and heaved himself over.

Bill, who was hiding behind a rowan bush on the other side just a few yards to the left, spun round when he heard the soil crunch as Sir Stanley landed, he was mightily relieved when he saw who it was. He put his index finger to his lips and beckoned Sir Stanley over.

"What the fuck, Stan, you scared the shit out of me".

They had a good view of the rear of the house from behind the bushes. They were no more than twenty yards or so from the house. Between them and the back doors was a row of well kept, rectangular vegetable patches separated from the back lawn by a flower border. The lawn sloped gently upwards to a small ha-ha beyond which were three rows of semi circular steps to a patio. The patio was about twelve feet wide and enclosed with a two and a half foot ornamental wall. The back doors onto the patio were wide and glazed with clear glass, the curtains were open and they could see easily into what looked like a large dining room. There was a small summer house on the top of the ha-ha about five yards from and slightly to the left of the patio steps.

Another car pulled up in the front driveway. Some people got out and they heard voices and laughter accompanied by the slamming of doors and footsteps in the gravel. They decided to make their way to the summer house so they would be closer and better able to see through the patio doors. They made their way over to hide behind it keeping low and using the ha-ha to obscure them from view.

"Damn! I never thought to bring some field glasses" whispered Sir Stanley.

"Unscrew the barrel and unclip the stock, push this button on the back and adjust the focus of the sights with this thumb screw".

"My God, Stan, this is one hell of a piece of kit".

"There are more tricks up its sleeve than that, Bill".

They took it in turns to peer into the house through the telescopic sights. After about an hour, four men came into the dining room and laid two briefcases on the table and sprung them open. One looked to contain bundles of money and the other small black pouches.

"They're exchanging the goods" said Bill, "how long before your men get here?"

"Too long, Bill. There are four men in that room and we can assume that there are at least a couple more in the other rooms but we don't know for certain how many in total, and how many of them are armed. Put the gun back together, we'll have to try to get into the house".

Just then, two of the men opened the patio doors and came out for a smoke. The others picked up the briefcases and left the room. The men on the patio lit up and sat on the patio wall with their backs to the summer house.

"We could do it with a knife, Stan. If we get rid of these quietly we can go in and start the party".

"Here, press the bottom of the stock forwards until it clicks then pull it back".

Bill was very gently so as not to make any noise, two short bayonets were exposed, they grabbed one each.

It was only about five paces from the summer house to the men, both of whom were deep in conversation gesticulating and laughing as they talked. Sir Stanley and Bill crept up to within a couple of paces of them and then rushed forwards. The men started to turn but it was too late. They pulled them backwards off the wall covering their mouths with their hands and thrust the bayonets into their lungs and jerked them upwards into their hearts. They rolled the bodies tight against the bottom of the patio wall and vaulted over it.

They kept in tight to the back wall of the house and moved across to the open door, Bill peered around it cautiously. The coast was clear so he stepped inside beckoning Sir Stanley to follow him. They crept through the dining room around the table and could hear voices in the adjoining room, which was probably a lounge just off the hallway. Bill peered round the door post and saw that the door was half open, he could see the shoes and bottom half a man's legs that were stretched out as he sat in a chair just behind the door.

"We have a man on the inside so any time you want more we can do further business with you" they heard someone say.

Bill stepped out followed closely by Sir Stanley and kicked the door fully open and entered the lounge. There were five men inside all of whom jolted into an upright sitting position with surprise, a wine glass fell to the carpet and broke.

Bill covered the left side of the room and Sir Stanley the right. The man in the chair behind the door shoved his right hand into the left hand side of his suit jacket, a shot rang out and the man's head jerked backwards splattering blood on the wall behind. Sir Stanley's revolver smoked. Within a split second, one of the men sitting on a sofa against the far wall directly in front of Bill leant forward and tried with one motion to stand up and pull out a gun that was tucked into the waist band of his trousers. Bill pulled the trigger, the man snapped backwards into the sofa as if he'd been attached to it with a rubber chord. He slid sideways slowly onto the left arm of the sofa leaving a smear of blood on the back rest as if someone had run a thick paint brush across it crudely. There was a hole in the front of his shirt about the size of a cricket ball, blood gushed out and dripped onto the carpet. The two men on the sofa beside him stared at Bill and Sir Stanley having second thoughts about going for their guns, if indeed they had any. The third man who was sitting in an armchair to Bill's left leant forward gripping the chair arms tightly, his knuckles as white as they could possibly be.

Bill had nearly been knocked off balance with the force of his gun's kick.

"Sorry, old boy, I forgot to warn you of the kick".

Sir Stanley barked an order at them "You three, all of you, kneel down and arms on the coffee table in front of you....now!"

Bill picked up the briefcases, one that was beside the chair behind the door and the other that was leaning against a lamp stand to his left, and put them by the door.

"You will be sorry" said one of the men, "this is small country and you won't get away".

"You have no idea who we are, do you" replied Sir Stanley.

"Bill, take some of that curtain chord and tie the hands of those two on the left together so that they are back-to-back. Nice and tight now and make sure that they are so close that they get to know each other intimately".

"Are you in charge?" Sir Stanley demanded of the one who had spoken out. He lifted his right foot and shoved the man's shoulder with it pushing him onto the floor sideways.

The other two were tethered together and sitting back-to-back on the floor the other side of the coffee table.

"Bill, go and check upstairs and then check the cars, make sure we have them all....and be careful".

As bill got outside he heard shots in the distance, he couldn't see anything and it seemed as if the shots were outside the grounds. There were no others anywhere inside the house. The old chauffeur who was in the Rolls Royce outside had jumped out and cowered behind the offside wing of the car when he heard the shots indoors. Bill brought him in. He was clearly neither a threat nor one of them and was shaking with fear.

"It's alright, sir, we won't harm you if you are good" said Sir Stanley. "Bill, tie him up anyway, can't be too careful".

"Stan, I heard shots outside in the distance but I'm not sure how far away or where exactly they are coming from".

Sir Stanley commanded the man who was lying on the floor to take his jacket off, then his shirt and trousers. Sir Stanley kicked them across the floor away from him.

"You are both dead men" the chap protested as he lay there in his briefs and socks, one of which was half off.

"Bill, this chap here won't talk but with the men coming I wouldn't want to spoil their fun anyway".

They tied him up securely and sidled over to the window so that they could peek through the gaps between the curtains and edges of the window.

"Stan, can I have a quick word with you?" said Bill under his breath, "what organization exactly do you work for? Now that I've blown someone's heart and lungs out whilst standing right beside you I think you can tell me, don't you?"

"Have you heard of the Baker Street Irregulars a.k.a. the Special Operations Executive? We were set up by the wonderful Winston Churchill, the best leader this country has ever had".

*Author's Note: Queen Elizabeth II knighted Winston Churchill on 24<sup>th</sup> April 1953 so he was not known at that time as Sir Winston Churchill.*

*Author's Note: Queen Elizabeth II knighted Winston Churchill on 24th April 1953 so he was not known at that time as Sir Winston Churchill.*

"As you know, we were set up initially to carry out espionage, sabotage and reconnaissance in occupied Europe but the organisation was broken up in January 1946. Both during and immediately after the war we became known as Military Intelligence, Section 6, or MI6 but our portfolio of 'services' is somewhat different now, of course. You must come to me in London tomorrow to fill out a statement of what took place here. The diamonds are obviously stolen so if their original rightful owners cannot be identified they will become Crown property. Most likely they have been stripped from other artefacts and changed hands so often that they will end up belonging to His Majesty King George VI".

Bill opened one of the briefcases to count the money. There was £100,000 in cash.

*Author's Note: £100,000 at that time would be worth around £3.5 million in today's money.*

"Where the hell do people like this get their hands on this kind of money?"

"I expect they are just the runners, Bill. Looks like you've earned yourself a Silver Wraith for your services to King and country. I will take the jewels back to London to be catalogued and checked and will make sure that you get the proper paperwork for your new car. I'll probably be here for a while when the lads arrive so it's best if you head back to join Horace."

Just then two cars and what looked like an armoured car came roaring up the driveway at great speed and screeched to a halt outside. Little stones from the driveway pinged against the glass. Bill ran up to the window to join Sir Stanley. They picked up their guns and watched intently. Someone got out and crouched behind the rear wing of the lead car and shouted "We're coming in".

"It's alright, Bill, stand down. That's Skip, one of my men".

"Skip!" Sir Stanley shouted, "it's secure in here. Come in but make sure you all wipe your feet, we don't want to make it any messier than it already is" he jested.

Skip told them that when they arrived they had to engage with others on the outskirts of the property. They'd killed two of them. They'd heard gunshots coming from the house just before the gun battle started and they didn't want to let the gunmen return to the house mainly because it would have endangered Sir Stanley and Bill but also it would have been more difficult to capture or kill them if they'd found refuge indoors.

"Change of plan Bill" said Sir Stanley, "this place is a hot potato. Martin, put these three in the battle wagon, they're already tied up. Be gentle with the chauffer, poor chap, he needs a cup of tea and to be let go if and once you can confirm his innocence, and please remove these bodies, there are two more outside by the patio. Bill you go and join Horace, here is the address in London to come to tomorrow. The sooner we get this all down on paper the better. My men will get more information out of these crooks back at base. Oh, and Martin, please get someone to clean up this mess. After all, we haven't been here".

Bill drove to Birmingham in his Rolls Royce to get Horace. He parked in front of the hotel and went into the restaurant.

"Horace, we have to go now, come on mate".

"I'll go and get my things and tell Mr. Montrose".

"No, leave them, Sir Stanley will sort it out. We have to go now. He put his hand on his arm, come on lad".

"What's the problem, Uncle Bill, you seem a bit on edge, you're looking more in the mirrors than you are in front, and where the bleeding hell did you get a Rolls Royce Wraith? Aunt Mavis will think you've gone bonkers, and her next question will be the same as mine, where did you get it?"

"We're not going home. I said come on I didn't say where we were going. They don't expect me back in Burton 'til Monday so we will go and see Sol in Luton, he can sell this for us, once we get the paperwork".

"Us, Uncle Bill? This is your car. The car suits you better than the Daimler, you look like a real country gent in this".

"That's why it's going to Luton. Our Mavis will think I've won the football pools. When I took the Daimler home the first thing she wanted to do was go to her mother's in Manchester to show it off to her sisters and all the neighbours. I went down the Hope and Anchor while she banged on about it. I can't be doing with all that shit, we're a working family".

They arrived in Luton at ten o'clock and went straight to the Horse and Jockey.

"Bill, Horace what a surprise". Ray was behind the bar and poured them a drink.

"Their money is no good in here" someone shouted.

They spun around to see Bert, Dot, Sol and Piglet sitting around a table in the corner. Dot ran over and threw her arms around Horace.

"I am so sorry to hear about Charmaine, Horace" and gave him a big kiss, "come and sit down with us".

"Ray" said Bert, "put all the food and drinks on my tab".

"You have a tab, Bert? You must be spending all of your hard earned in here".

"Well boys, there's news on that front as well, as from last Monday I own this place".

"You bought a pub? Where the hell did you get the money for that?"

"Now, my old son, there was a safe in the house. No key for it so Sol spent two days solid trying to open it with the combination. He got so mad that he kicked the handle and it sprung open. The bastard Lawrences didn't set the combination properly so it never took and we never thought to just try the bloody handle. I've got everything back now that I lost to my uncle and cousins, and more. Horace, son, we are all very sorry for your loss in the whole mess and we will try and make it up to you, one way or the other".

Dot put her arm in his and held his hand.

"We all will, me especially. You helped me on the long road

towards being able to trust a man again after what the Lawrences did to me".

"Charmaine was a lovely girl, Dot. People say that you never forget your first love. I don't know whether that's true but after losing her I can understand why they say it".

"I've not had a first love yet, Horace, not someone I can say is truly close to me, you're the first I've met that comes anywhere near".

"Were you a virgin before the Lawrences abused you, Dot?"

She put a hand to her face and cried. Horace put his arm around her to comfort her.

"I'm so sorry, Dot, that was so insensitive of me. Please forgive me".

She grabbed his hand and just held it tight then put her head on his shoulder.

"It's alright, Horace, it was six months ago now, I had only been here two weeks when it happened. I was new and trying so hard to be nice to everyone. When Arthur Lawrence asked me to go to see his collection of dog racing memorabilia I went with him. I suppose that was the height of naivety".

"Look, Dot, don't blame yourself. The Lawrences are the ones to blame and you will never see them again. There are decent people, Dot, and you will find them and be happy".

"I know, Horace, but I still feel dirty, and I'm only sixteen. Right now I don't think that I'll ever be able to trust another man let alone sleep with him".

"Dot, have you been able to talk to anyone about this, other than Beth and me? Have you been able to talk to your mum and dad?"

"Dad died in the war fighting for King and country. I don't see much of mum, she lives on her own and has done ever since she had me. I wish we were closer but there's something not right with her so my grandma looked after me since I was born. My mum looks even older than my gran, she always wears a scruffy grey dress".

"Drink up, let's go upstairs to be alone and talk. Ray, what room am I in?"

"Let them have the top room, Ray" shouted Bert, "there's a bathroom up there and you won't have to share it with anyone".

"Thank you, Bert, that's really kind of you, I fancy a bath too".

"My boy, we wouldn't all be here together if it wasn't for you and the grace of God. I wouldn't have my car business back, I wouldn't have bought this place and we wouldn't have been rid of those Lawrence crooks, plus Sol and Piglet have come into my life as good friends".

"Well, Bert, if God had anything to do with it then he's really shit on you from above sending that pair of losers into your life".

Sol and Piglet leapt up, grabbed Uncle Bill and tried to lift him out of his seat but Uncle Bill was still too strong and sharp for them. He got Sol in a neck lock and using him as a support swung his legs up and around Piglet's neck twisting him to the floor.

"One day, you big bastard" said Sol playfully, "I will get you but I suppose the fact that we can't is why we look up to you".

"That's three off us then. I'm going up to the room now, come on Dot. Hang on, I'll tell you what, I'll go and get some fish and chips for us being as we're in the big room, we can leave the window open".

The others protested because they too wanted a fish and chip supper so Horace offered to get them all some, including Ray behind the bar.

"Can you get some for the missus too?" asked Ray.

"No problem, mate" said Horace, "there was plenty of cash in the car so I'll use it to get everyone's".

Horace left to get their supper so Bill explained the real reason they had come to Luton.

"Well, Sol, Piglet, the reason we're up here is that I have a car for you to get rid of, once I get the paperwork for it. If you can keep it hidden for a few days then flog it".

"Where is it skip? We will put it in the lock up now, I need a cheap runner to get back anyway".

Bill threw the keys in their general direction. Bert caught them first.

"You are joking, you have a Rolls Royce? Where the hell did you get it from? What do you want for it, Bill, name your price".

"If you want it, Bert, you have it. I can just see you running about in that but that's guaranteed free lodgings for me and Horace every time we come here. Where are those damned fish and chips?"

Ray came out with a pot of tea.

"Here, Dot, take this up to your room. I know Horace likes his tea when he has something to eat".

Dot asked Ray where he will go now that Bert had bought the pub off him.

"Don't worry, Dot, we sold the pub but will continue to manage it for him. The mortgage was getting a bit much so it'll be the best of both worlds for us, still being here but not having all the outlay. Bert and Mr. Saunders reckon they can increase the clientele with their dog track customers".

Horace returned with the fish and chips, distributed the vinegar soaked newspaper parcels to everyone and bade them all goodnight.

"Horace, before you go, how much was in the car and where was it?"

"In the glove box, Uncle Bill".

He put his hands in his pocket and brought out handfulls of notes.

"Did you ever check the boot, Uncle Bill, the back seats lift up, I noticed that on the drive up and I don't think they're supposed to. Let's check it out in the morning. Goodnight".

Horace went upstairs with Dot and the first thing she did was to check the bathroom out. Horace's first job was to open the chips.

"Come on, Dot, while they're still hot".

"Have you seen this bathroom Horace?"

"I'll have a look when I've have had these fish and chips. Any bathroom will be better than ours at home. Come and eat your food, you can have a bath afterwards, and I've poured out the tea for us".

"What sort of bathroom have you got then, Horace?"

"A tin bath....once a week in front of the fire and the toilet's down the bottom of the garden".

Dot had a bath while Horace put his feet up and smoked a fag.

"You can leave the water in, love, I'll have a bath afterwards".

"Horace, you can have some fresh, clean water, this isn't a tin bath in here. My granddad used to have one of those hanging on a hook in the outhouse, luckily I never saw him use it".

"It's open house on Friday nights at ours. When I was a child as many as seven of us had baths, one after the other, never emptying the water but taking some out then putting some hot in so that it didn't get too cold. It was my granddad, my grandma, then dad, George, then mum, Eva, then my brother and my sister. If I was really unlucky my auntie and uncle would join in the fun, I'm sure my uncle used to piss in the bath, the bastard. But, they were good days, so I'm told".

Horace had a bath after Dot. She came into the bedroom with just a towel wrapped around her barely covering her rear end. She bent over to adjust the pillows and he tapped her playfully on the buttocks. She got undressed and waited for him naked while he had his bath. He dried himself and got in beside her. She put her arms around him.

"Can we just have our bodies close together so that I can feel your warmth?" she asked.

Just as she was falling asleep she felt Horace's penis against her, it was getting hard. She felt aroused, and so did Horace, but they just lay there and drifted off to sleep in each other's arms.

Horace was the first to wake the next morning. The sun shone brightly through the window and fell on the bed. He pulled the covers back and admired the wonderful contours of her body and her silky smooth skin. He sniffed her hair, it smelt divine. He ran his little finger down the middle of her stomach, which tickled and she awoke suddenly. She looked at him and told him not to stop.

"Please, Horace, keep doing that it is so gentle, it makes me feel warm inside".

But her eyes watered as she spoke.

"You are so gentle and kind but I can't help being scared. You're the first to touch me in that way since....that thing happened....since that disgusting man violated me".

"Dot, close your eyes and just lie there. You know I won't hurt you. All I want you to do is guess where I will touch you next".

The game went on for half an hour, Horace getting close to but never touching her intimate regions. She squirmed and smiled every time he got close. Then he stopped, swung his legs off the bed, stood up and got dressed.

"Horace, why have you stopped? Please don't stop loving me".

"I want you to take things slowly, Dot. You cried a moment ago and that tells me that you are not ready yet, I want you to be sure".

"But Horace, I think I'm ready now, you're the one I want, you know I want you".

"You said you 'think', but I want you to be sure".

Dot got dressed and they went down to breakfast. Bill was there with the woman that he'd met at the track during their last visit.

"Good morning, Uncle Bill, how are you this morning, and who is the lovely lady?"

"This is Rosemary, she is the book keeper for the race track....she knows I'm married by the way".

"That's nice, I will tell Aunt Mavis that she knows you're married, that will make her feel a lot happier".

Bill threw a table mat at Horace and laughed, they all laughed.

# CHAPTER TWENTY ONE

When they had finished breakfast Horace told Uncle Bill that they should go and check the back seat in the Rolls Royce. They went to the lock up where they'd left the car the night before and opened the back doors.

"How do you know the seat lifts up Horace?"

"I heard a noise when we were driving up yesterday. When I turned round to look in the back I saw it bouncing slightly whenever you went over a bump".

Horace opened one of the back doors and put his hand in the middle of the seat and tried to pull it upwards, the seat didn't move. He wiggled it and tried to pull it forward towards the back of the front seats and it started to slide.

"Uncle Bill, release the catches and move the driver and passenger seats forwards as far as they will go".

As the front seats moved forward the back seat moved with them until it stopped and raised itself on four small hydraulic pistons. Uncle Bill and Horace were transfixed, they couldn't believe what they were seeing. In a large compartment underneath the seat was a collection of arms fit for a militia. Horace opened the boot and patted his hound around the carpet. It wasn't long before he found a small lever under a flap which he flipped up. The floor of the boot emulated the back seat and raised itself up on four pistons revealing yet more ammunition, even hand grenades. Horace and Uncle Bill stared at each other.

"Horace, how does it go back to normal?"

Horace pushed the lever back down and the floor of the boot dropped back into position. He slid the back seat backwards and it lowered down as it went until it was almost back in position. He noticed that it hadn't quite gone back fully so he pushed it down and it clicked into place.

"That's why I noticed the seat moving yesterday, the piston on the front right is sticking and whoever closed it didn't do it properly".

They went back into the pub, collected their belongings and bade farewell to those who were up and about, the ones that had decided to tackle their hangovers head on. Horace kissed Dot goodbye and got into the car.

"Where are we going now, Uncle Bill, you said London didn't you?"

"Yes, we are going to meet Commander Carpenter, we arranged it yesterday. I have to give a statement about the events at Mullion Hall".

"You're being formal, Uncle Bill, why are you calling him Commander it's normally Stanley or Sir Stan. I still don't know what happened and what and where is Mullion Hall?"

"I called him Commander because he's a true soldier. He demonstrated that to me yesterday. After you alerted him at the hotel about the suspicious people you'd seen at the jewellers we sat outside in his car watching the place. The men came out and we followed them all the way to Oxford. They pulled into a place called Mullion Hall just off the A40. We sneaked into the gardens at the back and disposed of two of the crooks outside before making our way indoors. We burst in on them and had to shoot two of them. Stanley's men arrived with the bodies of two others they'd shot in or just outside the grounds. They took the three surviving crooks and their chauffeur with them to London to interrogate. They also took one briefcase full of diamonds and another containing £100,000 to London".

Bill followed Sir Stanley's directions to Baker Street just off Marylebone Road not far from Regent's Park. They parked just a few yards away from the building that Sir Stanley had indicated and went down a side alley to the back door. Bill knocked and a small head-height hatch opened partially. A voice asked them what they wanted and bill asked to speak to "Hill". The hatch snapped shut and they waited outside for about ten minutes.

"Are you sure you have the right place? That ignoramus behind the hatch could at least have asked us to wait".

There was the sound of bolts being drawn back followed by a lock turning and the door opened. Martin stood in the doorway.

"Good Morning Bill, it's good to see you again. I gather that this is your nephew Horace, pleased to meet you. We will take you to Hill shortly we've found out a thing or two but it's early days yet".

"Martin, before we go in we need to show you something, it's truly unbelievable".

They walked Martin to the Rolls and Horace went through the routine of lifting the back seat up and the floor of the boot. There were not many people about in the street and they wouldn't have been able to see inside the car anyway.

"Well boys, I say, what the fuck have you got here?"

"This is the car that some of the crooks turned up in yesterday. Hill gave it to me, pending his sorting out of the paperwork today. We found these compartments and their contents this morning before setting off".

"This is an amazing find. Well done, Bill, the commander will be chuffed".

"I can't take the praise for finding them, it was Horace".

"This is incredible, but your nephew is still a child. How old are you, Horace, are you at school?"

"You want to be careful, Martin, this kid will kick your arse if you're not careful".

"No offence meant, Horace. I am just so surprised to see someone so young here and involved in all of this. We normally only have the more, shall we say, experienced, the elite coming here to train or work".

"Then why is Uncle Bill here, Martin?"

Bill cuffed him playfully around the back of the head, "You

cheeky little bastard".

Martin called Perkins to drive the car around the corner into the secure basement car park and put it in a holding bay for a thorough examination.

"I wonder, Bill, Horace, why they have all these weapons, the must have been planning something. It certainly wasn't for last night, for one thing they weren't expecting us. It must have cost hundreds of pounds to get the car converted to accommodate that amount of weaponry not to mention the extra weight".

Just as Perkins had started the engine and started to pull forward Horace shouted "Stop!".

"There is something else at the front. Do you see those two holes under the bumper? That's not normal".

Perkins stopped and Bill and Martin crouched down to have a look but told Horace that they couldn't see anything unusual. Horace opened the driver's door and lifted the bonnet catch, opened the bonnet and had a look around.

"Look down here under the lights. There is a section on each side that wouldn't normally be there, the engine compartment has been modified too".

"What could possibly have been modified, Horace, isn't it just the normal front of the car?"

"I'm sorry, Martin, but there is something fishy about the front. We need to get this thing over a pit so we can see it properly. I will stake my next three meals on the fact that there is something different about the front of this car".

"Well, Martin, when Horace said there was something wrong with the back seat I didn't believe him at first. But he was right about that so I would give him the benefit of the doubt if I were you".

"OK, agreed, we will get someone to take it apart bit by bit to see just what we have".

The three of them went inside and upstairs to meet Hill.

"Just sit here, chaps, until he has finished his meeting. I will get someone to bring you tea and biscuits".

They were sitting in a cubicle in the corner just across from what they believed to be Hill's office. A large window in the cubicle offered them a good view of a busy open plan office. People were scurrying about between rows of desks upon each of which was a type writer and piles of files and paper that looked as if they were leaning over so far that they would fall at any moment, a row of neatly labelled metal filing cabinets ran down the entire length of one wall. Most of the desks had an ashtray that was overflowing with cigarette ends and the smoke had formed a haze that wafted about as the men and women walked through it. It was very noisy too. Over the hubbub of conversation there was the constant clatter of typewrite keys and the incessant shrill ringing of the telephones.

"Look, Horace" whispered Uncle Bill.

The door had opened and Hill walked out of his office accompanied by a not very tall, rotund gentleman with a cigar in his mouth, a very large cigar. Bill stood bolt upright suddenly and his chair slid backwards making a loud scraping noise on the floor.

"Horace, it's Winston Churchill....in the same building as us".

Martin had joined Hill and Winston and they were talking as they walked past the cubicle. Bill and Horace could just make out Martin saying something about a car with ammunition in it. Martin turned and pointed at the cubicle, in other words, straight at Bill and Horace. The three men walked over and entered it. Horace didn't know whether to curtsey, bow or salute so decided to just stand there and go red in the face instead. Hill introduced them to the Prime Minister.

"Sir, this is Bill and his nephew Horace. Gentlemen, the Prime Minister of the United Kingdom".

They all nodded to each other politely.

"This young lad, sir, saved my wife's life nearly three years ago. She was attacked by a thug and Horace, who was only fourteen at the time, leapt into action and stopped him. The man was arrested at the scene and is now in jail".

The prime minister took off his hat and held his hand out to Horace for him to shake.

"Well done, young lad, you seem to have gained the respect of the Commander, which is not a claim that many can make. So you are seventeen then, what do you want to do next year when you're eighteen and doing national service?"

"Prime Minister, I would like to go into the transport division of the R.A.F. I'm still sixteen but will be seventeen in two weeks".

"I hear you found a cache of arms in a Rolls Royce, how did you find that?"

"Well, Sir, I work as a mechanic and I noticed that the back seat was wobbling as we travelled last night. I told my Uncle Bill and we checked it this morning and found the stash. The seat is lifted up by four small pistons and we found a similar compartment in the boot".

"Prime minister, he is a very resilient and modest young man. He even disarmed two men with a spray gun in his workshop, they were threatening a young lady there. In addition, his girlfriend was kidnapped and raped a few weeks ago. Horace and two of Bill's men found the girl and Horace killed one of them in self defence".

"So, Horace how did you feel taking another man's life, and was it hand to hand or with a gun?"

"It was with a knife, Prime Minister. I put the knife straight through his throat and, Sir, I would do it again if i had to".

"Well, son, you seem very sure of yourself for someone so young, and to kill someone up close and personal with a knife tells me that you are capable of killing from any distance".

Uncle Bill told Winston Churchill that Horace is an excellent shot too, he will do well in his National service.

"Right then, Commander, shall we go and have a look at this car, it will be good to see how it has been modified and to discover to whom it belongs. If there are as many arms in it as you say then it must be a big organisation and they need to be stopped in their tracks".

They gathered around the car that was in the basement parked over an inspection pit.

"I've seen this Rolls Royce before, Commander" said Churchill, "but where the devil was it? I will damned well remember. A businessman I think, quite recently, now who was it? I will have to check my diary it was within the last month I know that".

Horace pulled the catches to reveal the full extent of the find.

"Ah! Commander, do you remember that chap from that new helicopter company, the one who is trying to get a deal with the armed forces to build their flagship helicopter for next year?"

"Yes, I do Prime Minister, Sir Reginald Smithy Cooper. You met the gentleman and a certain Peter Salt on the twenty seventh of last month, and you are due to see them again with the Defence Minister in a week's time. Are you thinking what I am thinking Sir?"

"Commander we are on the same wavelength, I will turn up at the meeting in this car. He will see me pull up and get out, that ought to flummox him. Will you drive me there Hill? You can be my bodyguard for the day".

"Commander, we have found what Horace was telling us about and where the control mechanism is. We can try it out, but please stand clear of the car. Would you all please stand in the debrief room for your own safety".

"Thank you, Martin. This way, Sir, behind this bullet proof window please. This should be interesting".

Martin sat in the driving seat and reached forward to press a button on the dashboard. Suddenly there was a loud, staccato burst of machinegun fire. Everyone jumped. They were expecting the unexpected but not a machine gun to open up. The sound was so loud that it echoed around the cement walls and pillars of the basement, their ears were ringing for some time afterwards. Martin came into the debrief room and, well, debriefed them.

"Two four inch machine guns under the front bumper fed by a magazine at the back of the nearside glove box that juts into the engine compartment to hold extra rounds. A button in the panel just to the left of the rev counter sets the fireworks off. There is bullet proof glass in all the windows, hence the slightly unusual sheen. I don't know whether parts of the bodywork are armour plated but it wouldn't surprise me, it's like a gun ship".

"I thought I noticed something different about the optics through those windows when I took the car up to Luton. Things seemed to be slightly offset when I had the driver's window half down probably due to the thickness of the glass".

Hill told Bill and Horace that he would give them another car to go home in because he would have to hang on to that one for a few more days for Martin to complete his analysis and investigations.

The Prime Minister shook their hands, thanked them for all they had done and bade them farewell. Martin took him back to the office to arrange for him to be chauffeured to his next engagement.

"We owe you both our gratitude for all you have done for the country. This is a major discovery that will help us no end in our quest to identify the people behind it all".

"Thank you, Commander, but I will not take credit for this, it's all Horace's doing. The lad is very knowledgeable about all types of vehicle, plus he also has an acute awareness of his surroundings. If it's OK with you I will get the train back home, it's only three hours from here and Marylebone Station is just up the road".

"And I, Commander, will get the train to Romford. I have Charmaine's funeral to attend on Tuesday".

"In that case, gentlemen, I have some money here for your fares. I have no doubt that we will be working together again soon. We are fairly sure now that the jewels are not from Nelson's hat brooch. Before you go, Bill, I must get Martin to take your statement on our little escapade yesterday, it was a pleasure to work with a professional like you. I would like both of you to keep this whole affair quiet even though I appreciate that it will be difficult not to mention that you met the Prime Minister today".

"You have our assurance that neither of us will say a word. Meeting him was indeed something very special, he looks as impressive in person as he does in the news reels at the cinema and sounds as commanding as he does when we hear him on the wireless".

After Bill gave his statement, which took about an hour, they left for the railway station where they went their separate ways. Horace sat on the train watching the steam billowing past the window reflecting on his and Bill's meeting with the Prime Minister, the iconic Winston Churchill. How could he possibly go through life not telling anyone that he had met this great man.

When the train pulled into Romford his thoughts returned to Charmaine. His only possessions were the clothes he was wearing so he would have to buy a suit, shirt, black tie and shoes, not to mention toiletries and a place to stay. He had a lot to do but was relaxed. He had £130 in his pocket which was a combination of the money he'd taken out of the Rolls Royce and the money that Sir Stanley had given him. He'd never had that much money on him before in his life.

It was a Sunday afternoon, the town was busy but not crowded. There was an upmarket tailor's shop that did off-the-peg suits so he made a mental note of the address to return the next morning when it was open. His next priority was to find somewhere to stay for two nights. He found a reasonable looking bed and breakfast in King George Close overlooking the River Rom. He knocked on the door and an attractive young woman answered.

"Yes, sir, we have two rooms, please come in and choose which you prefer".

The first room was very pleasant, it overlooked the river and boats were plying their way up and downstream as they talked. The lady, Mrs. Dooley, asked him where he was from.

"My name is Horace Gray, I'm from a small town in Staffordshire called Burton-on-Trent and I'm here for a funeral on Tuesday. It's for a girl I knew who very sadly took her own life in tragic circumstances. Her family come from Romford and have a working boat on the canals and rivers. Seeing these passing by reminds me of her".

"I'm so sorry, Mr. Gray, if it upsets you the other room overlooks the road and playing fields".

"No, Mrs Dooley, thank you, this one his fine, and please call me Horace".

"The poor thing that's terrible to happen to a girl, how old was she?"

"She was only fifteen, soon to be sixteen. Mrs. Dooley, I came here from London. I don't have any luggage because I was working with my uncle in London and someone stole his car with all my things in it. Is there a shop nearby where I can get some toiletries? I have already seen a tailor's shop in Arcade Place where I can get some clothes tomorrow morning for the funeral".

"There is a hardware shop on the corner of Bridge Street, they sell everything and they are open 'til seven every day. Turn left when you go out of the house and keep along the A12, turn left into Eastern Avenue then right down North Street, the shop is just over the bridge".

"Thank you. The next place I need to find, Mrs. Dooley, is where the Hackett Family are staying, they told me it's Old Church Road".

"That's the same way, Horace, but a little further along. Jonesy in the shop will put you right but I can tell you that it's down Waterloo Street, only just over a mile from here. See you later, Horace".

Horace followed Mrs. Dooley's directions and soon found the shop. Romford seemed like a lovely and very friendly place, a number of people greeted him as he passed by. He went into the shop and the bell above the door chimed. He bought a razor some soap a pouch of Golden Leaf tobacco some cigarette papers and a few other bits and bobs. Mr. Jones gave him directions to Old Church Road.

Horace knocked on the door and waited for someone to come. He heard voices inside and after a few moments a young girl opened the door.

"Who are you coming knocking?"

"Good afternoon. Is the Hackett family staying here, Lizzy gave me this address and told me this is where they would be".

"Well, you must be Horace then. They haven't stopped talking about you. Aunt Lizzy tells me that you're a good shag, what you got to say about that then? It's OK, I'm just teasing you, come in".

She showed him to the sitting room and sat opposite staring at him, her hand grasped her crotch. Horace glanced around the room feeling a little embarrassed and pretended not to notice. After a minute, which felt more like an hour, Lizzy popped her head around the door, she squealed, ran in and hugged him tightly. She held him close.

"It's so nice to see you, Horace. I wasn't sure you would be able to come all this way what with you being so busy and everything else that is going on".

"Charmaine was very special to me, Lizzy".

"Aunt Lizzy, if you don't let go of him he will get a hard on, if he hasn't already".

The girl's mother came in.

"Our Billy, be courteous to our guests in this house please. You can take a girl away from the canal but you can't take the canal away from the girl. I am Sheila, Billy's mother. Pleased to meet you, you must be Horace. James and Tim, my husband, will be with us directly. Billy, don't just sit there playing with yourself be a good hostess and bring a cup of tea, and put the scones in the oven to warm up. Did you have a good journey here, Horace?"

"Yes, thank you, Sheila, I came by train. I feel that I am to blame for what happened, she would still be alive today if she had never met me. I am deeply sorry".

"No one blames you for what happened, Horace. She fell in love with you and you with her. You were brave to risk yourself to find her, to help her and bring her back. Not many would have gone to the lengths that you did. You even avenged the terrible things that those people did to her".

Billy brought in the tea and went back to fetch the warm scones.

"How long did you known Charmaine?" Billy asked him.

"I have been going to the canal for over two years to chat to the boaters but I only knew Charmaine for a few months".

James and Tim, Sheila's husband, joined them. They spoke for two hours or more, there was much to discuss, to remember. Horace reiterated to them his vow to kill Fisher, it would always be unfinished business for him until he had done so.

Afternoon was turning to evening and they still had much to do to prepare for Charmaine's funeral. Horace got up and bade them all farewell telling them that he would see them on Tuesday, Billy showed him to the door.

"Do you want to go out for a drink tonight?" the question came out of the blue. So blue in fact, it was more like a navy blue. "I can be ready in ten minutes if you do".

"Well, I haven't got anything to do so, yes, Billy, where will I meet you?"

"Just stay the fuck where you are and I will be out in a minute. When I go out with a fella he always comes calling for me afterwards. I will be ten minutes".

Horace waited outside for her to reappear. Her hair was down and she looked so pretty, rather like Charmaine in fact. They could have been sisters with Billy being the older by two years.

"Can I ask Billy, what's your real name, or should I just call you Billy?"

"You can call me anything other than Belinda".

"I can't see anything wrong with that name. It's a lovely name. It would suit you better than Billy, but that's your choice, Belinda".

# CHAPTER TWENTY TWO

Billy slapped him, laughed out loud, and put her arm in his. They went to a pub called the Fox and Goose. He bought the drinks and they sat and chatted about Charmaine.

"She was my best friend when we were on the cut" said Billy, "she was two years younger than I am and very intelligent. You get to meet some great people working on the boats".

"I agree with you there. I've met some very nice people but a few nasty bastards as well".

"That's why my dad gave it all up, people wanted him to move some dodgy goods and wouldn't take no for an answer. They told him they would kill all his family so he sold up and bought the house we're in at the moment. He also bought an old ambulance and turned it into a grocery van. He's never been happier driving around Romford selling top quality fruit and veg. I go and help him most days. My mum works as head cook at the Royal Liberty School up at Gidea Park and I work in Glenda's dress shop, we've never been so well off. I can afford all the best clothes".

"Well, that blouse and skirt you're wearing is a head turner I can tell you, Bel. Bel....that suits you better than Billy, it's a lot more lady like, and you are all lady in that outfit".

"That's sweet of you, Horace. Bel, I would never have thought of that name".

"What do they call you at the shop, I'm sure they wouldn't call you Billy there?"

"No, they call me Miss Evans or Belinda, which I hate. I don't know why but I just don't like it, it sounds patronising, always has. Maybe it's just the way that people say it, but when you said Belinda just now it sounded alright. You said it using a more gentle tone. The more I think about it the more I like Bel. I chose Billy because it sounds harder, around here you have to be or you get picked on. Talk of the devil, my nemesis just walked in".

"Who's that?"

"Len Drayton. He and his family are the worst of the worst, they're into everything, protection, loan-sharking, fencing stolen goods and the rest. Some say his dad, Rich Drayton, cut someone's throat because he wouldn't pay the protection money. He told my dad that if he still intends trading he will have to pay ten pounds a week".

The lad, Len, was around nineteen. He swayed from the waist up when he walked as to give the impression that he was entitled to occupy more space than his body warranted as well as to warn others not to try to invade it. Horace listened as he spoke to the people in the pub strutting about as if he owned the place. He was arrogant and talked down to everyone, he even picked up a packet of fags that belonged to someone else and walked off taking one out as he went and lighting it. He walked towards them past an old man sitting on his own at the table beside them, about the same age as Horace's dad and proudly displaying his medals on the breast of his blazer. Horace watched him intently just waiting, hoping, for an excuse to teach Len Drayton a lesson. It didn't take long. Len held his hand out as he passed knocking the man's pipe askew, he laughed at what he thought was a hilarious jape. Horace jumped up, his chair tilted backwards almost falling over and the table scraped across the tile floor as it slid forward about a foot, the glasses fell over. Horace grabbed Len's shirt front with his left hand and pushed him backwards whilst slapping him hard three or four times across the face with his right.

"Have some respect for your elders you cocky little shit".

Len was already back pedalling from the slaps so Horace took advantage of the momentum that had built and shoved Len through the front door and gave him a good hiding outside.

The pub was silent when he returned. Everyone's gaze was upon him as he went back to his chair, pulled it up and sat down.

"Sorry, Bel".

The landlord came over with two pints and set them down on the table.

"These are on the house. If I could just get rid of that scum my trade would be a lot better than it is. Beware, mate, he will be back with his brothers in a few minutes, you can bet on that".

"Well, I don't want them to mess this place up I will wait outside for them. I'll be back in a minute, Bel. How many are there in the family?"

"Four of them all together but there'll be some hangers on as well so if I were you I'd drink up and get as far away from here as you can, and Billy I would watch yourself".

"Landlord, thank you for the beer and the advice but I have never run away from anyone so I will go outside and wait for them".

Which is exactly what he did. The landlord asked Billy who he was and where he was from.

"He was my cousin's boyfriend. She killed herself and the funeral is tomorrow so he isn't in the best of moods. Oh, and my name is Bel now".

"OK Bel, if you say so. I prefer that to Billy anyway, you're far too pretty to have a lad's name. I think I'll call the police the poor lad won't be able to manage all of them, and we aren't brave enough in here to help".

Horace saw them walking down the road towards him, one was carrying a piece of wood. Horace had already formulated his strategy, and it was a good one. When they got close he charged at them aiming for the one with the weapon and knocked him to the ground, grabbing the wood off him as he fell. A few punches and kicks rained in on Horace but they soon stopped when Horace swung round flailing at them. Once they'd backed off a little he ran at them swinging the wood this way and that slapping cheek bones, clonking heads and wrapping knuckles. It looked and sounded very painful for those on the receiving end, and it was. One by one their enthusiasm for the fight diminished but Horace knew that he mustn't let the tables turn back against him so he pressed home his advantage and beat the living day lights out of each of them, in no particular order, until they were all bleeding from one place or the other. Hitting the legs and particularly the knees was a very effective way of neutralising them to prevent them coming after him, something that his Uncle Bill had taught him. Exhausted and panting, Horace leant over them.

"If you mess with the Lees at the gypsy camp, I will find out where you live and burn your house down".

Horace walked back into the pub to everyone's surprise and admiration in equal measure. He was greeted with pats on the back and the odd "Well done, lad" from the customers. He sat down beside Bel, his hair was a mess and he was, not surprisingly, slightly dishevelled. Bel gave him her comb.

"It looks like you've been pulled through a hedge backwards".

No one noticed his hands except Bel, they were bloody and looked very sore.

The police arrived and came in to have a word with the landlord. The old man won't be happy with whoever did this to the Drayton boys. They said it was one of the Lees from the gypsy camp but there aren't any gypsies near here at the moment.

"Sorry Ernie, I had to call you because there was a commotion outside, when I had a look there were bodies everywhere".

Suddenly, the door sprang open with a bang and a great big chap, broad, tall and with a large belly, walked in and barged the constable out of the way, he went straight to Horace's and Bel's table.

"My boy said the one who did for them outside was talking to you, you slag".

Before she could utter a word, Horace jumped up and punched him full-square in the mouth. His head jerked backwards, the skin of his cheeks rippled and two teeth flew out of his mouth, but he stood firm. It would have taken a fire truck to knock him off his feet. He launched himself at Horace but two police officers anticipated that this would be the inevitable result and grabbed his arms pulling him back, which was a feat in itself.

"You're coming with us, Drayton, you and your boys have caused enough trouble for one night. Go to the hospital with them and behave, I will come round and see you all at home tomorrow, now clear off".

Drayton put a handkerchief to his mouth and stormed out looking back at Horace muttering curses at him through the blood foaming between his lips.

"Right son, what's this all about? I gather that you're the one that beat Rich Drayton's kids up. Where are you from and why are you here, I haven't seen you around here before?"

"Constable, I travelled to Romford this morning for a funeral and came in here for a quiet drink, that's all".

"Name and address please, son, so I can check who you are".

"I will tell you my name and give you a contact to confirm it but I won't give you my address because I don't know you. I'm not being funny but I've known some bent police constables in my time. You can contact Inspector Smart of Burton- on-Trent Police Station, he will vouch for me. I've done a few things for him in the past. I don't like anyone attacking old war heroes, the people that do that are the lowest of the low".

"OK son".

"My name is Horace Gray and I come from Burton-on-Trent. I'm here for the funeral of a friend of ours, a young girl. She killed herself because of people like the Draytons, wasters that manipulate and rob everyone. I bet they've never done a day's work in their lives, and never fought for their country like the old gentleman over there with his medals on. Did you fight on the Somme sir?"

The old chap walked across, nodded to the constable and sat with them. He thanked Horace for sticking up for him.

"Yes, son, I fought in the Somme and in Belgium. It was a terrible war. I lost most of my comrades at arms in the three years I was there. There were people dropping all around us, most of them young boys many crying for their mother, a terrible time. Then a few years later you get people like that boy threatening us. So, I thank you, son, for sticking up for us old veterans and the others that can't fight back, I owe you a pint, it's the least I can do".

"No, sir, it is me that should buy you a pint for your courage and for fighting for your country".

The police constable thanked Horace for providing him with

his details and departed with his men.

They sat and chatted for another hour until the gentleman had to leave saying that he hoped that Horace would return so they could meet again and talk further.

"You like living dangerously, don't you Horace".

"Bel, trouble seems to find me but one thing I will never do is roll over for anyone, and definitely not toe rags like the Draytons. A lot of things have happened to me over the last three years and I have done things that I shouldn't have done at my age. I've met people I shouldn't have met and seen things I shouldn't have seen but I'm glad I did because it's made me see things in a different way. We found the people that took Charmaine and dealt with them, and they won't now be taking anyone else. What happened outside is nothing compared to that but I think I will need two of my friends here to help me".

Horace asked the landlord whether he could use his phone, he showed him into the back room and left him alone. Horace picked the phone up and stood there for a moment trying to remember the number, then dialled. Ray answered at The Horse and Jockey.

"Ray, it's Horace can I speak to Sol? I'm guessing that he's there".

Sure enough he was. Sol came to the phone and Horace told him what had happened.

"How many hours have you been there Horace and you're in trouble already. We will be there at seven in the morning, who is this family Horace?"

He told Sol that the name was Drayton and the father was Richard, known locally as Rich, but he didn't know where they lived.

"It can't be far from the Fox and Goose because Drayton only took a few minutes to get here after I beat up his kids, and another few to tell me what he would do to me".

"I will find out what I can about them on the grapevine. Do you think you'll be alright tonight? Go back to your lodgings but keep your eyes open, make sure you're not being followed and try to stay where there are other people, avoid being on your own if you can. Tell the girl you are with to be vigilant too because she is associated with you and could be in danger? But don't panic, you hurt them so they will take a while to regroup. Did you say that the girl was on the canal? If so, get the boat people involved".

"They used to be, Sol, but I'm sure that her family will know them on the River Rom. I'll ask her".

Horace went back to Bel and told her he would take her home and talk to her dad about getting some people together to be ready, just in case.

"I don't want you or your family in danger. Are there any people on the river that are handy in a crisis, because you will need some protection if old Drayton is as bad as you say he is? A couple of my friends will be here tomorrow to help get the ball rolling".

"I suppose it had to come to a head sometime, Horace. Yes, there are some boat people my dad knows that can help. I'm sure they will be glad to meet someone who is prepared to stand up for himself against layabouts and villains like the Draytons".

They walked home keeping to the main thoroughfares and looking around them all the while. Sheila came to the door and they went into the sitting room where Bel described the events at the Fox and Goose to everyone, including James and Lizzy who had joined them. Bel's dad, Tim, asked Horace if he would walk down to the river with him to meet Den, a friend of his.

Horace and Tim walked along the river. The dark water reflected the lights of the houses and street lamps on the far side as it flowed past. It was as if there was another place, another town beneath its surface just as lively as the one above it. The air was still and the sound of voices and laughter could be heard as people went about their business, a dog barked every now and then.

Tim talked about what happened on the waterways around there and why he'd left that life behind. There were a lot of gypsies around London that had broken away from their camps and moved onto the water. There were big profits to be made moving dodgy goods and the waterways were not being policed properly.

They soon came to a longboat that was moored with its stern facing them, a bright yellowish-white light illuminated the steering area, which was cluttered with crates, sacks, the odd piece of scrap metal and other objects that were covered with tarpaulins. The roof was equally messy. A rusty bicycle lay on its side atop the detritus. Two short poles bore lights near the prow, a red one on the port side and a green one on the starboard side, which threw a semicircular pool of light on green ropes that were tied to green wooden mooring posts. It looked as if the boat had just returned from its long journey to the Thames via the Beam River. The lights were on inside. Tim called out to Den.

Den emerged onto the steering area from the double-hinged cabin door.

"Alright, Tim?" he asked. "Who's that with ya?"

"This is Horace, a good friend of ours. We have a problem, Den, is Sherman still in the Smoke?"

"We're expecting him back tomorrow. What's your trouble, Tim, can I help with anything?"

Horace told Den all about what had happened in the Fox and Goose and explained that he had friends coming in the morning.

"But I would like the family protected until they get here" said Horace.

"We can send two lads with you for tonight if that's OK then you'll have to come back tomorrow to see Sherman. He will definitely be here for poor little Charmaine's funeral, he's her godfather. By the way son, I can tell you're not a boater, I haven't seen you around here before".

"I was Charmaine's boyfriend, Den, I won't go into it now but I was involved in the events that led to her death".

"Well, whatever they were you sound like the kind of bloke who would've done everything to help her. I will give you Mick and Al, they're both big lads and can stay with you 'til the morning. What time will your boys be coming, Horace?"

"They said they at seven in the morning, and they won't let me down".

Mick and Al walked back with Tim and Horace. Den had described them accurately, they both towered above them and were broad shouldered, very broad. They asked Tim about the family that was causing all the trouble, how many there were and what they did for a living.

"There's the dad, Rich Drayton, and his four sons but they have hired help too. They make their living by making everybody else miserable. They came from the Smoke originally and make a packet with loan-sharking and protection. Everyone has to pay from shops to pubs to big hotels, they've even tapped me. I'm sure that the police turn a blind eye".

Horace chipped in that they probably don't just turn their backs but probably take a cut as well.

"I know a bent copper where I live that recently hid evidence so a local crook wouldn't get sent down. The crook in question is the one behind Charmaine's death, he's the one who had her kidnapped and raped. Me and the boys who are coming tomorrow are the ones that got her back and killed the captors, but sadly we weren't able to do anything about the damage to Charmaine, no one could. I will live with that for the rest of my life".

They both put an arm around Horace and told him that he'd done more than anyone else could have and that they would do everything they could to help him, Tim and his family.

Horace offered to get some fish and chips and some bottles from the off licence. They accepted the offer of food but thanked him and politely declined the drink on the basis that they needed to keep their wits about them. They ate their supper while they walked.

Bel had a pot of tea waiting for them when they got to the house and fetched two more cups when she saw that Horace and her dad had two welcome guests with them. She ran to the door to open it.

"Uncle Michael, Uncle Al, you brought the best two back with you, they won't let anything happen to our family and with Horace's friends coming in the morning we will be just fine".

"Who are your mates that are coming in the morning, lad? Are they as tough as we boat people, we're renowned for getting this kind of job done if you know what I mean".

"Mick, I know to be true what you say, I have a lot of admiration for the boat people. You are loyal and stick together, which you've proved tonight just by being here. To answer your question, I've seen my friends do things that you wouldn't imagine to people that deserve it. I've seen them torture and kill and trust me, they are experts at it. They learnt their skills fighting in the Far East with my uncle who was their company leader and is now my mentor and trainer in the arts of self defence and shooting. He was a sniper amongst other things so knows to take into account everything from the temperature to the wind direction and speed".

"Well, we look forward to seeing them in action, Horace. We've heard bullshit before from bank walkers but your dealings with Charmaine's captors and these Drayton's in town tonight shows us that you are the genuine article, and thank you for dinner by the way".

Horace bade them good night and headed back to his lodgings. There were two men about fifty or so yards behind him so he slowed down. Strangely, the men maintained the same distance behind a sure sign that they were following him otherwise they would have carried on and walked past him. He turned a corner and hid in the recess of a wall in the shadows. A couple of minutes passed and they eventually walked by looking around but couldn't see him so carried on. The prey became the predator, he followed them. He kept just off the road crossing people's front gardens stepping over low hedges and climbing over picket fences but keeping tight to and in the shadows of the houses. When they reached the end of the road he heard them talking.

"He must have gone into one of the houses in this row. Let's get back and tell Rich that he's staying somewhere in this road".

Horace followed them until they came to a long row of semidetached prefab houses in the Harold Hill Estate only a few streets away. They walked into the end house of the row. Horace crept up to peek in the window but it was dark inside so there wasn't much point. The end house was two semis that had been converted into a single, large detached house. It was late so he headed back to his lodgings.

He was up at six o'clock the next morning. He didn't want to go for breakfast too early so sat at the window looking down at the river. The boaters were toing and froing along the river taking their cargos of amongst other things, coal, sand, grain and scrap metal to their waiting customers. It was considerably less busy than it would have been a few short years ago with most things, particularly perishables such as food, being transported now by train and then road. The odd pleasure rower pulled themselves up the river.

*Author's Note: Various items were rationed during and after the war starting with petrol in 1939 and lasting until 1954 when all restrictions were lifted. The end of rationing began in 1948 when restrictions were lifted on flour.*

*The end of rationing was staggered for other items such as soap, clothes, tinned and dry fruit, sweets, chocolates and meat with all rationing ending officially on the 4th July 1954.*

Horace decided to go for a walk and have a cigarette. He didn't want to smoke in his bedroom, he didn't at home so didn't think it was fair to do so here. After about half an hour he went back for breakfast.

"Good morning, Mrs. Dooley, how are you this morning? It's a beautiful day".

"What do you want for your breakfast, Horace, and do you have anything planned for today?"

"I would like a full breakfast please, when I have a good breakfast I don't need anything 'til evening. The first thing is to meet some friends in the market who are travelling here then to get some clothes for the funeral tomorrow. I met some nice people yesterday who are part of the family".

Mrs. Dooley brought his substantial breakfast and put it on the table.

"Mrs. Dooley, I could stay here regularly, what a breakfast of fried potatoes and homemade waffles with lovely, thick bacon. It's just like the bacon I cut off the pig we have hanging at home".

"So you have one as well do you? We get through half a pig every week with breakfasts and dinners. We have gammon and chips at night time if people are staying in to eat".

Others who walked in for their breakfasts greeted Horace before sitting down in the small but comfortable dining room.

"Well that looks a good full meal, Ethel, they're not like that where we come from are they?"

"No, Sid, if you're lucky you might get an egg that's not broken and bacon that's not cremated".

"Where are you from son? We are from Skegness in Lincolnshire".

"I know Skegness very well, I've been there a lot with my brother, auntie and uncle, and my two cousins. Not all places are bad some do a very good breakfast in Skeggie".

"No, son" she laughed, "he means the ones I cook for him at home. You old fool, Sid".

Horace ate his breakfast and said goodbye.

"Nice to meet you and sorry to rush off but I have some friends to meet".

As he was leaving he saw Mrs. Dooley.

"Mrs. Dooley, you said that you do gammon and chips for evening meals, would it be possible to bring my two friends that I'm meeting today? I would pay the full amount or more if you could make them double the size, they are big lads and like their food. I will give you five pounds for your trouble, but I don't mind if you can't".

"Horace, you don't have to pay that sort of money, I like to see fully grown men eat well".

"Will it be alright if we get back at around six o'clock?"

"Off course, Horace, six will be fine and it will be nice to meet your friends".

Horace got to the marketplace for a quarter past seven and waited, the smell of coffee filled his nostrils. Someone tapped him on the shoulder and he turned around startled. It was Sol and piglet.

"Jesus! I wondered who it was, you buggers. Where have you parked, your car's not here?"

"You've known us long enough to know that we always employ the element of surprise".

"Shall we walk to Tim Evan's house? It's under a mile from here and it will keep your car away from any trouble, have you had breakfast?"

"We did at the railway station, which is where the car is parked. Yes, better get round there in case anything kicks off early. How many of the Draytons are there, Horace?"

"Fewer than there were yesterday morning, I put four in hospital, plus their dad. I know that three won't feel like fighting and the other won't be able to walk unaided but the Evan's family say that there are lots of runners who do their bidding. I did find out where they live. I was followed when I left the Evans last night but I turned the tables on them, they were thick as shit".

Mick and Al were still at the Evans' house and came to the door to let them in.

"Morning lads, I'm Mick and this is Al" he said to Solomon and Piglet. Mick and Al looked them up and down and were a bit disappointed that they weren't as big and broad as they are.

"I'm pleased to meet you. I'm Sol and this is Piglet. We are freelance fighters and protect our own for free but we take our share of the spoils, if there are any to be had. Horace wouldn't have called us if he didn't think it would be worth our while. Is there anyone else on our team?"

"Yes, one other, Sherman. He's our leader. He's on his way back from the Smoke, should he here later this morning and we can't take any decisions until he arrives".

"Fair enough, Mick. Shall we go in and talk about strategy? We can't give them time to regroup or recruit others. Horace has already put some in hospital so we need to press home our advantage, hit them tonight or tomorrow night. My preference would be tonight".

They went into the sitting room to meet the Evans.

"I'm Tim Evans, this is my wife Sheila and this is my daughter Belinda, or Billy as she likes to be called, or is it Bel now Billy....I mean Bel? Anyway, we've had trouble with the Draytons ever since we came off the canal, they were trying to get protection money off us. Sherman does what he can but he's not around a lot of the time and they know it. I'm a family man not a fighter and the same goes for all the other people they fleece".

James Hackett entered the room.

"Tim's right, our family is the same, just ordinary boaters, family people not accustomed to violence, nor are we the rogues and vagabonds that many think we are. I lost my daughter because of crooks like the Draytons and from what Horace told me I have you two to thank for helping to rescue our Charmaine. It's tragic that she died and there was nothing you could have done about it but the three of you did everything you could to save her".

"I've tried to get Jim off the waterways to come on the bank and join me" said Tim, "to get away from the prejudice and Drayton's exploitation. If he buys an old ambulance like I did and converts it to a greengrocer's van I could do the north and west of Romford and he could do the south and east. Anyway, that's not for now. The Draytons are nothing but crooks and Horace standing up to them last night might just be the spark that was needed to start the revolt against them".

"Alright, Tim" said Mick, "let's head down to the Rom with Horace, Sol and Piglet to see the others and check if Sherman is back early".

When they got to the river, Sherman was there with a group of boaters. He'd just arrived back from the Smoke. He too was a mountain of a man, although slightly older that Mick and Al. When he saw them all walking down the towpath he walked up to them holding his hand out.

"Well you know who I am, introduce yourselves".

"Sherman, I'm Horace Gray. I don't know if you heard about what happened last night with the Draytons but I'm the one who started all the trouble, well, they started it and I finished it. I was Charmaine's boyfriend and me and these other two gentlemen, Sol and Piglet, found her and I took her back to the Hacketts. I came here today to attend her funeral. I am consumed by grief, sir, and I will never forgive myself for what happened to her".

"Well, Horace, news travels fast so, yes, I know what happened at the pub, that you beat up the Drayton boys and that you belted old Drayton himself. That takes some doing, especially for a young lad your age. I understand that you were defending Billy's honour which on its own merits our full support but I also know that you risked your life to help Charmaine and that others are ultimately responsible for her eventual death and most certainly not you".

He turned to Sol and Piglet.

"Boys we sort out our own house, where have you both come from?"

"We're in Luton at the moment, Sherman. We stayed there after freeing Charmaine with Horace. We killed the crooked family members that were running the place and holding her. We took over their businesses and with your blessing we will help you to rid this town of the Draytons, nothing would give us greater pleasure. We would, of course, be interested in sharing with you and your people any of the benefits that might accrue to us".

"Boys, you helped our family in Luton and I am very grateful to you for that. It's only right that we repay you and do this together here in Romford, best to strike while the iron is hot. We will do this together tonight and bury them before we bury the poor girl tomorrow. They have goods and riches in their properties and we will gladly share them with you. You are honorary members of our family and welcome at our doors and tables anytime you are in the area".

# CHAPTER TWENTY THREE

Sherman told Horace to go to the Harold Hill Estate and put the word around that he was going to kill Len Drayton that evening. Although it seems counter intuitive to warn them it meant that they would all congregate there and could be dealt with in one go. The second part of the strategy was that they would be expecting only Horace with maybe one or two others rather than a full-on attack with the number of people they were planning to send. The third part was that they planned to attack at midnight. The Draytons would be tired having kept watch all evening and by midnight would start to wonder whether anything at all was going to happen thereby letting their guard down.

"I will get two boys to stay with Tim and his family just in case they send some people over there. It will be good for these people to meet their maker so meet me here at midnight, lads".

Everyone dispersed.

"Right, I have to go and get some clothes for Charmaine's funeral, if you two want to hang around here then I will meet you both later. All three of us have to be at my lodgings for dinner at six o'clock and you won't be disappointed I can tell you".

"We'll stick with you, Horace, just in case. We know you can't look after yourself" Piglet jested, "and we need some clothes ourselves as we're staying for the funeral now".

"Then you will need some lodgings too. It's best to be near Mrs. Dooley's. Some rooms may have become available, I know of one couple that is leaving today".

They walked back to Mrs. Dooley's. Sol and Piglet were exceptionally polite and Horace was sure that they were putting on a slightly posh accent to impress her.

"Good morning, Mrs. Dooley" said Piglet, "do you think you might have two rooms available for a couple of nights? We are here for the funeral tomorrow that Horace is attending. My apologies, I didn't introduce us. My name is Selwyn Squiller and this is my friend and associate, Solomon Salzman, very pleased to meet you".

"That's an unusual name, Mr. Squiller, I haven't heard it before".

"My family roots are in America, my father stayed here after the First World War".

"Well, three rooms are now available so, yes, that will be fine. Are these the two friends you booked for dinner tonight, Horace? Please be here for six o'clock for your meal".

"Yes, it's these two gentlemen. Well, Mrs. Dooley we'd better be off to the tailor to get our suits, we will see you later at six o'clock".

They wandered casually into town to the shop that Horace had seen the day before. They fitted themselves out with the best off-the-peg suits they could find and also bought shirts, black ties and shoes. Horace offered to pay but Sol insisted that he would pay for everything saying that the Draytons would ultimately foot the bill. There would be plenty of cash in their house from their nefarious loan shark activities.

On the way back Horace went on his own to the Harold Hill Estate and bragged to a few of the people he met that he was planning to kill Len Drayton tonight, that he would cut him up and feed bits of him to the dogs. With the number of stooges that the Draytons had around it wouldn't be long before word got back to them.

Horace, Sol and Piglet went about their business for the rest of the afternoon either investigating the town or walking by the river. They met up at the lodgings at just before six o'clock and sat in the dining room expectantly, they'd been saving themselves for their meal and were all ravenous.

Mrs. Dooley greeted them and brought in their dinner and put it on the table; dishes piled high with gammon, egg and chips.

"Mrs. Dooley, this looks amazing" said Piglet, "thank you very much. Your husband is a very lucky man to have such a delightful woman and wonderful cook as his wife".

"Well, Mr. Squiller, my husband ran off with my sister a year after we married so this is my life now, to run this bed and breakfast and to serve and talk to such pleasant gentlemen as your good selves".

"I'm so sorry to hear that, Mrs. Dooley, and please call me Selwyn. You run a fine establishment and it is a pleasure to be staying here".

She smiled and left them to tuck in.

"Piglet, I think you pressed a button there. She is indeed a very attractive young woman but how can she afford a house like this with eight bedrooms, plus her own living accommodation?"

Horace told them that he'd heard her tell a guest that it's the house she grew up in and that her father left it to her when he died, cutting her sister out the will because she had run off with her husband.

"I'm glad we're not meeting 'til midnight, it'll take me that long to get through all of this. I will have a word with Mrs. Dooley about a spare key as we're going to be late tonight. You're quiet, Sol, what's up with you?"

"Horace, I was always told not to speak with my mouth full, so I will leave it to you to ask for the key".

Horace finished and slumped back in his chair, he was stuffed to the gunnels.

"Leave it to me" said Piglet, "I mean, I'm the most charming of the three of us after all. It seems strange that no one else is in here eating dinner".

"Ah! Piglet" said Horace, "she'd probably put a sign up saying that you can't eat with monkeys and being as the dining room was full yesterday and it's empty today, and you two are the new guests, she must surely have meant you".

"And the other sign beside it said that only pigs can eat with the monkeys so she must have meant you, Horace, you little bastard" said Sol.

"Right, it's time to find that pub you had a drink at yesterday, Horace, and it's your round".

Piglet went to see Mrs. Dooley to tell her that they were going to see the boat people to drink the health of the Hackett family and that they would be late both tonight and the next night too because of the wake. He also told her that she was welcome to come if she wanted.

"That's very kind of you, Selwyn, I haven't been asked out since before I was married. My husband left eighteen months ago and I haven't been out from that day to this. You don't when you're on your own do you, some friends have asked me to go out with them but you just don't do you".

"Mrs. Dooley...."

"Please, Selwyn, call Me Dianna. Mrs. Dooley is far too formal for two adults".

"You're still young, Dianna, and there's nothing wrong with letting your hair down every now and then so please think about it. Would it be possible to have a key to the front door please, because we will only be back after midnight?"

Piglet went back with the key and they set off to the Fox and Goose. The landlord came over to Horace and shook his hand.

"Hello, Horace, I didn't get a chance to introduce myself properly last night. I am Gordon Neal and thanks for sticking up for old Norman. If I'd said or done anything they would probably come back and burn the pub down, never mind the money they take off me for protection. And the bloody police close their eyes to it, they know it goes on. I reported it but all they say is it goes on everywhere and that they can't do anything about it until someone makes a statement and sticks to it, which is unlikely given the intimidation".

"These two are my friends" said Horace, "I can't tell you their real names but you can call them Sol and Piglet. We are going to give the Drayton Family a taste of its own medicine."

"Horace, be careful what you say and who you talk to in here. That one going to the toilet is Len Drayton's cousin. He's either going to the toiler or out the back way, maybe because he's seen you".

"Thanks, Gordon, I will go and find out which one. Have your drinks lads I'll sort this one out".

While Horace followed the chap towards the back of the pub, Sol talked to Gordon about the Draytons; how long they've been here, what they do, and more importantly, why anyone hadn't yet done anything about them.

"Sol, to be honest we all have something to lose. The ones who have stood up to them are either crippled or dead. They cut the throat of my dog a few months ago so I sent my wife and kids to stay with her mother. I've got the pub up for sale but no one will buy it".

"Do you want to leave here Gordon, are your family unhappy here?"

"No, Sol, we are happy and like it here, it's where our friends and most of our family live but we just don't feel safe".

Horace had followed the chap out the backdoor. He was walking up the path towards the back gate.

"Excuse me, please could you tell me how to get to the Harold Hill Estate? I need to give some money to Rich Drayton".

"How much do you have for him, because I'm one of his runners?"

"Fifty quid, mate, will you take me to him please. If I don't pay by tomorrow he will break my legs".

Horace stepped forward so that he was close to the man. The Drayton runner slid a long knife out of his jacket and held it to the side of Horace's neck.

"No need to do that, mate. Here, I'll give you my wallet".

Horace reached down to his pocket ostensibly to grab his wallet but instead thrust his hand into the chap's crotch and grabbed his testicles and squeezed as hard as he could, twisting as he did so. The man's face contorted and the knife fell to the floor. Horace gave him an uppercut with his left fist to the underside of his chin, there was a loud crack and he sank backwards to the floor. Horace stepped back and kicked him in the face several times then his ribs and kidneys. He picked up the knife with his handkerchief as the man lay hunched on the ground groaning and parted his legs with his right foot. He located the general area of the femoral artery and pushed the knife in as far as it would go. There was a gasp as the man arched his back and grabbed his leg. Horace opened the gate, put his hands underneath the man's armpits and dragged him outside, shut the gate and left him there.

"You were there a while, Horace" said Sol, "I thought we would have to come and find you".

"No need, we were becoming good friends. He even showed me his lovely knife so I taught him how to use it".

"How is the chap now? I hope he's well enough to go back to Drayton's house to give them the message that we're in town".

"I don't think he'll be going back there, Sol, with the way the knife ground on his thigh bone and the amount of blood that came out, and even if he did he wouldn't be able to speak properly because his jaw's broken".

"Another drink please, Gordon, and have one yourself, this is going to be an interesting night. Do you know how many there are in the Drayton family? I suppose it's a large one, these scum tend to breed like rats".

"Rich Drayton has three brothers, they all live in the Harold Hill Estate, well, in the same road actually. Rich is the main man, the other three are thick as shit. Then there are all the kids but over half of them are under fourteen. So, immediate family you're talking around twelve to fifteen plus he has his stooges and runners".

"Gordon, tonight will be a watershed for the Draytons, it'll be Armageddon for them. You will soon be able to get your family back under one roof and live like a proper family".

"Thank you, Sol. You seem confident that you can eradicate the scum. I and many others hope that you can, believe me".

"The Element of surprise, Gordon, the element of surprise. One more please, landlord".

They stayed at the Fox and Goose 'til around eleven, shook hands with Gordon and told him they would see him before they returned to Luton. They left by the backdoor and made their way to the river to meet with Sherman and the others. The Drayton runner was there lying just outside the gate. He was dead with his eyes wide open staring skywards at nothing in particular. The moonlight that shone through the wispy clouds above was reflected in what remained of the sheen in his eyes. Horace looked at him intently for a moment. The dead man's face was as white as a sheet, most of his blood having vacated his body forming a shiny pool in the gutter.

"Come on, Horace, have you fallen in love with him?" Piglet shouted, "What's up with you?"

"Have you ever looked deep into a dead person's eyes? There's nothing there but emptiness".

"Horace, we've never even been sick enough to look into the eyes of our dead quarry when we go hunting".

They walked to the river and had a bottle of beer with the boaters. They already knew Mick and Al but four others they hadn't met before were also there. That made a total of fifteen men, roughly six to attack the main house and three each for the others.

Sherman told them that the four new men were from London, they knew a lot about the Draytons and wanted them eliminated. The Draytons had been trying in the last few months to encroach on the territory that another much more powerful family, the Messinas, was running. Mick had gone to the Smoke in the afternoon to get some gen on the Draytons and in the process had ended up coming back with reinforcements from the Messina family. As a young man, Eugenio Messina had become the head of the biggest crime syndicate in London. His father, Giuseppe Messina was deported from Egypt but having a Maltese passport went back to Malta and settled there. Giuseppe's eldest, Eugenio, was the black sheep of the family. He moved to London with Colette, his French prostitute wife, and his four brothers and built up a prostitution empire. They moved into gambling and in the 1920s blackmailed several high ranking police officers and politicians, one of whom was believed to be Oswald Moseley and another a cabinet minister. They drew on Colette's knowledge about the art of compromising and blackmailing high ranking French officials.

The Messinas took English names when they moved to London. Eugenio became Edward Marshall, Carmelo, the second eldest, became Charles Maitland, the next eldest, Salvatore, became Arthur Evans and the youngest, Attilio, became Raymond

Maynard.

Two hundred of the most expensive call girls in the West End were Messina girls. The family as a whole ran over thirty two whore houses. Colette made sure that she had the prettiest women and took eighty percent of their earnings. Salvatore a.k.a. Arthur spent two years in prison for living off his girlfriend's immoral earnings and for trying to bribe Superintendent Guy Mahon, the policeman who arrested him.

But the Messinas were also involved in other ventures, they moved between Belgium and London on a boat called the Martinet, which was a Belgian registered trawler, it was re-registered later on to sail under the French flag. They used the trawler to ferry stolen and elicit goods between Belgium, Holland and the UK, cocaine was often hidden and transported inside the fish. Scotland Yard had been following closely the vessel's movements and on one occasion observed it landing in Poplar, but the family had one of the inspectors of The Yard on their payroll so nothing ever came of the investigations. Fast forward to the meeting with Sherman, and Eugenio a.k.a. Edward was in his mid fifties.

"Gentlemen" said Sherman, "this is Edward Marshall and some of his lads. They want to make sure that Rich Drayton has his head removed and impaled on the railings at the entrance to the Harold Hill Estate. As soon as my men come back we will make our move".

"Horace already started two hours ago" said Sol, "he killed one of them at the Fox and Goose, by the way did you empty his pockets Horace?"

"What do you think, Sol? Whoever kills one has to take his belongings".

He took a gold lighter out of his pocket together with a wallet that was packed with notes.

Sherman's brother, Scott, came back with two of the boaters and told them that the Draytons appeared to be getting ready for a fight but their enthusiasm seemed to be waning given that it was getting late and all of them had returned to their four individual houses. This was a vindication of Sherman's strategy.

"Well that makes things easier for us" said Sol. "Edward's men come with me and Horace. Piglet, you take Mike and Al to number thirty six, Sherman and your do number forty and that leaves number twenty".

Sherman told the last three of his men to take number twenty.

"Take the men outside to finish them off if possible. We are not barbarians, the women and children needn't see them die. Sol, you go first and I will bring up the rear. Edward, do you want to do Rich Drayton or do you want one of us to do it?"

"No, he came onto my turf and now I am on his, the head belongs to me".

He took slid a sword out of his walking cane. It shone as he turned it and the stern light of the boat caught it at just the right angle.

"I'm a bit rusty because I haven't removed a head since we left Malta".

The men left the River Rom towards their allotted houses. The Draytons and their 'soldiers' had clearly given up waiting and were lax no to post lookouts along the way or in the windows of the houses. Sol's men crept up the driveway and kicked the door open splintering its hinges. They rushed into the house with pistols and knives at the ready shooting and slashing people as they ran out of the rooms. Horace saw Len Drayton leaning against the wall in the front room, he'd either been shot or stabbed in the left shoulder and was clasping it with his right hand. Horace ran over to him, grabbed the sides of his head and pushed his thumbs into his eye sockets, the eyeballs were firm but yielding. He could feel the orbs moving about beneath the eyelids as Len let out a deafening scream. He angled his thumbs inwards and they eventually perforated the lacrimal caruncles near the bridge of the nose and entered the eye sockets. There was a squelch as the orbs bulged out at either side and blood gushed out. Len fell to the floor with a thud. Horace took out the knife he'd tucked into his belt and drove it through the right eye socket into Len's brain.

Meanwhile, Sol and Edward and two of his men had been working on the giant of a man, Rich Drayton. They dragged him out of the house and held him down. Edward unsheathed his sword and began cutting the neck, sawing and thrusting through the flesh, muscles, tendon and bone until eventually it was separated from the torso. It looked the exact opposite of a clean surgical procedure.

All of the men were dead, the women and children were streets away by now having fled screaming. Sol and Edwards' men went through the house and took everything of any value that they came across and could carry, which was mainly cash, jewellery and other small items of gold and silverware. They threw Rich Drayton's body inside the house and set fire to it, which being a prefab went up pretty quickly. The same process was replicated by Sherman's men at the other three houses. After years of oppressing the entire community the whole of Drayton's organisation had been eliminated in around thirty minutes. Parts of the street were ablaze. The Drayton Empire was no more. It is inevitable that the police had got wind of what was happening but more than likely had decided to let the events unfold. They wouldn't have been able to summon sufficient men that late at night and with such short notice and, in any case, whoever was behind the attacks had saved them from putting themselves at risk not to mention months if not years of trying to apprehend and prosecute the Draytons to no avail.

If Horace had already changed before, then the events of that night had cemented his transformation irrevocably.

All of the men convened back at Sherman's boat on the River Rom. They sorted out the spoils and shared them out equitably.

Edward Marshall took Sherman to one side. They walked down the river bank path a few yards out of earshot.

"Sherman, would you be able to move some goods for me on your boats? I need some things to be moved from Liverpool and Manchester to London to be loaded onto my trawler. There is, of course, an element of risk but you and your men will be paid handsomely, cash on arrival of the goods".

He gave Sherman a phone number to contact his organisation in a few days to make arrangements. Edward went back to the boat and spoke to Sol, Piglet and Horace in private.

"There is a person coming to England who I need to be protected for three days. The way you all worked together tonight impressed me and my men".

He gave Sol a phone number too and he and his men departed

into the night as quickly and quietly as they had arrived.

The next morning, Horace, Sol and Piglet went down early and sat in the lounge before breakfast. They talked guardedly about the Messina's and their offer of protection. Sol told them that he wanted to take up the offer and that he was intrigued that Edward had not told them who it was. Piglet was also keen to get involved, anything that resulted in large amounts of cash was always of great interest to him, but Horace was not so sure.

"Mr. Rush has been good to me and I don't want to let him down".

But in reality he didn't like the sound of it, not knowing who the person to be protected was. He was also in Sir Stanley's good books and protecting someone for a criminal organisation conflicted with what he and Uncle Bill had done to help him. But he made a mental note of the Messina name and thought that it was one he would come across again at some point in the future.

Mrs. Dooley brought a pot of tea into the lounge and set it down on the coffee table.

"Good morning, lads, I thought I heard you talking in here. This tea will keep you going 'til I've got the breakfasts ready. What time is the funeral today, Horace?"

"Midday, Mrs. Dooley. The boaters say that the wake will go on until the early hours".

She turned to go to start preparing breakfast but stopped and turned back again.

"Selwyn, I would love to join you tonight".

Both Sol and Horace did a double take and looked at Piglet.

"What does she mean, Piglet, join you tonight?. Where and how is she joining you?"

"I asked her last night to come to the wake with me. I feel sorry for her, a young lady on her own".

"Piglet, how long have I known you? I think you have an ulterior motive with Mrs. Dooley".

"I asked Dianna out of the goodness of my heart, just being a kind guest that's all".

"I see, it's Dianna now is it? Well, you've been busy, and when did you ask her out and tell you her name?"

"Last night, Sol, when I asked her for a front door key. She is a mighty fine woman you must admit, a really good looker....and I felt sorry for what happened to her".

They went into the dining room when she shouted that breakfast was ready. Horace didn't waste any time poking fun at Piglet.

"Hmm, looks like your breakfast is bigger than ours, Piglet. There's an extra rasher of bacon underneath those potatoes and his sausage is bigger than ours, Sol".

"My sausage has always been bigger than yours, you little squirt. I have enough with this one taking the piss all the time so don't you start".

"I'm only a little squirt, Piglet, because you're the one who gets all the grub on your plate".

After breakfast they went upstairs to have a bath and get ready for the funeral. They had to take it in turns because it was a shared bathroom so Horace went out for a walk while he was waiting and decided to call Sir Stanley to see whether he was at home and to find out whether there had been any further news on the Rolls Royce.

"Morning, Helen, is Sir Stanley home this morning?"

"Good morning, Horace, yes I will get him for you. Are you alright?"

"Yes, thanks, Helen, I'm fine. Have you arranged your wedding day yet?"

"Not yet, Horace, Jacob has been sent to Africa for six months so I'm feeling a little trepidation at moving things along too quickly. He's a high ranking officer and can't refuse to go on the tours of duty they assign to him. I'm a little worried that I'll spend too much time on my own like mum did. Anyway, I'll get my dad. Take care of yourself, Horace".

"Hello, Horace, what time's the funeral today and how are you feeling? Let me tell you, thanks to Uncle Bill and you we've found out a great deal about the ones from Oxford, but I can't tell you much at this stage, unfortunately. The best thing is we're meeting the owner of the Rolls Royce tomorrow at lunch time so I will be returning to London later today. What can I do for you?"

Horace told Sir Stanley about the chap called Eugenio Messina a.k.a. Edward Marshall and the Messina family that runs crooked operations in the West End of London.

"I know that they have at least one high ranking police officer on their payroll and there is someone who comes over in a boat, from France I think, possibly Belgium. I thought I would tell you because I know I can trust you and I'm also intrigued about what is going on".

"Thanks for that, Horace. I will try to find out what I can about the Messinas and this boat of theirs. I will see you soon when I'm back in Burton although I'm not sure when that will be. Thanks again and look after yourself, young man".

Horace returned to the lodgings. Sol asked him where he'd been.

"I went to the phone box to make sure that everything is alright at home, I've never been away for so long. Everyone's fine particularly my dad. He's my main worry what with his poor health. I'll go and see whether Piglet's finished and is ready for his big date tonight".

"Get off with you, young bugger, let's go and see Charmaine off to a better place".

"Do you believe in all that, Sol? You've sent lots to their graves, those that were fortunate enough to have a grave that is. I don't believe in any of it. Once you're gone that's it, there is no such thing as a better place".

"Well, you are cheerful this morning, I hope you don't share all this when you go to your local church".

"I don't go to church, Sol, I don't believe. I don't trust any of them anyway, all those men living by themselves, sleeping, eating and bathing together. Not to mention all the young ones they come into contact with, what with the choirs and everything".

"From what I've seen and read, Horace, everyone reacts differently in the last few seconds of their life. Some see light and feel warmth and peace, others see darkness and feel fear. The brain does strange things when it is shutting down but I tend to agree with you, I don't believe in an afterlife either".

## CHAPTER TWENTY FOUR

Horace was the last to have his bath and they all got changed into their black matching suits. They walked to the canal as Charmaine's coffin was being readied to be moved to St. Bede's Roman Catholic Church. Everyone was waiting at the canal for the horse drawn hearse to pull up so that they could follow it. The horses were jet black with upright black plumes attached to their halters. It was a very sobering moment to see the bright white coffin inside the glass casing and Charmaine's name spelled out in flowers on either side with lilies and other flowers scattered around it. Horace's wreath leant against the foot of the coffin, it was a two-foot tall white heart surrounded by red roses with the two words in yellow – I'm Sorry.

Horace stood next to Lizzy and James as the horses came to a halt in front of them, nodding gently and neighing. James and Lizzy looked a lot older than a couple in their early thirties, the skin on their faces was heavy with the strain and sorrow. Horace's eyes were filled with water and his moist eyelashes blurred his vision.

The previous night's activities had been a part of Horace's subconscious crusade to rid the world of the vicious, nefarious people who knowingly hurt others, like Fisher and the Lawrences who had been directly responsible for Charmaine's death. But none of the terrible things he'd seen and done to avenge her had eased the pain he felt at losing the first love of his life. His pain was as acute as it was before but now, on top of that, he also had the mental images seared into his brain of the atrocities that he'd both witnessed as well as perpetrated.

The priest had initially refused to carry out Charmaine's burial service because he thought that the events leading to her suicide had been indicative of a poor upbringing and he wasn't sympathetic towards the boat people, but he relented after Sherman had visited him. Bank notes rather than appeals to his Christian faith and humanity played a big part in his decision to do it. When he got wind of what Sherman had done, Horace decided to pay the priest a visit before leaving Romford. The priest would be at the church ringing his bell, waiving his incense thurible from side to side and speaking words that Horace knew had been paid for and that he didn't mean. But for now, he had to hold himself together and be calm for the sake of the Hackett family, and the whole boating community.

The horses tossed their heads and the hearse started to move with the clipping of hooves on cobbled stones. The black plumes fluttered in the breeze. They moved very slowly down the road watched, Horace thought, by the whole of Romford. It was silent save for the sound of the horses' hooves and the footsteps of the mourners interspersed with the occasional sniffle or cough. Horace walked beside James and Lizzy holding her right hand in his left very tightly. Lizzy held the hand of Charmaine's eldest brother and James the hand of the next oldest. Sherman carried the youngest boy who had not yet started to walk. Tim's family walked immediately behind the Hacketts.

Behind them there were over a hundred people; boaters, Tim's customers and residents who lived near the river who had heard about this poor young girl who'd been raped and taken her own life fearing that she was pregnant with the child of one of her tormenters. Other onlookers stood at intervals beside the road and doffed their hats as the entourage passed by.

Charmaine's post mortem had confirmed that she was indeed pregnant but the size of the foetus confirmed that only Horace could have been the father. James and Lizzy hadn't yet had the heart to tell Horace.

When they drew up outside the church, they slid the coffin

slowly out of the glass casing and James, Horace, Sol, Piglet, Sherman and Al carried the coffin slowly inside. The priest stood by the entrance and nodded to everyone as they entered holding the hands of those who proffered them to him.

The priest read from the scriptures and began his eulogy, talking about the young, innocent girl who had enjoyed a wonderful life on the canals and waterways and the sadness of her untimely and tragic end. Then came the piercing blow to Horace's heart. He mentioned that Charmaine had been carrying a child of approximately eight weeks, a boy. Horace's legs buckled but Sol and Sherman caught and supported him until he was able to regain his composure. The family had given the priest strict instructions not to mention the child that had perished inside Charmaine. Horace was too shocked to listen to or assimilate anything else that the priest said.

*Author's Note: Eight weeks is too early to easily determine the sex of a baby even by today's standards. However, the post mortem had indicated that in all likelihood that baby was a boy.*

When the service was over, James and Lizzy went over to Horace who was standing at the graveside. They both held his hands and gave him a rose to throw onto the coffin and walked away. At the appropriate moment when Horace was walking back to join the throng, James approached him and took him to one side.

"We were going to tell you about the child at the wake. These services are always very emotional and we wanted to let you know when things had calmed down a little. We gave the priest specific instructions not to mention anything. We are so sorry, Horace. Lizzy is devastated and I hope you will understand why we did what we did".

Lizzy walked over to them and held both their hands then gave Horace a kiss on his lips.

"James, Lizzy, please could we put something on Charmaine's headstone to remember the baby? Do you know a name that Charmaine would have liked for a boy? I have one in mind....here I will write it down on my handkerchief and fold it, open it when you have both thought of a name".

"I think we can tell you now, Horace. She liked this person for his strong, firm but gentle voice and his ability to appeal to everyone. She said that if she had a boy it would be a force to be reckoned with and that this name would be very suitable for him. The name she would have chosen is Winston".

Horace lifted his folded handkerchief and held out his hand. Lizzy took it and unfolded it slowly, she raised her eyebrows and passed it to James. They both managed a weak smile and they hugged each other. Horace couldn't tell them that he'd met the man in person, and that hurt. He walked slowly back towards the grave and stood over it.

"Sweet Charmaine, out baby will be given the name that you chose for him, Winston. It will adorn your headstone and I promise that I will come regularly to visit you and Winston and to tend to your grave. I didn't find out about our son the way I had wanted to, from your lips, and I will ensure that the man who disobeyed your parents' instructions pays for what he did".

He walked back to the rest of the mourners and told James and Lizzy that he would be coming to Romford regularly to visit Charmaine and baby Winston's grave and, of course, them if they were there.

Horace joined the others and spoke to and embraced them. Sol asked him how he was.

"This must have come as a shock to you, me old mate, knowing your child died with your girlfriend, but you have to be strong. This sort of thing would take the stuffing out of anyone but try to focus and think of James and Lizzy, they need you to be strong as they will draw comfort from it".

"You're right, Sol. I know that but I can't help but feel angry about the way that I found out. Not because of James and Lizzy but because of the way that the priest disobeyed them and the fact that Sherman had to speak to him to get him to agree to bury my Charmaine. I will visit him tonight to have a quiet word. Come on, Sol, let's send Charmaine off with a bang and go to the wake to get a drink".

They walked back to a small field beside the river not far from Sherman's boat alongside which many others had moored for the commemoration. People were milling about outside a large tent that the boaters had erected, about as large as a small marquee but lower. Sherman assured them that it was a Nomad's tent with rugs draped over the entrance and spread around the floor inside. Also inside were a number of trestle tables each of which held kegs of beer or bottles of spirits of various types. Bottles and glasses chinked together amid the gentle hum of conversation and as the day wore on, the hum grew to a hubbub interspersed by the occasional flurry of laughter. The alcohol was doing its job of dulling the senses and lowering inhibitions. Soon there would be music and real merrymaking would break out, as was the plan and the tradition.

James and Lizzy asked for quiet to make an announcement, you could hear a pin drop.

"We are thinking of selling our boat to Sol and Sherman's new company, the Albescu Carrying Company".

Albescu was Sherman's surname.

"The company now has twenty boats, raise your glasses to Sol and Sherman's new venture".

The hubbub returned briefly before silence fell once more.

"If selling is what we finally decide to do, we will be sorry to be leaving the waterways, it's been our life for as long as we can remember, travelling with our parents when we were young as they did with theirs before them. But Charmaine's leaving us spells the end of an era. The British railways and roads are gaining traction and the lorries are getting bigger by the day, smaller independent companies are being bought by larger enterprises and squeezing out our way of life. Sol believes that the waterways still have their place for another ten years or so and I hope that he is right but for us our priority is our children. Whatever we decide, you will always be our family and in our hearts".

The crowd raised their glasses, cheered and clapped but many wiped away a tear. Piglet and Dianna came over to Horace to say how sorry they were to hear about the baby. Piglet put his arm around him.

Horace picked his moment and snuck away quietly from the wake. He walked the ten minutes or so to the rectory and looked through the windows to see if he could spot the priest inside. He eventually saw him through a side window in his office sitting at his desk drinking whisky. Horace went around to the back and found a door that was unlocked and walked in. He went straight to the office and opened the door. The priest sat bolt upright startled.

"Who on earth are you and what are you doing here this time of night? Get out of my house now".

Horace walked up to him.

"You were asked not to say anything today about Charmaine's baby, the parents gave you explicit instructions not to mention it but you did, why?"

"What on earth has this got to do with you anyway? God needs to know about the people entering heaven, as do all the other good Christians at the funeral".

"What about both the parents? Don't they get a say in the matter?"

"No, they brought up a wayward girl, and not in a manner that God would condone. These young girls and boys should have more respect for themselves and for God".

Horace was beside himself but went calmly over to the priest who started to rise but he pushed him down firmly into the chair. He grabbed the stole that was on the desk and wrapped it around the priest's neck pulling his head back and twisting the cloth so that the man had to open his mouth to breathe properly. He leant over and picked up the open bottle of whisky and proceeded to pour the contents down his throat, not all in one go, but pausing to allow the priest to take the occasional gulp of air. He poured until the bottle was empty. The priest slumped forward on the desk choking and trying to get his breath back.

Horace walked over to a cabinet against the wall and retrieved a fresh bottle. He pulled off the metal casing and pulled out the stopper as he walked back beside the priest.

"I bet you bought these with the money that Sherman Albescu gave you to perform the funeral, and what's this wad of money behind the glass on your desk, is that the money?"

"No, No, No more please, no more".

Horace grabbed him from behind again repeating the procedure but pouring more slowly this time to ensure that nothing was spilled. It took the best part of thirty minutes until the bottle was empty. He contemplated fetching another one but the priest had almost passed out not only due to the much reduced oxygen intake but also the sheer quantity of alcohol in his system.

Horace covered his left hand with the stole, slid the palm of his right hand underneath the priest's forehead that was wet with sweat and lifted it off the table sufficiently to be able to hold his left hand over his mouth whilst pinching his nose. He held him like that for ten minutes telling him that he was going now to meet his Lord and Saviour. The priest's shoulders relaxed and the rest of his body went limp. Horace laid him forward on the table and made sure that he was sitting in such a way as to not slide off.

Horace picked up and cleaned one of the bottles and stood it upright in front of the priest's body. He put the empty glass in the priest's hand, wrapped his cold fingers around it, tidied up the desk and folded the stole putting it on another chair in the corner. He took the other bottle with him and threw it into the hedge of one of the fields that he walked through on his way back. When he got back to the wake he immersed himself in the crowd and started chatting to people as if nothing had happened. No one had missed him. Dianna came up and asked him how he was feeling.

"Mrs. Dooley, I am ready for a drink, that's what, how are you getting on here with the boaters? I think they're a great crowd, don't you think so too?"

"I'm so glad you look a bit happier now, Horace, I haven't seen you smile like that before".

"Mrs. Dooley, it's me that should get you a drink, you are a very lovely lady" and went into the tent to get some drinks.

He bumped into Piglet on the way.

"Where've you been, you look very pleased with yourself?"

"I've just been to have a drink with the priest, he really likes his whiskey. He supped two bottles while I was there. Can you believe it? No wonder he runs his mouth off".

"So, what did you drink while you were there and how did you leave him?"

"The last question first and the first question last, Piglet. Dead and nothing, I just wasn't thirsty".

"You killed the Priest Horace? What the fuck! Did anyone see you go in there? Jesus!"

Sol had observed Horace's return and came over when he saw the expression on Piglets face.

"Piglet, you look worried. It's not like you to show your feelings. Horace what've you done, lad, it must be you the way he's reacting".

"Sol, he's only been and bumped off the priest, for God's sake".

"Well, lads" said Horace, "I don't think they'll think much of him, drinking himself to death like that. They're not keen on suicides in the Church, and dying by drinking yourself to death is practically suicide. Why, it's almost as bad as a girl hanging herself after she'd been raped".

"Horace, this getting a bit too much now, you need to be careful, lad. You don't kill everyone because they don't do what you want. My God, mate, you're only seventeen, even Jack the Ripper didn't start at your age".

"Look, both of you, it's done now. Charmaine will rest in peace now and so will Winston".

"Winston, why would Winston be at peace now, what's the Prime Minister got to do with this?"

"Not the Prime minister you moron, my son Winston".

"Mate, you need to get a grip on yourself. Get back home to some sort of normality, go and have a talk with your Uncle Bill".

"Solomon, I'm ok now. It's been a terrible few hours and I will get myself together, I promise. It was the shock of finding out that that Charmaine had my baby inside her. The poor girl must have been frantic thinking it belonged to one of those bastard Lawrences. I just went mad when I found out that the priest had been paid to conduct the funeral and that he'd been told not to say anything about the baby but did. I found and brought back the money he was paid, I have it here. This will help James to start his new venture, could you give it to him? I don't want this dirty money and he won't know where it came from. If he turns it down then give it back to Sherman. Christ! The boaters even had a whip round for the funeral so some of that must have gone into this pile".

Dianna who'd been waiting outside for Horace to return with her drink had come into the tent looking for him and Piglet.

Horace changed the conversation immediately.

"Selwyn" Horace said semi sarcastically, "when you are back in Luton could you get your hands on a vehicle suitable for James to start his business? There is a hundred pounds here if you think you can get something".

"Well there is this Austin K2 furniture van, it's a former Carter Paterson and Pickford one, only two years old. They're getting rid of some assets at the moment due to a downturn in business. I reckon we can probably get it for around £100 and if that's not enough, Sol and I will make up the rest".

"Of course, mate" said Sol, "it would help him on his way to getting his new venture started. We'll take him to Luton in the morning if he's free and wants to go. Let's go and ask him about it now".

They went outside and found James and Lizzy talking to Tim, Sheila and Sherman.

"Can I ask you both, are you sure that you want to leave the boating life? It's a big leap in the dark for you, you've spent all your lives living and working on the waterways".

Neither was yet certain whether they would or not.

"James, Horace has put one hundred pounds towards a vehicle for you" said Sol, "it's a large furniture van and we might have the very thing in Luton to start you off, if you're able to come with us tomorrow morning".

"The idea does sound a good one, James" said Tim.

"Thanks, Horace, but I can't take your money, it wouldn't be right".

"James, I'm doing it for your family and that includes Charmaine and Winston. Please accept the money, it would mean a lot to me. If you do decide to sell up and start your business and live here I could come down more often to see you and visit Charmaine and Winston's grave".

"I haven't had time to think about things really, Horace. I only discussed the possibility last night with Lizzy after Sherman offered to buy the boat and butty off us but we haven't made our minds up. Every time we travel down a cut, every lock we negotiate, at every mooring place we stop we see our beautiful Charmaine. We remember her crawling on the grass by the bank and taking her first steps on the boat. It would break our hearts to leave the canal family, we've always looked after each other. The Draytons are gone from Romford for now but soon there will be another family doing exactly the same just as there is in every town or city".

"If you do decide to come on the bank and buy the van I will do it up for you, I haven't got a project at the moment. My brother is a joiner so I'm sure he will help me board it out and make a counter and shelving. I will take care of the bodywork and strip down and rebuild the engine so that it's as good as new. You will need something reliable if you sell to Sherman and take Tim up on his offer to go into partnership".

Horace decided not to press them too hard for now, today wasn't the right time or place. He spent the rest of the night talking to Sherman and his mates. Sherman wasn't in a hurry for the Hacketts to make up their minds about his offer but said that he would understand fully if they didn't stay on the waterways.

"Horace, I would rather keep the families in the system, as long as we can make a living but Fellows Morton and Clayton are selling or scraping boats within hours of the families losing their contracts to the Railway. The market for boats isn't as buoyant as it used to be, if you'll pardon the pun. I haven't told many people and please keep this to yourself, I bought shares in Southern Railways five years ago when I saw that goods were coming off the water and going onto rail. That's why I only haul fragile goods these days like pottery or bulky items like sheep's wool. The perishable things are all going on the railway to distribution points then on the roads to their final destinations with British Road Services".

"What does your family think about you joining the opposition and supporting the railways, Sherman? I mean Jake and Grayson seem as happy as you are on the canals and rivers".

"Horace, whatever people think of the working boaters we are business men and women, just like our forefathers. My two boys will take over when I can't do it anymore and I will always live on the water. They will continue to move scrap metal and bulk liquids, they'll be the last thing to go off the water. Grayson moves paraffin and tar for all the new roads that are being built. It's ironic that he is making a profit moving the very materials that will ultimately result in the end of the income that he now enjoys. But boats are still well suited to haul those cargos of twenty tons or more and that may continue for a while yet even though that too will come to an end eventually".

"I'm going back home first thing in the morning, Sherman. I wish that the circumstances could have been better but it was a pleasure meeting you and the families. I just hope that I haven't brought trouble to your door with the Draytons. The police are bound to inquire about your and the boaters' involvement in the events that took place".

"I think that the police will be glad to see the back of them, just like the rest of Romford. Getting evidence won't be easy, the bodies were burnt beyond recognition and the bullets removed from the ones we shot. That's why some of my men returned a little bit after the others. As far as your helping the priest to meet his boss is concerned we helped to tidy that up too. There may have been questions asked with the way that you left things".

"How did you know I went there, Sherman, no one followed me and no one saw me there?"

"I knew what was probably running through your mind from the moment he mentioned the baby in the church and your legs buckled. You are right, you weren't followed. I sent Mel and Mat there to keep an eye on things, they were there before you even arrived".

"What did you mean when you said they tied up after me? I made sure that everything was as tidy as it could be when I left his office".

"That was a figure of speech, Horace. It was too tidy. It would be unusual for someone to drink themselves to death with both the bottle and glass completely empty. Either the bottle is empty and the glass is not, or the other way around and, drinking as much as he did, he would probably have been sick as well, either well before or just before he died".

"But you can't make a dead man be sick".

"Horace, you're young and have a lot to learn. But you can make it look like a dead man's been sick. Mel made himself throw up while Mat opened the priest's mouth, they made sure that some of it went over his clothes, on the desk and on the floor. They also made it look as if he'd slumped back in the chair and tilted his head backwards. It's more likely that someone would fall asleep in that position rather than slumped forward neatly on the desk. Misadventure is the most likely verdict".

Horace was absolutely amazed. They grasped each other's hands and said that they would meet again before long. Sol and Piglet came over and told Horace they were going with Dianna back to the boarding house.

"Do you know it's half past one and you have to be away first thing Horace?"

The throng had all but left to go home but each and everyone one of them had respectfully picked up their glasses or bottles and returned them to the crates that were behind the tent. Someone would have a big job sorting all that out in a few hours time but that was the last thing on Horace's or anyone else's mind right now.

Horace rushed over to hug James and Lizzy, Tim and Sheila and Bel and bade them all farewell promising to see them again soon.

Horace, Sol, Piglet and Dianna walked back slowly to Dianna's house. Horace thanked her for her hospitality and told her that he would be gone before she was up.

He caught the milk train back to Burton at five in the morning.

## THE END

To be continued....

Made in the USA
Columbia, SC
07 October 2020